SIBERIA

D0374798

Perm

Ekaterinburg

I A

Volga River

Kama River

Ural Mts.

Ufa

Kazan

Belaya River

K A Z A N

Volga River

ASTRAKHAN

URALSK

KEY

RED TRAIN ROUTE
••••••••••••••••••••••••

EASTERN FRONT 1917
—•—•—•—•—•—•—•—•—

0   25   50   75   150
MILEAGE

N

THE
SILENCE
OF GOD

THE
SILENCE
OF GOD

a historical novel

GALE SEARS

DESERET BOOK

SALT LAKE CITY, UTAH

To my sister Teri

for all the years of wisdom, love, and laughter

Map by Bryan Beach

This novel is based on a true story and contains real historical figures, facts, and places, in addition to fictional characters, places, and events which are a product of the author's imagination.

DESERET BOOK is a registered trademark of Deseret Book Company.

Visit us at DeseretBook.com

Library of Congress Cataloging-in-Publication Data

Sears, Gale.
   The silence of God / Gale Sears.
     p. cm.
   Summary: At the turn of the century St. Petersburg offered the best of Imperial Russia. Few realized that the glitz and glamour of the Silver Age would soon dissolve into mass rebellion and revolution. For the wealthy Lindlof family, the only Latter-day Saints living in St. Petersburg at the time, life would never be the same—changed forever by an ideology that would persist for more than a century. The ravages of the Bolshevik Revolution are seen through the eyes of Agnes Lindlof and her lifelong friend, Natasha, in a powerful, extraordinary novel of devotion and loyalty.
   ISBN 978-1-60641-655-6 (hardbound : alk. paper)
   1. Mormons—Soviet Union—Fiction. 2. Soviet Union—Religion—Fiction. I. Title.
   PS3619.E256S58 2010
   813'.6—dc22   2010003417

Printed in the United States of America
R. R. Donnelley, Crawfordsville, IN

10   9   8   7   6   5   4   3   2

ACKNOWLEDGMENTS

I extend my thanks to the many people who helped make this book a reality: my first readers—George Sears, Teri Boldt, Shauna Chymboryk, and Roderic Buttimore; G.G. Vandagriff for her endorsement; Kahlile Mehr for the history concerning the Lindlof family, and for his great knowledge of the LDS Church in Russia; Elder Dennis Neuenschwander for his guidance with background information and doctrine; my tour guides in St. Petersburg and Moscow, Ylena Gavrilova and Vera Zhuravleva, for bringing the history and the heart of Russia to life, and for answering my many questions.

A special thanks to Jana Erickson at Deseret Book for her encouragement, Heather Ward and Tonya Facemyer for the great look of the book both inside and out, and Lisa Mangum for her deft editing hand.

Author's Note

Sometimes we are given a precious gift. Such is the case when, in my research into the fascinating and splendid history of Russia, I found the story of Johan and Alma Lindlof. The first members of The Church of Jesus Christ of Latter-day Saints in Russia, they and their children endured during some of the most difficult times in history for people of faith.

The book is one of fiction, but the Lindlof family was a real family and were eyewitnesses to the tumultuous years surrounding the Bolshevik Revolution. The events depicted in the novel actually happened to them. To these elements I have been true.

It was an honor for me to place their story on paper.

THE LINDLOF FAMILY

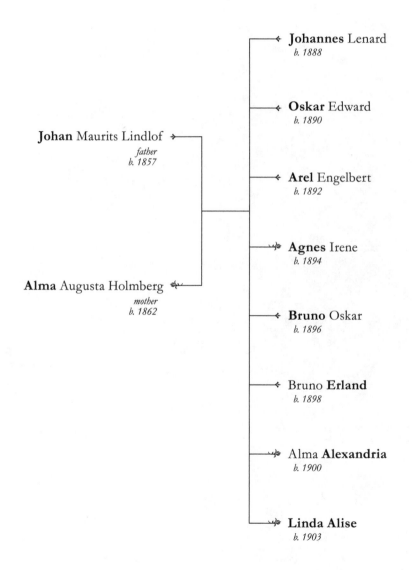

Johannes Lenard
b. 1888

Oskar Edward
b. 1890

Arel Engelbert
b. 1892

Agnes Irene
b. 1894

Bruno Oskar
b. 1896

Bruno **Erland**
b. 1898

Alma **Alexandria**
b. 1900

Linda Alise
b. 1903

Johan Maurits Lindlof
father
b. 1857

Alma Augusta Holmberg
mother
b. 1862

PROLOGUE

KIEVAN RUS

988 A.D.

Smoke and superstition whispered through the forest the morning that Perun fell. The thunder god's great carved image stood mute in the village gathering place—blank eyes staring east to where the sun would rise, and through the misted world a warrior ran—Erlendr, messenger of the prince. Erlendr of the beautiful form and long yellow hair, descendant of the Norsemen who had come to mingle and fight with the tribes of Kievan Rus.

As he neared the village, he heard the crackle of morning cooking fires and smelled roasting meat. But food would have to wait.

He called in a clear voice. "Men and women of Kiev, come to the gathering place! Come! Your prince is riding out from the fortress! He brings his new bride!"

Murmurs passed among the villagers who drew into the open area. His bride? Our prince has many brides. What will this one be like?

From the depth of the forest they heard the sound of horse's hooves, jangling bells, and beating drums. The worshippers in the gathering place fell silent as every heart pounded in cadence with the drum—pounded hard against their ribs as the sound drew near.

Prince Vladimir's giant black horse broke cover first, tossing its head and snorting. It squealed and turned in circles when it saw the blazing cooking fires, its massive hooves pounding the soggy grass into pulp. The creature's leather harness was adorned with silver bells, which made a sweet sound in the morning stillness, but did not allay the villagers' trepidation, and the nearest group stepped back. A young child started wailing, its eyes fixed on the stamping beast, while the rest of those gathered stared in wonder at the horse's magnificent rider.

Vladimir sat tall and sure on the back of his high-spirited steed. The prince's long, unbound hair and bushy beard added fierceness to his form. He was dressed in wool leggings and shirt, covered with a leather tunic that was branded with the images of elk, bear, and wolf. A red fox cloak covered the ruler's large shoulders, flowing down to drape over the rump of his horse. His sword was slung across his back, and a dagger hung on his belt. Vladimir reined in his horse and shoved his hand into the air. In his grasp was a beautiful silver object encrusted with pearls.

More members of the royal entourage poured into the clearing: warriors, women on horses, drum beaters, men in brown tunics, and men with axes. The villagers looked to each other. Why the ax carriers? Would someone be losing their head this morning?

The drums stopped, and the villagers gasped as the prince's bride rode into the clearing. Riding stately upon another of the prince's black horses came the lady from Constantinople. Her long, dark hair fell to her waist, and she wore it unbraided under a diadem of silver leaves encrusted with rubies and pearls. Her silver gown shimmered beneath a heavy gold cloak that had been exquisitely embroidered with hundreds of images which looked much like the object the prince of Kiev was holding aloft. In the crook of her arm, the bride held a wooden panel painted with the face of a man. The people wondered if it was her brother or perhaps her father.

Vladimir rode his horse to the side of his bride. "My people!" he called. "I present to you, Anna, Greek imperial princess, sister to Basil the second, emperor of Byzantium." He looked at her proudly. "My consort and co-ruler of Kievan Rus!"

The people cheered their consent and welcome.

"She brings great gifts from Constantinople. A gold coin for every member of the village and two pigs for every household!"

The people cheered more loudly.

Prince Vladimir dismounted, and the people grew quiet as he walked among them. He pressed the silver object against his chest. "She also brings something much greater."

What could be greater than gold and pigs? the villagers wondered.

The prince moved to the statue of Perun in the center of the gathering. "The time of darkness for the Rus is over. For years my heart has longed not only for stability with our neighbors but also for connection between our own people. Kievan Rus is growing. Our people spread across the mountains and the steppe like clouds across the sky, so we must have something to keep us strong and united!" He strode about the gathering place and every eye followed him. "I counseled with my boyars, and we have sent emissaries to the far reaches of the world to study the beliefs of our neighbors, their belief in one great God. The emissaries traveled far in search of knowledge—to the synagogues of Jerusalem, the mosques of the Bulgars, the Christian cathedrals of Rome—and indeed they saw marvelous things, but none, they say, as marvelous as what they beheld in Constantinople. They reported to me that God dwells there with the Byzantine people."

The drummers began a throbbing cadence and the brown-robed figures moved forward to form a circle around the god Perun, turning their backs on the great carved figure. The villagers stepped back, waiting for the fire arrows of Perun to fall from the sky and kill the disrespectful men. Who was this god that lived with the Byzantine people? Did these brown-robed men truly think the Byzantine god was more powerful than Perun? The villagers' attention was diverted as the beautiful, and now frightening, Anna was helped down from her horse.

She walked calmly around the gathering place, her heavily embroidered cloak dragging over the muddy ground.

"Dear people, I come here as your ruler and your friend." Her soothing voice carried to all, and they smiled to hear her speak to them in their own tongue.

"In my hands I carry a sacred image." She held the painted panel out to them, and they squinted to get a better look when it passed near. The skin, hair, and beard of the man were dark, and he wasn't handsome, but there seemed to be a light shining from his face.

"This is the Apostle Paul, a messenger from the Son of the one great

God. This Hebrew man came to my people almost a thousand years ago. He told us stories of one Jesus of Nazareth, the Son of God, born into the world to bring light, to heal our wickedness, to promise life after death."

A murmur passed through the group. Stories and legends of a Jewish man with mystical powers had been told by adventurers on the trade routes, but their tales were mostly fantastical and not taken for truth, and the holy men who might have brought messages of soberness, deigned not to venture into the dangerous, uncivilized regions of the north. The people of Kiev looked at one another. Had they heard the words correctly? The consort's accent was strange, so they could not be sure. Had she said that Jesus promised life after death?

Anna interpreted the rumbling voices and the looks of disbelief. "Christ Jesus, the Son of God did many miracles when He was on the earth: healing the crippled and the blind, feeding thousands of people with a loaf of bread, raising the dead—"

"Impossible!" someone shouted.

Prince Vladimir moved to stand beside his regal wife, and the noise stopped. "I know it seems impossible, my people, but you must realize that this is not a god of stone or wood, but a living God." He moved again to the statue of Perun. "A God made without hands."

"Where is he then?" a man called.

Princess Anna turned and looked at him kindly. "The Jewish leaders were afraid of Him, afraid of His power. They convinced their Roman rulers that Jesus must be put to death, so the Romans crucified Him."

The gathering grew quiet. They all knew the cruel stories of Roman crucifixion.

"He died?" a voice finally broke the silence. "How can He be a god if He died?"

The empress moved around the group again, tears glistening in her eyes. "The Apostle Paul saw the Christ and spoke to Him after His death."

No one dared contradict their new ruler, but how could anyone believe such unnatural foolishness? A dead person coming rotted from the ground to speak to another? It was madness. The villagers were sad that their prince had married a mad woman, yet as they looked at the empress's face, she did not seem mad. Her body was still, her hands gentle, and her eyes soft with surety.

Prince Vladimir put his arm around his dark-eyed beauty and spoke. "The Greeks have a written text which holds the history of the Hebrews. It has many testimonies of people who actually knew the man Jesus and saw Him alive again after His death."

Many of the women wept—hoping the prince's words were true, hoping that their dead children would come alive again.

The prince held the silver object above his head. "This is a symbol of the cross upon which the Romans killed the Son of God. But this lady and I are symbols of the living Son of God, for we have been baptized into His kingdom."

Baptized? This was an unknown word.

"A holy man has taken me into the water and put me down into it as though I were in a grave—as though I had died. But then my burier brought me up out of the water into new life!" He paused, and all the villagers stared at him. When the prince spoke again his deep voice rumbled with emotion. "I have been a pagan all my life. I have many pagan wives and hundreds of concubines, I have placed pagan statues around all of my dwellings, I have lived a life of excess and cruelty, but that old life has been washed away. I am done with excess. I have put away my pagan wives and concubines. And now the old gods will be rooted out, and we will worship the one true God of power and Christ His Son!" Vladimir gestured to the brown-robed men. "You will be taught the words of truth by these holy men, and tomorrow we will meet at the river where you will all be baptized into a new faith." Vladimir motioned to the ax carriers and they stepped forward.

Is he going to cut off our heads if we don't want to be baptized? the people wondered.

The prince made a sharp indication with his head toward the statue of Perun. "Chop it down."

The ax carriers stepped back. They were big men, but fear showed in their eyes.

"It is only wood," Vladimir told them, but still they did not advance toward the sacrificial circle.

Many of the villagers backed away, their faces shadowed with confusion and terror.

Suddenly Erlendr moved forward. Erlendr of the beautiful form. Erlendr the admired. He took an ax from one of the quailing men and walked with determination past his ruler to the waiting god. In one fluid motion, Erlendr raised the giant weapon and let it fall at the base of the idol. A deep gash scored Perun's side. Men cried out and women screamed, but Erlendr swung again and hacked away a large chunk of wood. No one stopped him. The people were mesmerized by the look of passion and assurance in the Norseman's vivid blue eyes.

The second ax carrier fell to his knees as Prince Vladimir took the weapon out of his hand. "You will see, my people! It is only wood!" he yelled as he raised the ax.

The two men were powerful and the axes sharp. Soon there was only one narrow shard of wood keeping the statue standing. Prince Vladimir moved forward, put his hand on the statue's head, and shoved the wood to the ground. The people waited for the wrath of Perun; it did not come. Warriors brought out leather cords, wrapped them around the fallen god, and tied the bindings to the tail of Vladimir's horse. The prince mounted his horse and dragged the statue to the river. Princess Anna followed with the holy men, while the people trudged behind, stunned into muteness.

They came to the river Dnieper, which flowed swift and cold with the spring thaw. Perun was untied from the horse's tail and hoisted onto the shoulders of four of Vladimir's strongest warriors. When the men reached the river's edge, they lowered the statue into their hands, swung it back and forth several times, and heaved it into the deep water. There was a loud crack when it hit and white sprays of water flew high into the air. Then, there was silence. The water rippled and swirled, and flowed on.

Vladimir turned to his people. "We are changed forever! We will never again be a people of superstition, a people worshipping lifeless, false gods. I declare to you that I will tithe my riches and build a church to the one great God in gratitude for my new life. A church where we may listen for His voice."

The villagers stood for a long time looking at the grave of their god.

Then insisting circumstance pulled them from the river's edge to gather wood, tend to fires, and eat.

"What will this mean for them?" Vladimir asked as he watched them go. "What will this mean for them, and their children, and their children's children on down through the passages of time?"

Anna took his hand. "It is as you said. They will be able to listen for the voice of the one true God."

Vladimir nodded. "Come, let us go and break bread with our people."

NOTES

1. Prince Vladimir brought Christianity to Russia in 988 A.D., as the Slavic historian Nestor the Chronicler (1056–1114) records in the Povest' vremennykh let (*The Russian Primary Chronicle*). In 996 A.D. Vladimir built the Church of the Tithes on the very mount which had formally been sacred to the pagan god Perun.

In 1037 Vladimir's son, Yaroslav I, laid the foundation for the Saint Sophia (Holy Wisdom of God) Cathedral in Kiev, which still stands today.

CHAPTER ONE

ST. PETERSBURG, RUSSIA

August 6, 1903

"And Elder Bloom was thrown into prison for preaching the gospel?" Johannes Lindlof asked, walking with long strides to keep up with his father.

Johan Lindlof nodded at his son. "Yes. Sentenced to twenty-eight days on bread and water for baptizing my mother and another woman there in Helsinki."

"But, that was Finland."

"A republic of Russia, my son. A republic of Russia."

"And why didn't you join the Church at the time? You were twenty-six."

"I wasn't ready, Johannes. Perhaps I was a bit of a coward."

Agnes Lindlof took her father's hand. "You are not a coward."

"Well, not now, but then . . . It was very dangerous to go against the state. A person was only supposed to see God one way."

"I would have been thrown into prison for the gospel," Oskar declared.

Johannes clapped a hand on his brother's shoulder. "That's because you're a hothead."

"No, I'm not!"

"Boys, no fighting," their mother reminded. "We wouldn't want to spoil this special day, now would we?" Alma Lindlof put her hands into the pockets of her light coat and turned to her husband. "Are you sure Brother Cannon said we were invited?"

"Yes," Johan assured her.

"And all the children?"

"Yes."

"And me in this condition?"

Johan gave his pregnant wife an understanding grin. "Yes, yes, and yes." He shifted his two-year-old daughter, Alexandria, in his arms and turned to look at the rest of the children walking behind them. "See, Arel is taking care of little Bruno and Erland, and Agnes is never any trouble."

Eight-year-old Agnes beamed up at her father and took her mother's hand. "We'll be good, Mommy. And if Erland starts to run about during the prayer, I'll take him to the other side of the gardens."

Alma Lindlof stopped on the Hermitage Bridge to catch her breath, and her family gathered around her.

"Are you all right, Alma?" Johan asked softly. "I should have had the carriage bring us all the way instead of dropping us at the Winter Palace."

"Don't be silly," Alma said. "It's a beautiful day for a walk along the river." She placed a hand on her protruding abdomen. "I'm just tired. This child is very active."

"Maybe you're going to have another Erland," Johannes teased. He knew he should have kept quiet the moment the words were out of his mouth, for on hearing his name, five-year-old Erland began jumping up and down.

"What about me? What about me? Is the new baby going to be like me?"

Johannes caught hold of his brother's suit coat. "Erland, calm down. Sorry, Mother."

Alma put her hand on Erland's head and he stopped jumping. "It's all right, Johannes. In truth, I would love to have another little boy just like our Erland." She looked earnestly into the eyes of her five-year-old, and he smiled. "Would you like to hear a story while I rest?"

Erland's head bobbed up and down.

Alma looked at each of her seven children. "Move closer."

Agnes glanced around at the great number of people walking along the prospect: laughing, talking, and enjoying the sunshine. Agnes moved in with her brothers.

"I want to tell you of the miracle that happened the day your father and I were baptized."

"June 11, 1895," Johannes said.

Agnes smiled. She and her older brothers knew this story by heart. It was one of their favorites.

"Eight years ago, your father and I were baptized in the Neva River."

Agnes leaned over the stone embankment to watch the water of the great river flow by. As her mother spoke of Elder August Hoglund coming all the way to St. Petersburg from the Swedish mission office, Agnes imagined the big man on the day of the baptism, rowing the wooden boat—rowing her father and mother up the river to find a quiet spot for the ordinance.

Alma Lindlof's gentle voice brought Agnes's thoughts back to the bridge. "There were many people out that day, crowding the river, the prospects, and the parks. We had to be careful for it was not a welcomed thing to join another church, but your father and I had spent several days being taught the gospel by Elder Hoglund, and we knew we wanted to be baptized."

"But you couldn't find a quiet spot," Arel interjected.

"No, we couldn't find a quiet spot." Alma turned and pointed up the river. "Just about a half a mile up that way, Brother Hoglund decided we should row ashore and have a prayer. As soon as Brother Hoglund finished praying, we looked up and all the boats and people just seemed to drift away from the place we'd chosen for the baptism."

"It was a miracle," Arel said.

Johan Lindlof put his hand on Arel's shoulder. "It was, son. We were baptized and confirmed members of The Church of Jesus Christ of Latter-day Saints with only nature and heaven looking on."

"See, you were very brave, just like Grandmother," Agnes said.

Her mother smiled at her.

"And now all of you will be part of another miracle," Johan said. He looked over at Erland and Bruno who were picking up pebbles to throw into the river. "Erland! Bruno! Come here, please."

The boys dropped the pebbles and came to their father's side.

Johan took the moment to school his children. "Now, we are almost to the Summer Garden and I want to make sure you understand how important your manners will be today."

"Father, you went through all of this at home," thirteen-year-old Oskar stated frankly.

Johan looked at his son with raised eyebrows. "And I obviously need to go over it once again."

Oskar reddened at the slight chastisement as his father continued. "Elder Francis Marion Lyman has traveled all the way from Salt Lake City, America. He is the European Mission President and an apostle of God. Imagine that . . . a member of the Quorum of the Twelve." Alma interrupted by clearing her throat. "Johan, your instructions?"

"What? Oh, yes. Yes, of course." He looked at his children who were being unusually quiet. "Anyway, Elder Lyman is an apostle of God and has come here to say a special prayer for our country."

"Is he more important than the tsar?" Bruno asked. Although only seven, Bruno was captivated by the royal family and their splendor.

"Tsar Nicholas is important to Russia, and Elder Lyman is important to God," Johan answered.

Bruno nodded as though that made perfect sense.

"Now, I do not know how long the prayer will take," Johan continued, "but you must be perfectly still while the apostle is speaking. Do you understand?"

The children looked tentatively at each other, and then nodded.

"If you must move about," Alma Lindlof said empathetically, "do it quietly. Just move away from the group and I'm sure no one will notice."

"What if Alexandria cries?" Erland asked, making a face at his little sister who was held in his father's arms.

Johan patted his daughter's back. "She's not going to cry. She's a big girl now."

The sun came out from behind a bank of clouds, transforming the Neva River from steel gray to sparkling blue. Johan took a deep breath. "Let's be on our way. We don't want to be late."

The family started east again soon arriving at their destination.

Agnes ran her hand along the ironwork railing that enclosed the huge garden. "Daddy," she said in a reverent tone, "do you think Peter the Great ever touched this railing?"

"I don't think so, sweetheart," Johan said, putting his hand on one of the massive granite columns which supported the grille work. "This was built long after Peter the Great died."

"Oh," Agnes said, disappointed.

"But I have a feeling the grand duchesses have run their hands along it."

"Oh, Daddy," Agnes drawled, quite sure that her father was teasing her.

"No, I'm sure of it. Do you think Tsarina Alexandra and Tsar Nicholas would not bring their girls here for a picnic?"

Agnes frowned at him. "Well . . . maybe." She brightened. "And you truly think they've all touched this fence?"

"Well, perhaps not Anastasia," he said, "she'd be too little. But I'm fairly sure Olga, Tatyana, and Marie have probably touched right where you're touching."

Agnes felt a thrill at the thought. She, like Bruno, was quite taken with the royal family, especially with all the beautiful grand duchesses about whom she could dream—imagining herself being invited to their country palace at Tsarskoe Selo for parties and pony rides.

"Agnes, pay attention," she heard her father say, and she looked up abruptly. She had walked right past the gate her father was holding open for the family. She hurried back to join the others as they entered the glorious garden. It held an impressive magic which enchanted the children into awed silence. Thousands of stately maple and elm trees stood sentinel near wide pathways and throughout the grassy acres. The foliage of the trees created a shimmering canopy of light and shadow. A breeze blew through the leaves, and Agnes imagined she could hear Mother Russia whispering.

Johannes took Erland's hand as the family walked the pathway to the central courtyard. Standing on the opposite side of the circular flowerbed were four men.

"Oh, look," Alma whispered excitedly. "That must be them."

"Isn't Brother Cannon an editor at a British paper, Father?" Johannes asked.

"Yes, the *LDS Millennial Star*," Johan answered.

As the Lindlofs approached the group, an older man in very American dress turned to look at them. He was stately and handsome with a well-trimmed beard and mustache. He had a high forehead, which spoke of intelligence, and his eyes held a look of earnestness and welcome. He didn't wait for the family to arrive within the circle of the group; a broad smile lighting his features, he strode to Brother and Sister Lindlof, his hand outstretched. He took first Alma's hand then Johan's.

"My friends, my dear friends, I am Elder Lyman. What an honor it is to finally meet you, Brother and Sister Lindlof—indeed an honor. The first LDS saints in Russia."

Johan was speechless. *He* was honored? Didn't the man realize what an honor it was for *them* to be meeting one of the Lord's apostles? Before Johan could find his voice, Elder Lyman continued.

"I understand that your interest in the Church came because of your mother, Brother Lindlof."

"Yes, sir. She joined the Church in Finland."

"Which is your birthplace."

Johan nodded. "Yes, mine and Alma's." He took his wife's hand. "Then, of course, Alma and I married and moved to St. Petersburg, where opportunities for plying my craft were better."

"And I understand you are a respected merchant in the community . . . a gifted gold and silversmith?"

Johan brushed off the compliment. "I have a small shop here in the city."

Brother Lyman smiled. "Well, I shall have to find a little treasure in your shop to take home to my wife. She has to carry on without me much of the time."

Alma found her voice. "Truly, Elder Lyman, we are honored to have you in our country."

The apostle gave a slight shake of his head, a kind grin crinkling the corners of his eyes. "I am just a busy servant, Sister Lindlof." His energy was infectious as he guided them back to the group. "Now come, we all want to meet your stalwart family."

The others in the company smiled as they drew near. Elder Lyman made the introductions. "You have already met Brother Cannon, Brother Lindlof, as I sent him to your shop with the invitation, and these two fine gentlemen—Elder Crismon and Elder Horne—are missionaries in Germany! They have been to Christiania, Norway, and Stockholm, Sweden, and are now in St. Petersburg for a few days. Gentlemen, may I introduce Brother and Sister Lindlof."

"First Latter-day Saints in Russia," Brother Cannon interjected, vigorously shaking Brother Lindlof's hand. "My, my, my . . . imagine. And the gospel shall go out to every nation, kindred, tongue, and people."

Elder Lyman laughed and clapped his traveling companion on the back. "The Lord is aware of all His children, Brother Cannon. He surely is!"

After everyone shook hands with Alma and Johan, Elder Lyman addressed Brother Lindlof in a gentle tone. "And now Brother Lindlof, if you would be so kind to introduce your dear children, I am anxious to make their acquaintance. Do they all speak English?"

"Yes, we've taught them several languages. The little ones know only a few words of English, but they can understand, and we can translate."

Elder Lyman smiled. "I would speak to them in Russian, but I know only a few words, and I'm sure my pronunciation is dreadful."

Johan motioned to Johannes. "This is our oldest child, Johannes. He is fifteen and helps me in the shop."

Elder Lyman took the young man's hand. "How do you do, Johannes? Are you keeping true to the faith?"

Johannes's eyes filled with tears. "I am, sir."

Elder Lyman nodded. "Yes, you are. I can tell. Wonderful. I will pray for you."

"Thank you, sir."

Elder Lyman started to move away, then stopped. He stood quietly for a moment, returning to Johannes's side. He looked searchingly into the young man's eyes. "Fifteen, are you?"

"Yes, sir."

"About the same age as the boy Joseph when he received the First Vision."

"Yes, sir."

"May I tell you something, Johannes?"

Johannes nodded, overwhelmed that an apostle of God would be standing there sharing stories with a young man of no significance.

Elder Lyman placed his hand on Johannes's shoulder. "My father, Amasa Lyman, knew the Prophet Joseph Smith very well. In fact, they were good friends. All the years of my father's life, though he had some sore spiritual trials, he always defended the Prophet Joseph's character. I remember him saying on many occasions that Joseph was one of the best men he'd ever known. I believe what my father said."

Johannes nodded.

Elder Lyman's voice took on a soft intensity. "I also want you to know that I have my own firm testimony of the Prophet Joseph Smith, and the Restoration of the gospel. The year before he was murdered, Joseph had been inspired by the Lord to send missionaries to this great country. He saw the empire of Russia in vision, and he appointed Elder Orson Hyde and Elder George Adams to that great calling. These dedicated men were preparing to leave in June of 1844 . . . and then . . . the Prophet was murdered." Elder Lyman hesitated, working to regain his composure. "The Prophet Joseph was a good man who died a martyr for the truth. To his last breath he held firm to what he knew was right."

The entire company felt the power of the Spirit as the words were spoken, but Johannes felt them seared into his heart.

"Will you remember what I've said to you, Johannes?"

"Yes, sir. I will."

Elder Lyman moved away to meet the next boys.

Brother Lindlof's voice was husky with emotion as he introduced Oskar and Arel.

"And they've been baptized?" Elder Lyman asked kindly.

"Yes, several years ago when Brother Anderson came for a visit from the mission office."

Agnes stepped forward.

"And this is our daughter, Agnes."

Elder Lyman took both her hands with his. "Dear sweet Agnes, in the middle of all these brothers."

Agnes giggled. "Yes, sir." She felt very comfortable in the big man's presence. "I'm eight and a half, but I haven't been baptized yet."

Elder Lyman smiled. "Oh, no? Well, we might have to take care of that before I leave."

Agnes looked over excitedly at her mother and saw a tear roll down her cheek.

Bruno, Erland, and Alexandria were introduced next. Bruno seemed impressed at meeting someone important, Erland didn't run around, and Alexandria didn't cry—even when Elder Lyman asked to hold her. He turned to talk with the group.

"Brother Cannon and I arrived a bit early in order to choose a secluded spot for our prayer. If you will all follow me."

They walked along a side path, passing flowering bushes and beautiful marble statues. In an area of the garden that was fairly deserted, Elder Lyman stopped near a statue of a woman holding a sunstone. "This reminded me of the sunstones on the Nauvoo Temple, so Brother Cannon and I decided it would be a fitting place for our prayer of dedication." He kissed Alexandria on the forehead and handed her over to Sister Lindlof. "Now, Sister Lindlof, please don't worry if the younger children get fussy. Their presence here is a blessing, and I understand they will probably get bored during such an extended prayer. I will not be troubled by them in the least, so set your mind at ease." He addressed the others in the group. "Brother Cannon will be acting as scribe, so please don't mind as he scratches away."

Brother Cannon had pulled his supplies from a satchel and was sitting down on a nearby bench. He looked up at Elder Lyman. "I will attempt to be as quiet as possible."

Elder Lyman smiled at him, and then looked over at Brother Lindlof. "It is fitting that you and your sweet family should be present at this dedication, Brother Lindlof. You are the only Latter-day Saints in all of Russia. It must be lonely, and I know you have prayed for kindred worshippers. God is very aware of this great land—vast and beautiful, and filled with His children whose hearts are true and good." He looked at the group. "The Prophet Joseph wrote that the vast empire of Russia was attached to some of the most important things concerning the advancement and building up of the kingdom of God in these last days." The apostle took a deep breath. "Joseph was never able to expand on that statement, but I believe it to be true. Since arriving here I have felt a great power in this country."

Agnes felt proud at the apostle's words.

"And in February of this year," he continued, "Tsar Nicholas II issued a proclamation of freedom of conscience. This is a very significant act—a miracle really. It means that people will be able to look about for truth and testimony." Emotion showed on the apostle's face. "Nearly a thousand years ago, Prince Vladimir of Kiev brought Christianity to this wondrous land, and since that time the Orthodox Christian churches here have kept the light of faith alive. We honor their devotion." He paused. "Now, shall we see what the fulness of the gospel may offer them?" He held out his hands to the small fellowship of believers. "If we can gather close, I shall begin."

Under the stately trees through whose foliage could be seen the blue heavens, Elder Lyman lowered his head and began praying. He offered a fervent petition for the Lord to open the great land so that His servants might preach the gospel in Russia. He dedicated the land for this purpose and turned the key that salvation and truth might be brought in. He prayed that religious liberty might be given so that all might worship unhindered and without persecution, and he petitioned the Lord to send servants full of wisdom and faith to declare the gospel to the Russians in their own language.

He prayed for the tsar and his family that they might be preserved from violence, and that this ruler might live to extend the religious freedom that his subjects needed so that all men might exercise their agency. He called upon the Lord to bless the great empire—in many respects the greatest in the world—and endow its rulers with wisdom and virtue, that there might be peace and progress, that darkness would flee, and that the voices of His servants could sound the glad tidings to the uttermost parts of the great land.

As the prayer ended, a profound stillness encircled the gathering. Agnes opened her eyes and lifted her head. She found her mother and father weeping, and, to her surprise, Alexandria asleep on her mother's shoulder. Erland sat on the ground, apart from the group, with his head in his hands.

Agnes went to see if he was sick, and she reached him the same time as Johannes did. Her big brother knelt by Erland's side and placed a hand on his back.

"Erland, are you sick?"

Erland shook his head and looked up at his brother. His eyes were red-rimmed from crying, and his dirty hands had smudged the tears on his face. "He loves us, doesn't he?"

"Who?" Johannes questioned.

"The apostle."

"Did you understand the prayer?" Johannes asked, surprised by his little brother's uncharacteristic demeanor.

"No, not most of it, but I felt that the apostle loves us."

"I felt that too," Agnes said softly.

"Me too," Johannes agreed, helping Erland to stand. "Here, wipe your face with my handkerchief."

"Are you all right, son?" Brother Lindlof asked as he moved to his children.

Erland nodded as he wiped his face.

Agnes piped up. "It's just that he was . . . Well, it's just that the prayer was . . ."

Johan Lindlof smiled. "I know what you're trying to say, Agnes."

"You do?"

"Yes. It's very hard to find the words, isn't it?"

Agnes nodded.

"Indeed," Johan continued, looking over at his oldest son, "I think we will be pondering the words of that prayer for many years."

At that moment, Sister Lindlof rushed up to them. "Johan! I don't know what got into me. I just invited everyone to supper at our home!"

Johan chuckled. "Calm down. Calm down, my dear. You always make enough food to feed all the tsar's relatives. A dinner party will be marvel-ous—the perfect ending to a perfect day."

Johannes hoisted Erland up piggyback. "I will never forget this day for as long as I live, Father." He nodded at Agnes, and then walked over to talk with the missionaries.

Filled with serenity, the company moved toward the garden entrance to find their carriages. Agnes lolled behind, listening contently to the murmur of voices on the summer breeze. She smiled as she heard again the voice of Mother Russia entwining itself into the conversation. Agnes twirled around and around. Her heart was happy, for now missionaries would come to Russia and there would be many families who would join the Church. Her best friend and neighbor, Natasha Ivanovna Gavrilova would be one of the first to be taught the gospel! And then, of course, Natasha's parents would want to be baptized. Agnes stopped short. The tsar! Surely the tsar would want to hear about the beautiful prayer that Elder Lyman had just given, and then the Grand Duchesses Olga and Tatyana would be baptized right away, and Marie and Anastasia when they were eight, and—

"Agnes, hurry along!" her father called.

She twirled one more time and ran to join the group.

NOTES

1. The miracle attendant with the baptism of Johan and Alma Lindlof was recorded by the missionary who baptized them, August Joel Hoglund. He wrote of the entire incident in a letter to the Swedish Mission Office. It was also recorded in an article in the Latter-day Saints' *Millennial Star.*

2. In October 1843 the Prophet Joseph Smith posted an article in the *Times and Seasons* concerning missionaries being called to Russia and asked faithful Saints for donations.

3. LDS apostle Elder Francis Lyman pronounced two prayers of dedication for Russia, one on August 6, 1903, in the Summer Gardens in St. Petersburg, and one on August 9 of the same year in the garden outside the Kremlin in Moscow. I have combined selections from each prayer. Both prayers were recorded by Brother Joseph Cannon, and published in the *Times and Seasons.* An article about the visit also appears in the August 20, 1903 *Millennial Star.*

4. The Russian naming system requires that people have three names: a given name, a patronymic, and a family name (surname). The patronymic uses the father's name followed by a suffix meaning either "son of" or "daughter of." Males use either "-ovich" or "-ovitch," while females use "-ovna," e.g. "Ivanovitch," which means "son of Ivan," or "Ivanovna," which means "daughter of Ivan." In standard usage, both the given name and patronymic are used together when referring to a person, but for the sake of brevity and English-language convention, I often use the given name alone.

CHAPTER TWO

St. Petersburg

January 22, 1905

People poured like rivers of water from the lanes and prospects—surging forward within a tide of intent; thousands upon thousands of people marching toward the center of the tsar's solitude. Men, women, and children pushed into the maelstrom by hunger and hopelessness. They held aloft the tsar's image amidst sacred icons and flowing banners. Many shouted, many sang "God save the tsar," many hearts prayed silently—*Surely he will hear our petition. Surely he cannot ignore the suffering of his people.* Onto the Nevsky and Voznesensky Prospect the workers' boots stamped the snow into gray sludge. It was only one o'clock in the afternoon, yet the sun had already begun its descent toward darkness.

"Oskar! Stop!" Johannes yelled as he ran after his brother. He shoved past a mass of human beings. "What are you doing?" he gasped, yanking his sibling back by his coat sleeve. "You are defying Father's word. He says you are not to march with the workers!"

Oskar glared at him.

"Don't look at me like that. You know what the Church teaches, and it teaches you to honor your mother and your father!"

Oskar tried to yank his arm free. "Let me go! I *am* honoring them by being a part of this!"

"Of anarchy?" Johannes spat.

"It's not anarchy."

People bumped them on every side, and Johannes shoved his brother into an alcove of a storefront. "What would you call it then? Thousands of people marching against the tsar?"

"We're not marching against the tsar. We just want him to hear our voice."

"*Our* voice? What are you talking about, little brother? These people are poor and desperate; you've never gone hungry in your life."

"Does that mean I can't care about my countrymen who eat only bread and porridge?" Oskar bit down on his rage. "And just because I sleep in a bed every night, does that mean I can't care about the men who sleep in squalor on the factory floors or in tenement housing? And just because I have a warm coat, does that mean I can't care about the beggar in rags?"

A cheer went up a few hundred feet from them as a group of university students pushed their way into the throng. "To the people!" they shouted.

Oskar's eyes flashed and he moved to follow.

Johannes grabbed him by his coat lapels. "Oskar, you're only fifteen!"

"So what? Look into this crowd, brother. There are families marching with their young children. Our little neighbor, Natasha Gavrilova begged her father to let her come along, and she's only eleven. She's a brave little citizen!"

"And her father said no, just as our father said no. Yet here you are, defying him and placing yourself in danger."

"We are not violent. No one carries a weapon. We just want the tsar to hear our voice. To hear the voice of a hundred thousand Russians!"

"Oskar, I know you've seen the placards posted all across the city. The people have been warned that if they march to the palace they will be met by resolute measures."

Oskar looked past his brother. "Johannes, just see how many are uniting. Do you think the tsar will not hear the voices of so many? They will call out to him like the cathedral bells."

Johannes growled. "Brother, you are young. You are caught up. You don't realize the danger!" He shook him. "Do you think that these people will go peacefully to the Winter Palace, knock on the front door, and ask to see the tsar? And do you think the tsar's Cossack guards will simply invite you all in for tea?"

"Don't be ridiculous," Oskar said, struggling to break free. "Of course we don't believe that. Father Gapon leads us. He's written to the tsar and has asked him to stand before the people and accept our petition, that's all."

"That's all?" Johannes scoffed. "Tsar Nicholas is a Romanov. He doesn't understand or care about your petition. He is above your petition." He gripped his brother's coat more tightly. "Listen to me. Father Gapon is a good priest, but he's just a pawn in this game."

Oskar's jaw tightened. "You don't know what you're talking about. Father Gapon has tried to help the factory workers and the peasants. He himself is leading the march."

"Yes, he leads you," Johannes countered, "but you are missing my point. Even the head of the church himself could not convince Tsar Nicholas to come out into a crowd of wolves."

"We are not—"

Johannes cut him off. "Nicholas was a young boy when his grandfather's body was brought into the Winter Palace! Alexander II tried to do good things for the people, and still they murdered him . . . blew him apart with an assassin's bomb! Oskar, think. Nicholas was there. He stood and watched as his grandfather's blood spilled onto the marble floor."

"We are not assassins."

"Do you think you can convince the tsar and tsarina of that? A hundred thousand people pressing in against their front gate?"

"We mean them no harm!"

"Don't be stupid, Oskar. Do you think there aren't terrorists in this crowd—members of the People's Will?"

Oskar shoved his brother hard, causing him to lose hold of his coat. "I'm going!" He turned and became part of the flow of humanity.

Within moments, Johannes was beside him.

"You can't stop me," Oskar said, his voice hard with determination.

"I know," Johannes returned. "So I'm coming with you."

"No one asked you!" Oskar spat back, his anger unappeased.

"I know," Johannes answered. "But I am your older brother."

"Two years older."

"Older, stronger, and wiser."

Oskar grunted. "Huh! Has Mother been telling you fairy tales again about the clever older brother?"

Johannes grinned, glad to hear a calmer tone returning to his brother's voice. They passed St. Isaac's Cathedral and turned east toward the Winter Palace. Johannes studied the faces of the people around them: gaunt, determined, hopeful, desperate. *Please Lord,* he prayed. *Watch over us. These workers and their families are reaching out to the tsar for his help. Do not let their petition go unnoticed.*

"Johannes!" Oskar barked, grabbing his arm. "Look there! Imperial guards on horseback."

The pace of the enormous mob slowed as the vanguard of the marchers reached the Palace Square and as more and more citizens realized that they were flanked on either side by grim and anxious men with rifles and swords.

"Can you see if Father Gapon has reached the gate?" Oskar asked, straining to see above the heads of a thousand people.

"I can't see anything. I think there's a blockade," Johannes grunted, struggling to stay beside his brother.

They were shoved forward with the momentum of the marchers as an eerie and unsettled stillness enveloped the multitude. A few voices rang out with calls or questions.

"Is the tsar coming out?"

"Has Father Gapon seen him?"

"Some say the tsar is not at the palace!"

Like a wave, voices threw this last sentiment from the front of the crowd to the back.

"Not at the palace?" a man beside Oskar mumbled. "Where is he then?"

An old woman with rotted teeth looked in their direction and sneered. "Probably off to Tsarskoe Selo for a winter holiday. Bundled up the fragile little tsarevitch and the grand duchesses for a pleasant little sleigh ride out to the country palace." She bobbed her head. "Yes, yes. Far away from this mad crowd."

The man frowned at her. "Stop babbling, old woman. You don't know what you're talking about."

The old woman continued to smile. "Read books, I can't, but read the tsar?" She tapped her forehead with a crooked finger. "He never changes. Read the tsar? Yes. And I say he's not here."

"Why have you come here then?" the man spat at her.

"To die perhaps."

As if with shared breath, the crowd pushed in closer to the palace walls and the old woman was lost from sight.

Johannes grasped Oskar's hand. "Let's get out of this."

Oskar looked at the thousands of people surrounding them. "Impossible."

Johannes swallowed down his fear. "I believe the old woman, Oskar. I don't think Tsar Nicholas is at the palace."

Oskar opened his mouth to speak, then hesitated, looking at his brother's worried face. "Even if he isn't here, he'll surely send one of his ministers of state to listen to us."

The petitioners surged forward again, and Johannes fell onto his knees.

"Johannes!" Oskar yelled, stooping to help his brother.

From only one hundred feet away, a horse squealed, pinned between a wall and the press of people. The Imperial rider fired shots into the air, and the horse reared, trampling a young girl under its hooves. Men yelled and women screamed as the horrified citizenry attempted to rush back from the gruesome sight. Their effort to retreat was met by a wall of confusion. Shots sounded again, this time from many locations.

People were shouting. "Stop! Stop! Don't kill us! We mean no harm!"

Before Johannes could get to his feet, he was knocked sideways, and several people fell on top of him. They were up and running immediately, but Johannes did not rise.

Oskar reached him just as a horse and rider charged forward. He yanked his brother out of the horse's trampling path as the guard fired into the crowd. A bullet grazed a man's forehead, spraying blood onto Oskar's coat.

"The tsar will not help us!" was being shouted and screamed by a hundred voices.

Oskar tried to drag his brother to a place of safety, but he was terrified, and his thoughts would not stay still. *Where can I go? Where can I go?* He stumbled and fell backward against a corpse: a young mother shot in the neck—her child still alive in her death grip. As Oskar sat staring at the grisly sight, a university student pried the howling infant from the woman's fingers and disappeared into the melee.

People cursed as they tripped over the prostrate brothers. "Get moving!" someone yelled, and Oskar jumped to his feet, aimlessly dragging his brother's body over the rough cobbles. "Dear Lord, please help me!" he cried. His view fixed on the Alexander Column in the middle of the square, and he immediately headed in that direction.

Two more people were shot as they ran past. They crumpled onto the stones and Oskar howled in desolation. "Where is our tsar?" he screamed. The words from a hundred mouths pierced his head and heart like a spike. *Our tsar will not help us!* In that instant, the tsar's mask of protective father was stripped away, never to be replaced.

Oskar put his hand on his brother's face. "I'm sorry, Johannes. I'm sorry." He began moving again, and with every tug on his brother's body he cried out his loss and rage.

He was two feet from the column, his lungs searing with exertion, when the bullet struck. All he felt was a heavy punch that knocked his legs out from under him. He hit the ground, hard. Women's skirts and men's boots swirled around as he crawled to Johannes. He laid his head on his brother's chest as a voice whispered into his ear, *It is a good thing Natasha Ivanovna Gavrilova listened to her father.*

Then light and sound disappeared.

◆　◆　◆

He felt, rather than heard, the words of his father's blessing pouring through his body like amber light, clearing his head and pushing air into his lungs. He stretched his fingers, sliding them over the soft, cool fabric. He heard a woman's voice call out, but he couldn't understand the words. Blue light shimmered in front of his eyes, and he breathed deeply just to feel the sensation.

"Oskar?" said a voice from far away. "Oskar Lindlof, open your eyes."

Why is Mother bossing me around? Can't she just let me sleep?

"Oskar, open your eyes. Oh, please, son, open your eyes."

Don't be upset, Mother. If it's that important to you, of course I'll open my eyes.

"Johannes! Come here. Come here, everyone! He's waking up."

Oskar opened his eyes a slit and images wavered behind a gray blur. Someone took his hand and Johannes's face came into view.

"Johannes? Weren't you dead?" Oskar whispered.

Several voices laughed weakly as Johannes leaned close. "Yes, and now I'm a resurrected being."

"Oh, for heaven's sake," his mother's voice chided. "The first words to him have to be a joke?"

"Well, *he* asked the question," Johannes protested. Oskar smiled. "And look, it's cheered up his day."

"Step back and let your father talk to him."

Oskar blinked several times and an unfamiliar room came into focus. "Where am I?"

"In the infirmary, son." His father's deep voice was calm and reassuring.

"Why?" Oskar's voice croaked back.

"Would you like some water?"

"Yes, sir." He tried to position himself higher on the pillows and a sharp pain twisted the flesh of his upper leg. He cried out involuntarily.

His father put a gentle hand on his shoulder. "Here now. Stay still, son. Let me help you sit up."

As they slowly accomplished this task, Oskar gritted his teeth and took in his surroundings. It was a large room with pale green walls and seven other beds. His mind skipped back and forth from wondering if they used the same green paint as on the Winter Palace, to being angry about the pain in his leg, and finally to evaluating the other sick people in the room. He couldn't see them well because his many family members blocked the view. Perhaps that was best. The one man he could see had a large bandage covering his head and his skin was the color of old cheese.

Oskar pulled his attention back to his father's face. "What's wrong with me?"

Johan turned to the others. "Alma, will you please take the children home? Johannes and I will stay."

Alma nodded, but Arel protested. "I'm not a child. I'm thirteen."

"Yes, that's true," his father answered. "You are not a child. That's why I need you to help your mother—especially with Erland."

Erland looked up abruptly. "What did I do?"

"Nothing," his mother assured him. "Come on now, everyone, say good-bye to your brother. You will see him later."

Oskar's head ached, but he cherished the tender pats and kisses he received from his younger siblings. Four-year-old Alexandria started crying as she moved close for her farewell. And the baby started in too. Alexandria's tears came from sympathy, while Linda Alise's weeping was unadulterated fear. He didn't blame her. He had never been in an infirmary before and even he was finding it stark and melancholy. His littlest sister quieted when Agnes held her close. *Sweet Agnes.* She stood bravely by the bed gently patting Linda Alise on the back.

"You're going to be all right now, Oskar. I've said many prayers."

Oskar put his hand on her arm. "Thank you, Agnes. We won't have to worry then, will we?"

She smiled at him. "No." She stepped away from the bed, then turned back quickly. "Oh! I almost forgot! Natasha Ivanovna sent you a card to cheer you up." She shifted Linda Alise on her hip and rummaged a letter out of her pocket. "She felt terrible that you were injured, so she made you this."

Oskar took the letter and grinned. "Hmm, even though I tease her all the time?" Agnes laughed. "Well, that was nice of her." He opened the envelope and took out the letter. He began to chuckle as he read.

Agnes looked indignant. "Don't laugh at my friend."

"No, no. It's wonderful. She's drawn a picture of me riding off on one of the Cossack's horses. And she sent me a riddle to figure out while I'm recovering."

Agnes brightened. "How fun!"

"Fun for you and Natasha," Oskar said. "I'm afraid trying to figure out a riddle might make me sicker."

"Oh, Oskar, riddles aren't hard. I'll help you. What does it say?"

Alma Lindlof touched Agnes on the shoulder. "Not now, little riddler, he needs his rest."

Agnes stepped back. "Yes, Mother."

Alma kissed Oskar on the cheek, and he could tell she was holding back tears. "I will bring you some bread and soup."

At the mention of food, Oskar's stomach ached. "Ah yes! I'm starving."

Johannes laughed. "Now that's a good sign, Mother."

Alma nodded. "I will get the children settled and come back with food."

With the family gone, Oskar was painfully aware that he would have to face the consequences of his disobedience. His throat was dry, and when he spoke, his voice was raspy. "I'm sorry, Father . . . Johannes. I was wrong to not listen. I'm sorry."

His father handed him a glass of water. "Yes, you were wrong, and now we're done with that. You had no way of knowing. Drink your water." He turned to look out the hospital's small window. "You're alive. That's all I care about." He turned back. "You and Johannes are both alive."

Oskar handed his father the empty glass, then looked over at Johannes. "What happened? I thought you were dead."

Johannes nodded. "So did I, but it turns out I was just knocked unconscious. I guess you must have pulled me to safety before being shot."

"Shot? I was shot?" Oskar pushed back the covers to gape at the bandages covering his upper thigh. "I don't remember."

"The bullet just missed your main artery," Johannes continued. "Even still, you about bled to death before the ambulance wagons arrived."

"Johannes, not so much. He's young."

"No, Father," Oskar said firmly. "I want to know everything." He looked at his father straight on. "And I am not so young anymore."

His father's view wandered back to the window.

"How long have I been here, Johannes?"

"Two days."

"Two days?" Oskar grimaced as pain jabbed into his leg. "I don't remember. All I remember were voices screaming, and people shoving and running." He paused in painful silence. "How many were hurt?"

Johannes looked at his father, but realized he would make no reply. He pulled the covers back over his brother and sat down on the bed. "They don't have an exact count yet—some reports say a hundred dead, some say five hundred with several thousand injured."

Oskar felt like vomiting. He lay back on his pillows and sucked air into his lungs. "Why didn't he come? Why didn't the tsar come out to hear us?"

Johannes lowered his head. "He wasn't at the palace. He'd taken his family to Tsarskoe Selo."

Oskar choked back a sob. "Safely away in the Tsar's Village." Tears ran from the corners of his eyes. "Just like that little old woman said." There was silence for several moments. "I wonder if she's dead."

"I'm sure Tsar Nicholas never meant for any of this to happen," Father said sadly.

"How can you defend him?" Oskar demanded. "His blindness has murdered hundreds of his people! They were reaching out for help. Their blood is on his hands." The next words came at a cost. "We will never love him again."

"Oskar!"

"No, Father, he's right," Johannes said flatly. "The people may have to endure more years of Romanov rule, but only the country people will say the tsar's name with any kindness again."

"Joseph Smith taught that we must honor the laws and rules of our country," Johan said.

Johannes nodded. "Yes. But we can also encourage change if change is needed."

Oskar was agitated. "Father, the Prophet Joseph honored the laws of America, and he was murdered! He and his brother Hyrum—killed without mercy!"

"Shut up there!" a visitor of another patient called. "This is a hospital not a union house!"

Johannes held up his hand in apology, then turned to his brother. "We must not talk of this now, Oskar. You must rest so your wound will heal."

Oskar slumped back onto his pillow, tears streaming from his eyes. "And what about here?" he asked, laying his hand on his chest. "What do I do about the pain here?"

It took Johannes many moments to compose himself before he could answer. "That wound may never heal."

Timidly their father approached them. "I . . . I think I'll get back to the shop." He put his hand on Johannes's shoulder and smiled at Oskar. "Now that I know you're both all right."

Oskar reached out for his father's hand. "I'm sorry, Father. Sorry that I disobeyed you, and sorry for what I said about the tsar. Maybe he'll change. Maybe things will get better."

Johan gave his son a smile. "We can pray for that."

Oskar forced brightness into his voice. "And thank you for the priesthood blessing. I should be ready to come home tomorrow."

His father chuckled. "Ah, the strength of youth." He patted his son's hand and turned to leave. "I'll tell your mother to hurry along with your soup."

"Yes, thank you. I'm starving." As Oskar watched his father walk away, he noticed for the first time that he moved at a slower pace. "He doesn't understand what's happening."

Johannes shook his head. "No. It will be hard for his generation to admit the need for change."

Oskar closed his eyes. "I love my country."

"I know you do."

"But I want to see her strong and healthy, and her people content."

Johannes chuckled. "Such words from a fifteen-year-old."

"If only the gospel would come, Johannes. Don't you want to see Elder Lyman's prayer fulfilled?"

"Yes, but there is much upheaval in Russia right now. People are listening to other voices—finding promise in talk of revolution. It is not a safe time. It might be years before the missionaries are sent to us. We have to trust God."

Oskar did not respond.

Johannes smiled at his younger brother's earnest discontent. "Sleep now, brother. Get your strength back. We'll just have to wait and see what the months and years bring."

NOTES

1. Lenin referred to the workers' uprising of January 1905 as "the dress rehearsal" for the revolution of October 1917. Prior to the revolt of workers in 1905 there had been strikes, insurrections, and the emergence of a great *soviet* (worker's council) led by Leon Trotsky. Provoked by horrible economic conditions and political oppression, workers in St. Petersburg marched to the Winter Palace to petition Tsar Nicholas for relief. They were led by a respected Orthodox priest, **Father Georgii Gapon,** who had been ministering to factory workers and organizing them into unions. On January 22, 1905, an estimated 200,000 workers marched to the Palace of the Tsar. The tsar's Imperial Guards used swords and rifles against the peaceful crowd. It is estimated that between 500 to 1,000 men, women, and children were killed or wounded. After the incident, which became known as **Bloody Sunday,** Tsar Nicholas and his family never again lived in the Winter Palace. Though participation in the march by Oskar and Johannes Lindlof was possible, the account of their involvement is fictional.

2. The assassination of Tsar Alexander II (Tsar Nicholas's grandfather) was accomplished by members of **The People's Will,** a terrorist organization founded in 1878. The small militant group included workers, students, and members of the military. They wanted to wrench power from the tsar and place it in the hands of the people. On March 13, 1881, several members of the group assassinated Tsar Alexander II as his carriage traveled the roads of St. Petersburg. One bomb stopped the carriage, but did not kill the tsar. After he exited the carriage to inspect the damage from the bomb, another bomb nearly blew off the tsar's legs. He was rushed to the Winter Palace where his family members watched helplessly as he bled to death. Unfortunately—for it is said this forward-thinking tsar had the plans for a Russian Parliament in his pocket. The Resurrection Church (The Church of Our Savior on the Spilled Blood) was erected over the place where the assassination took place.

3. A foiled assassination attempt by **The People's Will** occurred on March 1, 1887, against Tsar Alexander III, Tzar Nicholas's father. One of the captured would-be assassins was Aleksandr Illyich Ulyanov. He was found guilty by the court and hanged on May 8, 1887, at the age of twenty-one. His younger brother, Vladimir Illyich Ulyanov, would later change his last name to **Lenin** and become the driving force behind the Bolshevik Revolution.

4. **Cossacks:** Imperial guards of the tsar. Also the cavalry branch of the army. Regiments of Cossack cavalry fought in the Great War.

CHAPTER THREE

Petrograd (formerly St. Petersburg)
March 15, 1917

"The towers grand where fires burn—Father and Mother of two boys and two girls."

"Is that your riddle?" Natasha Ivanovna Gavrilova asked with mock disdain. "That's such an easy one. The answer is the Rostral Columns, of course. The copper bowls on the top are lit to guide boats safely into the mouth of the river."

Agnes Lindlof stopped in front of the deserted milliner's shop and scowled at her friend. "And their children?" she insisted, drawing the fur collar of her coat closer around her face.

Natasha returned a crooked grin. "They are the statues at the base of the columns. The male statues represent the rivers Dnieper and Volkhov, and the female statues represent the Volga and the Neva."

Agnes stamped her foot. "I can never outsmart you! *Tu est tres intelligente, mon amie.*"

Natasha shook her head. "Don't speak French."

"But I love French," Agnes protested.

"You love French because the tsar and the royals use French more often than their native tongue," Natasha chided.

"Well . . ."

"And the aristocrats use it because they think it elevates their status.

You may be the spoiled daughter of a rich merchant, but you don't need to act like one."

"I am not spoiled," Agnes said in a wounded tone.

Natasha noted the pained look on her friend's face, and relented. She put her arm around the girl's waist and gave her a squeeze. "No, you are not spoiled. In fact I think you are the most innocent girl in Petrograd." Agnes's expression altered only slightly. "Come on, little squirrel," Natasha coaxed, "don't be angry with me."

Agnes pouted. "But Russian is so harsh, and besides, you speak French."

Natasha laughed. "Yes, once in awhile, but I also know German and English."

Agnes narrowed her eyes. "Don't brag just because you go to the university and are the daughter of a university professor."

"I'm not bragging. You know English too."

Agnes turned to look into the empty shop window. "Only a little." She put her hand on the glass. "Madame Orlovskya used to make the most beautiful hats here. Father bought me my first hat from this shop."

"Bourgeoisie," Natasha said teasingly.

Agnes glanced at her. "You don't like the vacant shops any more than I do."

"Ah, that's true," Natasha answered, continuing their walk down Voznesensky Prospect. "But, I care about the food shops, the fruiter, and the bread makers, while you lament over the chocolatier, the milliners, and the flower shops."

"You can still buy flowers!" Agnes said brightly.

"Only if you have the money," Natasha corrected. "White lilacs in winter—it's disgraceful. The Duma should put a stop to it, but they are just silly puppets of the tsar."

"Well, the country gardeners can't stop growing things," Agnes protested. "They have to maintain their greenhouses, you know, and they have to eat just like everyone else."

"Let them grow potatoes and cabbages." Natasha saw Agnes bite her bottom lip and knew her friend was about to get emotional. "Little squirrel, I'm sorry. I know you don't like to talk politics."

"I don't like many things," Agnes said, stamping her foot. "I don't like how the other young women tease me just because I won't cut my hair short. How dare they criticize me? Most of them don't even wear corsets anymore." Natasha covered a grin as Agnes continued. "I don't like how I'm almost twenty-three and not yet married. I don't like how everything is dreary and sad. St. Petersburg used to be a sparkling city, and now . . ." Tears wrapped themselves around her words. "Now we've had to change the name of our beautiful city to Petrograd because of the stupid war, because St. Petersburg sounded too German."

"Agnes, calm yourself."

Agnes stopped walking. "No! You think I'm foolish and care only about foolish things, but there are many serious things I think about . . . things that make me sad and angry." She smacked her hand on a store window, frightening the merchant inside. "Do you think I like my brothers being away in the war? Do you think that it's easy for my family to worry every day if Arel and Bruno are still alive?"

"Of course not."

Tears rolled down Agnes's cheeks and she dashed them away as soon as they appeared. "I don't like how there's little food to feed us and little fuel to warm us—but what can I do?"

Natasha handed her a handkerchief. "Here, blow your nose."

"My father tries to help. He buys extra bread for the neighbors when he can, but we have less money now too, you know. Not many people buy silver goblets or gold chains these days."

The wizened shopkeeper opened his door. "Hey! Get away from my shop!"

Agnes moved quickly down the street, talking to herself until Natasha caught up. "We are not wealthy merchants anymore, Natasha Ivanovna, but we are certainly not Bolsheviks. We want change, but we don't wish to harm the tsar."

"My friend, stop!" Natasha said firmly. She lowered her voice. "You never know who may be listening."

Indeed, several people glowered at them as they passed.

"And that's another thing I don't like," Agnes said. "I don't like how everyone looks cross or suspicious. People used to smile more."

Natasha tempered her response. "Perhaps there's not much to smile about."

Agnes nodded. "Perhaps not." She took a deep breath and wiped away the last of the tears. "I'm sorry. It's just that we've not heard anything from Arel or Bruno from the war—not for a long time. And Mother has been snapping at everyone. My nerves are worn-out. That's why I thought this walk might do me good, might help me forget about my troubles for awhile."

"Of course."

Agnes took Natasha's arm and they walked along in silence.

Natasha pondered the unique bond they shared—a bond that tied them together even though their lives were so different. Their families' apartments stood side by side on the lovely Griboyedov canal promenade, looking across the water to the St. Nicholas Cathedral. Natasha smiled to think that while her family occupied only two of the four stories in their building, Agnes's family took up all the levels in theirs. Johan Lindlof's gold and silver shop was on the ground floor with the kitchen at the back, and the other three floors were living space for the large family.

When visiting the Lindlof home, Natasha had often been overwhelmed by Agnes's five brothers and two sisters. They made so much noise. Natasha was an only child of a mother who had grown up in the country and a father who was a professor of language and literature at the university. Agnes's father, on the other hand, was an established artisan and merchant selling jewelry to the wealthy bourgeoisie. He also supplied ornate and costly trappings for the homes of the St. Petersburg elite.

Natasha shook her head. *Foolish frills.* She glanced over at her friend and saw the frayed cuffs and patched pockets on her once fancy coat, evidence that even the upper-class merchants were beginning to feel the economic demise of a flawed system. *Good,* Natasha thought. She bit her bottom lip and chided herself for such unsympathetic feelings.

She did not wish her friend ill, but life in Russia was changing, and if anything tested their friendship it was their opposing views on politics and religion. Agnes had been raised in an obscure American religion called Mormonism and taught to honor the tsar and the government he dictated. Natasha was raised according to her father's wishes, and was therefore separated from any form of faith, and encouraged to question every injustice and edict.

Natasha pulled her mind away from weightier issues and thought instead of their physical differences. Agnes was average height and curvaceous. She had golden brown hair that reached halfway down her back; she normally wore it pinned up with soft curls around her face. Her eyes were pale blue, and people often commented on her open and innocent expression. Natasha had always been taller than her friend, and now, at almost twenty-four, her physique was slender and boyish. She had brown eyes and chocolate brown hair, and, like other emancipated young women of her day, her hair was cut short. She liked it—it suited her heart-shaped face. She recalled Agnes's shocked reaction when she'd first seen her after the shearing.

"Natasha, what did you do? It's frightful! If your hair was yellow, you'd look just like one of those boys in Holland."

So many differences.

"Are you angry with me?" Agnes asked, bringing Natasha's thoughts back to the present.

Natasha looked at her and shook her head. "No, of course not. I was just thinking how different we are, and how long we've been friends."

"We've been friends all our lives," Agnes answered, patting Natasha's arm. "We played together as babies."

"I don't remember," Natasha said flatly.

Agnes laughed. "Well, of course you don't. We were babies."

"I do remember your brothers being dreadful to me, though."

Agnes laughed again. "They weren't being dreadful. They were just being boys, and you weren't used to it." Her voice became conspiratorial. "Remember when we figured out that several of them liked you?"

Natasha grinned. "Yes."

"And you gave Oskar a black eye to set things straight."

"They were afraid of me after that."

"And now you have the handsome and intelligent Sergey Antonovich Vershinin to occupy your thoughts and ruin our friendship."

"Don't be silly." Natasha prickled. "Sergey Antonovich and I are associates at the university."

"No, no, no, Natasha Ivanovna. I know you, and you are very attracted to this man," Agnes stated emphatically.

"You've only seen us together a few times."

"And that has been enough to know."

They crossed a bridge over the Griboyedov canal and a cold wind sent needles of pain into the exposed skin on their faces. Both young women groaned and pulled their scarves higher over their cheeks.

"Good thing we're almost home," Agnes mumbled through the cloth. "Should we continue our game?"

"Why not?" Natasha answered. "I hope our brains aren't frozen."

"It's your turn to think of a riddle for me," Agnes said.

Natasha smiled. How long had they been playing these riddle games? She remembered sitting in Agnes's bedroom when they were nine or ten and trying to outsmart each other with hidden names or locations.

"Don't make it too hard," Agnes added. "I think my brain *is* frozen."

"This should be easy," Natasha assured. "Are you ready?"

Agnes nodded.

"The palace we eat."

"What?" Agnes asked loudly. "The palace we eat? Is that what you said?"

"Yes. The palace we eat."

"The Stroganoff palace," came a deep voice behind them.

The two women jumped and Sergey Antonovich laughed.

"Sergey Antonovich!" Natasha scolded. "Have you been following us?"

"I have—since the bridge."

Natasha could tell that Agnes was captivated by the striking young man with his shoulder-length dark hair and smartly styled beard and mustache. Like Natasha, Sergey had brown eyes and a tall lean body. She could just imagine Agnes knitting them together as the perfect couple, and she knew her friend well enough to know that she would willingly sacrifice their friendship if a higher order of love came along.

"Good morning, Miss Lindlof," Sergey said, nodding his head in her direction.

"Good morning," Agnes returned shyly.

"What are you doing here?" Natasha asked, noting the suppressed excitement infusing Sergey's smile. "And so early?"

"You haven't heard?"

"Heard what?" Natasha asked, a hint of irritation in her voice. "We have been out walking."

"Tsar Nicholas has abdicated his throne."

"What?" the women chorused.

"As of early this morning he gave up his throne. We no longer have a tsar. Well, he turned things over to his incompetent brother, Mikhail, but that won't last long."

Natasha was first to recover from the shock. "This is not just a rumor?"

Sergey shook his head. "No. It's been officially announced. Nicholas came back from the war where Russian soldiers are deserting by the hundreds to find chaos at home: strikes by factory workers, women marching against him, and mutinies by his Imperial guards!" Sergey picked up Natasha and spun her around. "He had no choice! He's finished!" They laughed together. "They are putting him and his family under house arrest at Tsarskoe Selo."

"He should have listened to his people and not his German wife," Natasha said.

"And someone should have killed Rasputin sooner than they did," Sergey added. "But it's done now! It's done now, comrades! Three hundred years of Romanov rule is ended!"

Natasha's heart was beating fast. "And now perhaps the people will be heard."

"Yes! Yes, of course. A new government will now be free to further the Socialist ideals." Sergey's voice filled with passion. "And soon Lenin will return from exile in Switzerland!"

Natasha turned excitedly to Agnes. "Agnes! Can you believe this?"

The grief on Agnes's face stunned Natasha into silence.

Agnes backed away from her friend, and when Natasha reached out a hand to her, she ran.

"Agnes, come back!"

"Let her go," Sergey said, and Natasha noted the derision in his voice. "I think your friend is a White Russian."

"Don't!" Natasha commanded. "You know nothing about her."

"Well, I believe she is crying for the fallen royal family."

"Yes, I'm sure she is. Many Russians will cry when they hear of it." She turned and moved quickly down the street.

"Where are you going?"

"To be with my friend."

NOTES

1. **Russian Social Democratic Labour Party:** Marxist Socialists. In 1903 the party split on the question of tactics into the **Bolshevik** and the **Menshevik** parties (roughly translated, "Bolshevik" means "majority" and "Menshevik" means "minority"). The Menshevik party included all shades of socialists who believed society must progress by natural evolution toward socialism. This was the party of the socialist intellectuals. The Bolsheviks believed in rapid change through upheaval and insurrection. In 1918 the Bolsheviks became the Communist Party, to emphasize their complete separation from the tradition of "moderate" or "parliamentary" socialism. The Bolshevik party proposed immediate working-class insurrection, seizing the reins of government in order to hasten the coming of socialism by forcibly taking over industry, land, natural resources, and financial institutions.

2. **Bourgeoisie** (adjective: bourgeois): The term "bourgeoisie" in sociology and political science historically denoted the middle or merchant class where social and economic power came from gained employment, education, and wealth, as opposed to the aristocracy, whose power derived from inherited wealth, and the proletariat, or the working class. Marxism defines the bourgeoisie as the social class that owns the means of production in a capitalist society. In modern society, after the collapse of the aristocratic class, the bourgeoisie became the ruling class. Often used as a term of disparagement.

3. **The Great War** (or **World War I**) embroiled most European countries, occupying four bitter years of fighting from August 1914 to November 1918. We are probably most familiar with the battles on the Western Front which involved Germany, Austria-Hungary, France, England, America, and several other countries. Russia fought on the Eastern Front against Germany, and lost some 1.6 million Russian soldiers during the conflict. Ironically, the seeds of the Russian revolution were sown during the Great War as Russia struggled to free itself of the worldwide conflict.

4. The city name of **St. Petersburg** changed several times between 1914 and 1991—from St. Petersburg to Petrograd during the Great War because St. Petersburg sounded too German; to Leningrad to honor the Bolshevik leader after

his death in 1924; and back to St. Petersburg in 1991 after the fall of the Soviet empire.

5. **Duma:** The debacle of Bloody Sunday in 1905 weakened the power and stature of Tsar Nicholas II. To forestall rebellion, the Tsar established a *duma,* or legislative assembly, to help govern, but their actual power was limited. Over the next twelve years, economic conditions worsened, acute food shortages increased, and Russia became embroiled in the Great War. February 1917 saw strikes, rioting, military insubordination, and mutiny. Tsar Nicholas II attempted to put down the workers by force and dissolve the Duma. The Duma refused to obey, and Petrograd insurgents took over the capital. Nicholas was forced to abdicate and a **Provisional Government** was put into place. The leaders of this government were Constitutional Democrats (**Cadets**—see the notes to chapter nine).

6. **Gregori Efimovich Rasputin:** (January 2, 1869–December 29, 1916) A self-proclaimed holy man and wandering mystic, Rasputin was brought into the life of Russia's royal family by Tsarina Alexandra, when it seemed he could miraculously ease the suffering of her son, Tsarevitch Alexis, who suffered painful episodes attendant with his hemophilia. Rasputin was murdered by a group of nobles who considered him a charlatan, a meddler in government affairs, and a depraved braggart.

7. **White Russian:** A designation for anyone with anti-Bolshevik sentiments or opinions.

CHAPTER FOUR

PETROGRAD

April 16, 1917

"Here you have Lenin who eats, sleeps, breathes, and dreams the revolution, and Tsar Nicholas who wanted nothing more than to take care of his family."

"And his people. Didn't the tsar wish to take care of his people?"

Sergey Antonovich turned a spurious look at his bear-like friend. "Nicholai Lvovitch, you know the answer to that. Nicholas never wanted to be tsar. He wanted to putter around in his garden, sail about on the *Standart,* and play games with his children. He would have given the honor of being tsar to his mother if the government had allowed it."

Nicholai grunted. "When he ran from all his troubles he gave it over to his brother Mikhail to be tsar."

"Who held the empire for two days," Sergey scoffed. He downed his glass of vodka and poured another. "The tsar was always far from the people, up there on his golden pedestal. He never saw us or cared about our suffering."

"Well, now we have Kerensky and the Provisional Government to take care of us," Nicholai Lvovitch slurred.

"Kerensky is a fool. A Socialist who dances with the wealthy merchants. He is not a true Socialist."

Nicholai reached out a beefy hand for the bottle of vodka, and Sergey snatched it away.

"Hey!" the big man protested.

Sergey wagged a finger at him. "You've had enough, my friend."

"And what of you?" Nicholai growled. "You've been drinking as much as I have."

"True, and we must stop now." Sergey stood, the vodka bottle in his hands. "We have our meeting soon and our heads must be clear."

Nicholai grunted. "My head is never clear anyway, so let me have that bottle!" He lunged for it and Sergey sidestepped.

Sergey's voice took on a hard tone. "Leave it, Nicholai Lvovitch! You're done." He shoved the bottle into the cupboard and slammed the door.

Nicholai stared at him a moment, then swallowed hard, and sat down in his chair. "Sorry, comrade, you're right. I would spoil the meeting if I passed out from too much vodka." He slapped his hand on the table. "I did want to make one more toast to the grand duchesses though."

"Make it with your empty glass," Sergey answered.

Nicholai laughed and held up the smudged glass. "To Olga, Tatyana, Marie, and Anastasia! May they all marry peasants and live in izbas and hoe their own potatoes!"

"Well said!" Sergey concurred. "But no toast for their little brother, Alexis?"

"Of course, of course!" Nicholai barked. "We certainly can't leave out the former tsarevitch. You, Sergey! You give the toast."

Sergey gave a mock salute and raised his glass. "To Alexis, the once proud son of Tsar Nicholas and Tsarina Alexandra—may Rasputin's ghost come to haunt him. May his attendant, Boatman Derevenko, fall off the *Standart* in perilous seas. May the innocent tsarevitch never be able to grow a beard, and may he marry a butcher's daughter, become a butcher, and work with knives all his life." Sergey gave another mock salute and thumped Nicholai on the back. "Breathe, my large friend, breathe."

Sergey had taken his time pronouncing the toast, and through it all Nicholai Lvovitch had roared with laughter and pounded the table. Now Nicholai's pudgy face was red and tears leaked from the corners of his eyes.

He gulped several times, sucking in large quantities of air, and wiping his eyes with his shirtsleeves.

"Oh! Oh, that was good, Sergey Antonovich. You are a great speaker. I want to write that down."

Sergey heard voices in the hallway moments before his apartment door was shoved open, revealing his friend Dmitri Borisovitch. With him came a woman and two men. Sergey figured they must be from Dmitri's neighborhood for they certainly were not university students. Nevertheless he was glad that his clever friend had talked them into coming to the meeting. They needed more and more young people to embrace the Bolshevik ideology.

"Dmitri Borisovitch!" Sergey called as Dmitri stepped into the room.

Sergey caught a glimpse of the smile dropping from Nicholai Lvovitch's face, and he wondered if Nicholai would ever give up his jealousies.

"So you have brought friends, Dmitri Borisovitch," Sergey stated, taking all their coats and shaking hands.

"Yes," Dmitri answered. "These are my neighbors from the Demidov family. May I introduce Vanya Stephanovich, his brother, Anton, and their sister, Yulia."

Sergey greeted them warmly, amused to see Yulia staring at him. She and her brothers were plain creatures, to be sure, so he tried not to add to the young woman's discomfort by looking at her directly.

"And I have news," Dmitri said.

"Yes? What?" Sergey asked.

"Natasha Ivanovna is not far behind us."

"I knew she was coming," Sergey answered with a shrug.

"Ah, but did you know her father is coming with her?"

Sergey came to attention. "Is he?" He paced the small room as people settled themselves. "Is he? This is good news. Very good!"

"Is he important?" Yulia Demidov asked.

Sergey's enthusiasm was blunted by her question and the almost masculine quality of her voice. He stared at her a moment trying to decide whether to point out her ignorance with his answer or to be magnanimous.

"Of course, Comrade Demidov, you do not attend the university so you would not know the brilliant Ivan Alexseyevitch Gavrilov. He is a professor of language and literature, and is highly regarded, but more important to us, he is the head of a soviet and he knows Trotsky."

Yulia's brother Vanya broke in. "Leon Trotsky? Do I understand you correctly? This man who will join us knows Leon Trotsky—the brilliant revolutionary?"

Sergey put his hand on the man's shoulder and smiled down at him. "Yes, comrade, you heard me correctly. But, remember, we must not be intimidated by position anymore. We are all equals now."

There was a knock at the door and everyone came to attention. Sergey wiped his hands on his worn coat and went to admit the newcomers. He had met Natasha's father a few times for only moments, yet he remembered his own feelings of inadequacy in those encounters. The man's dark brown eyes were penetrating, and you felt as though his searing appraisal went directly into your thoughts. Sergey Antonovich also had the impression that the man could discern a lie before it was spoken. Ivan Alexseyevitch's physical stature was as intimidating as his intelligence; he stood well over six feet tall and he carried himself with calm assurance—a trait Sergey worked hard to possess. He forced the strain from his face and opened the door.

"Professor Gavrilov! What an honor to have you join us." He looked at Natasha, who was watching him carefully. "Natasha, you neglected to tell me your father was coming."

"He decided on his own," she said.

Sergey's smile broadened. "Wonderful! Come in, come in." He made introductions and attempted to take their coats as the two stepped into the room.

"We won't be staying," Ivan Alexseyevitch said. "In fact, we are going to the train station."

Sergey looked to Natasha, his disappointment evident. "Train station? I don't understand. Are you going somewhere?"

"No," Professor Gavrilov said. "We are going to the train station to meet someone, and all of you will be coming with us."

The tension in the room rose perceptibly, and Sergey felt a prickle of fear run along his spine. Perhaps he'd misunderstood. Perhaps Natasha's father was actually sympathetic to the tsar or the Provisional Government.

Was it a trap to have them taken away by tsarist loyalists? He couldn't imagine it, but perhaps Natasha's father knew Trotsky only enough to loathe him. Sergey chided himself. He was letting his fear get the better of him.

"Is there a problem?" Professor Gavrilov asked. "Does no one wish to go with us to meet our friend? He's been on a long and painful journey, but now he's coming home."

Nicholai Lvovitch plucked up his courage. "But, Professor, we . . . we don't know your friend."

"Ah, yes, comrades, indeed you do."

"We do?" Dmitri Borisovitch asked, his puzzled expression reflecting the feelings of the others.

Professor Gavrilov nodded. "Yes, of course. For, you see, if my sources are correct, Vladimir Ilyich Lenin arrives at the Finland station today, compliments of the German government."

♦ ♦ ♦

Spring was allotting winter darkness smaller and smaller increments of time, and Natasha Ivanovna knew that in a month the White Nights would bring shimmering light well past midnight. She loved those soft evenings when she and her friends from the university would sit at the café, eating blini and talking philosophy and poetry. Of course in recent years they ate bread and talked about the war and the revolution. The youth of St. Petersburg were a blazing force for the ideals of Socialism. Her group of friends spoke loudly of insurrection—impatient to burn away the last vestiges of evil capitalism and the blight of religion.

Natasha's mind drifted away from the memories of the café. She saw herself at her aunt and uncle's enchanting cottage in the country. Her hair was long and braided. It was the summer that Agnes was allowed to accompany her. They were fourteen and they made crowns of wildflowers for their hair and pressed ripe strawberries to their lips. The warm sun played lightly on their skin as they walked the golden meadows.

"Natasha, where are you?" Dmitri Borisovitch teased, poking her in the ribs.

Her mind snapped to the present and she stepped away from the impudent young man. "Don't poke me, Dmitri Borisovitch."

"Well, I had to wake you up, comrade, or Vladimir Ilyich Lenin might have come and gone while you were daydreaming."

Natasha looked around. *How odd,* she thought. *I'm standing here in the large parade room at the train station with a thousand revolutionary disciples, and I'm thinking of meadows and strawberries.* She turned to find her father debating with Sergey Antonovich.

"You don't think Lenin should have come?" her father questioned. "You think that he should have stayed in Zurich, raging like an animal in a cage?"

"Of course not, Professor. I only meant—"

"You imagine that he and his wife and the other exiles haven't thought of every possible way to get back into Russia?"

"All I'm saying is that the counterrevolutionaries will say that Lenin is a pawn of the Germans—that the Germans put him and his comrades on this sealed train and gave them free passage across Germany for a price. And what price will that be, they will ask? The anti-Bolsheviks will question what Lenin has promised the German imperialists."

Professor Gavrilov nodded. "Lenin has never made it secret that the Bolsheviks would put an end to Russia's involvement in the war. I'm sure that's what the Germans are hoping will happen when he comes to power. That is no secret, Sergey Antonovich."

There were many people in the crowd listening to the debate, and several voiced their support of the Professor's words.

Sergey's tone became commanding. "But we know the German imperialists. They do not believe in our cause. They care nothing for our struggles. I just wonder about the pound of flesh the Hessians will require of us when payment is due."

Several more people in the crowd applauded his statement, and Sergey Antonovich took in their approval with a nod and a slight bow.

"He's coming!" people began shouting. "I see him!"

The thousand workers and soldiers who had been gathered by the Petrograd soviet to make a show of Lenin's arrival turned as one in the direction of the train platform.

"I see Kamenev of the Central Committee!" Dmitri Borisovitch called out excitedly.

"And Cheidze, president of the Petrograd soviet!" Sergey Antonovich added. "They are getting ready to greet him."

"Yes, I see Lenin—there!" Professor Gavrilov said, pointing. "Someone has given him a bouquet of flowers. See there—in the round hat."

"Ah, yes!" Sergey yelled. "He's hurrying to the committee!"

By now most of the crowd had seen the Bolshevik leader, and an excited roar of approval ebbed and flowed throughout the hall. The official welcoming party stepped forward, and Lenin stopped short as if in coming upon Chairman Cheidze he'd come upon an unexpected obstacle. The thousand voices stilled in intense anticipation. Most people had read Lenin's words in essays and articles smuggled out of Switzerland, but many had never heard their leader speak.

Natasha pushed around in front of her father to get a better view. "Don't tell me Cheidze is going to speak," she said crossly.

"Oh, he is," Sergey responded, shaking his head.

"The old sourpuss," Dmitri added. "Lenin is going to chew him into pieces."

Chairman Cheidze gave a curt bow. "Comrade Lenin, in the name of the Petrograd soviet and the whole revolution, we welcome you to Russia . . . but, we consider that the chief task of the revolutionary democracy at present is to defend our revolution against every kind of attack both from within and from without. We hope that you will join us in striving toward this goal."

Natasha looked back to see her father scowling.

"What's he trying to be," Sergey hissed, "Lenin's moral instructor?"

"Don't worry," Professor Gavrilov said. "Lenin will know how to deal with that hypocritical Sunday school greeting."

"Comrade Lenin!" a clear voice rang out.

Lenin turned his back on the committee members to acknowledge the young naval commander who had stepped forward.

Face to face with an icon, the man swallowed and stood straighter. "I speak in the name of all the sailors, Comrade Lenin. We welcome you home and hope sincerely that you will soon become a member of the Provisional Government!"

The crowd cheered as Lenin shook the sailor's hand. The young man's companion came to stand proudly beside him. She carried a banner which read "Peace! Land! Bread!"

Lenin bowed to her and gave her the bouquet of flowers. Keeping his back to the committee, he addressed the people.

"Dear comrades, soldiers, sailors, and workers, I am happy to greet in you the victorious Russian revolution, to greet you as the advance guard of the international proletarian army! On the journey here with my comrades, I was expecting we would be taken directly from the station to prison at the Peter and Paul Fortress. We are far from that, it seems. But let us not give up the hope that it will happen, that we shall not escape it."

Sergey leaned close to whisper in Natasha's ear. "Ah, Lenin would love for the bombastic politicians to throw him in jail and bring attention to the cause."

Natasha was caught by Lenin's next words.

"We wish our cause to incite, to inflame, to burn away the last scraps of capitalist oppression. Only the Bolshevik stands guard over the proletarian interests and the world revolution. The rest are the same old opportunists, speaking pretty words, but in reality betraying the cause of Socialism and the worker masses."

Chairman Cheidze's face flushed with anger as Lenin continued.

"We don't need any parliamentary republic. We don't need any bourgeois democracy. We don't need any government except the soviet of workers', soldiers', and farmhands' deputies!"

The crowd cheered, but Natasha could not find her voice.

"The hour is not far when, at the summons of our revolutionary comrades in other countries, the people will turn their weapons against their capitalist exploiters. The Russian revolution achieved by you has opened a new epoch. Long live the worldwide Socialist revolution!"

The crowd erupted into noise. A band played and people sang. Some of the soldiers led Lenin to a waiting convoy of armored cars and insisted that he climb up on one of them.

"Look at the spotlight on his car," Nicholai Lvovitch shouted. "Look how it stabs through the darkness!"

"Yes, Nicholai!" Sergey Antonovich agreed, slapping his big friend on the back. "It is symbolic, isn't it?"

Nicholai Lvovitch beamed, his head bobbing up and down. "Yes. Yes, it is symbolic."

"It will be a triumphal march through the city!" Dmitri Borisovitch exclaimed as he waved his hat in the air. He looked over at his friends from the neighborhood then back to Sergey. "My friends and I are going to follow. Are you coming?"

"Of course!" Sergey answered immediately.

"Am I invited?" Nicholai asked petulantly.

A spasm of irritation crossed Sergey's face, but it was momentary, and he covered it with an enthusiastic smile. "Of course, Nicholai Lvovitch. We are all one in this!"

The group moved off with the crush of followers. Suddenly, Sergey Antonovich turned back. "Natasha Ivanovna, are you coming?"

"No. Father and I are going home."

Sergey returned to the twosome.

"Father wants to write a paper on tonight's happenings, and he wants to do it while the recollections are clear," Natasha said.

Sergey looked up at Natasha's father and gave him a charming smile. "Of course. I understand." He shook his head in wonder. "His speech, Professor, what did you think of that? I feel like I've been flogged over the head with a flail! I don't think Chairman Cheidze expected anything like that."

Professor Gavrilov nodded. "No. I'm sure he didn't."

Sergey shook hands enthusiastically with the man. "Thank you so much for bringing us along, Professor."

"Of course. We are all one in this."

Sergey smiled, and Natasha could tell he was flattered to hear his own words repeated by her father.

"Sergey, come on!" Dmitri yelled.

Sergey turned. "I will see you tomorrow, Natasha Ivanovna."

Natasha watched as the group of believers marched away into the night. A cold wind bit at her cheeks and she pulled her scarf higher on her face.

"Shall we see if we can find a ride?" her father asked, putting his arm around her.

"Oh, that would be very nice," Natasha answered. They went to the taxi area, but no vehicles were in service.

"The drivers must be Bolsheviks," Natasha said, "and have all driven off to be in the parade."

Her father chuckled. "We will catch a streetcar."

They walked together in the lingering atmosphere of the momentous event, now and then catching the distant sound of singing and a band playing songs of the Bolsheviks.

Natasha Ivanovna twined her arm around her father's. She kept to her silence, unable to articulate the emotions and images bumping around inside her head. Finally a feeling surfaced which she felt impelled to express. "Father?"

"Yes?"

"I was a little frightened by what happened here tonight."

"That is very wise of you, and while I am not frightened, I *am* stunned." Natasha stopped and stared at him. "Oh, yes," he replied. "I am stunned by the power and pace of the movement. You young ones don't see it clearly, but I have studied the cultures of much of the world's history and nothing like this has happened before."

"The French Revolution?"

"Yes, but the French still wanted government, they still wanted democracy. In Russia we are casting away capitalistic government. We declare that we will be a country of councils—of soviets, and those councils will be made up of soldiers and workers and peasants."

"'All Power to the Soviets.'"

"Yes."

"But led by the Bolshevik leaders."

Her father gave her a sideways look. "Of course. You must have a Lenin or a Trotsky to show the way."

They found themselves standing on the Liteyny Bridge, the wide expanse of the Neva River flowing beneath them. Released from the icy bonds of winter, the dark cold water was pulled inexorably toward the Gulf of Finland.

Natasha felt the turbulence and the danger under her feet. She closed her eyes and put herself again in the summer meadow with Agnes. It was safer there. It was quiet.

"Natasha, are you all right?"

She looked at her elegant father and felt her heart twist. "I don't know," she answered truthfully. "I feel as though the world is shredding."

The wind whipped her short-cropped hair into her face and her father reached over and tucked it behind her ears.

"Let us remember what the Bible says, 'Don't take thought for tomorrow, for tomorrow will take thought for the things of itself. Sufficient for this day are the evils thereof.'"

"But you don't believe in the Bible."

"As a holy book, no. But it still contains some very beautiful words. Now, let us get home before your mother worries herself into sickness."

Natasha smiled and leaned against her father's shoulder.

In another part of the city, the jubilant convoy of revolutionaries had reached the Smolny Institute, headquarters for the Bolshevik Committee.

Vladimir Ilyich Lenin had come home.

Notes

1. Sergey's toast to the Tsarevitch Alexis—that the young man should marry a butcher's daughter and work with knives all his life—is especially cruel in light of Alexis's hemophilia. He suffered from the painful illness all his life.

2. The character of Dmitri Borisovitch is patterned after an actual person, **Dziga Vertov**. Dziga Vertov was a young filmmaker in Russia who pioneered forms of documentary film. He was recruited by Lenin to use the artistry of filmmaking to advance the Soviet Socialist ideology through propaganda.

3. **Izba:** a traditional Russian countryside dwelling similar to a log cabin.

4. **Proletariat:** The class that lives by selling its labor.

5. **Soviet:** a council of workers.

6. **White nights:** Because St. Petersburg is situated only six degrees of latitude south of the Arctic Circle, from mid-May to mid-July twilight never gives way to night. The Russians refer to this time as "the white nights."

7. Lenin's arrival at the **Finland Station** in Petrograd was greeted with a mixture of euphoria and distrust. Many of the more strident proponents of socialism were emboldened with his arrival. Other, more moderate-minded constituents worried that Lenin and his company had come from exile in Switzerland on a secret train supplied by the German government. They wondered about the harsh

reparations Germany might impose for Russia's capitulation. Indeed, Lenin had made it clear that if the Bolsheviks were to come to power, they would end Russia's involvement in the Great War. Germany was counting on this eventuality, because it would release their forces on the Eastern Front, which could then be deployed to the Western Front. Many in the Provisional Government feared that Lenin would shred the fragile thread of power they'd established after overthrowing the tsar. Indeed, Lenin himself fully expected the Provisional Government to arrest him upon his arrival in Petrograd.

8. The socialist revolution in Russia was not meant to be an isolated event. The Bolshevik leaders were convinced that when other socialist movements in Europe and America saw the success of the Bolshevik takeover in Russia, they would follow suit. That was the dream of the socialists—a worldwide proletariat dictatorship.

9. **Peter and Paul Fortress:** Peter the Great built a walled encampment in 1703 on Zayachy Island to protect the city of St. Petersburg. Within the walls of the fortress stand military buildings, the Church of Peter and Paul, and a prison.

CHAPTER FIVE

PETROGRAD

August 1917

"You will never guess what Mother and I saw today when we were shopping, Natasha Ivanovna."

Natasha grinned at Agnes's bright expression. "I can't imagine."

"Dog collars!"

"Dog collars?"

"Yes. It was so odd. All along the Nevsky Prospect there were closed shops, one right after another, and then here was this run-down little shop selling dog collars. Some of the collars were studded with small jewels."

Natasha Ivanovna scoffed. "Such a waste. The shop owner will have a hard time selling those. Who would be bourgeois enough to have a dog these days, anyway? No one. That's probably why he had something to sell, because no one has a dog."

Agnes grunted. "You are so tiresome, Natasha Ivanovna. Let's not talk anymore. I say we pay attention to the soup and bread, and not talk about anything."

The women stood in the Lindlof kitchen, chopping vegetables for the evening meal of borscht.

"But don't you see how much better life will be under Communism? We are Russian, Agnes. We are not British or American. We know how to share. The ancient peasant ideology of sharing will slide easily into Communism."

"Must we talk politics?" Agnes protested, cutting through the head of cabbage with one stroke. "That's all you want to do anymore, Natasha Ivanovna—talk politics."

Natasha opened her mouth to share another opinion, then relented. "I'm sorry, little squirrel. I won't say another word."

They chopped in silence, adding to the colorful piles of thin strips of cabbage, carrot, beet, potato, and onion that waited for the soup pot. The dark brown dough of peasant bread was rising on the sideboard, and golden summer pears filled a bowl on the table. Even with Agnes's two brothers away at war, Natasha was amazed at the amount of food needed to feed so many mouths. Agnes's father still found places to sell his gold and silver trinkets, a fact that Natasha found disconcerting. Russian soldiers were starving on the front lines, factory workers existed on bread alone, and the country farmers were forced to send the bulk of their harvest to the cities. Yet, with the earth crumbling around them, the upper class still had lavish parties, went to the theater, and purchased silver wine goblets to toast their own good health. She shook her head and chopped vegetables.

"What?" Agnes asked.

"Nothing," Natasha said flatly, placing beets on the beet stack.

"Natasha Ivanovna, we are closer than sisters. I know when something is on your mind."

Natasha grinned. "No, I won't say, because it's politics again."

"Ugh!" Agnes protested. "I'm glad you are done with the university."

"Are you? Why?"

"Because they taught you only to think, think, think."

Natasha laughed. "Yes, I suppose that is the purpose of education."

Agnes picked up an onion and began peeling it. "Yes, but the Bolsheviks want us to only think their way. All these brilliant people running around insisting they can figure out the best way for people to live. Kerensky and the Provisional Government say this; Lenin and the Bolsheviks say that."

Natasha nodded. "And the monks in the church chant prayers, while the war goes on and people are starving."

"Politics again!" Agnes snapped, her eyes watering from the onion.

"Politics always, little squirrel," Natasha said.

They worked without speaking for several minutes.

Agnes broke the silence. "Father says it won't work."

"What won't work?"

"Communism."

Natasha carefully chopped a carrot.

"He says that the ideas of the Socialists are flawed."

Natasha worked to keep a sharp tone out of her voice. "Now who's talking politics?"

"In our Church we have this law called . . ." Agnes stopped chopping and concentrated. "Oh, I can't remember. The law of cons—of something."

"It was called the law of consecration," Johan Lindlof said, coming into the kitchen.

Agnes jumped. "Father! You frightened me."

"Sorry, dear one. I only came in for a drink of water." He moved to the sink. "How is the soup coming, Natasha Ivanovna?"

"Fine, sir. We've chopped half a garden's worth and only have the other half to manage."

Johan chuckled. "My wife is very grateful for your help."

Natasha nodded. She knew that Agnes's mother was often ill with worry over her two sons in the war.

"So, here you are, two intelligent girls, chopping vegetables and talking religion and politics."

Agnes frowned. "I'm tired of talking politics. Everyone is always talking politics, or going on strike, or protesting."

Natasha watched Mr. Lindlof's face, but it was full of tenderness as he set down his glass of water and gave his daughter a hug. "I know this is a hard time for you, my Agnes—conflict and upheaval on every side. Be patient. Trust God."

Agnes nodded.

"I know Agnes won't be pleased," Natasha ventured, "but I would like to ask about this law of consecration, Mr. Lindlof."

Johan searched the bright, inquisitive face of his daughter's lifelong friend.

Natasha returned his look openly, realizing that he was assessing if her inquiry was genuine. She knew he found her family to be an enigma—affable toward their neighbors, yet holding themselves aloof. She knew her mother's aloofness came because of her timid nature, but her father's distance came because of philosophical differences with the Lindlofs concerning occupation, politics, and religion—basic differences which affability could not bridge.

Unadulterated affection had bonded her and Agnes through the years since their childhood, and she hoped that Mr. Lindlof would trust upon that bond to answer her question.

He sat down at the kitchen table. "What would you like to know, Natasha Ivanovna?"

"What is the law of consecration?"

"It's a way of living. And when the law is lived properly it can lead to the total elimination of poverty."

"Excuse me?" Natasha said, her knife held idle over the vegetables.

Mr. Lindlof smiled at her. "Yes, a lofty goal indeed."

"An impossible goal."

"Well, ancient scripture tells us that it has happened on a few occasions."

Natasha's intellect bristled at the mention of scriptural folklore, but she was intrigued by such sweeping economic claims.

"How does it work?"

"With great difficulty," Mr. Lindlof answered. "It hasn't been achieved for thousands of years."

Natasha laid down her knife. "But your church practices this law?"

"Wait now, we're getting ahead of ourselves. Let me start back a bit." Mr. Lindlof hesitated, and Natasha surmised he was organizing his thoughts. She waited. "The law of consecration was received through revelation to the Prophet Joseph Smith," Mr. Lindlof stated.

Natasha struggled to keep listening.

"I know this is difficult for you, Natasha Ivanovna, but see if you can pull anything interesting from my fairy tale of faith."

Natasha found herself smiling. She glanced over at Agnes. "As long as you don't try to tell me that story of gold bibles and angels."

Johan Lindlof smiled with her. "No. We will have enough to consider with this topic."

"So, what is it?"

"First let me ask if you've read Lenin's newest writing—*The State and the Revolution?*"

Natasha stared at Agnes's father as though she'd never seen him before. "I . . . I have. Have you?"

"Of course."

Natasha came to sit with him at the table. "But you are not a Bolshevik."

"No. But it is a foolish man who is not aware of the forces pressing in on his world."

Natasha nodded.

"I found it fascinating that Lenin writes of a great utopian vision."

Agnes put onions into the soup pot. "Utopian?"

"A perfect society," her father said. "Lenin predicts that when the government of the common man sweeps away capitalism, then people will be transformed."

"What do you mean?" Agnes asked as she brought the lump of dough to the table for kneading.

"Lenin doesn't say how it will happen, he just says that man will no longer think in a selfish, capitalistic context, but in a new, brotherly communistic one."

Natasha sat straighter. "That man will behave in a natural, ethical manner."

"Yes," Mr. Lindlof agreed. "That's what Lenin believes. Marx had the same vague vision of what society would be like after the proletariat smashed the state machine. In the *Manifesto,* he expects the experience of the mass movement to show them the way to the next step."

Natasha stiffened. "You don't think their vision is possible?"

Johan looked at her straight on. "No. Neither Marx nor Lenin knows how this transformation will happen—how man will change from a selfish lout to a caring, hardworking comrade. They just believe that *somehow* it will."

Natasha spoke slowly. "Well, the *process* will change them. As we move through this great journey of the proletariat, men will see the benefit of equality—of working together in a communal effort." She looked again into Mr. Lindlof's eyes. "You don't believe that."

"No. You cannot change a man's nature or behavior by outside means, Natasha Ivanovna. There must be a change of a man's heart, and only God can do that."

"I don't believe in God."

"I know, and neither does Marx or Lenin. For them religion is to be purged from the system along with capitalism and class."

"Religion is the opium of the people," Natasha said, not looking at Agnes.

Johan smiled at her. "So I've heard."

"But we are off the subject," Natasha said. "I want to know why you think this law of yours will work and Socialism won't."

"But faith *is* the subject, Natasha Ivanovna. Faith is the difference between the two ideologies. It matters where you put your trust." He turned to his daughter. "Agnes, will you please bring me my Book of Mormon and the new book Brother Hoglund sent me? They're on my dresser."

"Yes, Father." Agnes finished kneading the bread and set it aside.

Natasha felt out of sorts and trapped. She did not want to hear anything from the strange Mormon books. She berated herself for asking about the stupid concept in the first place. She would have invented an excuse that her father needed her at home, but her parents were in Sel'tso Saterno visiting her mother's sister. She wished she were with them in the country with her aunt and uncle and cousin Irena—anywhere but here listening to religious nonsense.

"The law of consecration says that a person is to consecrate all their time, talents, and earthly goods to the building of God's kingdom."

Natasha brought her full attention to the subject matter. "Your God certainly asks for much."

"Actually He doesn't ask it for Himself at all. We live the law for each other—to become one in heart and mind."

Agnes returned and laid the books on the table.

"Thank you," her father said, patting her hand.

"I thought you promised not to talk about gold bibles," Natasha said.

Johan smiled. "Think of it as a history book." He flipped pages in the black book until he found the place he wanted.

Natasha heard Agnes's knife thunking on the wooden table and smelled the tang of onions simmering in the pot. *Indulge him,* she thought. How often had she indulged her mother's empty rituals, watching with pity as she knelt in front of the small bedroom table covered with miniature icons, or when she wore her scarf embroidered with crosses out into public. Natasha turned her face toward Mr. Lindlof, her eyes devoid of interest.

"There was a group of people in ancient America that, because of faith, changed their hearts so completely that they lived in peace for a long time."

Natasha set her jaw as he read.

"'And they had all things common among them; therefore there were not rich and poor, bond and free, but they were all made free, and partakers of the heavenly gift.'" He turned the page. "'And it came to pass that there was no contention in the land, because of the love of God which did dwell in the hearts of the people.'" He stopped reading and looked at her.

"For how long?"

"I beg your pardon?"

"How long did they live in peace?" Natasha asked.

"Almost two hundred years."

Natasha was shocked by that answer. "Two hundred years? I've studied a little about the ancient people of the Americas, but I've never heard of this."

Johan Lindlof nodded. "I'm not surprised."

"And you believe this folklore?"

Mr. Lindlof looked at her straight on. "Not folklore. I believe there actually was an ancient civilization that found a way to peace through living this law of consecration. From each according to their ability. To each according to their needs."

"Those are the words of Karl Marx. No man above another—all men sharing."

"Yes, but here is the difference. This consecrating of one's time, talents, and all earthly goods is done voluntarily, Natasha Ivanovna. It is not mandated by government. And because men's hearts are changed, they will not only share willingly, but they will not demand anything they do not deserve."

Natasha felt a coil of resentment snake up her spine. She thought of the gold and silver which constituted the Lindlofs' livelihood. "You don't live your church's law," she said before she could temper the harshness of her tone. She sensed Agnes staring at her, and she felt the heat of shame rise into her face.

"No one lives the law at this time," Mr. Lindlof answered without rancor. "The Prophet Joseph tried to prepare the people to live the law, but they could not move beyond their selfishness."

"Men's hearts again."

Mr. Lindlof gave her a kind look. "Yes, men's hearts again. We are asked to work hard and take care of our neighbors where there is need." He picked up the other book that Agnes had brought out. "For now, we live the lesser law of tithing, but that is a story for another day." He stood. "I must get back to the shop before Johannes and Oskar ruin the silver set we're working on." He held out the book to her. "I want you to have this, Natasha Ivanovna."

She sat motionless, not wanting to be rude, but not wanting to take the book.

"It is not the golden bible," he said gently. "It is a book I think you will find most interesting. Think of it as a philosophy book."

"A Mormon philosophy book?"

"Yes, a treatise on the basic tenets of our faith. It is written by a professor, James Talmage, considered to be one of America's great scholars." He waited patiently. "If nothing else, it will help you practice your English."

She took the book. She figured she could put it on the shelf in her bedroom where it would soon be lost among the clutter. She looked down at the title written on the dark blue cover: *Articles of Faith.* "Thank you, Mr. Lindlof. I . . . I will look at it."

"I think it will surprise you." He turned and walked from the room.

Natasha looked over at Agnes who was placing lumps of dough into the bread pans. "Here, let me help you, little squirrel." She stood. "And I promise, no more talk of politics." She set the book to the side. "In fact, I only want to hear about flowers and dog collars and the odd things you saw today on the prospect."

NOTES

1. When Natasha schools Agnes about the "peasant ideology of sharing," she is referring to the **Mir**, a system which dictated how a village community of peasant farmers functioned in pre-revolutionary Russia.

2. The book *Articles of Faith* by James E. Talmage first appeared in print in 1899. Its subject matter was taken from addresses delivered by Professor Talmage to university-level theology classes. The book is a study of the thirteen Articles of Faith set forth by the Prophet Joseph Smith.

3. Lenin's book *The State and the Revolution* was written in the summer of 1917 and published in 1918. It describes and defines the writings of Friedrich Engels and Karl Marx in relation to the theories of communism, the need for a proletarian revolution, and the role of the state in society. Johan Lindlof is aware of the book prior to its publication date in deference to my time line.

CHAPTER SIX

RIGA—THE EASTERN FRONT

September 1, 1917

"You are a madman!" Arel Lindlof hissed at his brother as he squatted next to him in the trench. "The colonel will shoot you if you try to run away."

"I don't care," Bruno spat back. "I don't care." He glared at Arel with red-rimmed eyes, and he swiped away the yellow ooze from his nose with a dirty hand. "I'm going home. I won't stay in this madness for another winter. I can't." Tears streaked the grime on Bruno's face and the eyes of the despairing soldiers nearby were locked on the pitiful sight.

Cold weather had set in, turning the barren landscape brittle and brown, and in the night rain had fallen. The men watched as the death detail floated through the early-morning fog like ghosts. They watched as twenty-three bodies were taken from the trench to the mass grave. The boots and coats of the dead did not go with them.

"There are more of us dying from sickness and starvation than German bullets," Bruno growled.

Arel could not dispute that fact so he changed the subject. "Look, Bruno, stay by me for just a few more days. I'm sure the war will be over soon."

Bruno stared at the ground.

"I'm sure of it," Arel insisted.

An older soldier with a full beard and creases around his eyes broke into Arel's speech. "Well, perhaps soon, comrade, but not in a few days. I came out of Riga and overheard a report that the Germans are on the doorstep. We will be taking a stand here."

A soldier with a skeletal face turned his head slowly in their direction. "Stand, Andre Andreyevitch? I don't even have a rifle. Kerensky and his Provisional Government are liars and cowards. They tell us we must stay in the war, but do they send us food and equipment? No. We common soldiers are not worth their time. I say, give me the Bolsheviks and peace."

"Peace?" the older soldier cut in. "You think you'll have peace if the Bolsheviks come to power?"

"Yes," the skeleton said, his rasping voice grinding the word to dust. "Yes. Peace, land, and bread." Several heads nodded. "They've promised to get us out of this senseless war."

Andre Andreyevitch shook his head. "I've lived long enough to know that the promises of politicians are hollow. Their hearts are well-meaning, but their hands are empty."

The thin man wagged his head. "Oh, we have a great thinker standing in the mud." He pointed at Andre. "Your brain won't keep you from starving and freezing along with the rest of us."

"Go get a rifle from the grave detail, you little rat, and quit complaining," Andre Andreyevitch snarled.

The other man glowered and moved to a different position on the line.

Andre Andreyevitch swore. "We have braver soldiers in the women's death battalion."

"My cousin is a member of that group," a soldier nearby piped in. "She sent a picture. They look like men in their uniforms and their shaved heads. Three hundred or so women. Can you imagine?"

Bruno stared at the soldier in disbelief. "Women? Women in battle?"

"No, no. They're not coming out here," the soldier corrected. "They're defending Petrograd . . . well, the government offices actually. They must be a sight, I'll tell you. Most don't have boots because the military supply couldn't get their sizes, so the girls just wear their own shoes."

Other soldiers were beginning to bunch around to hear the talk of women and shoes.

"Yes, it's true, comrades—uniforms, shaved heads, and pink dancing shoes," the young man continued, happy with the attention.

Some of the men chuckled at the thought, while others mumbled comments about the rotten government and the tragedy of women shaving their heads. Suddenly the commanding officer shoved through the group of men, grabbing the young soldier and pressing him back against the side of the trench. "What is this nonsense?" he snarled. "Think you're in a bar in Petrograd swapping stories?"

Arel pulled Bruno away from the knot of soldiers and the angry colonel.

"I said, what are you about, young fool?" The officer's grip around the struggling soldier's throat made it impossible for him to answer, but the colonel persisted. "Answer me." The officer was from the old guard and sure of his authority. "I said answer me."

The boy was strangling.

"He was just telling us a story," Andre Andreyevitch intervened.

The officer backhanded him across his cheek. "Did I ask you?"

Andre Andreyevitch staggered to the side, blood dripping from his lip.

Released from the choke hold, the young soldier slumped to the ground, gasping for air, as the men in the group stiffened and stepped forward.

The officer pulled out his pistol. "Get back there! What are you about?" He fired, and a soldier in a fur cap went down.

Bruno screamed and ran forward—directly into the sights of the waiting pistol.

"Bruno, no!" Arel yelled, struggling to grab his brother's coat.

Andre Andreyevitch swung his arm in a wide arc, knocking the gun out of the officer's hand. The look on the colonel's face changed from consternation to disbelief to fear. He fumbled to unsheathe his sword.

The sound of an incoming artillery shell pulled everyone's attention to the battlefield. The shell exploded a hundred feet to the left of their position, blowing all of them against the back of the trench or onto the slimy ground. The officer scrambled to his feet and stumbled down the line, screaming orders.

Crying and muttering at his younger brother, Arel stood and pulled Bruno to his feet. "What were you doing, idiot? Going against the colonel?

What good does it do that I pray for you if you're going to behave like such an idiot?"

Another shell hit and then another. "Flamethrowers!" someone yelled, and the terrified cry of "Poison gas!" coursed down the line.

"We don't have gas masks!" Bruno cried. He grabbed Arel and shoved him over the back side of the trench. "Run!"

"Fall back! Fall back!" Andre Andreyevitch called out, and soldiers began pouring out of the trench in waves, abandoning starvation, doubt, and duty. Weak, yet determined, they ran, fighting for breath and life.

Arel fell and Bruno pulled him up.

"Stop! Stop there!" they heard the colonel ordering. "Hold your line!" No one obeyed.

Bullets began zinging past as Arel and Bruno ran with their comrades. With a grunt, Bruno fell onto his knees, but was up a moment later, lurching forward. Andre Andreyevitch grabbed him around the upper arm and dragged him forward until they were even with Arel.

"Hey! Hey!" The older soldier had to yell to be heard above the din. "Your brother's been hit!"

Arel checked his panic and spun around. Hit? What did the man mean? Bruno was up and moving. He heard a bullet zip past his head and looked to see who was firing. The colonel was doggedly pursuing the retreating men, firing at them with intent. Arel stared as the butcher aimed straight at him.

Suddenly a soldier shoved the colonel from the side, and he crumpled into the mud. Before the officer could rise, the gaunt man rushed forward, stabbing him with a bayonet. Several others kicked the downed officer, and another pulled the pistol from his hand.

Arel's mind slipped sideways and he stood frozen in place like a child watching a dogfight.

Someone yelled at him. "Get moving, soldier! Now!"

A yellow mist of poison gas crawled over the colonel's body, and panic pushed Arel away from the grisly scene. Bruno cried out in pain as Arel ducked under his injured arm and gripped him around the waist. Andre Andreyevitch took Bruno's other arm, and the three stumbled off across the uneven pasture. They ran east, away from the chaos and toward the rising sun.

◆　◆　◆

The peasant woman brought the soldiers black bread, pickled cucumbers, and a cross.

"Thank you, little mother," Andre Andreyevitch said, handing the food to Arel and setting aside the cross, "but we need a doctor. The boy must be looked after."

She shook her head at the bearded man. "As I told you before, the doctor was killed in the war. No one has come since to fill his place."

Arel stopped pacing. "Perhaps another town?"

The woman shook her head again. "There is no doctor, but our priest knows something of medicine."

Andre Andreyevitch was about to refuse when Arel broke in. "Yes. Yes, go and get him, please."

The woman left and Arel resumed pacing. "I should have stayed with him. I should have been the one."

"Shut up about that, friend," Andre Andreyevitch said. "War is war— the bullet does not care who it hits." He moved an old wooden box to the wall of the shed and sat down. "Eat something. You need to build your strength." He held out a large piece of bread.

"I can't," Arel answered.

"You must, comrade. How will you get your brother home if you don't have strength?"

Arel took the bread and slumped onto the ground next to the makeshift pallet they'd arranged for Bruno. He stared at the blood-soaked wad of cloth he'd bound around his brother's shoulder. *What will I tell my family if he dies? If I had gone with him when he wanted to run, he wouldn't be lying here bleeding to death.* He glanced at his brother's face, sickened by the clammy gray skin and bloodless lips.

Arel's thoughts came in disjointed fragments. *Bruno, the best looking of all the Lindlof children. Bruno, my partner in fun. Oh, the tricks we played on Agnes and Natasha Ivanovna. Natasha Ivanovna . . . so beautiful. When we were boys, we both tried to win her favor. But how can Bruno love her? She is a Bolshevik and doesn't believe in God. Poor Bruno. Poor me.*

Arel sat back against the wall of the shed, brought his knees to his chest, and put his head on his arms. Exhaustion was making him weep.

The shed door opened and Agnes walked in. She wore her pink dancing dress and shoes, but her head was bald. Her ears protruded from either side of her skull, and her blue eyes were filled with tears. She looked at him without flinching, and then she raised her hand and pointed at him.

Arel gasped and sat up, shaking the dream away. A man was kneeling by Bruno's pallet, poking at the wounded shoulder. Bruno was moaning in pain.

"Hey! Get away from there!" Arel yelled, lunging forward and bumping the man sideways.

"It's all right, Arel," Andre Andreyevitch said from his place. "It's the priest. He's come to help."

Arel tried to clear the ache of sleep from his brain. He saw the long black dress of the priest and the full beard. *How long have I been asleep? I didn't even hear him come into the shed.* "I'm sorry, Father. I . . ."

"It's all right," the priest answered. "You've had a hard time of it."

The deep base of his voice was soothing and reassuring, and Arel's fears retreated a step. He moved to Bruno's side. The priest had removed Bruno's shirt and was washing the skin clean with vodka.

"The man tells me this is your brother."

"Yes," Arel answered.

"And that you are running away from the war."

Arel's eyes flew over to Andre Andreyevitch, and the man made a brief inclination of his head.

"Yes," Arel affirmed. "One of our own officers shot my brother."

"The world is a mad place," the priest said softly. "Now, I need you to hold your brother on his side as I examine the entrance wound. It seems as though the bullet's gone straight through, but I want it clean. With his body in such a weakened state, we can't afford infection."

Arel looked at the priest in wonder. Did he study medicine at night after prayers?

Bruno's eyes opened a slit, and he groaned when Arel rolled him onto his side. "Don't . . . don't," he rasped.

"Be still, Bruno. We need to look at the wound."

Bruno gritted his teeth as the priest probed the wound, cleaned it, and covered it with several layers of cloth. Blood seeped through to the outer layer almost immediately, and the priest made the sign of the cross.

"He's not a bleeder, is he?"

"Bleeder?"

"A hemophiliac—like the tsarevitch?"

"No. No, of course not," Arel said. "He has always been very healthy."

The priest applied more dressing, overlaying it with a band of cloth which extended around the shoulder. When they laid Bruno down, blood streamed from the exit wound. The priest washed it clean and hurriedly applied thick padding, tying it tightly with the strip of cloth.

"Healthy or not, he cannot afford to lose much more blood," the holy man offered, pressing down on the wound. Bruno yelled.

Arel's panic returned. "We . . . we should give him a blessing," he sputtered.

The priest looked over at him. "I have been praying for him since I arrived."

Bruno writhed in pain.

"Of course, and I'm grateful, but . . ."—Arel placed his hands on Bruno's head—"may I say a prayer for my brother?"

"Most assuredly."

Arel closed his eyes and immediately the prayer was on his lips. In the name of the Lord and by the power of the holy Melchizedek priesthood, he blessed his brother that he would recover to make the journey home. He blessed those traveling with him that they would be guided to find the safest path. He blessed the kind woman who'd given them sanctuary, the priest for his goodness, and Andre Andreyevitch for his courage. He promised Bruno that he would see his family again, but as he opened his mouth to add words of future events, they would not come. Tears streamed down Arel's face as he felt the warmth and solace of the Spirit confirming that it was enough. Arel finished the prayer in the name of the Savior. He stood quietly for a moment enveloped in the affirmation of the blessing.

When he looked up, three pairs of eyes were staring at him. The peasant woman stood just inside the doorway, her fingers pressed against her lips—slowly she made the sign of the cross. Andre Andreyevitch's brow was furrowed, and he leaned forward as if to study Arel more closely. The priest drew his hand away from the bandage on Bruno's shoulder.

"I have never heard a prayer such as that," he said reverently. "Are you a minister?"

Arel shook his head. "No, Father. All the worthy men of our faith hold the priesthood."

The priest looked bewildered. "All the men? I have never heard of such a church."

"I would imagine not," came Bruno's whispered reply.

Arel looked down quickly into the eyes of his brother, and smiled. "You are alive then."

"I am."

The others in the room drew close.

The peasant woman reached out to touch Arel's arm. "You have healing power, young master."

"No," Arel replied kindly. "*God* has healing power."

The woman bobbed her head and smiled a toothy smile. "I will bring soup." She turned quickly and waddled from the room.

The priest untied the bandage and carefully lifted the cloth from the wound. "The bleeding has slowed," he said quietly. He looked into Bruno's face. "I think you will be fine now."

Bruno smiled weakly. "Thank you, Father."

"Yes, Father, thank you. You have great skill," Arel said.

"Skill? Ah, perhaps . . . yes. I suppose that is something." He looked deeply into Arel's eyes. "If I could, I would ask about your faith."

Arel nodded. "If there was time, I would tell you."

The priest handed Andre Andreyevitch extra bandages and the bottle of vodka. He gave the man a stern look. "Not for drinking. Only for cleaning the wound."

"Of course," Andre said indignantly. "What do you take me for?"

"A Russian," the priest answered. "I will make sure the village keeps you safe and I will try to find other clothing for you to wear. Perhaps the widow has some of her husband's old things." He gathered up the bloody cloths and put them into a bucket. "There is a train out of Aluksne, but that is a hundred miles away. I would drive you, but no one here has an automobile."

"It would be too dangerous for anyone to help us, Father," Andre Andreyevitch said. "Besides, you have done much already. We will manage."

The priest turned to Arel. "He should stay down for a few days. Then take it slowly."

"Yes, Father."

"God go with you."

"And with you," Arel answered.

The priest hesitated as though he had something more to say or a question to ask. Finally, he picked up the bucket, nodded to the men, and left.

"I'll go and chop some wood for the widow," Andre Andreyevitch said. He grabbed another piece of bread and headed for the door.

"I will come and help in a moment," Arel replied. "I want to make sure my brother is settled."

When Andre Andreyevitch was gone, Arel brought a second ragged blanket and laid it over his brother. He lifted Bruno's head and gave him a drink of water, and then he made sure the two small shed windows were closed tightly.

"Soon the little mother will come with hot soup, and I will be just outside chopping wood," Arel said.

Bruno nodded. "About time you did some work."

Arel chuckled and gave him another sip of water.

Bruno took his hand. "In a couple of days I will be able to help you."

Arel gave him a doubtful look. "In a couple of days I hope to be heading home."

"Yes," Bruno said. "We're going to see the family again." He took a deep breath. "*I* will see them again, thanks to your blessing."

"The *Lord's* blessing," Arel countered. "It will take us some time, little brother, but we'll make it."

Bruno closed his eyes. "I wonder if we'll find it much changed?"

"Changed? What do you mean—changed at home?"

"I mean everything."

Arel heard the thwack of an ax against wood. "Yes. I'm sure everything will be different," he said softly. He tucked the blanket around Bruno's shoulders. "Rest now." He turned to help with the chopping.

NOTES

1. Russian troops were defeated by German forces in the battle of Riga on September 3, 1917, just two days after I have the Lindlof boys deserting. By this point in the war, dispirited Russian soldiers were deserting by the thousands and it was not uncommon for officers to use brutal (and deadly) force to keep soldiers in line. Although Bruno and Arel Lindlof could have been soldiers in the war, their participation is fictional.

It was because the deserting Russian soldiers kept their weapons when they returned home that there was an armed populace when the revolution occurred.

2. **Women's Death Battalion:** All female combat units formed by the Provisional Government. Fifteen formations were created in 1917 including the 1st Russian Women's Battalion of Death. The women who joined believed they would be fighting to defend Mother Russia, when in reality they were pawns of the Provisional Government to stand against the Bolsheviks, shame the Russian soldiers into maintaining the fight on the Eastern Front, and guard the offices of the Provisional Government located in the Winter Palace.

CHAPTER SEVEN

Petrograd

September 20, 1917

"I don't understand why your mother comes every day to check the death lists," Natasha Ivanovna whispered to Agnes. "They only change the standings once a week."

Agnes looked at her mother walking ahead of them and holding the hands of Alexandria and Linda Alise. "You saw her face. It brings her comfort. When she comes and looks at the posting and doesn't see their names, it brings her comfort."

"It's a ritual then?"

Agnes stiffened. "Yes, it's like a ritual, if you want to call it that."

Natasha noted the tension in Agnes's voice. "I'm sorry, did I offend you?"

"I just don't see why you came with us today if you find our *little ritual* so pathetic."

Natasha stopped walking. "Oh, my friend." Agnes turned to look at her. "I'm sorry." She walked quickly to Agnes and took her gloved hands. "I don't find your ritual pathetic at all. I find it . . ."

"What?" Agnes snapped, pulling her hands away. "Sad? Meaningless?"

"No. I—"

"I don't believe you. You have been cross all afternoon, Natasha Ivanovna."

"No, I haven't."

"And what about all *your* rituals? What about all the meetings you attend with Sergey Antonovich, all the banners you carry and the slogans you call out?"

"Those aren't rituals."

"Aren't they? 'All Power to the Soviets!' How many times a day do I hear that pathetic sentiment chanted in the street? And how many really know what that means?"

Natasha quickly scrutinized the people closest to them on the walkway. "Agnes, stop."

"I suppose you find much of what our family does pathetic—believing in God and saying prayers. You think we are mindless sheep. Well, what of the way Sergey Antonovich leads you around? You are blinded by his brightness."

Alma Lindlof was beside her daughter. "Agnes? Natasha? What's the matter?"

Agnes quieted immediately. She took a deep breath and looked away from Natasha. "Nothing, Mother . . . truly. We just had a little disagreement about something."

"Friends should never disagree," Mrs. Lindlof stated flatly, as though surprised by the very idea. "Friends are dear treasures, especially lifelong friends like you and Natasha."

Agnes's eyes welled with tears. "Yes, Mother."

Natasha could feel the stony glares of Alexandria and Linda Alise, questioning her part in the misunderstanding. She avoided looking at them, looking instead to Mrs. Lindlof. "Yes, yes of course, you're right. It was my fault. I'm sorry, Agnes."

"Agnes?" her mother prompted. "Have you nothing to say?"

"Yes. I'm sorry too."

"Good. That's settled then," Alma Lindlof said, patting her daughter on the arm.

Natasha glanced at Agnes as she gave her mother a forced smile, realizing that her friend had meant every word of her invective against her and that she'd apologized only to lessen any worry or sadness her mother carried. Natasha was miserable. She and Agnes would always be friends, but their friendship was changing. Perhaps the playful bonds of youth could not stand against the sharp differences that now molded their characters.

"Now, I have a favor to ask of the two friends," Mrs. Lindlof said innocently. "Would you please take Linda Alise home while I go with Alexandria to find a new pair of gloves?"

"I want to find a new pair of gloves," Linda Alise whined.

"You don't require gloves," Mrs. Lindlof stated. "Tonight, Alexandria is going with friends to the ballet at the Mariinsky Theater and must have indoor gloves."

"I don't mean I want to buy any gloves," Linda Alise answered in frustration. "I just want to go with you to shop."

"Not today," her mother said kindly. "You have lessons waiting at home that must be finished."

Natasha watched the sour expression on Linda Alise's face deepen. The girl was fourteen years old, yet she often acted much younger.

Agnes stepped in. "Come on, sister. Natasha and I will play our riddle game with you while we walk."

Linda Alise's mind changed abruptly. "Really? You never play that game with me."

"Well, today we will test your brilliance." She reached out and took her sister's hand.

Natasha admired her friend's ability to set aside her own heartaches and irritations for the needs of someone else. It was a quality she herself found difficult to emulate. The truth was she *had* been irritated during the outing, and her words had been colored by that annoyance. It had started when she saw how Mrs. Lindlof and her daughters were dressed: smart hats, heavy cloth coats, and warm mittens. Natasha had given her own excess clothing to the factory workers and wondered why Agnes's family did not do the same. And as the outing progressed, she had been put off by the women's easy chatter. They did not intentionally exclude her, but the flow of words formed a language that they easily interpreted, and often she could not. Natasha squirmed as she evaluated her peevish behavior. As they'd stood around the large board where the names of the war dead were posted, she'd dallied in the background, envious of the Lindlofs' attachment to each other.

As Linda Alise was giving her sister instructions on what type of gloves to buy, Natasha went to Agnes and put her arm around her waist. "Agnes, I'm sorry. I have been cross today—jealous and out of sorts. It made me say terrible things. I do treasure our friendship."

Agnes lowered her eyes and nodded. "I'm sorry too. I'm ashamed of the things I said."

"No. And what you said is true. I do let Sergey lead my thinking at times. There is no halfway for him, and I need to be careful of his influence."

Agnes looked up. "Oh, yes, Natasha Ivanovna. I worry about you. There is so much passion and anger now. Johannes said that he saw a young man who was a counterrevolutionary being horsewhipped by some Bolsheviks. I don't want you caught up in anything that would hurt you."

Natasha gave her a squeeze. "Dear friend, how I wish for your sake we could live in a world of beauty and kindness."

"I think that will only be in heaven."

"I'm ready," Linda Alise said cheerily as she came up beside her sister. "Do you have a riddle ready for me?"

"Yes," Agnes said as they started walking. "No tears, no trials, no turmoil."

Linda Alise frowned at her. "That's not a riddle. That's a Sunday lesson from Father."

Agnes smiled at her. "We're starting easy. So, what's the answer?"

Linda Alise shrugged. "Heaven, of course."

◆　◆　◆

"Wait! Wait, don't tell me!" Linda Alise shrieked as Natasha Ivanovna laughed.

"You've been trying to figure this one out for the past eight blocks," Agnes said. "There is a time limit, you know."

"That's true," Natasha confirmed. "If you're going to play, you have to play by the rules."

"But this one is so difficult," Linda Alise protested.

Agnes nodded in agreement. "Natasha Ivanovna is the *grand duchess* of riddles."

Linda Alise frowned at her. "Are you giving me a clue? Don't do that. I want to figure it out by myself." She stopped walking. "Treasured pictures that will never be sold, encased in a heart of flowered gold."

"Hurry, or it will be *Easter* before you figure it out," Natasha said solemnly.

Linda Alise's face brightened. "I know!" she shouted.

"Amazing!" Agnes teased.

"It's the Faberge eggs that the tsar gives to his family for Easter!"

"But which egg?" Agnes encouraged.

"The one with the lily of the valley and the pictures of his family that magically pop up from the inside!"

"Well done!" Natasha congratulated.

Linda Alise beamed. "I love this game! No wonder you two have been playing it for so many years."

"Hello there, you three!" Alma Lindlof's voice interrupted the merriment. She and Alexandria were soon beside the trio. "You've certainly been taking your time," she scolded good-naturedly. "We've been to the shop, made our purchase, and nearly arrived home ahead of you."

"We were just having so much fun playing our game," Linda Alise defended.

"Yes, and now you have schoolwork to finish, Alexandria has to dress for the evening, and Agnes and I must prepare supper."

They started walking. When they turned the corner onto the Griboyedov promenade they saw Erland standing out in front of the Lindlofs' apartment.

Mrs. Lindlof shook her head. "What in the world is that boy doing out in front of the house?"

"Father probably sent him outdoors as punishment for one of his pranks," Agnes said, trying hard not to laugh. "Poor Erland can never keep still and out of trouble."

As soon as Erland saw the women he ran to them. "Mother, Mother, come," he said, grabbing her arm and pulling her ahead. He was crying uncontrollably, and Natasha was sure some sort of tragedy waited inside the Lindlof home.

The women ran, Natasha staying a few steps behind.

They burst through the door of the shop and saw the Lindlof men gathered there—*all* the Lindlof men. There was absolute silence as Arel Lindlof walked to his mother and fell into her arms, weeping.

♦ ♦ ♦

"How could they walk over two hundred miles?" Agnes asked. "How?" She paced in front of the apartment, weeping and mumbling, and then weeping again.

Natasha Ivanovna stood as a mute companion, allowing Agnes's grief to release itself in a gush of words.

"And did you see their bodies? So thin! They've wasted away to nothing." For several minutes Agnes cried. "They have been living in a nightmare. Can you imagine how horrible it must have been? Walking through the forest, hiding from people, afraid of being caught." She crossed her hands over her chest to keep in the anguish. "They slept on the cold ground without blankets . . . and Bruno shot . . . shot by one of the officers. He doesn't look good, does he?" New tears coursed down her face. "I mean they both look horrible, but Bruno . . . Bruno looks . . ." She stopped, bending over and placing her hands on her knees. Her breathing came in short gasps and Natasha moved to her, rubbing her back and making soothing sounds.

"My dear friend, perhaps you should go in with your family. Perhaps—"

"No! I can't go back inside. It hurts me too much to see Arel and Bruno in such a horrible condition." The sobbing returned.

Natasha cried with her. "I understand. I do." She felt a knife point of pain in her chest. "Oh, my friend, what can I do?"

Agnes slowly stood up. "I must stay at your house for awhile. I will ask Mother if I can."

Natasha noticed that the thought seemed to quiet her friend.

Agnes continued. "Perhaps after the doctor comes tomorrow I will be able to help Mother care for them, but not now."

"Yes, of course you can stay with me." She held her friend's hand. "Your brothers are young and strong, Agnes. The doctor will come and give them medicine to get better, and you and your mother will tend to their every need. I'm sure in a short time they will both be well and pestering us again."

Agnes took a shuddering breath and nodded. "I must get ahold of myself. I will pray and pray and pray that the Lord will help us through this."

Natasha was stunned. If her friend truly believed that there was some cosmic being that had power over her life, how could she not but hate him for his lack of care and concern? This was a riddle that confused and angered her.

"Please come with me while I talk with Mother. Please, Natasha, I need your strength."

Natasha set aside her bitter feelings, not for her friend's hollow faith, but for their years of companionship. She took a deep breath and followed Agnes into the house.

NOTES

1. **Mariinsky Theater:** Erected in 1860 and named in honor of the Tsarina Maria, wife of Alexander II. It is the premier opera and dance theater of St. Petersburg.

2. Agnes makes reference to a young counterrevolutionary being horsewhipped by a group of Bolsheviks. Though the Bolshevik leaders discouraged violence between citizens of differing political factions, the fervor of socialist ideology often translated into physical attacks.

CHAPTER EIGHT

PETROGRAD

October 6, 1917

Natasha Ivanovna stood at her bedroom window watching large snow-flakes fall onto the Griboyedov canal promenade. She squinted to see across the canal, barely able to make out the golden domes of the St. Nicholas Cathedral. She loved how the church's pale blue façade shimmered in the frosty morning light. She shivered and drew her shawl closer around her shoulders, trying to unravel the dream she'd had in the night of a young peasant girl who took care of a magical cow. She was sure it was part of a country fairy tale her mother had told her years before, but she could not remember the details of the story. It was giving her a headache.

There was a tap on her door.

"Yes?"

The door opened and her mother came into the room with a basket of mending. "Good morning."

"Good morning."

"Be aware of your gray skirt. It has a three-corner tear near the hem."

Natasha nodded. "Yes, ma'am, but I won't get to the mending until this afternoon. Remember Father asked me to go with him to the Smolny to do some work for the Revolutionary Committee."

"I remember," her mother said, straightening the runner on the side table. "This afternoon will be fine." She turned to leave.

"Mother?"

"Yes?"

"Do you remember the story you used to tell me about a peasant girl and a magical cow?"

Svetlana Karlovna smiled and Natasha knew that she was pleased that she'd asked her a question. Usually her mother was content to sit and listen as Natasha and her father discussed economics, politics, and books. She never participated or gave her opinion, and Natasha figured the conversations were beyond her reasoning. But fairy tales were as familiar as the birch trees that surrounded her wooden house in Sel'tso Saterno or the sparrow song she knew as a child.

"Of course, the little orphan girl and the magical cow," her mother said, nodding shyly and touching her fingers to her lips. "It is the same story my mother told me many times." She moved to look out at the falling snow. "'There are in this world good people, people who are not so bad, and those who simply have no shame.'"

Natasha's face broke into a broad smile. "Yes, that was it! That was how it started! And the little orphan girl was taken in by a mean woman with two daughters."

"Three daughters."

Natasha nodded. "Ah, yes, three daughters."

"'The eldest was called One-Eye, the middle was Two-Eyes, and the youngest Three-Eyes,'" her mother recited.

Natasha clapped her hands. "And they were always spying on the orphan girl to make sure she got her work done."

Natasha's mother chuckled. "Yes. You wanted to poke their eyes out with a stick."

"I remember."

Svetlana Karlovna smoothed a wrinkle from the coverlet. "What made you think of that story?"

"Last night I dreamed about the orphan girl and the cow. But it was all mixed up and I couldn't remember the ending." Natasha watched as her mother made the sign of the cross on her pillow, knowing that she was blessing it to give her daughter a better night's sleep. *Such empty superstitions.* "So what happened?" Natasha asked, a note of irritation in her voice.

"The mean woman gave the poor peasant girl many chores to do, and if she didn't finish them by the end of the day, the woman would beat her."

Natasha nodded. "But the magical cow helped her."

"Yes. The girl went out to the pasture, put her arms around the cow's neck, and cried. Then the cow spoke to her and asked her why she was so sad. She told the cow all her sorrows, and the cow promised that she would help."

At that moment, Natasha's father came to the bedroom doorway. "Natasha, I must leave in a half an hour. Will you be ready?"

Natasha straightened. "Yes, sir, of course."

"When is breakfast, Svetlana?"

"Things are ready now. I have everything finished." Natasha's mother moved quickly to follow her husband. She stopped at the door and turned back. "I can tell you the end of the story after supper tonight, if you'd like."

Natasha found her mother's eagerness a bit pathetic, but forced a bright tone into her reply. "Yes, that would be fine. Only tell me one thing beforehand. Does it turn out well?"

"Well?" Natasha's mother questioned. She shrugged. "I suppose that depends on who you are in the story."

"Svetlana?" Ivan Alexseyevitch called from the kitchen.

Svetlana Karlovna jumped. "Yes, I'm coming!" And she was gone.

Natasha sighed and went to dress. Her mother was the peasant girl from every story: a pretty, but unpretentious, face; plain clothes and country shoes; and a simple, predictable response for every situation. As Natasha stood at the mirror to brush out her hair, she examined her features. Where was her mother in her? She had her father's dark hair and eyes, her father's intellect, and her father's temperament. *Perhaps if there had been another child,* Natasha thought, *he or she might have favored Mother's side of the family.* She shook her head. *Pity the boy who inherited such a meager personality.*

She finished her grooming and turned to choose her reading book for the day. She moved to the shelf and closed her eyes. She would play her game. She ran her hand along the line of books, stopping at one and drawing it out. She opened her eyes expectantly, and then glared at the blue book in her hand. It was the book Agnes's father had given her, and this was the second time it had presented itself for choosing. The last time she'd quickly lifted her fingers from the cover, choosing instead the book on its right.

Natasha blew out a breath of air. Several times she had thought of throwing the gift into the trash bin, but always relented when she imagined the pained expression on Agnes's face if she ever found out. Her friend did not need any more pain in her life right now. She spent the majority of her day caring for Bruno whose recovery was erratic. While Arel's body had responded to the medicine and food, and strengthened daily, Bruno's body seemed unable to conquer the vicissitudes of the war.

Natasha opened the book. It was one of the few books she owned in English, so even if the words were rubbish, it would afford good practice of the language. She looked down at the page to which she'd opened. *The Articles of Faith, Appendix 2—notes relating to Chapter 2. Natural to Believe in God.*

"Natasha?" her father called up the stairs. "Time to leave."

Natasha closed the book quickly. "Yes! Yes, sir. I will be right down." She placed the Talmage book back into the line and chose a book of short stories by Chekhov.

Natural to Believe in God—what did that mean?

A calm feeling poured into her body. It was a summer feeling—the feeling of running in a meadow.

"Natasha?"

"Yes! I'm coming!" she called back. She gathered her belongings and rushed downstairs.

Her mother helped her on with her coat, scolding her for making her father wait, and shoved a roll into her pocket.

Natasha and her father stepped out onto the street. Her father opened his umbrella and took her arm. The beautiful snowflakes had turned into a chill sleet and people passing by hunched into their coats and grumbled about the horrid weather. Natasha leaned against her father's shoulder, sad to discover that the sensation of calm she'd felt in her bedroom had vanished.

Notes

1. Fairy tales are woven into the heart and soul of the Russian people; even Russia's great writer Alexander Pushkin wrote a book of fairy tales in the 1800s. The tale of the orphan girl and the white cow is a fairy tale which Natasha and her mother would have known.

CHAPTER NINE

Petrograd

October 15, 1917

Sergey Antonovich looked dashing in his long bohemian coat. His listeners spent as much time looking at him as they did listening to his fiery words, and he was a compelling speaker.

The lecture hall at the university was filled with students, sailors, and factory workers. Several speakers had preceded him, but their words had turned colorless and meager after Sergey's opening lines.

Natasha glanced over at Dmitri Borisovitch and Nicholai Lvovitch, amused by their open adoration. She pulled her thoughts to the speech.

"Yes, comrades, we hoped Kerensky and his government would have served the proletariat, but what have we received? The factories do not belong to the people, the bourgeoisie still own the land, and thousands are starving on the streets of Petrograd!"

An angry cheer went up.

"Every soldier, every worker, every real Socialist, realizes that there are only two alternatives to the present situation. Either the power will remain in the hands of the bourgeois-landlord—and this will mean every kind of repression for the workers, soldiers, and peasants, continuation of the war, and inevitable hunger and death—"

Shouts and jeers from the floor.

"Or . . . or, the power will be transferred to the hands of the revolutionary workers, soldiers, and peasants. In that case, it will mean a complete abolition of landlord tyranny, immediate check of the capitalists, immediate proposal of a just peace. *Then* the land is assured to the peasants, *then* control of industry is assured to the workers, *then* bread is assured to the hungry! I say to you that we must either drop 'All Power to the Soviets' or make an insurrection—there is no middle course!"

Dmitri and Nicholai stood and cheered with the rest.

"And in the muddy trenches of the front, our men give their last feeble breaths to fight for Mother Russia—noble, forsaken souls who fight without coats or boots or food!"

A roar of condemnation arose, and Natasha saw many of the sailors shake their fists and stamp their feet. Natasha's stomach clenched as she thought about the wretched condition of Agnes's brothers when they'd returned from the front. She would never forget the scene of Arel weeping in his mother's arms. She was jostled sideways as Dmitri and Nicholai joined the factory workers as they called out, "Peace, Land, and Bread!" Yelling matches erupted as some of the anti-Bolshevik students shouted their distrust. It took several minutes for the pandemonium to quiet.

"The Provisional Government does not care how many young men it slaughters! Kerensky does not care how many rotting corpses are piled up on the eastern front!"

The yelling broke out again.

"Will the Bolsheviks leave the soldiers out in the barren wasteland to fight a senseless war?"

"No!" the audience yelled.

"Will the Bolsheviks forget the poor peasant toiling in the field?"

"No!"

"Will the Bolsheviks allow the factory workers and their families to starve on the streets?"

"No! No! No!"

"So, comrades, as Soviets, will we hold a revolver to the head of the government?"

"Yes!"

"As Soviets, will we rise up and take the land from the bourgeois landowners?"

"Yes!"

"What is Kerensky? A usurper, whose place is in the Peter and Paul Fortress! A traitor to the workers, soldiers, and peasants who believed in him! Kerensky is finished! Long live the worldwide proletariat struggle! Long live the revolution!"

A storm of shouting and cheers swept through the crowd and chanting began of "All Power to the Soviets!" Signs and posters of the Bolsheviks were lifted into the air, as the counterrevolutionary factions were shoved about. A score of students rushed onto the stage—many to congratulate Sergey Antonovich on his brilliant speech, many just to be near him.

Natasha was caught up in the fervor, but she did not add her voice to the cacophony. In the back of her mind she heard Agnes's words about shouting slogans, and it tempered her enthusiasm. The storm swirled around her, but she was in the center and it was calm, quiet. Her mind was not thinking of Kerensky or the revolution—not even thinking of the handsome Sergey Antonovich—instead, her thoughts touched soothingly on the precepts of consecration as she considered the qualities of men's hearts. The shouting continued, but Natasha Ivanovna sat pondering the words from a small blue book that was again presenting itself.

NOTES

1. Much of Sergey Antonovich's speech is compiled from speeches given by Lenin.

2. Following is a partial list of the factions vying for power in post-tsarist Russia:

Cadets: Constitutional Democrats or "Party of the People's Freedom." Composed mostly of liberals from the propertied classes, the Cadet party formed the first Provisional Government. The Bolsheviks saw them as puppets of the bourgeois elite.

Left Socialist Revolutionaries: Followed the theoretical ideas of the Bolsheviks, but were reluctant to follow their tactics. This was the party of the peasant and firmly supported the confiscation of the great landed estates without compensation, and disposing of the properties by the peasants themselves.

Bolsheviks: The majority formed at the split of the **Russian Social Democratic Labour Party.** See the notes to chapter three for more information.

Mensheviks: The minority formed at the split of the **Russian Social Democratic Labour Party.** See the notes to chapter three for more information.

Red Guards: The armed factory workers of Russia. At every crisis in the revolution the Red Guards appeared in the streets, untrained and undisciplined, but full of revolutionary zeal.

White Guards: Bourgeois volunteers who emerged in the last stages of the revolution to defend private property from the Bolshevik attempt to abolish it.

CHAPTER TEN

PETROGRAD

October 18, 1917

"Natasha, will you bring me another cloth?"

Agnes held out a limp rag, warmed with Bruno's fever, and waited. Natasha reached into the basin of cold water and drew out a square piece of fabric. She squeezed out the excess water and traded her friend for the used one. Agnes placed the cloth on Bruno's forehead. He groaned. Natasha swallowed down her concern as she noted the gray pallor of his skin. It matched the dingy color of his nightshirt—the gray of the afternoon clouds—the drab color of death. She chided herself for such morbid thoughts, turning her focus to her friend.

"Agnes, you must get some rest. You've been here all morning."

Agnes looked over, a puzzled expression washing her face. "Oh, Natasha, I'm so sorry. We've been at this for hours. You must be exhausted."

"I'm not concerned for myself," Natasha answered, bringing a small chair over to sit beside Agnes. "I'm concerned for you."

"I know, and you are a dear friend for helping me, but I'm fine, really. Why don't you go home for awhile?"

Natasha shook her head. "No. I want to stay."

Bruno's body shivered and his arm came up jerkily to his head. "Don't want it," he hissed. He knocked off the cloth as he babbled a string of incoherent words.

Agnes stilled his arms while Natasha retrieved the cloth from the floor. "Should I get someone?"

"No, he's calming down now. Mother said he did this off and on through the night."

Bruno's body relaxed and his eyes opened a little. "Tatyana," he whispered.

Natasha moved forward. "Did you understand that?" she asked.

Agnes shook her head. "No." She rubbed her brother's arm. "It's all right, Bruno, we're right here."

"At the hospital," he slurred.

"He said hospital," Natasha reported. "I thought I heard hospital."

"Yes, me too."

"Olga," Bruno rasped.

"Olga?" Agnes repeated, leaning nearer.

"Walking by."

"Who's walking by?" Agnes asked softly. Bruno did not respond. "Who's walking by, Bruno?"

"Tatyana . . . hospital."

"I heard Tatyana," Natasha said. "Olga and Tatyana? Is he talking about the grand duchesses?"

"He's having a fever dream," Agnes said sadly. "I think he believes that Olga and Tatyana are taking care of him at the royal hospital."

"That's odd," Natasha said before thinking.

"He thought the grand duchesses were very heroic when they became nurses and cared for the wounded soldiers." Agnes smiled down at Bruno. "We both loved the Imperial family. Bruno and I would pretend to be their servants at Tsarskoe Selo, or sailors on their yacht." Bruno's breathing deepened. "Once we actually saw them go by in one of their carriages. We couldn't stop talking about it for weeks."

Natasha frowned. "And you liked them even after your brother, Oskar, was hurt in the uprising?"

Agnes paused before answering. "It wasn't an uprising . . . and, yes, even after that." She sighed and stretched her back. "We saw them as a family, Natasha Ivanovna. We weren't political at eight or ten. We were just enchanted by these regal persons who, we thought, lived a fairy-tale life. I decided to keep a diary because the grand duchesses kept diaries; Bruno desired to attend military school because he thought he could impress them in his uniform." She took Bruno's hand. "Isn't he handsome? So handsome and so funny." She shook her head as if to clear her thoughts. "Once Father was commissioned to make a set of silver inkwells for the tsar's study at their dacha at Alexandria. Just before they were shipped, Bruno and I wrote notes to Olga and Tatyana and slipped them inside." She stroked Bruno's hand. "Silly, I know. Just silly little children."

"You never told me about doing that," Natasha said.

Tears fell freely. "It was our secret," Agnes said. "Besides, you were never really interested in anything to do with the tsar and his family."

"I was interested," Natasha protested. "A little."

Agnes wiped her eyes and gave her friend a weak smile. "It's all right, Natasha. You loved your books and writing your stories, and now you have the revolution and your work with Sergey Antonovich, but I still care deeply about the little Romanov family. I know you must have feelings about what they've been through—first house arrest in Tsarskoe Selo and now shipped off to Tobolsk in Siberia . . . and Tsarevitch Alexis with such serious health problems. They're people, Natasha. They're a family, and they've lost everything. I feel sad for them." Agnes's voice filled with emotion but she kept it subdued. "I feel sad for them."

Arel walked into the room. "Alexandria is cooking while Mother sleeps. She says to come and eat something."

"But—"

"No arguments. I'm here to give you a rest."

Natasha looked into Arel's grayish-blue eyes, seeing nothing but exhaustion and sorrow. He was only a year older than she was, but it seemed that intense suffering had stamped excess years onto his features.

Agnes shook her head. "You are tired too, Arel. It looks like you could fall asleep on your feet."

Arel straightened. "I am tired—we are all tired—but I'll be fine. Besides, Alexandria's insisting."

Natasha spoke up. "I'll stay. Agnes, you go and get something to eat and I promise to keep Arel awake."

Agnes gave her a half-grin. "And you'll take a rest when I'm done?"

"I will," Natasha agreed.

"I don't need someone to prop me up," Arel said, lifting Agnes out of the chair. "Besides, Father went for the doctor. They should return at any time."

The women shared a look. There was fear in Agnes's eyes. She turned and walked quickly from the room.

An awkward silence ensued as Arel checked Bruno's breathing, and then sat down by the side of the bed. "Has . . . has he come around at all?"

"He mumbled something about Olga and Tatyana, but nothing else."

Arel made a strange sound in his throat—a mixture of mirth and pain.

Natasha knew that Arel was the quiet one of the brothers. Johannes and Oskar were confident and opinionated, Bruno was the outgoing trickster, and Erland was . . . well, Erland was high-strung and unpredictable.

"He fancied them."

"Excuse me?" Natasha said, leaning toward him.

"Olga and Tatyana, and later Marie and Anastasia. Bruno fancied them."

"Yes, Agnes told me. You'd think he would have found a girl within reach."

Arel swallowed and gave her a slight grin. "Well . . . he did, but after you punched Oskar in the nose for teasing you, Bruno returned his affection to the grand duchesses."

Natasha put her hand over her mouth to quell any sound of laughter, and Arel smiled at her. She realized that she had never been alone with this Lindlof brother—with any of the brothers, actually—but Arel had an easygoing way about him that made her feel comfortable. "And I suppose that my unwomanly conduct scared you away from women. Is that why none of you older boys are married?"

Arel blushed.

"I'm sorry," Natasha said quickly. "That was quite a forward question." They'd been talking in subdued tones so as not to disturb Bruno, and Natasha figured that the intimacy of the exchange, coupled with the remark about marriage, was the cause of Arel's embarrassment. "I am sorry, Arel. It's none of my business."

He smiled at her again. "No. Now I feel it's my duty to defend our honor," he whispered.

Natasha pressed her lips together to keep from smiling.

"You see, when women find out we don't belong to the Orthodox faith, or that we're not Bolsheviks"—he paused for effect—"or that we belong to a strange American church, they tend to find us less than desirable."

"I see."

"Do you? And do you agree that we're odd?"

Natasha shrugged. "Actually, I don't find you odd at all."

"Really?" Arel gave her a crooked grin. "Not odd at all?"

She grinned back. "Well . . . your Mormon faith *is* unusual."

"Yes, I'm sure it seems so—an angel appearing to a young man and handing him a book written on golden plates."

Her grin faded. "Do you truly believe that, Arel?"

He nodded. "I do. Joseph Smith was an uneducated farm boy. He couldn't have written the Book of Mormon. It would have been impossible. And he gave up his life for the things he believed in and preached. Yes, I do believe it, Natasha Ivanovna."

Natasha studied him for a long moment, so long in fact that Arel turned away. When she spoke her tone was solemn. "I don't believe in God or Jesus, Arel, so you can imagine what I make of angels and golden plates." She was surprised when Arel smiled.

"Yes, I expect they sound like fairy tales," he said without rancor. "Well." He stood and laid a hand on Bruno's face, then walked over and retrieved a cool cloth from the washbasin, returning to place it on his brother's head.

"I should have helped with that," Natasha said.

"It's fine, Natasha Ivanovna. You have done much already . . . especially being a support to Agnes. She is such a porcelain doll."

Bruno groaned and opened his eyes.

Arel took his hand. "Bruno?"

"Where are we?" Bruno whispered.

"We're at home. Do you remember?"

Bruno's eyes drifted out of focus. "Yes . . . you brought me . . ."

A moan caught in Arel's throat.

" . . . brought me home." Bruno's eyes closed.

They heard deep voices and footfalls coming up the stairs, and Natasha knew the doctor had arrived. Arel laid down his brother's hand and stepped back while she rose and walked away from the sickbed. She stood against the wall at the far end of the room attempting to make herself as unobtrusive as possible. There was an ache in her chest from the scene she'd just witnessed, and she pressed her palms against the cool wall to distract her emotions.

Mr. Lindlof entered the room, followed by the doctor. The man carried his doctor's bag and an aura of efficiency. He was not tall, nearly a head shorter than Mr. Lindlof, with a remarkably bushy mustache. Arel nodded to him and moved back until he was standing next to Natasha.

Mrs. Lindlof, Agnes, Alexandria, and Linda Alise came quickly into the room—Alexandria still in her apron, and Mrs. Lindlof rubbing the sleep from her eyes. Agnes held Linda Alise's hand; her focus on the doctor. No one spoke as the doctor took out his instruments and examined Bruno. He calculated the boy's temperature, listened to his breathing, and gingerly probed and cleaned the infected shoulder wound.

At length he gathered his things and turned. "Mr. and Mrs. Lindlof, if I could speak with you in the hallway."

The two nodded and moved out of the room with the doctor, closing the door behind them. Agnes burst into tears and knelt down by the side of the bed, as Linda Alise patted her shoulder, and Alexandria turned to look out the window.

Only Natasha heard Arel's tortured whisper. "It's my fault, my fault, my fault."

◆　◆　◆

The Lindlof family stood mutely around Bruno's bed, and Natasha felt like an intruder. She would have left with the doctor, but Agnes had begged her to stay. The plea had carried such desolation that Natasha submitted without thought for her own distress.

Mrs. Lindlof had drawn her close. "Please stay, Natasha Ivanovna, you are part of our family."

So she stayed and watched as Mr. Lindlof, Johannes, Oskar, and Arel gathered around Bruno's bed and laid their hands on his head. Mr. Lindlof said a prayer with words full of comfort and love. Then, with tears streaming down his face, he whispered, "Thy will be done," and closed the prayer.

After the prayer, Natasha had eased herself away from the group, back to her little space along the wall. She'd found much of the language of the prayer odd, yet many of the words had made her catch her breath for their beauty and consolation. Even now her emotions vacillated between pity for belief in such empty ritual and inexplicable feelings of comfort.

Arel came to her. "May I walk you home, Natasha Ivanovna?"

"Arel, I live ten steps from your front door."

"Then I'll walk you ten steps. Please, I need a reason to leave the house."

She saw the haunted look in his eyes. "Yes, of course."

They moved out into the cold October afternoon. It was the kind of murky weather that brought so much illness to Petrograd's already suffering populous.

"I know it's a miserable day, Natasha Ivanovna, but would you mind a short walk? Perhaps just to the cathedral?"

"No, I wouldn't mind."

"Thank you." He nodded and handed her his scarf.

They walked along the canal and over the bridge. The sun had almost set, but small fingers of light were trying to reach through the shredding cloud cover.

"It would be better if it would just snow," Natasha said.

Arel didn't respond. He stumbled along, unaware of his surroundings.

"Arel, do you want to go back?"

He put his gloved hands over his mouth and took several deep breaths. He shook his head. "I can't."

She remembered his tortured words. She touched his arm. "It's not your fault."

The bells of the cathedral rang out, and Arel put his hands over his ears and wept. "Bruno wanted to desert. He wanted to come home. I said no. No! If we'd run just a day sooner he wouldn't be dying."

"You can't know that," Natasha said firmly. "Arel, listen to me. You can't know that."

He started walking again, heedless of direction or destination.

Natasha caught up to him. "Arel, stop. Stop!" She was angry. "The war has taken millions of our men. The war is a demon who doesn't care who it takes. You think you can fight that? You think you can change things? To try to stop who the war takes is like pushing against air." Arel howled and paced back and forth. Natasha persisted. "If it were you in that bed, would you want Bruno out here lamenting about how it was his fault?"

"No!"

"No. So grieve for him—grieve for yourself and your family, but don't take the burden of death onto your shoulders."

Arel put his hands over his face—the tears coming freely.

Natasha placed her hand softly on his back. "You brought him home, Arel. You were with him every step." She held him as he wept.

Arel stepped back, wiping his eyes on the sleeve of his coat. "I need to keep walking." He put his hand tenderly on the side of her face. "It's cold, Natasha Ivanovna. Why don't you go home?"

"I'll go with you."

"No." He put his hands on her shoulders. "Please, go home." He turned in the direction of the Neva River and didn't look back.

Natasha felt the cold seep into her skin. She tied Arel's scarf up around her face, watching him until he turned the corner.

◆　◆　◆

For hours she sat by her window staring down at the empty Griboyedov canal promenade.

Near midnight, her mother came timidly to her room, announcing that the Lindlof boy had died. Natasha nodded, keeping her emotions in check until her mother was gone. She pressed her forehead against the window glass and cried, aware that somewhere in the dark night Arel Lindlof still wandered the streets, searching for absolution.

NOTES

1. With the beginning of the **Great War** (World War I) in 1914, **Grand Duchesses Olga** and **Tatyana** passed a two-month nursing course. They worked at the Palace Hospital named for Grand Duchesses Marie and Anastasia in Tsarskoe Selo. They, with their mother, assisted during operations, made bandages, gave injections, and looked after wounded soldiers.

CHAPTER ELEVEN.

PETROGRAD

October 23, 1917

Johan Lindlof and his daughter backed away from the gathering crowd and the flames. Agnes looked at the side of the building where the Red Guards had just pulled down a large, double-headed eagle insignia. The destructive act left a scar of plaster adrift in the building's pale blue paint. Agnes looked sadly at the barren spot. Three hundred years of Romanov rule reduced to a smudge of gray. She wondered distractedly if it would ever be fixed. Perhaps the Revolutionary Council would simply hang a red banner over the scar and declare it repaired.

Red banners, Bolshevik slogans, and red flags were everywhere in Petrograd. Several weeks ago she and Arel had been walking in front of the Alexandrinsky Theater and noticed the statue of Catherine the Great. There stood the regal Grand Empress with all her favorite courtiers sitting at her feet, and on her scepter—a red flag.

Agnes's eyes flicked back to the fire as the burly soldiers threw another tsarist standard onto the burning pile. Gray smoke curled and twisted in a cold afternoon breeze and a cinder flew into Agnes's eye. She moaned; stepping back, she bumped into a young woman who yelped in surprise.

Agnes stood mute, staring at the tall, big-boned girl. She had large green eyes and a shaved head. She wore a baggy military jacket, and a pair of pants which were too short. Her ill-fitting trousers exposed brown-buttoned shoes and yellow stockings. The girl picked up her cap and secured it on her head.

"I'm . . . I'm sorry," Agnes stammered.

"Don't worry," the girl said. "I'm not hurt."

Agnes's eye watered as her tears worked to clear the cinder. She pulled at her eyelid with irritation.

"Are you all right?" Johan Lindlof questioned, finally noticing his daughter's discomfort.

Agnes blinked several times. "Yes, yes—just something in my eye from the smoke. I think it's gone now. I stepped on this poor girl though."

Mr. Lindlof turned a compassionate eye on the young woman, but before he could speak, she held up her hands in protest. "No, no. I'm fine, truly."

"Are you a soldier?" Agnes asked, looking again at the military jacket.

"Yes," the girl said. "I am with the women's battalion."

"We've heard of your group, of course," Mr. Lindlof said.

The girl at once became wary. "Have you?"

"Yes, you protect the members of the Provisional Government," Mr. Lindlof said reassuringly.

The girl nodded and relaxed. "Yes, we are at the Winter Palace. Things have been especially tense with the thousand or so delegates in the city. They've come from all over Russia."

Mr. Lindlof nodded. "Ah yes, the meeting of the Russian Soviets."

"The vote is in a few days," the girl pronounced as though divulging insider information. "Perhaps that will stop all the arguing and chaos."

Johan Lindlof nodded.

"You're not a Bolshevik, are you?" she said bluntly.

"No."

"No, I didn't think so. You and your daughter don't dress like Bolsheviks." She turned to Agnes. "And your hair is lovely." She pulled her hat closer onto her head. "They made me shave off my hair when I joined the battalion. I came here from Il'linskya. It is a small place near Lake Ladoga."

Agnes was amused by how much the girl was talking to complete strangers. "It must be a beautiful place," she said.

"Yes, it is, but very small—nothing like the great St. Petersburg . . . I mean, Petrograd. See, I *am* a country girl. I can't even remember to call Petrograd, Petrograd. Many of us from small towns answered the call for the women's battalion—a chance to come to the grand city." She looked down at her boots. "We had no way of knowing. We thought we were going to fight for Mother Russia—to fight for the revolution, but . . ." Her voice trailed away.

"Often things are not what we expect," Mr. Lindlof said kindly.

The girl looked at him and nodded. "Do you have sons in the war?"

Agnes turned quickly to check her father's reaction. He looked away from the girl's face, took a breath, and looked back. "Yes, two sons actually, but they're both home now."

The girl's face brightened. "Oh, well that's good then. I'm glad for you. I wish I could go home to our simple wooden itza . . . our big stove in the main room. My sister and I slept there when it was cold. I miss the chickens and the cow." She took a step toward them and whispered, "I hate the Winter Palace—all cold and hard with the gold and marble. I mean, it's beautiful, truly, but you can never get warm there. I'm on my way back now. I was sent out to find bread." She touched the satchel slung over her shoulder.

"An important job," Mr. Lindlof said. He was being his usual polite self, but Agnes could tell that the girl's banter was wearing on his grieving sensibilities.

"Well, we won't keep you, comrade," Agnes said, reaching into her pocket and bringing out a gaily wrapped box. "Here is some chocolate to share with your friends."

The girl's mouth opened and closed several times. Her green eyes stared at the box, but her hands stayed motionless by her side.

"Please, I want you to have it," Agnes insisted. "For my bumping into you."

The young woman reached out slowly and took the chocolate. "You have a golden heart," she whispered.

There was a loud crash and the three turned to look at a wooden placard which had just been thrown onto the fire. It was some sort of announcement concerning the grand duchesses. Agnes watched as the flames licked away part of the royal emblem and the name—Anastasia. One of the Red Guards kicked it with his heavy boot, sending smoke and sparks into the air.

Agnes and her father turned back to talk to their soldier, but she was gone.

"Oh," Agnes said, disappointment registering in her voice and expression. "I wanted to ask her name." She shaded her eyes and looked about. "Do you think she'll be all right?"

"I think so," her father answered. "Even if there is a fight, any countryman would find it very difficult to injure a Russian woman."

Agnes nodded.

"I hope she makes it home to her little village someday," Mr. Lindlof added. He squinted to see if he could catch a glimpse of the green-eyed soldier in the milling crowd, but she had become part of the mass. "We'll include her in our prayers tonight."

They walked away from the crowded square, each lost in their individual thoughts. Agnes wondered if her father was thinking about the political chaos of the day, the soldier out scavenging for bread, or their visit to Bruno's grave. He surprised her when he finally spoke.

"It was kind of you to give her your chocolate—one of the few presents you'll have for your upcoming birthday. Very kind."

Agnes shook her head. "I don't think she's had chocolate for a long time."

A group of Cossacks shoved their way past. They were elegant and intimidating, and though they carried little of their former authority, their fierce reputation still made people lower their eyes and make room. Agnes stopped to watch as a babushka in old boots and a tattered coat held out her bare hands to them. "Tell me of the tsar. Is he well? And the tsarina? Are you still watching over them?"

Two of the Cossacks stopped and moved back to her. Those nearest the old woman quickly found other destinations, but Agnes found herself transfixed by the scene. The younger of the two guards bent down so his face was level with the old woman's.

"Are you well, little mother?"

Her head bobbed, and Agnes could tell by her bright expression that she was pleased to have the royal guard speaking to her. "Yes, yes, I'm well," she said, offering him a toothy grin. "And you? Are you well?"

The young guard chuckled. "I'm well, thank you, little mother."

The babushka's face became serious. "And the tsar—have you seen him?"

"No, we haven't seen him. They've sent him away."

She frowned. "Who sent him away? This new man—this Kerensky?" She crossed herself. "He's a devil." She spit. "May he come to a bad end."

The Cossack straightened. "Now, little mother, you must be careful what you say."

Weathered fingers reached out to touch his sleeve. "You must try to bring the tsar back. Everything is bad without him." Her rheumy eyes filled with tears. "I don't understand what's happening anymore. Mean soldiers yell at me when I try to go into the church to pray. They call me names."

The other Cossack soldier looked around to their retreating comrades. "Come on, leave her. We have to go."

The young soldier seemed reluctant to abandon the ragged woman. As he backed away, he bowed to her. "I will try to find the tsar, little mother." He turned and hurried after his companion.

The woman crossed herself and put her prayer hands to her forehead. Agnes watched with pity as the babushka hobbled toward the bonfire to find some warmth.

Agnes looked up at her father. "It makes me sad. I keep thinking of the beautiful prayer Elder Lyman gave in the Summer Garden."

"You were only eight." He touched her cheek. "You remember it?"

"Yes, much of it, and we've talked enough about it over the years. Mostly I remember how it made me feel. I felt that God was aware of us. That He loved the Russian people."

Mr. Lindlof nodded. "That hasn't changed, my sweet girl."

"But Elder Lyman prayed that missionaries would come. He promised that they'd come to preach the gospel."

"Perhaps certain freedoms have to be in place before that can be accomplished."

"And do you think that can happen under a Soviet government?"

Mr. Lindlof shook his head. "No. I'm afraid the Soviets will leave God out of their plans."

Agnes grunted. "I don't understand politics. Even among the Socialists there are different groups, each wanting different things. I'm sure God doesn't like the chaos and contention."

"I'm sure He doesn't."

"So who will ever be able to unravel the political mess?"

Johan Lindlof didn't answer her question. He put his arm around her shoulder and gave her a slight hug. "Let's go home. Your mother said she was making apple cake."

"How did she manage that?"

Johan Lindlof smiled. "Didn't I tell you? She knows magic."

◆　◆　◆

Natasha had gotten used to the din—the constant buzzing of voices, the feet walking in the hallways of the Smolny Institute, the discussions and arguments pouring from other offices. She had even learned to block out the hum and rattle of the sewing machines that occupied the room in which she worked. Her small desk sat twenty feet away from them and next to a lovely coped window, which provided sufficient light for her to write even on cloudy days. The electric lights were turned on from dusk to midnight and during the day only in an emergency. She'd been given a handful of candles, but at five rubles each, she rarely thought of lighting one.

A typewriter sat neglected by the side of her desk. She had told the supply committee that she'd never learned to use one and preferred to write with paper and pencil. Nevertheless, she had arrived at work one morning to find the odd contraption sitting smugly on her desk. She'd planned to take it back to the supply room, but hadn't found the time. Perhaps someday she'd try to learn how to use it, but the men who did the typesetting told her they liked her writing and could easily read every word, so the typewriter sat on the floor, gathering dust.

"Natasha!"

She looked up from her scribbling to see Sergey Antonovich striding toward her. He held a pamphlet in the air and waved it as he approached. Several of the girls stopped sewing and watched his every movement. Only when he knelt down at Natasha's side did they pull their eyes back to the red cloth at their sewing machines.

Sergey had his hair tied back at the nape of his neck, which made his brown eyes the dominant feature of his face. He was looking at her with such admiration that it made her blush. "Oh, my friend! My dear, dear comrade! I have just come from the printers with your latest work." He took one of her hands. "It is brilliant! Brilliant! What beautiful propaganda!" He slapped the pamphlet down on her desk, put his hands on either side of her face, and kissed her hard on the mouth.

She was so stunned by his impulsive act that she did not pull away. She had never been kissed like this before and she figured Sergey's passion for her work was what made his lips so warm and his hands tighten on the sides of her face. He pulled away slightly, grasping her hair, and breathing deeply. She was breathing deeply too.

"Oh, Natasha Ivanovna," he whispered. "I'm sorry." He looked at her and stroked her cheek. "It's just that I'm captivated by you—your brilliance and your beauty."

Natasha noticed suddenly that the room had gone very quiet. She was embarrassed and angry as she imagined the seamstresses gawking and giggling at the private scene. She turned to glare at them, surprised to see they weren't looking at her and Sergey at all, but were staring at the door.

Natasha turned to look. "Oh, no!" She stood quickly, bumping an array of items off her desk.

Sergey stood too. "Commissar Trotsky!"

Leon Trotsky stood smiling in the doorway. It was not an expression he wore often. Usually he was intense and preoccupied. He chuckled and walked calmly to one of the seamstresses and laid his hand on the sewing machine. The girl bowed her head.

"Ah, comrade, none of that," he said. "We are all equal here." She looked up at him and smiled. "That's better." He picked up the side of the banner she was sewing and let the smooth red fabric run through his fingers. "You do beautiful work."

"Thank you, Commissar. The sewing machines are good."

Trotsky smiled. "Yes. We must write the Singer Sewing Company and thank them for such a wonderful invention. And what will your banner say?"

The girl sat straighter in her chair. "Workers of the World Unite!"

His look turned reflective. "And do you believe that's possible?"

The girl hesitated. "It's a lofty goal, Commissar."

He nodded. "Lofty? Yes." He let the fabric fall back onto the floor. "Well, we shall just have to work for it." He turned. "Like our Comrade Gavrilova." He walked toward her.

Natasha had never seen Comrade Trotsky up close. He and his pretty wife lived in one room on the top floor of the building. Sergey had been there once and told her it was very meager, portioned off like a poor artist's studio—two cots and a cheap little dresser on one side, and a desk and three wooden chairs on the other. The few times she had seen Trotsky in the hallways it was at a distance and he was always surrounded by people. She knew it was because everyone was too intimidated by Lenin to approach him, but they could go to Trotsky with every small detail and problem.

The commissar reached out his hand and she took it, looking past his thick glasses to his dark eyes. "Comrade Gavrilova," he said, shaking her hand and returning her look with interest. "I came to congratulate you on your stirring sentiments, but I see that Comrade Vershinin has rushed here ahead of me."

Natasha blushed and Sergey smiled.

"Truly, comrade, it is a great piece of writing. I especially like the part where you compare Kerensky's government to a chicken that continues to run about the courtyard even though its head has been cut off. It struggles and it fights, because it doesn't know it's dead." He nodded at her. "Yes, very good. The Provisional Government does not speak for the proletariat—they are merely puppets of the bourgeoisie, and so the workers have left them and banded behind the promise of the Bolsheviks. We know that Kerensky will stab at us, but that will only make us stronger."

Natasha felt the determination in his words.

Trotsky continued. "Even though Kerensky is a lawyer, he's a fool. And so the Provisional Government runs about with no head and no support." He removed the pamphlet from his pocket and tapped it on his hand.

"Yes, it is a great image—an image that the country peasants will well understand."

Natasha started. "Country?"

"Why, yes. We are sending thousands of copies out into the countryside—the small towns and villages. We Bolsheviks are strong in Petrograd and Moscow, and our message is understood by the soldiers, but we must win the hearts of *all* the people." He leaned closer to them. "And when our revolution has swept away petty selfishness—when men's hearts are changed—we will work together to build a new order." He placed his hand on Sergey's shoulder. "You two will be part of that. We are in this together. You cannot tie a knot with one hand." He looked into both their faces. "A great orator and a great writer? Yes, we will use you. We will see that you are kept very busy." He shook both their hands.

"Thank you, Comrade Trotsky," Sergey said, his voice layered with gratitude and pride. "We are waiting for the insurrection!"

Trotsky looked at him intently. "Not much longer, comrade. Many plans are in motion."

"So everything is set?" Sergey asked anxiously.

"Set?" Trotsky shook his head. "It is the fog of revolution, Comrade Vershinin, and I think you will see that the outcome will surprise the victors as much as it will stun the defeated. No, things are never set, but we have heard some good news." He looked at Natasha. "You see, I understand that our friend Lenin has defied Kerensky and has snuck back into town from Finland."

"What?" Sergey blurted out.

Trotsky smiled and put his finger to his lips. "I hear he's in disguise. Our secret." He noticed the typewriter on the floor. "You don't like your typewriter, Comrade Gavrilova?"

Natasha shrugged. "I don't know how to use it."

Trotsky laughed. "Me either. I was writing everything by hand and getting crankier and crankier until the Committee told me I had to get a stenographer. Now, I have two to keep up with me!" He turned to leave, and then turned back. "Oh, Comrade Vershinin," he said gravely. "Don't distract Comrade Gavrilova too much. The revolution needs her."

Sergey nodded and relaxed. "Yes, Commissar. I'll try to remember."

Trotsky raised a hand to the seamstresses and left the room.

The sewing stopped as the girls gathered excitedly together to talk.

"He knows our names," Sergey Antonovich said. "And he has taken a special interest in you, Natasha Ivanovna." He pulled his gaze from the door to stare at her.

For some reason the thought was unsettling and Natasha knelt quickly to retrieve the things she'd knocked off her desk. Sergey joined her.

"Now that I've kissed you, though, I may find it impossible to leave you alone to write."

Natasha looked over at him, expecting to find a smirk on his face, but his expression was one of complete sincerity. She stood and dumped the articles onto her desk, making a show of arranging them.

Sergey Antonovich placed papers and a book on the other side of where she was working. "I'm sorry, Natasha Ivanovna. If you'd rather, I won't kiss you again. Perhaps you don't care for me, like . . ."

She looked at him straight on. "I never said that."

Sergey moved to her side and kissed her lightly at the corner of her mouth. She felt her body warm with his touch.

"When your work is done, let me take you out to supper."

Natasha smiled at him. "That's rather extravagant of you."

"I've been saving some money." He touched her hair.

"Hmm. There's only one problem—my work for the revolution is never done."

"Nor is mine," Sergey agreed, "but we must eat once in a while."

"True. All right, give me two hours."

He ran his hand down her arm and picked up her pamphlet.

Now that she'd expressed her mutual interest, it seemed that Sergey Antonovich could not stop touching her. Natasha was overwhelmed by a feeling of belonging.

Sergey backed away from her, his eyes never leaving her face. "Two hours." He held up the pamphlet and announced to the room, "This is absolutely brilliant, comrades! You must read it!"

When he was gone, Natasha tried to maintain an air of efficiency and detachment, but her body kept remembering Sergey's touch and her mind kept exalting over what Commissar Trotsky had said. He had encouraged her writing and indicated that she and Sergey would be important to the revolution. *From each according to their ability. To each according to their need!*

For some reason the sentiment sounded hollow and her euphoria retreated. She continued straightening her desk, trying to ignore other words and phrases that kept jumping into her reasoning. She stacked the papers that Sergey Antonovich had retrieved and set the blue book on top—the blue book from Agnes's father: *Articles of Faith.* Trotsky had talked so powerfully about the government of the proletariat sweeping away petty selfishness—of changing men's hearts—of building a new order. In his words she could feel the force of the revolution. The Bolsheviks had inflamed the hearts of the workers in Petrograd and Moscow to insurrection and there was no turning back. How often had she heard Lenin and Trotsky preach to the proletariat that their brother workers in Germany, Hungary, and France—indeed all the workers of Europe—would throw off bourgeois capitalism and establish a new order—a united order? And religion, which had for so long dominated the minds of the common man with meaningless ritual and empty hope, would give way to true brotherhood and caring.

Her fingers pressed into the book. *Yes! Yes, that would be the way of things. Surely that is the right way.* She reached up and touched a tear on her cheek. Why was she crying? How foolish. Into her head came clearly the words of Agnes's father, *"You cannot change a man's nature or behavior by outside means. There must be a change of a man's heart, and only God can do that."*

Only God can do that.

Natasha strode to the window and shoved it open, taking in deep breaths of cold air. She gritted her teeth and fought against the feeling that somehow those words had meaning—somehow those words were true.

NOTES

1. The double-headed eagle was the insignia of the Romanov family who ruled Russia for three hundred years. Just weeks before his abdication on March 14, 1917, Tsar Nicholas II was cheered by crowds of adoring subjects in Petrograd as they celebrated the 300-year anniversary of Romanov rule.

After the abdication of Tsar Nicholas II, the Socialists took great delight in tearing down any plaque or insignia of the Romanov dynasty and burning them in a public demonstration of disgust. I placed Agnes and her father passing by one such rally where royal objects are being burned.

2. Russia is a huge country. It is the only country to span two continents—Europe and Asia. It crosses eleven time zones, and in 1917, was home to approximately 150 million people. The ideas of the socialists had been slowly filtering to outlying areas, and *soviets* (councils) were being established in many cities, towns, and even villages. **The All-Russian Congress of Soviets** was a meeting in Petrograd of a sizable number of heads of soviets to discuss issues and take votes on which of the many socialist parties would chart the course and take over the reins of government. The Bolsheviks overthrew the Provisional Government the day before the meeting of the Congress and declared themselves the party in power.

3. **Leon Trotsky** was a leader in the socialist movement in Russia, and head of the Petrograd soviet. An intense advocate of the ideals of socialism, Trotsky stood side by side with Vladimir Illyich Lenin in bringing the Bolsheviks to power. He was appointed to be the Foreign Affairs Commissar, and later the commander of the Red Army and Commissar of War. After Lenin's death in 1924, Trotsky was embroiled in a power struggle with the ruthless Joseph Stalin. Stalin used his position as General Secretary of the Communist Party to eliminate all rivals. Trotsky was exiled. In 1940 he was murdered in Mexico City by a Stalinist agent.

4. In July 1917 there were Socialist demonstrations in Petrograd against Alexander Kerensky and his Provisional Government's continued support of Russia's involvement in the war. Many Bolshevik leaders were arrested, including Leon Trotsky. Lenin also wanted to be arrested so he could challenge the government in a public trial, but his Bolshevik colleagues, fearing that he would be assassinated in jail, convinced him to go into hiding. Lenin eventually escaped to Helsinki, Finland. On October 20, he returned in disguise to a Petrograd suburb where, from a secret location, he helped orchestrate and drive the revolution.

CHAPTER TWELVE

PETROGRAD

October 24, 1917

Natasha laid her head on her desk and let her hand drop to her side. She flexed her fingers and stretched her back, attempting to ease the cramp that had settled there an hour ago. Even with all the noise surrounding her, her mind began to drift, conjuring images of magical cows, birch trees, and barges floating down the Neva River filled with treasures from the Winter Palace. She sat on one of the barges watching the dark water flow away beneath her. She wore a crown, and a servant in a blue coat adorned with gold buttons offered her a cup of tea. She took it and the bold gentleman sat down beside her and began singing. His voice was strong and low and she felt an ache of emotion at the back of her throat. She hummed with him as he sang.

> *"Then comrades come rally*
> *And the last fight let us face.*
> *The Internationale*
> *Unites the human race."*

There was a slight pressure on her shoulder and she looked over to the servant. "Agnes?" Why was Agnes Lindlof on the barge? Natasha sat up and squinted at her friend. "Agnes?" She was surprised by the gravelly timbre of her voice. She cleared her throat and pushed her hair away from her face. She heard distant singing and her disorientation lingered. "What are you doing here?"

Agnes took her arm and helped her to stand. "First, let's get you awake." She led her to the window and opened it. A rush of cold damp air hit Natasha in the face and made her gasp. The singing intensified and the two friends looked down into the courtyard. Several dozen soldiers were singing a song of the revolution with voices filled with passion and power.

"There is no more beautiful sound than when we Russians sing together," Agnes said. "It breaks the heart."

Natasha nodded slowly. Her senses were returning and with the awareness came a cacophony of noise that beat against her eardrums. A dull ache banded around her head and she reached up to rub her temples.

"Here, sit down, Natasha Ivanovna, before you fall down," Agnes directed, helping her back to her chair.

"Actually, I need to go to the water closet and splash some water on my face."

"Good idea," Agnes said, maneuvering her toward the door. "It looks like you haven't slept in days."

"I haven't," Natasha answered. "Perhaps an hour or two, but no more." She gave her friend a quizzical look. "What are you doing here, Agnes?"

"Mother sent me with sweet bread. We're worried about you. She said she saw you leave your house at four o'clock in the morning."

Natasha nodded. "But how did you get here?"

"Streetcar. This is the end of the line. I used to go to school here, you know. Of course, now that the Bolsheviks have taken over, the white marble floors are caked with mud."

"Agnes . . ."

"There are still some of the class placards over the doors, but everything else has changed."

Natasha's head throbbed. "Yes. Yes, I know." She looked at Agnes's bourgeois attire. "But what I meant was, how did you get in here to see me? The guards are being very strict."

Agnes smiled. "I must not look dangerous."

A woman, carrying a bolt of red fabric, pushed past them with a surly look and a grunt.

"Besides," Agnes continued, belatedly stepping aside, "it's chaos— people coming and going in a mad rush. I've never seen anything like it."

"And probably won't again," Natasha said. "We're preparing for something big."

"The Second Congress of Soviets?" Agnes asked.

Natasha shook her head. "We've heard rumors that the Bolsheviks will soon take control of the telephones and telegraphs, and the train stations."

Agnes stared at her. "Take control?"

"Shhh. I can't say more. I don't know for sure. I just know they've had me writing leaflets and flyers for days."

Agnes nodded. "Everyone on the street is reading some sort of paper— devouring every bit of information."

Natasha lowered her voice to a whisper and brought a paper from her pocket. "This is the last statement they had me write." In a conspiratorial tone, she read it aloud. "'Citizens! The Provisional Government is deposed. State power has passed into the organ of the Petrograd Soviet of Workers' and Soldiers' Deputies.'"

"What?" Agnes said loudly.

They stepped out into the hallway and were caught in a press of humanity: Red Guards stood tense and awkward, waiting for their next orders; typists ran from one office to another carrying paper; members of different soviets stood arguing, while couriers entered and left the building without bothering to remove their hats or wipe the mud from their boots.

Agnes clutched at Natasha's arm. "The insurrection is happening now?"

"Shhh," Natasha scolded. "That's why I'm surprised they let you in here. Things are moving very quickly, and—" Her words were knocked out of her as a young woman came hurrying from a side hall and smashed into her. The two fell onto the floor.

"Natasha!" Agnes yelled.

A knot of people crowded around, shouting and swearing, as the two women were lifted to their feet.

"What's the idea, comrade?" a Red Guard barked as he held onto the frantic girl.

She seemed unaware of the chaos she'd caused. "Where's Lenin?

Where's Trotsky?" she screamed. "I have to see them right away!" Her eyes bulged from her head and she gasped for breath.

"Calm down. Calm down, little comrade," the soldier said. "You don't want to pass out."

"You . . . you don't understand!" the girl cried. "I've run . . . run all the way from the newspaper building. The editor sent me." She was crying in earnest, and several people patted her on the back and shoulder.

"Get the commissar!" Natasha called, stepping forward.

The girl glanced at Natasha. "Thank you. I'm sorry I hit into you . . . it's just that . . ."

"Yes, it's all right," Natasha said dismissively. "Now, what's this about the newspaper building?"

The girl put her hands on her knees and sucked air into her lungs. "The editor sent me to find Lenin or Trotsky. They . . . they need to know . . ." She ran out of air again.

"Something about *Pravda?* Something about the Bolshevik paper?" Natasha demanded.

The girl did not respond.

The crowd parted as Trotsky approached, his dark wavy hair unkempt and his clothing rumpled. The girl's head jerked up, a mixture of fear and determination on her face. "Comrade Trotsky! Oh, Comrade Trotsky, I'm just a typist, but no one else could come. Should I tell you or Comrade Lenin?"

Trotsky smiled at her. "Well, Lenin is addressing the assembly at the moment, so I think you should tell me."

The girl wiped tears away with the sleeve of her coat. "I'm sorry. I just don't know what to do. I'm just a typist."

"What is your name?"

"Yelena."

"It's all right, Yelena," he said gently. "Tell me what has happened?"

"Kerensky sent guards—Junkers . . . you know . . . the young soldiers from the military schools, and some other soldiers, not as young." She looked around at the pressing crowd of people.

"Yes, good. Go on," Trotsky encouraged.

Natasha was amazed at Trotsky's patience. All she wanted to do was wring the information out of the silly typist.

"They have shut down our newspaper! The soldiers scattered the print, tied up some people, and sealed the door." She looked at the commissar and began crying again. "They smashed my typewriter."

Natasha felt Agnes take her hand as everyone privy to the scene went quiet. All eyes were on Trotsky. He did not move—he did not speak for what seemed a very long time. Finally he turned to the soldier. "Lieutenant, find me the head of the Litovsky regiment and send him to my office." He turned to one of his stenographers. "Bring me the forms I need." He looked around at the waiting faces. "We will answer this outrage. The last remnants of the fetishism of authority is about to crumble to dust."

The typist squared her slight shoulders. "If you send out a guard against the Junkers, Commissar, we workers will bring out the paper!"

Trotsky looked at her intently. "Yes, comrade, the workers will not be stopped. Come with me while I fill out the needed forms." He took her by the arm and turned from the group. "Insurrection must be documented."

The gathering dispersed as people went back to the urgent business they'd abandoned. There was a smattering of elevated voices, and several people ran past to deliver messages, but Natasha Ivanovna did not move.

Agnes shook her arm. "Natasha, what is it?"

"Kerensky and his government have just lit the match of revolution."

Agnes started. "What? Kerensky? Why would he do that?"

"He doesn't realize he's done it. It's just another of his blunders."

"Another?"

Natasha led Agnes to a less crowded area of the hallway. "Sergey Antonovich told me yesterday he'd heard rumors that the Provisional Government plans to prosecute the leaders of the Bolshevik movement. They've also ordered the military cruiser *Aurora* out of the Neva River—out to sea."

Agnes's frown deepened. "Father says Kerensky doesn't trust the sailors' loyalty."

"He shouldn't."

Agnes bit her bottom lip. "What do you think the sailors will do?"

"I think they will do whatever the Revolutionary Committee tells them to do. The workers at the Bolshevik newspaper and the sailors on the *Aurora* are the proletariat—the people, Agnes, the common masses— and they're standing against the edicts of an unwise government. Since Kerensky has taken the offensive, any action taken by us will be in defense. We will not seem the aggressors." Natasha felt a chill of enthusiasm and apprehension run through her body. "In his attempt to suppress us, Kerensky has lit the match."

Agnes leaned back against the wall. "I don't feel well, Natasha Ivanovna."

Natasha turned quickly to her. "You must get out of here, Agnes. You must get home as fast as you can." She began pulling her down the hallway.

"But what about you, Natasha? Why don't you come home with me?"

Natasha kept walking. "I can't, Agnes. I have work to do."

"I'm frightened, Natasha. I don't understand any of this."

"I know, little squirrel. Most citizens don't really understand what's happening. Things will be difficult for awhile, and then it will be better. Our lives will be so much better."

They reached the front door and stopped. Agnes's eyes filled with tears. "Will they, Natasha? Will our lives be better?"

"Yes. Now go. You can still catch the streetcar."

"Oh, wait!" Agnes reached into her satchel. "I almost forgot to give you the bread." She handed it over and took Natasha's hand. "I want to go back to when we were girls—sharing riddles and braiding each other's hair."

Natasha nodded. "Yes, that would be nice, wouldn't it? Now go. Be safe."

Natasha watched as her friend walked through the courtyard, past the soldiers standing around their warming fires, past the machine guns and artillery, and out through the front gate.

As she turned and raced to her office, Natasha Ivanovna knew there would be no going back.

NOTES

1. The song Natasha hears in her dream is the Socialist revolutionary song "The Internationale."

2. The pamphlet written by Natasha concerning the takeover by the Bolsheviks is based on an actual notice written by Lenin and distributed the night of the storming of the Winter Palace.

3. **Pravda:** "Truth," the main Bolshevik newspaper.

4. Before the Bolshevik revolution, Russia calculated its time according to the Gregorian calendar, which was thirteen days behind the Julian calendar. In March 1918, the Bolsheviks converted all their calendars to the Julian system. To avoid confusion I have calculated all dates according to the Julian calendar, with one exception—I kept the date for the Bolshevik revolution as October 24, 1917. Most people are used to referring to this insurrection as Red October.

CHAPTER THIRTEEN

PETROGRAD

October 25, 1917

"The cruiser *Aurora* has fired a blank shot at the Winter Palace!" Dmitri Borisovitch yelled as he ran into the Smolny. "And now the sailors are firing artillery from the Peter and Paul Fortress! They are bringing down Kerensky!"

Natasha Ivanovna flew out of her office, mixing with the throng of people pouring into the hallway and out the front door.

Dmitri saw her and rushed to her side. "Comrade Gavrilova! The revolution begins! Come! Come with me! Sergey Antonovich sent me to get you. We're in a truck. We're going to the Winter Palace!"

There was a distant boom, and the people already on the front steps roared out their consent.

Dmitri and Natasha emerged into the courtyard and the slap of cold air made her gasp. "I've forgotten my coat."

"Here, take mine," Dmitri Borisovitch said, stripping off his coat mid-stride, and handing it to her.

"But—"

"I have my jacket. Don't worry." His face shone in the firelight. "Besides, who could be cold on a night like this?"

Natasha shrugged on the coat without slowing. She was determined not to lose Dmitri in the crowd. As they ran through the courtyard, she noticed that most of the Red Guards were gone. Only a few remained to protect the entrance of the building and the strategists inside. She could imagine Trotsky, Lenin, Marie Spirodonova, and some of the other leading Bolsheviks calling on the telephones, yelling to couriers, bending over maps, and sending telegrams to orchestrate the unfolding drama; ordering the bridges to be kept down so that the workers from outlying areas could march into the center of the city to fortify the cause; calling for increased security at the already taken train stations, postal offices, and utility departments; and sending soldiers to storm the Winter Palace.

"Here! This way!"

She heard Sergey's voice before she saw him.

Dmitri yanked her arm and they turned left toward a large truck. Sergey was standing in the truck bed with Nicholai Lvovitch. The flaps of the canvas covering had been tied back and Natasha could see a few other people in the truck bed's dark interior. They seemed to be sitting on piles of paper. One man looked familiar—one of the typesetters from the printing office—while another looked perfectly foreign with wild, dark hair and a long, black cloak. The truck lurched forward and Natasha saw Nicholai catch Sergey before he fell.

"Come on! Come on!" Sergey yelled as he righted himself. "It's moving!"

Natasha and Dmitri ran serpentinely past several people and jumped a small bonfire in their eagerness not to be left behind. The truck was moving at stops and starts to avoid hitting workers who ran heedlessly out into the street. As Natasha and Dmitri neared the lumbering vehicle, Sergey and Nicholai reached down their hands for them. They pulled the pair up over the back gate and into the truck. Immediately Sergey brought Natasha into a crushing embrace.

"I can't believe it! Can you believe it?" he yelled.

The truck lurched forward again and the four friends dropped quickly to their knees.

"What have you seen?" Natasha asked. "Has the Winter Palace been taken?"

"Yes! Yes, I think so," Sergey answered, putting his arm around her. "On our way here we saw hundreds of guards moving in that direction."

Someone in the rear of the truck bed shoved papers in their direction. "Here, comrades," came a disembodied voice. "Pass these out to the people."

It was near midnight and darkness had crouched in the streets since four o'clock, yet in the flash of passing lamplight, Natasha could see that the flyers carried the message she'd written from the Military Revolutionary Committee. *Citizens! The Provisional Government is deposed!* She looked up quickly to find Sergey smiling at her.

"Yes, comrade, those words will be read by thousands of happy workers this night."

"Well done, Comrade Gavrilova!" Dmitri and Nicholai yelled, grabbing handfuls of the missives and shaking them in the air.

Natasha felt color come into her cheeks and she turned her face out to the dark night. Even with the lateness of the hour, she noted that the streets were crowded—some people still out from the supper hour, while others had obviously been dragged out of their homes by the sound of cannon fire.

As the truck rumbled down side streets and onto Nevsky Prospect, the four friends scattered the leaflets from the back of the truck. Some people scrambled over the cobbles, fighting for copies, while others snatched them out of the air.

As they crossed over the Ekaterininsky canal, the truck was forced to stop. A burly sailor came to the back carrying a torch, his rifle slung casually over his shoulder. "Sorry, comrades, the road is blocked here. If you wish to go on you must walk, and you must have a reason for entrance. You must also have the proper passes."

"Of course! Of course, comrade!" Sergey said enthusiastically. "We work with the Military Revolutionary Committee," Sergey said. He grabbed a handful of leaflets. "We were sent to hand these out." He shoved a paper at the big man.

A grin spread across the sailor's face as he read. "Well, they certainly had faith that we'd do our job, didn't they?"

Sergey and Nicholai jumped from the back of the truck and lowered the back gate. As the others exited, Sergey held Natasha around the waist and helped her down. They moved to the front of the truck and were confronted with a barricade and a guard of twenty Kronstadt sailors.

"Did the Red Guards do this?" Sergey asked, indicating the barricade.

The guards smiled and shook their heads. "No. The Junkers put this up to stop the revolution," one of the sailors quipped. "You may as well brush aside the tide with a broom."

The other sailors laughed.

"May I take your picture?" Dmitri Borisovitch asked, bringing his American-made Kodak camera from his bag.

"I don't see why not," one of the sailors answered. "I've never had a picture taken. Will it hurt?"

One of his fellows smacked him on the back. "Your village is so small, it doesn't even have a name—right, Boris Alexayvich?"

His comrades laughed.

"Everyone move together a bit," Dmitri instructed.

The sailors did the best they could while still being diligent to their office.

Natasha found it an odd scene. In the midst of a revolution with chaos and urgency all around, this band of sailors had stopped to have a picture taken.

"Now, your passes," the burly sailor said, taking on a serious tone and demeanor. Just as he was examining Natasha's pass, gunfire and the heavier boom of artillery shelling was heard in the distance. Open concern showed on the sailor's face. "You realize you're going into a dangerous area?" She nodded. "We're doing our best to harm as few of our countrymen as possible, but there still may be a stray bullet or two."

"Yes, comrade, thank you," Natasha said.

Sergey stepped to her side. "I'll watch out for her."

The sailor frowned at him, and Sergey artfully turned the subject. "What have you heard? Has the palace been taken?"

The sailor nodded. "We think so, but we don't know for sure. Rumors are going around that Kerensky snuck away from the city yesterday."

"Yes, disguised as a Sister of Mercy," another guard added, amusement evident on his face.

The first sailor ignored him. "We've also heard that many of the Junkers and members of the women's battalion have come out and surrendered their weapons."

He finished looking at the passes, rejecting the dark-haired man in the long cloak. The man started to protest, but thought better of it. He trudged away down the prospect, muttering to himself.

The guard turned to Sergey. "Go no further than the Red Arch—stay on the fringes. Do not attempt to go into the palace. No one in there will be interested in your flyers anyway."

"Yes, comrade," Sergey answered, already starting to move forward.

Natasha followed closely as did Dmitri and Nicholai. The sound of shelling had stopped, making the thump of their boots on the cobbles seem strangely loud.

"It is so quiet now," Natasha said. "I have never heard it this quiet."

"Well, until the gunfire and the shelling starts again," Dmitri said in an attempt at humor.

No one smiled.

To Natasha it was a silence which reigned more terrible than all the thunders of the world. She felt as though the ground shifted beneath her. In her mind she saw the masses of peasants and workers pressing forward and the present rulers fading away like smoke from a dying fire. So much talk of revolution, so many years of persuasion and propaganda, of exile and struggle, and now the history of her beloved country was being rewritten in a night.

They were passed by a knot of armed workers and Red Guards running toward the square.

"Come on," Sergey whispered. "I think they're going to the palace. Let's follow."

"We said we wouldn't go near there," Nicholai Lvovitch said. A nearby shell blast sent the four friends running to the side of a building. "See," he took up the argument, pressing his bulk as close to the plaster wall as possible. "Maybe we should go back."

"You can if you'd like, but not me. I'm going forward," Sergey answered. "Natasha, what do you want to do?"

Her heart was beating fast and her face felt hot even in the frigid temperatures of the night. "I want to be a part of it," she said.

Sergey took her hand and pulled her close. "Dmitri?"

Dmitri pulled out his camera. "You think I'm going to miss this?"

"All right! All right!" Nicholai said fiercely. "Just don't get us killed."

They made it safely to the Red Arch where they came upon another contingent of soldiers, all of whose eyes were turned toward the palace. Light from their bonfire danced on their haggard faces, and each face carried an expression of astonishment.

"Comrades!" Sergey said, coming shoulder to shoulder with one of the smaller guards.

The guard snapped to attention. "Who are you?" He pointed his field pistol at them. "Are you counterrevolutionaries?"

All the guards snapped to attention. The officer of the watch came forward, his rifle at the ready.

"No! No, comrades," Sergey assured them, taking out his pass. "We are from the Smolny. Commissar Trotsky sent us to document the glorious event."

"Trotsky?" the soldier questioned, taking Sergey's pass.

Dmitri Borisovitch pulled out his camera, nodding confidently. "That's right. The insurrection must be documented."

The officer checked each pass carefully then gave them a distrustful glare. "All right, go on then. You'll probably be shot, but it's up to you." He handed them their papers and waved them off. "You'd better be quick or you might miss it."

"Has the Provisional Government surrendered?" Natasha asked.

"Yes, just now. The commandant of the Junkers has surrendered the palace." Dmitri and Nicholai shouted, but the officer merely gave them a measured look and continued. "The radio report said that some of the ministers were hiding but some were just sitting in a grand room around a big table—like they were having a meeting. They should be bringing them out anytime."

"Come on!" Sergey yelled.

The four ran across the square, stooping low and bunching together in case of sniper fire. When they reached the Alexander Column, Natasha looked up into the windows of the palace. Light streamed out onto the square and she could see people moving about inside.

They continued on, clambering over barricades that had been hastily constructed from firewood. Sergey was leading the group, and as he maneuvered around one of the obstructions near the palace, he stumbled over a pile of rifles and fell.

Swearing, he picked himself up and kicked at one of the weapons.

"Hey! What are you doing there?" a guard asked.

"Nothing. Nothing." Dmitri Borisovitch offered quickly as Sergey composed himself. "We're here to document the insurrection, that's all." He showed the soldier his camera, but the man looked baffled.

Sergey Antonovich stepped forward. "Here, take a picture of these rifles," he said with authority. He turned to the guard. "These were taken from the Junkers, I would imagine."

The soldier grunted. "Just keep out of the way."

Natasha was just catching her breath when five of the military school boys were escorted out of the palace and their guns thrown onto the mound of weapons. One of the aristocratic youth was weeping, but the others carried themselves with the dignity and aloofness of high position. As Natasha watched them being scolded by the Red Guards she felt sad. Russia had moved several centuries beyond these precious young men, and their manners and ability to speak French would be of little use in this brutish new world.

Nicholai Lvovitch spoke in a whisper. "Sergey Antonovich, my hearing's not so good. Can you hear what the guards are saying to them?"

Sergey nodded. "They're calling them traitors against the people. They're telling them they have supported the wrong government and that now they have the chance to serve the people. If they will promise on their word of honor not to fight against the soviets, they are free to go."

"They're not being arrested?" Natasha asked.

"It seems not," Sergey answered, a hint of amusement in his voice. "The magnanimous Bolsheviks. At least we're not being naïve enough to let them keep their weapons."

"Look! Look!" Dmitri called clandestinely to them. He had a better view as he stood on the other side of the pile of rifles, closer to the door. "They're bringing out the ministers!" He tried to steady his camera as the men came through the small door single file, flanked on either side by soldiers.

Natasha recognized several of the group: Kishkin, his face drawn and pale; Konovalov, looking straight ahead; Tereshchenko, looking sharply around. He stared at the gathering crowd of soldiers, Red Guards, and members of the workers' committees with cold fixity.

Sergey leaned toward her. "Tereshchenko is ridiculous," he scoffed. "He does not work for the people. Look at his pompous manner and smart suit. He is groomed for the theater, but he's headed for the Peter and Paul Fortress."

Natasha had to agree that none of the ministers seemed much like representatives of the people.

Rutenberg came last, looking sullenly at the ground. He glanced up and saw Dmitri taking pictures. "Are you with the newspapers?" he croaked. "Well, you tell the people that democracy is to blame. She lured us into government and set a mighty burden on our shoulders, and at the moment of danger she left us without support."

"Not true, old man!" someone shouted. "You had a choice!"

The pent up anger and spite against the conquered unleashed from the crowd in waves of recrimination.

"You had a choice!"

"You betrayed the people!"

"Where is our land?"

"Death to them!"

"Shoot them!"

Several of the soldiers in the crowd leaned past the guards and attempted to strike the ministers.

Antonov, the military commander, stepped forward, raising his arms and shouting. "Comrades! Comrades! Do not stain the proletarian victory. We have conquered a nation with very little bloodshed and we will not take judgment into our hands. These men will be taken to the fortress and there imprisoned until they can answer for their crimes against the people."

"And Kerensky? Where is Kerensky?" Sergey shouted.

Antonov addressed his answer to the crowd. "Like a coward he has fled." The people shouted their outrage and Antonov held up his arms again to quiet them. "But . . . but he will be found and punished!"

The people shouted again, this time approving the declaration.

Dmitri took pictures.

"Comrades, we will walk these criminals through the Milliony and across the Troitsky Bridge to the dungeons of the Peter and Paul Fortress," Antonov announced. "You are welcome to follow, but if you interfere in any way with my command, I will deal with you harshly." He ordered the troops forward and the vanquished ministers were herded east out of the square. A large contingent of people followed, calling out curses and mocking the ousted officials, but restraining themselves from force.

"Let's go with them!" Dmitri said, beginning to move after the disappearing group. "Come on!"

"Hey! You there!" someone called. "You with the camera."

Dmitri stopped.

The foursome turned to see an important-looking Bolshevik officer coming from the palace.

"Oh, this doesn't look good," Dmitri said.

Nicholai Lvovitch shuffled from one foot to the other. "Should we run?"

"With fifty guards ready to shoot us?" Sergey said. "I don't think so."

The officer rushed up to them. "Are you Bolsheviks? Are you with the newspapers?" he demanded.

"Ah . . . well . . ." Dmitri stammered.

"Yes, we're with *Pravda*," Sergey lied, stepping forward. "We have instructions from Commissar Trotsky to document."

The officer's face lit up. "Ah, good. Good. Come with me."

The friends exchanged doubtful looks, but followed the officer, entering the palace through the same door the ministers had exited only a few minutes before. They came into a great vaulted room from which issued a maze of corridors and staircases.

"This way," the officer said. He led them down a hallway lined with packing boxes and into a large room. Here too were packing boxes—hundreds of packing boxes nearly filling the room, but these had been smashed open, the contents strewn about the floor.

Natasha gaped at the opulence and quantity of the goods: damask curtains, tapestries, clocks, linens, glassware, porcelains, small exquisite portraits in gold-leaf frames, silk dresses, and gilt-edged tables. *Did all of this belong to one family?* She knew of course that it did, but it was still hard for her mind to accept.

Two guards were working to place the goods back into their boxes, and the officer went to stand beside them. "Here, take a picture of this," he ordered Dmitri. "Some of the peasant soldiers wanted to loot the place, but we said no. No! This is the property of the people. Don't steal from the people."

Dmitri collected his wits and took several pictures.

The officer nodded. "Good, now come with me."

A few minutes later they emerged from a side door to face the grand staircase of the palace. Natasha's breath caught in her chest and unexpected tears sprang into her eyes. She heard Sergey swear, and Nicholai Lvovitch kept muttering, "Impossible . . . this is impossible."

The white marble staircase swept up like two circling arms and was surrounded by walls festooned with carved garlands, flowers, and swirls. Most of these ornamentations were covered in gold. Thirty-foot-tall malachite pillars topped in gold cornices held up the ornate arched ceiling, while marble statues kept watch over the hidden excess.

Natasha blinked and saw Dmitri slowly raise his camera. Sergey Antonovich came to stand beside her. "Now you know why we struggle," he said, his voice cold and determined. "Now you know why we fight."

NOTES

1. **Marie Alexandrovna Spirodonova** (1889–1941): Member of the Left Socialist Revolutionist party. She was a revered leader of the revolution.

2. Kronstadt Island sits outside the mouth of the Neva River in the Gulf of Finland. It served as the main naval base for the Kronstadt fleet. The **Kronstadt sailors** were sympathetic with the Bolshevik agenda, and on the night of October 25, 1917, the naval cruiser *Aurora* sailed up the Neva River, and at a signal from the Naryshkin bastion, fired the cannon salvoes that started the attack on the Winter Palace.

3. The rumor that Kerensky escaped Petrograd disguised as a Sister of Mercy was exactly that, a widespread rumor.

CHAPTER FOURTEEN

Natasha slumped on a brocaded sofa in one of the minister's private offices. She watched through half-lidded eyes as two soldiers ripped the elaborate Spanish leather upholstery from the chairs.

"I . . . I thought," she said without energy, "that this was the people's property and not to be taken."

The soldiers stopped for a moment and looked at her good-naturedly. "That's true, comrade, but *these* chairs belonged to the Provisional Government and we need boots."

"Of course." She nodded and closed her eyes. Her body was tired from lack of sleep, her mind was spinning from days of unending work, and her emotions were numb with all she'd seen in the palace over the past few hours—room after room of such excess and opulence that she could no longer take it in.

Had it truly only been hours ago that they'd stood next to the Bolshevik lieutenant in the grand staircase foyer? She remembered people being ushered out through the one unlocked door. A self-appointed committee had set up a table over which guards stood with drawn revolvers. A young soldier sat at the table with pen and paper to note confiscated items. As the armed workers and soldiers passed by, they were searched, and the lieutenant called out a litany.

"Comrades, this is the people's palace. This is our palace. Do not steal from the people . . . do not disgrace the people."

The officer had Dmitri take several pictures to document that the Bolsheviks were not a lawless band of robbers. Natasha found it sad what the soldiers had taken: the broken handle of a Chinese sword, a coat hanger, a wax candle, cakes of soap, a blanket. The thieves had laid out the bits and scraps on the table, their faces red with shame. These simple people had walked through halls of wealth beyond their imagining and thought only to take insignificant souvenirs.

Yet, hadn't she felt the same as she'd gazed on paintings and sculptures of the masters, silver clocks, gold candlesticks, and intricate marble floors that glistened under crystal chandeliers? Hadn't her mind thought only of picking up a little piece of bric-a-brac to take out and look at later on— something small and real to convince herself she'd actually been inside the great palace of the tsars and been witness to its glory?

What will Agnes say when I tell her I actually walked the same hallways where the grand duchesses walked? A cool breeze blew across her face. Someone must have opened a window.

"Natasha Ivanovna."

Is someone holding my hand?

"Natasha Ivanovna."

She opened her eyes.

"I leave you to rest for two minutes and you fall soundly asleep."

She sat up and tried to compose herself.

Sergey Antonovich chuckled. "Are you awake?" She nodded. "The lieutenant wants to show us one last place before we leave."

She took a deep breath and stood. The soldiers, just finishing their work stripping the leather chairs, smiled at her. "We hope we didn't disturb your rest, comrade," one of them said.

She gave him a brief smile. "No. No, not at all."

"Bring that leather, any clothing, and all papers to the sorting area," the lieutenant ordered the soldiers. "The commissars wish to see everything. Chairman Lenin especially wants to see the papers of the Provisional Government. Take a picture of this, comrade."

Dmitri obeyed.

The lieutenant led the four friends down several hallways to a large room of malachite and gold with crimson brocade hangings. There was a long table surrounded by chairs, but little else in the way of furniture.

"This is where we found most of the ministers," he said. "They were sitting here like regal jackasses still trying to figure out how to save their pitiful government."

The four moved to the table.

"It's just as they left it," Dmitri said. He tried to take a picture in the bad light and swore. "These will never come out."

Natasha put her hand on the table. "I will remember and write it down, Dmitri Borisovitch." She ran her fingers over the inkwells, the pens, and the papers. The papers were covered with scribbled writing: the beginnings of plans of action, rough drafts of proclamations, definitions of manifestoes. Sergey came to her side as she picked up one of the pages. "Most of the thoughts are scratched out," she said.

"Of course," he answered. "They knew their cause was futile."

She brushed aside his cold assessment. "Look, someone has covered his sheet with absentminded geometrical designs."

Sergey said something derisive, but looking at the paper in her hand made her sad—sad to think of the frustration, fear, and despondency mingling in the room during those last hours.

"Here's one with Konovalov's name on it," Sergey said, grabbing up another paper. He read it out, his voice mocking and disdainful. "'The Provisional Government appeals to all classes to support the Provisional Government.'"

Just then a loud crash occurred in the hallway and everyone rushed out to investigate. A young woman in army attire and shaven head was running down the corridor. A soldier ran after her, aiming his revolver at her back. "Stop! Stop, comrade!" he shouted. "Please don't make me shoot you."

The lieutenant reacted immediately. "Put your weapon down!" he shouted. "Comrade, stop!" he ordered the girl.

She stopped, turning abruptly to meet the new voice.

The lieutenant held out his hand to her and she stumbled down the long hallway back to him. She was a large, sturdy girl, but as she neared, Natasha could see tears swimming in the girl's vivid green eyes. From behind them came three more soldiers guarding a group of girls. The girls were also crying and Natasha felt a keen ache of compassion for the terror they must be feeling.

The lieutenant brought the first girl back to the group and several of her friends patted her face or rubbed her arm. The officer confronted the soldier with the gun. "What happened here?" he asked, his voice accusatory and harsh.

"We . . . we found . . ." the soldier stammered. He looked at his fellows and set his jaw against emotion. "Sir, we found eight members of the women's battalion hiding in a back closet. We were bringing them out as we have all the others, when this one"—he nodded his head toward the green-eyed soldier—"started crying loudly that she wanted to die. She said she had disgraced her family and could never go home."

The girls held hands and wept.

The soldier flinched at the sight, but went on. "She said she was going to throw herself out a window. Then she knocked over a large vase and ran."

The lieutenant stood silently, looking at the shiny parquet floor. Finally he took a deep breath and looked up into the faces of the girls. He moved to them, catching the eye of the girl who ran. "How old are you?" he asked gently.

"Nineteen."

"Ah, nineteen. A little younger than my own daughter. Well, here is the truth, comrade: you have not disgraced anyone. You were tricked by the Provisional Government into thinking you were serving Russia. Is that right?" All the girls nodded. "Yes. I understand. Many people believed— and still believe—that the Provisional Government served Russia, but tonight the people of Russia have spoken. And are you not the people of Russia?" The girls' faces were full of hope and pride as they nodded again. "Yes, of course, you are. And we would not think of harming our own people. We are sending all the women of the women's battalion back to your camp in Levashovo."

Natasha noted the look of unbelief mirrored on the face of each girl.

"Not to prison?" the green-eyed girl asked.

The lieutenant looked incredulous. "Prison? No, of course not. We would not think of it!" He spoke to them as a kind father. "Now, here is what I want you to do. I want you to return to your towns and villages, grow back your beautiful hair, and have families." The girls blushed. "Yes, families. Work hard for the Soviets and teach your children to do the same. Can you do that for me, comrades?"

They all nodded, smiling and crying.

Natasha saw Dmitri sneak a picture.

"Good," the officer said, taking the hand of the one girl. "And no more thoughts of throwing yourself out of windows. You are important to the country. You must live and work and share."

From each according to their ability. To each according to their need, Natasha thought.

"Yes, comrade," the girl answered. "I am a hard worker."

"Good." The lieutenant turned to the guards. "Walk them to the truck, please." His tone was mannered and even, evaporating the last modicum of the girls' trepidation.

The soldiers moved off and Natasha noted relief on their faces; probably because they would no longer be plagued with the young girls' caterwauling.

Nicholai Lvovitch followed them for a few paces. "I wonder where that green-eyed girl is from?"

His companions laughed and the lieutenant slapped Nicholai on the back. "I could find out, if you'd like."

Nicholai's ruddy face turned even redder. "No, no. I was just wondering."

"Come then," the Bolshevik officer said, turning the focus away from the embarrassed man. "It is time to get you back to Trotsky with your documentation."

"Yes, comrade, thank you," Sergey said. "We will be sure he knows what a splendid job everyone has done—especially you."

Minutes later the friends were standing outside on the palace square. It was cold and quiet and dark. The cobbles underfoot were littered with broken stucco. Natasha looked up and saw that a cornice of the palace had been hit by artillery and shattered. It seemed to be the only damage that she could see, but perhaps the morning light would reveal more.

"I want to go home," she said, speaking her thoughts aloud.

Sergey took her arm. "I will walk you, Natasha Ivanovna. You must be exhausted."

She nodded. "Good night, Dmitri Borisovitch. Nicholai Lvovitch. I will see you some other time."

"What a wonder, hey?" Nicholai said, kicking at one of the log piles. "A whole government changing over just like that."

"Good thing I brought my camera," Dmitri said, laughing.

As the two men moved off toward Nevsky Prospect, Natasha and Sergey walked out of the square toward St. Isaac's Cathedral. She thought of the mammoth empty church with its riches and splendor. *Is God hiding behind the icons and the gold angels? And now that the Soviets are in charge, will they dismiss God as a fairy tale—a fairy tale that has no place in their movement toward utopian brotherhood? And will the European governments follow Russia in the vision for worldwide Socialism? And what of men's hearts . . . men's hearts?* She groaned and rubbed her temples.

"What's wrong?" Sergey asked. "Are you ill?"

"No. It's just that so many thoughts are tumbling around inside my head."

"That is because you need to sleep. Stay here and I'll find us a cab."

"You can't afford that."

"Perhaps the driver is a Bolshevik and will give us a free ride in celebration of the victory."

Natasha stood on the sidewalk, trying to keep warm and trying to calm her mind, but she kept seeing Konovalov's scribbled note—his desperate cry for support. Only in her exhausted mind, the name at the top of the page was V. I. Lenin and the paper read, "The Soviet Government appeals to all classes to support the Soviet Government."

NOTES

1. Many of the images concerning the storming of the Winter Palace are taken from the books *Ten Days That Shook the World* by John Reed and *Six Red Months in Russia* by Louise Bryant. As American reporters sympathetic to Bolshevik ideals they were given access to the events of the revolution, thus serving as eyewitnesses to history.

2. Little damage was done to the Winter Palace during its takeover by the Bolsheviks. Hundreds of bullet holes and a few broken cornices were reported, but overall the Palace was miraculously unscathed.

3. St. Isaac's, one of the great Russian Orthodox cathedrals, was turned into a museum of religion and atheism during Communist rule.

4. Two to three hundred female soldiers from the Women's Death Battalion made an unsuccessful attempt to stand against the Bolsheviks during the storming of the Winter Palace.

CHAPTER FIFTEEN

At the horizon a ginger sun was sinking, a corona of gold fanning out in a wide arc around the half circle. The rest of the cloudless sky was palest blue, almost white, and Natasha reached out to brush her hand across the sun's brilliant surface before it slid behind the hill. She walked through the knee-high grass without thought or care of destination. It felt good just to move through the acres of green, smell the pungent smell of dirt, and hear the wind. This kind of stillness and peace had eluded her for a long time.

She caught movement at the corner of her sight and turned to glower at whatever or whoever was intruding on her solitude. She saw nothing but miles of grass. Now movement flickered on the other side of her vision. This time when she turned, she saw a white image in the distance. She began walking to it, but as she approached, the image retreated. After several attempts to reach the phantom item, she gave up and went back to her picnic.

Mother had packed meat pies, cheese, pears, figs, and loganberry tarts, and as Natasha brought the foodstuffs from the basket there was more to take out. The quilt upon which she sat expanded and was soon covered with more food than she'd seen in months. She reached into the basket to make sure it was empty, and her fingers felt a solid metal object. She brought it out and discovered that her mother had included a simple silver cross with the picnic lunch.

Natasha drew back her arm and threw the cross far out into the field of grass. By this time she was very hungry. She grabbed a wedge of cheese, but when she went to put it into her mouth, she found it was another silver cross—this one with scrolled edges. She threw the second cross out into the tall grass as she had the first. Now her hunger was terrible and she secured a plump, juicy fig, knowing that if she didn't eat soon, she would die. But, when she bit into the fruit, instead of the soft meat of the fig, her teeth met hard silver.

She held the third cross in front of her, blinking at the splendor of the piece: pearls and emeralds encrusted the surface and the etching on the metal was exquisite. She brought the cross closer to her face so she could make out the small words hidden within the loops and swirls of the etching. She read, "The light which shineth in darkness." She stood and threw the cross with great force. It disappeared into the darkening sky.

Her body trembled from lack of food and she turned quickly to her feast, but the dark was so complete that she could not find the place where she had spread out the quilt. She fell onto her hands and knees, crawling frantically in search of the soft fabric, but her fingers found only rocks and stickers. She cried out in fear and frustration. Finally she collapsed, weeping, onto the ground. The peacefulness she'd felt earlier was swallowed up in a night without stars.

She pushed herself onto her knees and turned toward the east. Sunrise gilded the top of the hill and the black eastward sky began to lighten. She saw the white image in the distance again. She stood and walked toward it. This time it did not retreat, but moved to her. As it neared, she recognized it as the orphan girl's magical cow, but instead of the orphan girl holding the lead rope, it was a formidable-looking peasant in ancient costume. He held a sword and there was a crown on his head, yet Natasha felt neither fear nor intimidation.

The man smiled at her. "What is it you want?"

"Wisdom."

"More than food?"

"Yes." As she watched, the sword and the crown disappeared. "Who are you?" she asked.

"I was once a prince of this land. I was a pagan and I fought many wars and built up a great kingdom, but my greatest achievement was not of conquering cities or accumulating wealth."

"What was it?"

"I brought the word of God to my people." He opened his hand and a small silver cross glittered in the first rays of the morning sun.

"I know you. You are Prince Vladimir of Kiev." She patted the cow's head. "But why do you have the orphan girl's cow?"

"You were the one who sent for it," he said simply. "You must have need of it."

She heard voices, strident and low, and she turned, looking for the source of the argument, but the world was gliding again from light into dark.

Natasha blinked several times, knowing that she was waking from a dream. A gray light filled her room and she heard the voices of her mother and father. Her bedroom door was ajar and she could hear snatches of a heated conversation coming from the kitchen. She pulled her shawl around her shoulders and crept out to the top of the stairs. She sat in the shadows halfway down the stairway and focused her attention on the words. Her father's voice came first.

"You will not try to influence her with your superstitions and symbols, Svetlana. They are making her agitated. She hardly gets any sleep as it is with her work at the Smolny, and for the past three nights I've heard her moaning and talking in her sleep. The superstitions and stories must stop."

Her mother's voice came softly, but with uncharacteristic firmness. That was odd. Natasha had never heard her mother use such an assured voice when speaking to her father. "You think her troubled sleep is from simple fairy tales?"

"You are discussing much more than fairy tales. You are filling her head with the nonsense of Christianity. Telling her the stories of Vladimir and Anna."

"I am only answering her questions. Does she not have the right to ask questions?"

Her father grunted. "Of course. I have always encouraged her to ask questions."

"But she must only ask certain questions about certain things?"

Her father's voice took on a gruff tone. "When I married you, Svetlana, I told you that you could keep to your archaic country faith, but if we had children, you were not to try to indoctrinate them."

Her mother's voice lost some of its confidence. "I have kept that promise, Ivan Alexseyevitch, but she is asking me. What can I do? Do you want me to lie and tell her I don't want to share my beliefs with her?"

"Just tell her it's not important."

Natasha felt a shiver run through her body, and she pulled her shawl closer around her shoulders. It was several moments before her mother answered.

"I can't do that."

"You will do that. Religion will ruin her, just as it's ruined everything throughout history. Your bible is filled with wars, and genocide, and acts of vengeance. And religious history is replete with atrocities enacted in God's name."

Her mother's voice was strong again. "You see only what you wish to see. My sister and I were taught kindness, compassion, and service by the monks in our little village church. That is what the church teaches. People with strong faith in God have always tried to live simple lives of kindness. Yes, there have been bad things done in the name of religion and sometimes the church loses its way, but . . ."

Natasha sat forward, straining to hear each word.

" . . . the teachings of Jesus are always about goodness and righteousness."

Her father's voice was mocking. "Like the empty ritual of worshiping icons and bowing before statues? Or the church's goodness at amassing fortunes and then turning its back as the ignorant parishioners starve?"

"And you think that the philosophies of men and the governments of men do a better job? What has been *that* record in history?"

Natasha had never heard her mother speak so many words, or reason so ably. Had she been forced over the years to keep quiet in deference to her husband's standing and intellect?

"Svetlana, this conversation is over. Natasha is important to the Bolshevik cause. She has work to do, and *that* work *will* make a difference to people. People will finally be released from the chains of servitude and myth and will come together in a glorious common purpose."

Her mother said nothing.

Her father's voice was full of authority. "When she wakes up, I want you to tell her that you will no longer share your silly country fairy tales with her, and you will especially not talk to her about religion."

"No."

"No?"

Her mother's voice trembled with emotion, but the words were sure. "If you want to end our talks, you must tell her yourself. You must be the one to tell her not to ask me any more questions."

Natasha heard the scrape of the kitchen chair and assumed her father had stood.

"By the devil, woman, I will!"

Natasha stood to flee to her bedroom, but her mother's next words stopped her short.

"And you'd better tell her to stop talking to the Lindlof family about faith, because I think they've been sharing their ideas about God with her."

Natasha heard her father's footsteps moving out of the kitchen and she ran quickly and quietly back into her room. She threw her shawl over the chair and slipped into bed. The sheets were cold and she struggled to relax and make it seem as though she was just waking.

Her father shoved open her bedroom door. "Natasha," he said, none too gently.

Her body jerked and she sat up. "What?"

Her father calmed his voice. "I'm . . . I'm sorry to wake you, but I need to make a request."

"A request?"

"Yes. I want you to stop asking your mother—or anyone else—questions about religion."

"How did you . . . ?"

"There isn't much I don't know, Natasha." He looked at her sternly. "So, hear me. Leave the topic of religion alone."

She faked a yawn and made her voice drowsy and disinterested. "Why?"

"Because it is a waste of your time."

"Hmm. I am twenty-four, you know. Besides weren't you the one who encouraged me to ask lots of questions?" She made her voice girlish and innocent, knowing that it would assuage her father's ire, and in the dim morning light she saw a grin brush his mouth.

"Don't be impertinent." He came to sit at the end of her bed. "Why all these questions anyway about a subject of no importance?"

"Merely intellectual curiosity," she said.

Her father nodded. "Ah, I should have known."

"When the Bolsheviks take over, there will be monumental shifts in society, especially when it comes to religion. I think it wise to have a feeling for how the Orthodox faithful will react."

"I see."

"And if I know their beliefs, I will be better able to write edicts against their archaic thinking."

"Subtly show them the error of their ways."

"Exactly. Especially when we offer them the brotherhood of the proletariat."

Her father chuckled and tapped her gently on her forehead. "I think up here you are more than twenty-four." He stood.

"So, I don't have to stop asking questions about religion?"

He hesitated. "No. I should have had more confidence in you. You are certainly smart enough to separate reality from myth."

"Indeed."

He kissed her on the forehead. "Why don't you and I spend the day together? Perhaps a trip to the science museum."

She yawned again. "I would like that." He turned to leave. "Ah . . . Father?"

"Yes?"

"You won't tell Mother about our conversation, will you?"

"Why not?"

"Well, she is . . . simple . . . naïve about her faith. And though you and I find it foolish, I wouldn't want to hurt her feelings."

Ivan Alexseyevitch looked at his daughter a long moment, then nodded. "As you wish. Now, get up, lazy girl, before your brain turns to porridge."

As soon as he left the room, Natasha jumped out of bed and ran to her shelf of books. She secured the blue book Agnes's father had given her, went to her dresser, and hid the book under her camisoles and stockings.

NOTES

1. **Orthodox:** meaning "the way" or "the right way."

2. **The Russian Orthodox Church:** Christianity was established in Russia in 988 A.D. by Prince Vladimir, and the Russian church resembles more closely its sister the Greek Orthodox Church than it does the Catholic Church of Rome. In the Russian Orthodox Church, priests are allowed to marry as long as they do not aspire to be members of the clerical hierarchy. There is no instrumental music in any of the churches. Music is provided by a cappella singing by monks. There are no seats in the churches. Parishioners stand for the service.

CHAPTER SIXTEEN

PETROGRAD

November 19, 1917

The pale afternoon sun gave off no heat, and though Natasha had put on two pair of socks, she could feel the cold seeping through the soles of her worn boots. She found it fitting that Sergey Antonovich had chosen the front courtyard of the Mariinsky Palace as the place for his speech to the people. The appropriated palace had been the meeting place for the disenfranchised Soviet factions who resisted the pace and intensity with which the Bolsheviks pushed the country toward revolution. But the qualms and consternation of the Cadets, the Menshiviki, and the Left Socialist Revolutionists had been blown aside by the whirlwind of insurrection—the storm of the people's will. The proletariat had spoken, and for now the ideas of the Bolshevik stood.

A crowd of a hundred had gathered, and those who had been combative or scornful during the beginning of the speech had either moved away to other pursuits or changed their minds. Sergey stood confidently on the makeshift platform addressing the people in a voice infused with just the right mix of passion and persuasion. Natasha marveled at the way he could captivate or excite with a phrase or even a word. And, of course his good looks only enhanced the connection.

Natasha blushed. She was glad that her father, who stood by her side, could not read her thoughts. If he saw color on her cheeks he would assume it was brushed there by the cold. She turned her attention to Sergey's words.

"With our revolution we have paid our debt to the international proletariat, and struck a terrible blow at the war, a terrible body blow at all the imperialists, and particularly to the German butcher, Wilhelm the Executioner!"

The crowd broke into enthusiastic applause.

"Dear comrades, we have been through the years of imperialism when the worker was only a slave, when this great city was built upon our bones, when the wealth of the tsar and the clergy and the landlords was acquired at the cost of our blood and toil. And for the last years Russia was ruled through the right of monarchic succession by Tsar Nicholas, a man inadequately endowed by nature for the task; a man who believed in saints and mummies; a man who listened to his German bride; a man who submitted to Rasputin."

Natasha noted that many faces in the crowd reflected the scorn on Sergey's own, and several men yelled guttural curses.

"But the people swept Tsar Nicholas and the privileged classes into the dustbin of history!"

A cheer went up.

"Then Kerensky's band of tricksters tried to make us believe that they had crawled out of the pocket of the bourgeoisie."

Shouts of derision.

"They said, All power to the Soviets, all power to the people—but you must let us guide you, for the people are not wise enough to run their own affairs. One hundred fifty million people of fifty nationalities—run their own soviets? Impossible. Can the janitor run the building? Can the soldier become a general? Can the train oiler become the station superintendent? Can the locksmith become head of the factory? The Provisional Government said, Impossible! The Provisional Government said, No! But the people said, Yes! And the people swept the Provisional Government into the dustbin of history!"

The crowd cheered and stamped and clapped.

Natasha glanced at her father and saw a bemused expression on his face as he clapped with the others. She looked back at Sergey and found him staring at her. His voice became intimate and infused with emotion.

"Tsarism and capitalism have divided the Russian people." His glance moved over the crowd, bringing each person into his realm of concern. "These false systems have separated us—made us distrustful of one another. These false systems have brought national enmity, massacres, pogroms, and slavery." His voice lifted. "I say to you, comrades, that we must put an end to these unworthy policies! The old ways must be replaced with honesty and mutual confidence—the mutual confidence in our Soviet system. Only as the result of such a trust will there be found an honest and lasting union of the peoples of Russia! Only as a result of such a union can the workers and peasants of the peoples of Russia be cemented into one revolutionary force—a revolutionary force that will never be broken!"

The crowd cheered for several minutes, and Sergey lowered his head.

"Comrades, our hearts are being emancipated," he said at last.

Natasha, who had been watching the crowd, snapped her attention back to Sergey. *Men's hearts.*

"Our hearts are being changed!"

Only God can change men's hearts.

"The Soviet system speaks of equality. The heart of the people yearns for equality. The voice of the people calls for equality! The will of the people fights for equality!"

Natasha felt palpable emotion surge through the mesmerized crowd.

"The Soviet system stands with its hand outstretched—anxious to take care of us. Will we take that hand?"

"Yes!"

"Will we take it?"

"Yes!"

A tear slid down Sergey's cheek. "We must take it, comrades! We must!"

All the voices united in consent, and as Sergey stepped down from the platform, he was brought into the embrace and enthusiasm of the people.

"Quite a speaker," her father said, his eyes focused on Sergey and his entourage of admirers. "No wonder Lenin wants to send him out into the country."

Natasha held her exclamation in check. Her father was always attempting to throw her emotionally off-balance. It was a game between them. He set the trap and she sidestepped.

"Well, of course," she replied nonchalantly. "He can do much good in the country." She smiled as her father's eyebrows rose.

"Then he's told you about it?"

"Who? Lenin? Well, we aren't exactly on speaking terms."

Her father laughed. "Don't be impertinent, young woman. Sergey has told you about Lenin's plans for the agitprop train?"

She turned abruptly. "The what?"

"Aha! I've caught you! You know nothing about it!"

Natasha was annoyed with her father's teasing. She didn't like the fact that he knew something about Sergey that she didn't.

At that moment, Sergey came up to them and her father took his hand.

"A moving oration, Comrade Vershinin."

Sergey lowered his eyes. "Thank you, Professor. We each do what we can."

Natasha was irritated with Sergey's mock humility, with her father's teasing, with the rhetoric of the revolution. She looked at the common Russian workers and peasants ambling away from the speaker's platform, concerned that their expectations that this government—or any government—would cure their ills. It was misguided.

"Natasha?"

She turned toward her father's voice.

"Have you nothing to say to Sergey Antonovich?"

"It was a good speech," she said.

Her father laughed. "Don't mind her lack of enthusiasm, Sergey Antonovich. I think she's angry with me. You see, I'm afraid I divulged the information about the agitprop train."

"Oh," Sergey said, taking her hand. "I'm sorry, Natasha Ivanovna. I was going to talk to you about it right after the speech today . . . truly."

His tone was warm and his words seemed genuine. She looked into his face and he smiled.

"There now," her father coaxed. "It's all mended."

"I think it may be better than mended when you both hear the news I have," Sergey said.

"Something my father doesn't already know?" Natasha quipped. "That will be news indeed."

The professor chuckled. "Watch your tongue, young woman."

She held up her hand as Sergey began to speak. "Before your news, I want to know about these trains. Why haven't I heard of them? I do work in the main offices."

Sergey smiled at her again, but this time the charm did little to appease her.

"Chairman Lenin has just released the plans, and Commissar Trotsky has just told me . . . well . . . us—a few of us." His face shone. "They are such brilliant men, Lenin and Trotsky, and—"

Natasha stamped her feet to encourage circulation.

"Shall we get out of the cold?" Professor Gavrilov suggested. "I know a little café nearby. I will buy us something to eat."

"The least you can do," Natasha answered, taking Sergey's arm. "Something to eat, Sergey Antonovich, while you tell us your news?"

Natasha knew he wouldn't refuse. Everyone in Petrograd was hungry these days.

♦ ♦ ♦

After the tea and potato pancakes arrived at their table, the conversation turned again to the plans of Lenin—plans which somehow included Sergey. Natasha tried to keep up the pretense of annoyance, but it was difficult with Sergey softly rubbing the back of her hand.

"Agitprop stands for agitation and propaganda. Lenin's going to send artists, speakers, writers, and filmmakers out on these trains to educate the Russian people about the Soviet system."

"It's brilliant," Professor Gavrilov said.

Sergey nodded.

"But don't most of the towns already have councils in place?" Natasha asked.

"Yes," Sergey answered, "but this will be a way to get the people enthusiastic about the movement and get the councils running smoothly. Can you imagine when a Red Train—"

"Red Train?" Natasha interrupted.

"That's what some of us are calling them. Red for the revolution. When these trains stop at different places there will be posters hung about the town, pamphlets given out, rallies held, street meetings, and films shown. Dmitri Borisovitch is taking a few movies that he's already made, and he'll make more as we travel. I've convinced them to let Nicholai Lvovitch come along as a worker."

"I see," Natasha said. "So how long will you and your friends be gone?"

"Several months."

"Oh." She glowered at him for his insensitivity to her feelings. Why hadn't she heard about any of this? Hadn't Commissar Trotsky said that she and Sergey would both be important to the revolution?

Sergey and her father shared a look. "Aren't you excited for me, Natasha Ivanovna? Aren't you excited that I will be helping to lay the foundation of the proletariat dictatorship?"

She swallowed and tried to mask her disappointment. "Yes, of course, Sergey Antonovich. It's just that I thought we'd be working together."

His smile faded. "Of course, I understand." He reached into his pocket, pulled out a letter, and slid it across the table to her. "Perhaps my bit of news will help."

She gave him a quizzical look and took the paper. Her heart thumped awkwardly as she noticed her name written prominently in black ink above the wax seal of the Smolny. She broke the seal and began reading silently.

"Well . . . what is it?" her father questioned, shoving a potato pancake into his mouth.

She looked up, her eyes filled with wonder. "I'm to go along."

Her father grinned. "What? Go along? Go along where?"

"On the train—the Red Train! The Propaganda Committee has requested that I go along as a writer!" She stared at Sergey. "Is this true?"

"Well, you read the letter, Natasha Ivanovna. I don't think the Propaganda Committee sends out things it doesn't mean."

She threw her arms around Sergey's neck and kissed him; in a public place and in front of her father, she kissed him.

NOTES

1. In Sergey Antonovich's speech he references **Wilhelm the Executioner.** This was an epithet given at the time to **Wilhelm II of Germany** who was the last emperor of Germany and king of Prussia. His lust for empire expansion and Germany's subsequent involvement in the Great War caused the suffering and death of millions of people.

2. Lenin conceived the idea of the **Red Train** or **agitprop train** as a means of spreading the ideals of Socialism across the vast expanse of Russia. He hired artists, writers, and filmmakers to man the trains and take Bolshevik propaganda to the Russian people. The term **agitprop** comes from **agitation** and **propaganda.**

CHAPTER SEVENTEEN

PETROGRAD

November 20, 1917

"Time! Time is up! What's your answer?"

Linda Alise glared at her sister. "Braid her hair more tightly, Natasha Ivanovna. She's being mean."

Natasha grinned at the young girl's animosity, but continued to brush and braid her friend's hair with gentle consideration.

"I am not being mean," Agnes said. "We told you before, if you want to play the riddle game with us, you must play by the rules."

"But we don't get much time for these," Linda Alise whined.

"You wanted to play," Agnes answered. "We told you these were quick riddles that had to be answered quickly. No more stalling. What's your answer?"

Linda Alise stood up from the bed and started pacing, mumbling. "What can't you see that is always before you? What can't you see—"

"Ten seconds," Agnes said.

"You can do it," Natasha coaxed.

"Five seconds," Agnes continued.

Linda Alise squealed. "Don't! Stop it!"

"Time!"

Linda Alise slumped onto the bed and threw a pillow at her sister.

"Time. My answer is time. I know that's not right, but at least I get points for trying."

"You're a trickster," Agnes said, smiling at her. "What do you think, Natasha? Should we give her one point for that answer?"

"Hmm," Natasha mused. "I don't know. It's a very thin answer." She selected a rose-colored ribbon and tied it at the bottom of Agnes's braid. "I suppose we can give her one point for all her anguish."

Linda Alise made a face. "Very funny. So what's the answer?"

"The future," Agnes said, standing and moving to look out her bedroom window. "The thing that is always before you that you can't see is the future."

"Well, that's not always true," Linda Alise scoffed. "The prophets see the future."

"Obviously you're not a prophet or you would have seen the answer," Agnes teased.

"It was a dumb riddle."

"You're only saying that because you didn't figure it out," Agnes said.

Linda Alise started to give a curt reply when Mrs. Lindlof came to the bedroom door.

"Linda Alise, I need you in the kitchen."

"Now?"

"Actually ten minutes ago."

"Yes, ma'am." She stood. "Mother, what can't you see that is always before you?"

"A riddle?" her mother asked, smiling.

"Yes," Linda Alise said, "and a difficult one."

"The future," Mrs. Lindlof stated.

Linda Alise's mouth fell open and Agnes and Natasha laughed.

"You can't have figured it out already!" Linda Alise protested.

Mrs. Lindlof chuckled. "Come on, there's work to be done." She put her hand on her daughter's shoulder. "And remember, I taught Agnes most of the riddles she knows." They moved out the door and Mrs. Lindlof turned back to address her smiling daughter. "And just because it's your birthday, Agnes, don't think you can get away with torturing your sister all day."

"Me?" Agnes said, dampening down her bright expression.

"Don't give me that innocent face." Mrs. Lindlof shook her head, and Agnes laughed. "We'll have your birthday dinner ready in a little while." She left the room.

"Your mother is so kind," Natasha said.

"So is yours."

Natasha shrugged.

"She is," Agnes insisted.

"Oh, yes. Yes, she's kind," Natasha answered quickly. "It's just that we have so little in common. In fact, I see most everything opposite from the way she does."

Agnes nodded. "You do tend to take after your father."

"I've actually been asking her a few questions about her faith."

"Have you?"

"Yes, and don't sound so shocked."

Agnes attempted to put on a bland expression.

"Oh, Agnes, your face hides nothing. I know how much your faith means to you."

Agnes grew still. "Yes, it's very important, especially now."

"What do you mean, especially now?"

"Oh, nothing." Agnes looked out into the dark night. "I'm glad you're learning a little about what your mother believes. She must be very happy."

"Well, it's not as if I haven't seen the rituals all my life," Natasha said. "Burning candles, chanting prayers, and bowing at icon stands. It's all habit and superstition. Not much different from the fairy tales she loves. She was obviously indoctrinated with both when she was a little girl."

Agnes looked at her friend. "I'm sure there's more to your mother's faith than what you see on the outside."

"Hmm." Natasha sat down at the dressing table and ran the brush through her short hair. "You know, my mother cried and cried the day I cut my hair—some silly country superstition that I'd never marry a handsome man if I cut off my long hair."

"Well, that didn't prove true, did it?"

"What do you mean?"

"You must admit that Sergey Antonovich is very handsome."

"And who's to say we're going to marry?"

"Oh, yes, of course. You're right. He's just your friend. A friend who wants to kiss you all the time."

Natasha threw the hairbrush at her. "I'm never telling you one more thing."

Agnes laughed. "Oh, yes you will. I'm your best friend." She picked the hairbrush off the floor and set it on the dressing table.

Natasha sobered. "It's true. You are my best friend."

Agnes went back to looking out the window. "And that superstition couldn't be true anyway. I've never cut my hair short, and a handsome man has never kissed me, let alone asked me to marry him. And here it is my birthday, and I'm twenty-three and without any sort of suitor. My younger sister Alexandria has more suitors than I can count."

Natasha laughed. "You're just more particular than she is."

"That's true."

Natasha stood and moved to the window. "Here's a love riddle for you. Why do you always find something in the last place you look?"

Agnes smiled at her. "Because when you find it, you stop looking."

"Yes, and when you find real love you'll stop looking."

Agnes sighed. "Finding just the right suitor might not be easy for me. You think it's difficult that you and your mother have little in common? What about me and all the men in Russia?" She took Natasha's hand. "Remember that summer at your aunt and uncle's cottage?" Natasha nodded and Agnes smiled. "We braided our hair with flowers and imagined that the Prince of the Wood Elves would come and spirit us away to his kingdom."

"Or that handsome Cossacks would carry us off on their horses."

"Yes, that's right. And your poor cousin Irena didn't understand that it was only make-believe. She kept begging us not to leave her, not to go off with the handsome Cossacks."

"Yes, it was my best summer."

Agnes quieted. "Yes, mine too, Natasha Ivanovna. Mine too."

Natasha watched as tears welled up in Agnes's blue eyes.

"Oh, little squirrel. What is it? You're trying to cover something over with this false birthday cheer, and it's not just worries about boyfriends and romance."

A tear slid down Agnes's cheek and she wiped it quickly away. "Natasha Ivanovna, you have to promise me that you will say nothing about this to anyone."

"Of course not. What is it, dear friend?"

"My father is trying to find ways to get us out of Petrograd."

"What? Out? What do you mean?"

"He wants to move us back to his hometown in Finland."

"But . . . why?"

"I think you know the answer to that. Our family is not in favor here. We won't declare our allegiance to the party, and even though my father does half of the work he used to, the Bolsheviks still consider us wealthy."

Inwardly Natasha flinched. She knew it was true. She'd once overheard Sergey and Dmitri talking about how the Property Appropriation Committee was preparing to confiscate goods and property from people they felt were not adhering to the Soviet promise of communal living.

"But . . . but your father helps other people," she spluttered. "And Arel and Erland are common workers . . . factory workers."

Agnes nodded. "I know, but still we've received threats."

"Threats? What do you mean?"

"Notes slipped in with our post. The boys shoved around at work. A rock thrown at my father."

Natasha took Agnes by the shoulders. "What? A rock? Was he injured? When did this happen?"

"Last week. He wasn't hurt. It hit him in the back."

"Who did it?"

"He doesn't know. Someone yelled 'White Russian' and then this rock hit him in the back. He turned quickly, but there was no one there. It might have been two people. They must have been hiding." Tears flowed freely now.

"Oh, Agnes, I'm so sorry."

"Mother thinks some of the anger is because of our faith. The Orthodox neighbors were wary of us before, but now the Bolsheviks are shutting God out of the churches and intimidating anyone who worships."

"But, how can they—"

"I know, I know. Father doesn't agree with her, but she says some of the secret police are looking for any excuse to arrest people."

Natasha felt her stomach cramp. "Arrest? Surely you're not afraid of that?"

Agnes was silent.

"Agnes?"

"We don't know. Father just wants to get us out, if he can." She took a step closer and lowered her voice. "Listen, Natasha Ivanovna, I have something to tell you."

It frightened Natasha to see the intensity in her friend's sweet face and hear the desperation in her voice. "What is it?"

Agnes hesitated. "We are hiding money . . . money and bits of gold and some jewelry so that if they come to take everything we will still have something to live on."

Natasha was stunned. "Why haven't you told me any of this?"

"I've had to keep it a secret."

"Even from me?"

Sorrow filled Agnes's face. "Yes."

Natasha gathered her into her arms. "Oh, my friend, I'm so sorry."

Agnes accepted the solace for a few moments then stepped back. "You mustn't tell anyone, Natasha Ivanovna, not even your mother or father. Then if the police ask them questions, they will be innocent of any knowledge. Promise me."

"I promise," Natasha whispered.

"Good." Agnes wiped the tears off her face and went to look in the mirror. "Ah, it looks like I've been crying." She smoothed some powder over her face and pinched her cheeks. "I'll just have to tell my family I was crying because I'm twenty-three and have no hope of suitors."

"Dinner's ready!" her mother called up the stairs.

"We're coming down!" Agnes called back. She turned and saw the look of loss on Natasha's face. "Natasha?"

"I don't want you to go to Finland."

Agnes took her hands. "Please don't make me start crying again. We don't know what's going to happen. We'll just have to hope for the best.

Who knows, maybe the Bolsheviks will see that they're not quite ready for the law of consecration and that capitalism isn't so bad after all."

"Agnes, please don't joke. It just makes it worse."

Agnes began pulling her toward the door. "Now you see why my faith is so important to me right now. It is the main thing helping me through this sadness." She stopped at the door and took a deep breath. "Maybe I shouldn't have shared my sorrows with you, Natasha Ivanovna, but I have, and now you must promise to keep my secret and help me through this." She turned to stare into her friend's eyes. "Will you keep my secret?"

Natasha nodded.

Agnes nodded also. "What can you break with one word?"

Natasha thought for a moment. "Silence."

"Silence," Agnes repeated.

The two friends put false smiles on their faces and went downstairs to celebrate Agnes Lindlof's twenty-three years of life.

NOTES

1. **The Commission on the Appropriation of Property** was established by the Bolsheviks to make sure that property was properly distributed among all the people in an equitable manner.

Any person who spoke against or fought against the power of the Bolsheviks was considered a White Russian or anarchist and was subject to confiscation of property, physical intimidation, and imprisonment in a work camp.

CHAPTER EIGHTEEN

PETROGRAD

December 5, 1917

"Oh, Papa," Agnes whispered. "What are you doing?"

She stood in the kitchen doorway gazing at her father asleep at the table. His head rested on papers and maps; his hand on an open book that had arrived in the post that morning: Talmage's book, *Articles of Faith.* Mother had sent to the Swedish mission office for a copy to replace the one he'd given away to Natasha Ivanovna.

Her father's messy hair and soft snores made him seem childlike and Agnes fought to control the press of tears behind her eyes. Her one candle glowed brightly in the dark kitchen and as she moved nearer the table she could make out the words on the page of the book: "Chapter 18. The Gathering of Israel."

Her father's other hand lay on a map of St. Petersburg and the surrounding area, his fingers splayed over Kronstadt Island and dipping into the waters of the Gulf of Finland. She imagined further west would be the ocean and the Finnish coast. Would their family be able to find sanctuary in the land of her parents' ancestors? Perhaps, if they could get there, but the Great War still held Europe in its teeth, which made travel dangerous if not impossible.

Agnes wanted to scream, or cry, or kick something. She wanted to go back to a time of calm. She closed her eyes, remembering the day in the

Summer Garden when Elder Lyman had said the prayer for Russia. As her mind conjured the blue sky and the rustle of the elm leaves, her heart searched for the peace that had enveloped her that day, the feeling of love and hope. *"Let not your heart be troubled, neither let it be afraid."* The words seemed to pour into her soul from heaven.

She opened her eyes and saw her father lifting his head off the table. He sat up, emerging slowly from the cocoon of sleep. He stretched his back, turning his head in her direction and blinking at the candlelight.

"Agnes?"

"Yes, Father."

"I . . . I must have fallen asleep."

"You did." She set the candle on the table and began rubbing his neck and shoulders. "A man of sixty should probably not fall asleep at the table."

"Probably not." He sighed with relief as Agnes rubbed a sore muscle. "You're an angel, but what are you doing out of bed at this hour?"

She kissed the top of his head. "Taking care of you, it seems."

The clock ticked and a persistent wind rattled the windows.

"I don't have to ask what you're doing up so late," she said finally. "You're still trying to find a way to get us to Finland."

He laid his hand on the map. "Yes."

"It doesn't seem likely, does it?"

"No, but we will trust God."

She nodded. It was always his answer for the vagaries of life he could not understand or for the events that were beyond his control. Trust God.

"Papa," she said, sitting in a chair to the side of him.

He smiled at her. "You haven't called me that in a long time." He patted her hand. "Tell me your troubles."

"I suppose if we just said we were Bolsheviks, it would save us from much of the persecution."

"Do you think so?"

She was still for a moment, and then shook her head. "No. I think the Socialists will always see us as middle-class bourgeoisie."

"I think you're right. Besides, I don't know how we could ever say we were part of a system which sees God not merely as an irritant, but as an enemy."

Agnes nodded. "I know. I love Natasha—she is like my sister—but I can't see how she can live her life without faith in God, how she puts all her hopes in men and earthly ideologies."

"Well, they are brilliant men, Agnes. She sees them fighting for the people, and it's a very noble cause."

"Yes, but—"

"Natasha Ivanovna is smart. She looks around her at the poverty of the people and their lack of representation, and she sees the government, the wealthy, and the church doing very little about it. In a way, I agree with her. As a country, we do have problems, and while I also agree that the landowners, the government, and the church need to be held accountable for their excesses, I don't agree with the Socialist methodology."

Agnes was mesmerized by her father's words. He had never shared so many of his feelings with her. He was speaking to her as he would to Johannes or Oskar, and as she looked into his beloved, aging face, she felt a distance close between them. She averted her gaze to the scattered items on the desk, absently worrying the corner of a photograph. She pulled it from under a pile of papers. It was a picture of her family standing together on the bridge over the Griboyedov canal. The year was 1910. She was sixteen and Bruno was fourteen. In 1910, Bruno was alive—alive and vying with Oskar and Arel for the attention of Natasha Ivanovna. It was a time when there was no war and no revolution, when she and Natasha shared riddles and secrets, when she believed in dreams of future happiness.

"You can't go back, little birch tree," her father said, seeming to read her thoughts. "You can only go forward."

"But aren't you afraid? I don't know what's going to happen to us."

Her father patted her hand. "None of us knows from day to day. Life is unsettled for everyone at the moment. That's why we must plan ahead." He reached into his coat pocket and brought out a small beige bundle.

Agnes knew immediately what it was: ruble notes, a few gold coins, and silver rings rolled tightly in soft wool cloth and tied with string. The packet was fashioned to fit in one hand—a size that could be easily hidden.

Her heart started beating as though she was running a race. "Where are you hiding this one?"

"The Rostral Column. There's a convenient nook behind Dnieper's trident."

She nodded and tried to calm her worried thoughts. Two bundles had already been hidden without any trouble, but each one was a risk.

"Papa . . . maybe if we told someone . . ."

He frowned at her. "What do you mean? Tell who?"

She took a chance. "Maybe the Gavrilovs."

His answer was swift and stern. "No. Why would we do that?"

"Maybe they could help us. Professor Gavrilov is an important person."

"Yes, an important person with the Bolsheviks."

"But he's also our neighbor. We've been neighbors for a long time."

Mr. Lindlof set down the bundle and took his daughter gently by the shoulders. "Agnes, I don't think the Gavrilovs would intentionally harm us, but loyalties change when people feel themselves threatened. We can't take the chance."

Agnes lowered her head.

"You understand, don't you?"

She nodded.

"This will be the final bundle, anyway. The few other pieces I have left are too large to hide easily." He yawned. "I'll try to sell those in the next few days." He lifted Agnes's chin. "So no more worrying."

She attempted a smile, but it did not reach her eyes or her heart. "I don't know if that's possible, Papa."

"Do the best you can."

The candle sputtered and Agnes picked it up. "I think it's telling us that it's long past our bedtime."

Johan Lindlof stood, gathering up the papers, maps, and book. Agnes noted that his pace was slow and counted the creases lining his face. She would talk to Johannes about her concerns. Since Bruno's death, she'd watched as her father relinquished more and more responsibility to her brother. Johannes had taken over what was left of the business, procured food and household items, and most recently had the job of hiding the bundles of money. Johannes usually took Oskar or Arel with him as a lookout. Nonetheless it was dangerous. She doubted she could convince him to trust the Gavrilovs. He would probably agree with Father.

She moved toward the stairs and her father followed. She had to think of a way to help her family. Her father was convinced they had to keep their plans a secret, but she'd already told Natasha Ivanovna, and she was sure her friend would not betray them.

Agnes took her father's arm and helped him climb the stairs. She would think of something—something that would give them extra protection.

CHAPTER NINETEEN

Petrograd
December 31, 1917

"Eeek!" Alma Lindlof shrieked, as a fox snuck up behind her and grabbed her around the waist. She tried to sound angry, but laughter crept into every word. "Stop, you terrible ugly fox! Get out of my kitchen. How will I ever get these blini cooked for the celebration if you keep scaring me?"

Erland's fox-like voice was muffled from behind the mask. "But it's my job to sneak and steal and scare." He reached for one of the thin golden pancakes, and his mother swatted his hand with the ladle.

"Ah! None of that! Go find your brother wolf and brother bear and see if they can keep you out of trouble."

"They've gone to frighten the Gavrilovs and bring them to the feast."

"Well, go and help them."

Erland slumped toward the door. "Professor Gavrilov frightens *me*."

Alma Lindlof worked at keeping the mirth out of her voice. "He is no match for fierce Master Fox. Besides, you'll have your brothers beside you."

Erland curled his gloved hands like claws and resumed his fox's voice. "That's right! If he growls at us, we'll just growl back."

She heard the front door close as Erland slipped out into the night. She shook her head as she poured a ladle of thin batter into the hot pan. It sputtered and sizzled, and a warm buttery fragrance filled the kitchen.

"No, no! Now stop that immediately!" came a voice from beyond the kitchen door.

"Oh, now what?" Mrs. Lindlof said in mock irritation. She deftly flipped the thin pancake as Johan Lindlof stepped grandly into the kitchen. He wore a white fur cap and was dressed in an impressive leather robe with white fur trim all around the edges. He looked so festive that Alma found herself tearing up with the joy of the season.

"You're very brave, Ded Moroz, to come into my warm kitchen. Aren't you afraid you'll melt?"

He moved to her. "Well, I had to come and tell you to stop cooking up these little suns or I shall melt for sure."

He grabbed the hot pancake she was about to place on the stack and juggled it between his hands. "Oh! Hot! Hot!"

Alma chuckled. "Yes. That will teach you, Father Frost. And there will be one less pancake for you at the feast."

"What two things don't like to be counted?" he asked, taking a big bite of the pancake.

"You're asking your riddles already, Ded Moroz?"

"Yes, and this one is very important."

She gave him a crooked smile. "The two things that don't like to be counted are pancakes and . . . kisses."

He nodded and kissed her on the mouth. "I think I'll go outside and look for the rest of our company."

"Yes, I'd imagine that robe is a bit hot."

As Johan moved toward the door, he stopped and turned in a circle. "I never thought I'd wear this again once the children were grown. Yet, there I was last night, rummaging in the trunk for our costumes."

Alma Lindlof looked over her husband's costume with a critical eye. "No worse for the wear, I guess."

Johan looked down at his robe. "What do you mean? I think I look splendid." He moved to his wife and gave her a squeeze. "And you're not going to be my helper this year?"

Alma put another pancake onto the stack. "No. Agnes wanted the honor this year. It will be good for her."

"She was very insistent on a New Year's celebration this year."

"You know why, don't you?"

Johan nodded. "A piece of her sweet childhood remembered?"

"I think so. It will also be a bit of gaiety in a dark time. And . . ." Alma's voice trailed off.

"What?"

Alma poured a ladle of batter and picked up the pan to swirl it around. "It was her and Bruno's favorite festival."

Johan Lindlof took a deep breath. "Of course . . . I remember."

Alma watched the pancake brown around the edges. "And it may be the last one we have for a long time."

"Really?"

"Yes. Agnes confessed to me that she'd overheard Natasha Ivanovna and Sergey Antonovich talking about how the new Soviet government is going to do away with all the old pagan festivals and holidays."

Johan shook his head. "It doesn't surprise me." He stood near his wife, breathing in the delicate aroma of the pancakes. "Will there be enough?"

Alma nodded. "I've been saving ration cards and hiding food from Erland for two months."

"And he didn't find it?"

"I threatened him with his life."

They laughed together, then Johan sobered. "Putting this together has been difficult for you."

Alma flipped the pancake and smiled. "Who can say no to Agnes's sweet face?"

"Who indeed."

Just then a racket sounded from the direction of the Gavrilov's house: animals growling, drums beating, and horns being blown.

Mr. Lindlof's face brightened. "I think our company is arriving!" He moved off through the shop and opened the front door. "Welcome! Welcome, friends!" He patted Natasha Ivanovna's shoulder. "I hope the wild beasts did you no harm, Natasha Ivanovna."

Natasha was laughing and beating a drum. "No, of course not, Ded Moroz. They are not frightening at all. I would say they were all as gentle as rabbits."

To this comment there were human howls of protest from beneath the masks, and the company laughed.

"Come in, come in, Svetlana Karlovna," Johan Lindlof said in his Ded Moroz voice. "Father Frost loves the cold, but doesn't recommend it for frail humans. We shall go out in the back courtyard later for some games, but until then, come and warm yourselves."

Oskar, Arel, and Erland took off their animal masks and gloves and helped the ladies with their coats.

Before closing the door, Mr. Lindlof looked out into the street. "Ivan Alexseyevitch is not coming?"

Svetlana Karlovna looked at her mittens as she handed them to Erland. "No . . . he sends his regrets. He's . . . not feeling well."

"Not in the festive mood," Natasha added with meaning.

Svetlana Karlovna shrugged. "Oh, well . . . more blinis for the rest of us."

It was such an uncharacteristic thing for her to say that everyone was momentarily stunned into silence. Then laughter erupted—first from the boys, then Natasha, and finally Mr. Lindlof and Svetlana.

"Come into the kitchen," Alma called. "I'm missing all the fun!"

The joyful gathering moved through the shop and parlor and into the kitchen. The women joined in making blinis together as the men loaded the sideboard with cold meats and cheese, sour cream, pickled mushrooms and cucumbers, jams, and honey. Mr. Lindlof temporarily set aside his heavy robe so he could help. Just as they were finishing their work and the stacks of pancakes were covered and set in the warm oven, Johannes arrived with Alexandria and Linda Alise. Natasha thought they all carried smug, satisfied looks of having accomplished some secret job.

Natasha looked around with a slight frown on her face. "You said while we were cooking that all the others had been sent off for special tasks," she said impatiently. "And now all the others are back . . . except for one." She looked at the bright faces. "So? Where is my friend, Madam Lindlof? Where is our Agnes?"

Alma Lindlof grinned. "She wanted it to be a surprise. Everyone sit down at the table."

"What? We're not eating right away?" Erland complained.

"Just sit down, son. You'll like this."

"Not more than eating," he grumbled as he slouched into his chair.

"Arel, turn off the lights, please."

Arel did as his mother asked and then slid into the seat next to Natasha Ivanovna.

She gave him a look.

"I know, I know. The seat is reserved for Agnes, but she's not using it at the moment, right?"

The two were about to get into a friendly whispered argument, when they noticed everyone else looking toward the hallway. There was a soft glow emanating from the corridor, melting the darkness.

Agnes came slowly into the room and the effect of her costume was so striking that even Erland was still. She was dressed in a gown of shimmering white with fur collar and cuffs. Ice-blue snowflakes sparkled on the bodice, reflecting the light of the single candle she held. On her head was a sequined headdress in the same ice-blue and white of her dress. Her golden brown hair was unbound and it cascaded over her shoulders and softly framed her face.

Natasha felt as though she was looking at an angel.

"I am Snegurochka," Agnes said solemnly, "granddaughter and traveling companion of Ded Moroz." She circled the table. "We have traveled far to find warm hearts in this cold world." She stopped and laid a hand on her father's shoulder. "And though Ded Moroz is a great wizard and the father of frost, he longs for companionship and the warmth that will melt his cold, cold heart." She patted her father's shoulder dramatically and many in the assemblage chuckled.

Snegurochka continued her sojourn around the table, looking each person earnestly in the eyes. "And so our journey has brought us here. I ask you, friends, is there one among you who can melt the cold, cold, *cold* heart of Ded Moroz?"

"Here now!" Mr. Lindlof roared in an offended Ded Moroz voice.

Erland hooted with laughter, and Agnes moved directly to him and put her hand on his head. "You, young master—do you think you know the secret?"

Erland's stomach growled loudly, and chuckles traveled around the table. Erland stood. "Yes, I know the secret! Feed him blini, right now! And the rest of us too!"

Arel, Oskar, and Johannes clapped and cheered their agreement as Erland bowed.

Linda Alise squealed with laughter, and Snegurochka moved quickly to her, laying her hand on her head. "You, little pig with her tail caught in the door—you must know a trick or two."

Linda Alise looked at her father, got up quickly, and ran over to kiss his cheek. The company applauded the tenderness as Mr. Lindlof put his hand over his heart and sighed.

"Well, it's a beginning," Snegurochka said. "But remember, it's a very cold heart."

"Ah! Be careful what you say!" Ded Moroz warned with a stern look.

Snegurochka clamped a hand over her mouth to keep from laughing, and Natasha watched with amusement as her friend struggled to regain the regal deportment of her character. Finally Agnes was again able to address the group as Snegurochka.

"Please, dear friends, don't tell me that Ded Moroz and I will have to go searching again. That we will have to go back out into the bitter night where my little candle light will be swallowed up in the darkness or blown out by a harsh wind."

The table was silent. Then, so softly that Natasha wasn't sure where it was coming from, a voice began singing a charming Russian folk song. As Natasha looked around the table, her eyes found Alexandria. Her head was bowed, but Natasha could see her lips moving. Alma Lindlof joined her daughter, then Svetlana Karlovna began singing, then Agnes and Linda Alise. When the men joined, the song swelled in volume and passion. Natasha found herself trembling and Arel reached over and took her hand. She did not have a voice for singing, but she sang anyway. She made sure her meager efforts hid behind the other, more accomplished, voices, but it lifted her heart to be part of the celebration.

When the song finished, Natasha clapped and cheered with the others, while Mr. and Mrs. Lindlof dabbed at their eyes with handkerchiefs. She looked over at her own mother and found her staring about in wonder. She leaned toward her. "Mother, are you all right?"

"Yes, yes. It's just that . . ."

"What?"

Her mother bowed her head and said softly, "I've never really known them."

"Dear friends," Agnes said, raising her Snegurochka voice above the din. "I think that Ded Moroz has finished wandering." She moved over and kissed him on the top of his head. "What do you say, dear Ded Moroz?"

"I will stay with you always." His voice was husky with emotion and he dabbed again at his eyes.

Another cheer went up and Arel turned on the light.

"Hurrah!" Erland shouted. "Is it time to eat?"

♦　♦　♦

After the superb meal, where for once everyone had had enough to eat, the revelers bundled up and went out to the back courtyard for games and contests. Mr. Lindlof put on his Ded Moroz robe, told silly stories and riddles, and handed out presents. All the gifts were either handmade or simple, but no one cared. A happiness filled the air that Natasha hadn't felt for months. Her mother had abandoned the party soon after dinner, and for once Natasha was sad not to have her near.

Agnes had wisely chosen to trade her beautiful, but impractical costume for a country dress, heavy coat, fur hat, and boots. Natasha watched her as she played a balancing game with Arel. They each stood on a patch of ice with one foot held in the air while their siblings either taunted them or cheered them on. After several minutes, Arel's leg began to shake and he wobbled sideways, putting his foot on the ground just before falling. The girls clapped for Agnes and the boys chided Arel good-naturedly for his weak leg.

Mr. Lindlof's voice broke into his children's revelry. "Your mother and I are off to bed."

"So early?" Agnes protested.

"It is not that early for us," he returned. "We're getting old, remember."

Agnes hugged him. "Don't say that."

"What about welcoming the New Year?" Linda Alise asked.

"We will welcome it tucked away in our warm bed," her mother answered.

"And do I have to go to bed too?" the youngest Lindlof asked plaintively.

"Of course not!" her father answered in his booming Ded Moroz voice. "Don't you and Johannes and Alexandria have a surprise for everyone?"

Linda Alise brightened. "Yes, we do!"

"Well then, if I were you, I'd continue your celebrating with all the other young people gathered out front by the canal."

Linda Alise squealed with delight and hugged her father and mother. "Thank you. Thank you. This is the best New Year's I've ever had!"

"I'm glad for you," her mother said softly. She lifted her voice as she looked around to her other children. "The best New Year's to all of you!"

They all returned the good wishes and, one by one, kissed her cheek.

When Alma Lindlof had finished patting Erland's face, she stepped forward and took Natasha's hand. "We loved that you were with us, Natasha Ivanovna."

"Thank you for having me . . . me and my mother. It was wonderful."

"Agnes's twin, that's what you are," Mr. Lindlof said, smiling at her. "Good night, my children!" he called as he and Mrs. Lindlof moved off to the house. "Remember your prayers."

Her parents had barely stepped inside the house when Linda Alise grabbed Alexandria's and Johannes's hands. "Come on! Let's get the surprise! The rest of you go to the front!"

"Quite bossy, isn't she?" Oskar said.

"I don't mind," Erland replied, "as long as the surprise is something to eat."

"You're *always* thinking of eating," Agnes said.

"I'm a growing boy."

"You're almost twenty, Erland," Arel piped in. "I don't think you're going to grow anymore."

"Unless it's out," Oskar teased.

Erland chased him through the house to the front, while Agnes scolded them.

The quick pass through the warm house and into the cold again made

Natasha's eyes water. As she searched for her handkerchief, Arel stepped to her side. "Don't cry for my silly brothers," he whispered saucily in her ear. "They're not worth your tears."

She giggled and turned her head to smile at him. Arel smiled back and kissed her at the corner of her mouth. Before she could react, he was running after Oskar and Erland.

"Did my brother just kiss you?" Agnes said indignantly as she came to Natasha's side.

"I . . . I believe he did," Natasha answered, her eyes wide in astonishment.

Agnes, on the other hand, frowned. "Well, I apologize for him. Just wait until I tell Father of his bad manners."

"Oh, please don't," Natasha said, laughing. "I'm sure it was just for friendship and from the happiness of the night." She locked her arm in her friend's arm and they began strolling toward a group of young people dancing to the music of a balalaika and an accordion.

"Well, I'm going to scold him anyway," Agnes insisted. "If Sergey Antonovich had seen that, there would have been trouble."

The smile left Natasha's face and she changed the subject. "I wonder what Johannes and your sisters have planned for us?"

They didn't have to wait long for the answer, as the three conspirators came dancing from the house carrying a life-sized straw scarecrow.

"It's Maslenitsa!" Agnes cheered. "I asked them to find one and they did!"

Alexandria led with a lantern held high, and Johannes and Linda Alise followed carrying the ugly female scarecrow with her big head and paper dress.

"Maslenitsa? But it's months before her festival," Natasha said.

"I know!" Agnes answered, dancing about as her siblings drew nearer. "But we're going to celebrate everything tonight! Christmas and Easter and New Year's and the end of winter! Everything!"

Tears were sparkling in Agnes's eyes and Natasha felt a momentary rush of sadness. She chided herself. If this was the way her friend chose to shake off the melancholy season, who was she to question? She grabbed Agnes's waist and joined the circle of revelers now gathering around Maslenitsa. Arel grabbed Natasha's other side to close the circle.

"Arel Lindlof!" Agnes hissed at him. "You let go of her this instant!"

Arel ignored her.

Johannes's voice sounded clear and strong in the cold, still night. "This is Maslenitsa, the witch of winter!" The circle of dancers booed and hissed and shouted insults. "She holds in her ugly hands the last vestiges of winter!" More boos and shouts. "But I tell you, Maslenitsa, that your reign is over!" The crowd cheered as Johannes took out two long wooden matches and lit them in the flame of the lantern. "This year, winter is leaving early!"

The dancers began moving clockwise as Johannes put the matches to the dry straw and the scarecrow burst into flame. The dancers shouted and sang as the ugly witch of winter perished.

Natasha's blood warmed as she danced and she wished for the long dark winter to end, for the cold to give way to the breath of spring, and for the gray of snow and ice to be brushed over with the green of life.

She held tightly to Agnes and Arel as they danced, feeling safe in their embrace.

NOTES

1. **Ded Moroz** and **Snegurochka:** Ded Moroz plays a role similar to Santa Claus. The translation of his name means Grandfather Frost. Ded Moroz is usually accompanied on his journeys by his granddaughter, Snegurochka. Her name translates to Snow Maiden.

During the reign of the Communists many Russian traditional holidays were canceled or modified. This was especially true of religious holidays such as Christmas or Easter. Even marriage was taken from the church and made secular. Couples declared their allegiance to the state and proclaimed their vows under the red flag.

CHAPTER TWENTY

Petrograd

January 3, 1918

There was thunder, or bombs falling, or someone was pounding . . . pounding on a door. Natasha sat up in the darkness, her heart thumping against her chest. She lurched out of bed, getting caught in the coverlet and falling with a thud onto the floor. It was cold. The fire in her small stove had gone out hours before. She heard footsteps in the hallway and her door opened.

"Natasha?"

"Yes?"

Her father came to her. "Are you all right?"

"Yes. I fell out of bed. What time is it?"

"About three."

There was another crash of wood.

"What's happening? The sounds are coming from the Lindlofs' home."

Her father helped her to stand. "I'll go and see. Stay here."

She heard the sound of shattering glass and angry voices. Her heart jumped so violently it made her cry out. She saw her mother run past her doorway.

"Mother?"

Svetlana Karlovna did not stop. "They've come for them!"

She ran on and Natasha heard her footsteps flying down the stairs. The panic in her mother's voice made Natasha stagger back against the bed. *They've come for them.* She found the matches on her side table, but her body was trembling so violently it took several attempts before she got the candle lit. She found her boots and pulled them on. She grabbed her coat and threw it over her shoulders as she ran down the stairs.

Yelling, gruff voices, and crying assaulted her ears as she reached the front door and threw it open. The cold was piercing, and she shuddered involuntarily. Two police trucks were idling on the street, their barred doors thrown open. Johannes Lindlof was being shoved inside by a Cheka police officer.

Natasha ran forward. "Johannes!"

"Natasha, no!" She heard her father yell and she spun around to find him. Someone knocked her sideways, and she had a blurred picture of her father and mother with a man pointing a rifle at them, before falling onto her hands and knees in the snow.

Someone grabbed her roughly and pushed her to her parents.

"Stay back," a disembodied voice commanded.

She turned her face to the Lindlof home as Oskar and Linda Alise came out the front door. Linda Alise was crying so hard she stumbled over the threshold. Oskar caught her and whispered something into her ear. The face of the fourteen-year-old girl was so pale with fear it shone against the dark night, but she nodded at Oskar's words and stood straighter.

"Father," Natasha cried, grabbing his coat sleeve. "Father, do something!"

"I can't."

"But you must! You must!"

"Now is not the time."

As Oskar and Linda Alise climbed into the lead police truck, Alexandria stepped out into the night. She wore a flowing green cape and held tightly to a little brown suitcase. She carried herself with such aloof assurance that only one of the policemen dared to approach her.

"Comrade, your suitcase—"

She cut him short. "I am not your comrade, and the head officer has already checked this. It carries nothing of importance to you."

The policeman stepped back, blinking, and Alexandria climbed regally into the truck.

Arel came next. He held a cloth against his cheek, and even though the light from the doorway was meager, Natasha could see that the cloth was bloodstained. Her mind pulled up images of the New Year's celebration—of Arel in his bear mask, of him sliding next to her at the dinner table, of the kiss he placed so sweetly at the corner of her mouth.

As soon as his eyes found her, he did not look away. He walked more slowly and it seemed as though he was trying to record in his memory each detail of her face. When he reached the truck, he stopped and held up a hand to her. His expression was one of sadness and innocent longing. She raised a hand to him just as a policeman rushed forward and pushed him into the truck.

Suddenly there was a crash from inside the house and Erland burst out into the night, followed by a police officer yelling curses and aiming his rife at Erland's back. Alma Lindlof came to the doorway, screaming for her son to stop and pleading for the man not to shoot. Svetlana Karlovna stepped sideways into the path of the policeman and he slipped on the ice and fell.

He scrambled to his feet, cursing and threatening her. "Stay out of my way, woman, or I'll shoot you too!"

Natasha stood frozen in place as her father yanked her mother back toward the house. She heard gunshots and turned numbly in the direction Erland had run. She expected to see him lying in a heap, but he had stopped abruptly and flung his hands into the air. The pursuing policeman ran up and jabbed him in the stomach with the butt of his rifle. Erland shouted in pain and doubled over.

Nausea moved into her throat and Natasha put her hands on her knees and sucked cold air into her body. At the sound of her name, she looked up and saw Agnes being herded toward the truck. Without thinking, Natasha ran toward her. A boxy policeman with a broad country face blocked her way.

"Stay back!" he barked.

"Please, please, please," Natasha whispered, looking up into his young face. "Please, comrade, I'm a Bolshevik. My father, Professor Gavrilov, is the head of a soviet." Tears sprang from her eyes and froze on her cheeks.

Her voice rose in volume and intensity. "This is my dearest friend!" The policeman did not move. "I am a Bolshevik! Let me see her!"

The policeman swallowed and his eyes flicked to Natasha's face, but he set his jaw and shook his head. "I have my orders."

An anguished cry strangled in Natasha's throat.

"Now, now, comrade, we must not be callous to friendship," an oily voice said, and Natasha looked around for the source. She caught the eye of the head Cheka officer and he smiled a cold smile. His large hands were clamped around the upper arms of Johan and Alma Lindlof as he dragged them from their home. The officer stared at Natasha with unmasked lust, and she took a step back and lowered her head. He laughed. "So, you are a Bolshevik, and yet you are friendly with upper-class, merchant scum. Not a good idea, comrade."

Natasha focused on Agnes's innocent face. "Why are you taking them? Why?" she pleaded.

"Natasha, be quiet!" her father hissed.

Natasha ignored him. "They are good people. They work hard and they cause no trouble."

At that moment, the policeman who'd gone after Erland pulled him past her, and Natasha saw a bloody lip and a bruise purpling on the left side of his face. "Erland," she said tenderly, reaching out to take his hand.

"Long live the Bolsheviks," he growled at her, and the policeman punched him in the kidney and shoved his crumpled body into the second truck.

"Stop! Stop it!" Natasha screamed.

Johan Lindlof's voice came reassuringly out of the dark. "Be still, Natasha Ivanovna. They're just taking us in for questioning. Everything will be all right."

"Get in the truck, old man," the head officer snapped as he yanked Johan and Alma to the second truck. His voice carried none of the former silkiness, and Natasha wanted to hit him hard in the face for his rough handling of the dear couple, but she held her anger and forced subservience into her voice.

"Please, comrade. Please, let me speak to my friend."

The head officer turned from depositing the Lindlofs in the truck and leered at her. Natasha's skin crawled with disgust, but she kept her face placid, even when the brute grabbed Agnes by the back of the neck and shoved her forward. Natasha concentrated only on the fact that her friend would soon be within reach. Agnes stumbled on a rough patch in the sidewalk and fell weeping into Natasha's arms.

"Have they hurt you?" Natasha whispered.

"No."

"We will get this figured out, little squirrel. My father will see to it."

"Here, Natasha," Agnes whispered urgently, shoving a wadded up piece of paper into her hand. "Take this."

Natasha closed her fingers quickly around the paper. "What is it?"

"It can save us."

"What's that there?" the officer barked, stepping close to Natasha and grabbing her wrist.

She cried out. "It's nothing. Just a note. A silly schoolgirl's note." She didn't actually know what it was, but she didn't think Agnes would be foolish enough to write anything incriminating in a letter. She kept her fingers clamped tightly around the missive.

The officer pried it out of her hand.

"They're just riddles," Agnes confessed. "We've shared riddles all our lives."

"You, shut up." The officer unfolded the paper and read over the content. He smirked at Agnes's angelic face. "How old are you—twelve?" He shoved the paper back at Natasha and put his large hands on Agnes's waist. "You don't look twelve." He drew her close to his body. "You don't feel twelve."

"Leave her alone!" Natasha commanded. "Or my father will have to report you."

The officer looked over to see Natasha's father and mother coming near. His men were all at the trucks now, waiting impatiently for the last prisoner, and a chance to get out of the cold. The officer let go of Agnes's waist, taking her arm and squeezing it so tightly that Agnes whimpered. "Don't get any ideas about reporting anything, Professor, or you might just find a few reports filed about *your* family."

Professor Gavrilov stood silently beside his daughter, and Natasha noted the anger washing his face. She looked quickly back to see Agnes step up into the truck. Agnes glanced back and nodded.

The bars were shut and locked, the policemen piled into the trucks, and the vehicles pulled away.

Agnes leaned over for one last look through the bars, and Natasha shuddered as a strand of her friend's golden-brown hair caught the faintest glint of light.

Natasha's mind could not accept the reality of what had happened. Just a few days ago they had celebrated the New Year with gaiety and hope, and now there was only a sense of emptiness.

"Natasha, come inside. I want to speak to you." Her father's voice was filled with anger and disapproval.

"No." She wanted no part of a lecture, besides she felt as if going inside was a betrayal. Go inside to a warm bed and security while her friend and her family were being taken away into an unknown darkness? No. She also feared that if she went into her house, her mind would snap. She already felt it slipping in and out of reason.

"Natasha!"

"No." She looked over at the Lindlofs' door and saw that it had been nailed shut and a notice placed on it. She moved numbly over and read the sign out loud.

For crimes against the state—
this property and all its contents are herby confiscated.
All possessions will be shared equally by the people.

Her mother came to her side.

"The law of consecration cannot be mandated," Natasha said.

"Please, dear one, you don't know what you're saying."

Natasha yelled out into the night. "The government cannot force men to live a communal law! And the government can't come in the middle of the night and take innocent people away!"

"Natasha, don't."

"Did you hear that, Father? Did you hear?"

"He's gone into the house, Natasha."

Natasha paced back and forth, her eyes darting from the Lindlofs' door to the deserted street. Her voice came loud and wild. "Interesting how none of the neighbors came out to help." She yelled again at the dark houses. "Didn't he give you bread, and potatoes, and cabbage? Didn't he and his sons find wood for you so your families wouldn't freeze?"

Her mother was frantic. "Natasha, stop. Please, dear one. This is not good."

"He gave you bread!" Natasha screamed into the deserted street. "I want to see them." Her body shuddered with cold. "I want to see them! I want to see my friend!" Her mind slid out of focus and she saw Ded Moroz handing out presents, the family singing together in the warm kitchen, and Agnes in her beautiful snow maiden costume. A knife point of pain pressed into her heart, but no tears flowed to ease the pressure. *Think, Natasha, think. You must figure out a way to free your friends.* She looked over to find her mother staring at her. "Father will be able to get them out, won't he?"

Her mother looked away. "I think he'll do what he can."

"That's not an answer."

"I know, but it's all I can give you."

A piercing wind blew across the canal and Natasha's ears and cheeks ached with cold.

"Ah, look," her mother said. "There is white on your cheeks where your tears ran down." She covered Natasha's cheeks with her fur mittens. "Frostbite. Please, we need to go inside now. Tomorrow we will see what we can do."

Natasha looked into her mother's face and saw calm determination. "If there is a God," Natasha said bitterly, "where was He? Where was He when this family who loves Him so much was taken away?"

Her mother did not respond for several moments. "Was it His name on the orders?" she asked gently as she removed her hands from her daughter's face.

"I don't understand."

"God didn't send the trucks or the policemen, Natasha. Someone in the Soviet Council did that."

Natasha stared at her.

"God gives men the right to choose, and sometimes they choose badly."

Natasha's mind went to the fairy tale of the peasant girl and the magical cow. "'There are in this world good people, people who are not so bad, and those who simply have no shame,'" she quoted.

Her mother nodded. "And sometimes the choices of others cause innocent people to suffer." She put her arm around her daughter's waist. "We need to go inside."

Natasha stiffened. "I don't want to speak to Father."

"We'll tell him you're not feeling well."

Natasha nodded and allowed herself to be led away. "I don't know what to think anymore," she said impassively into the night. Her mind had shut down, but her heart hurt so badly that it was hard to breathe. Still the tears did not come.

NOTES

1. **Cheka:** The secret police force established by Lenin in December 1917. The name derives from Chrezvychaynaya Komissiya (or "Extraordinary Commission"), which was eventually expanded to "All Russian Extraordinary Commission for the Struggle Against Sabotage and the Counter-Revolution."

2. The story of the Lindlofs' 1918 arrest by Cheka police was documented, as was the fate of the Lindlof children.

CHAPTER TWENTY-ONE

January 3, 1918

Natasha Ivanovna fell asleep as the rising sun sent shafts of light along the frozen Neva River. Thousands of others woke, had their tea and black bread, and tromped off to work under a brilliant blue sky—many saw the flashes of sunlight on the spires of the Admiralty Building or the Peter and Paul Cathedral—but exhaustion and grief had shut down Natasha's mind and senses, sending her mercifully into a land of forgetfulness. She slept with the open book from Agnes's father under one hand and the note from her friend in the other.

Svetlana Karlovna stood in her daughter's doorway, reluctant to carry out the assignment she'd been given. *Just let her sleep,* she thought, but Ivan Alexseyevitch had returned home from the Smolny desiring that his daughter be woken and sent to him immediately. Svetlana was acutely aware that the task had been given to her as a test of obedience, and for Natasha's sake, she would not refuse it and cause any more anger and contention.

She walked quietly to the edge of the bed and gently pulled the book from under her daughter's placid hand. She could not read the words as they were written in a foreign tongue, but she knew the book held meaning for Natasha as she'd secreted it away in her camisole drawer.

Svetlana leaned over and brushed back matted strands of short hair from Natasha's cheek. *How beautiful your hair once was, dear one—never with curls, but long and thick.* Svetlana sighed and Natasha's eyes opened a slit. Svetlana pressed her fingers to her lips. How sad it was to see her daughter's face blotchy and her eyes swollen and red-rimmed from crying. Natasha moaned and closed her eyes.

"Natasha, wake up. Your father wishes to speak with you."

Natasha moaned again and a frown puckered her face. "Go away." Her voice was raspy.

"He wants to see you."

"I need to sleep."

"I know, and I'm sorry, but he insists."

Slowly Natasha's eyes opened, but she stayed curled in the fetal position. "What time is it?"

"Two o'clock in the afternoon."

Natasha stretched out her body and the note fell from her hand. She fumbled for it and pressed it against her chest. "Why can't he leave me alone?" Her mother didn't answer. "I know what he wants to talk about and I don't want to think about it." Tears leaked from the corners of her eyes. "I want to sleep."

Svetlana sat at the end of the bed. "Sometimes the best way to avoid anger and sorrow is to let it brush past you."

Natasha pushed herself up against the headboard and stared at her mother, trying to clear the fatigue from her mind to make sense of her words. "I . . . don't understand." She wiped the tears away on the sleeve of her nightgown. "How can this sorrow ever brush past me? It is inside me . . . so deep inside me that I can't breathe."

Her mother handed her the blue book. "But if you can't breathe, you can't function, and if you can't function, you can't help them."

Natasha was quiet.

Her mother stood, placed a few small pieces of wood in the stove, and put a match to them. "You can seem meek and accepting on the outside and no one need know the strength you have on the inside. Sometimes you must play the game."

"I'm too tired."

"Of course you are tired now, but that will change. You *will* find the strength to do what you must do, Natasha." She smiled at her. "Now, get up and get ready. I'll tell your father you will be down, but to give you time." She moved to the door.

"Mama?"

Svetlana Karlovna turned back. "Yes, dear one?"

"I don't understand how the Bolsheviks can think that the Lindlof family is a threat."

"I cannot answer for the Bolsheviks, Natasha. Why do they see God as a threat?" She left the room.

Natasha stared at the door for several minutes. She had always been her father's child: she carried his coloring and temperament, she followed in his intellectual and philosophic pursuits, and she mimicked his political passion, but now uncertainty washed through her like cold water. Her feelings were changing. The arrest of the Lindlof family had changed everything.

Natasha looked at the paper crumpled in her hand. *"It can save us."* She carefully unfolded the paper and spread it out on the coverlet. She suppressed tears when she saw Agnes's all too familiar penmanship. *Riddles.* The connection had served them well over the years—with it they'd enjoyed girlish fun, kept innocent secrets from their families, and shared confidences. A day drifted into her memory of when Arel and Bruno had boasted that they could play the game, and asked to be given a riddle to solve. She and Agnes were surprised because the boys always said it was childish to spend time on such simple foolishness. To humble their arrogance, she and Agnes planned a riddle hunt for them. There were five riddles to follow to specific locations around St. Petersburg. If they made it to all five locations, and back home in three hours, they'd receive a prize. She couldn't remember what the prize was because it had never been awarded. The boys straggled in after five hours, having solved only four of the riddles, and confessing that they'd asked several people for help.

She ran her fingers over the precious words and heard again Agnes's enigmatic appeal: *"It can save us."* Natasha sensed the paper contained a secret meaning that Agnes wanted her alone to recognize.

She put more wood into the stove, checked to make sure no one was coming up the stairs, and climbed back into bed. She held the paper close and scrutinized the four riddles. The bottom three riddles were numbered, but the top one was not. That meant that the top riddle was the key to the others. If she could figure out the first one, she would have a much better idea what Agnes was trying to communicate. She read:

> *Whoever makes it, tells it not.*
> *Whoever takes it, knows it not.*
> *And whoever knows it, wants it not.*

Below this there was an arrow pointing south. That meant that whatever answer she deciphered, the true answer would be the exact opposite. The next riddle was numbered and it was one she recognized:

> *The towers grand where fires burn.*
> *Father and Mother of two BOYS and two girls.*

There was a clue here also as there had to be a reason for Agnes to capitalize the word *boys,* but not *girls.* She already knew the answer to this riddle. It was the Rostral Columns, and perhaps reference to the male statues seated at the base of the columns which represented the rivers Volga and Dnieper. She looked back to the first riddle: "Whoever makes it, tells it not."

There was a knock on her door and she jumped. "Just a minute," she called, stuffing the paper and the blue book under her pillow. She went to the door and opened it a crack. Her father stood there elegant and angry.

"Are you coming down?"

"Yes," Natasha said innocently. "I was just going to dress."

"I have a meeting with the Council in an hour, so hurry along."

"Yes, Father." He moved away and she shut the door. She found her own compliant behavior odd. Was she already accepting her mother's solution for anger and sorrow? She knew she'd do whatever was necessary to help her friend and her family.

She wondered where the Lindlof family had been taken. Certainly not to the Peter and Paul Fortress. She couldn't imagine Mr. and Mrs. Lindlof in a cell, or Agnes in a dark room, or Erland being questioned. She thought again of the dance she'd shared with Agnes and Arel on New Year's night, their faces bright with youth and hope. She started crying and rushed to bury her face in her pillow.

Please God, watch over them. Don't let anyone hurt them. She sat up abruptly. Where had those words come from? She didn't believe in God.

◆　◆　◆

"We will get the situation with the Lindlof family sorted out, Natasha, but you must not shirk your work at the Smolny or your responsibility to the soviet. Your name is known."

"What does that mean?"

Ivan Alexseyevitch narrowed his eyes and slowly pushed away his dinner plate. "What is that voice?"

Natasha softened her tone. "Nothing. I just wondered what you meant by 'Your name is known.'"

"The Central Committee is aware of you, Natasha, and of your writing." He paused for her to reply, but she said nothing. "You cannot be naïve of this fact."

"No, sir."

"Then you must not let this incident with the Lindlof family keep you from your duty."

"Incident?"

"I know you are upset, but this is a critical time for the Bolsheviks, and we must unite and work together if the goals of the proletariat are to be met."

Her stomach tightened, but the words she spoke did not betray her anguish. "I understand, and I will do the work required of me. I am just very concerned about my friend."

Her father's jaw relaxed. "Of course. We are all concerned."

"And when will we know what has happened to them?"

Her father poured himself more tea. "I've sent around some inquiries."

"Have you?"

"Yes."

"And does anyone know anything?"

"I just asked today, Natasha. It will take time."

"Of course." She looked down at her hands, unable to meet the uncaring expression on her father's face.

"You hardly ate anything," he said.

"I'm not hungry."

He reached over and took the untouched cheese roll from her plate. "So, have I made myself clear?"

"Yes, sir."

"It was very stupid of you to confront the Cheka officer, Natasha. He was simply following orders."

"I'm sure his orders did not include molesting innocent young girls."

Her father's face set again, and he drummed his fingers on the table. "Do you want my help in finding Agnes?"

She swallowed her anger. "Yes."

"Then do as you're told. This is not a time for arrogance or to question the system. Keep strong emotion off your face, lower your head, and serve the state."

A cold sadness poured into Natasha's body. Her father had never told her to lower her head.

"In a few months you will leave on the agitprop train with Sergey Antonovich to spread the ideals of the Soviets. It will be a grand adventure, and will help secure our family's place."

"What do you mean?"

"Svetlana!" Ivan Alexseyevitch called to his wife. "We're done now. You can come clear the table." He stood. "I must leave or I'll be late for my meeting."

Her mother came from the kitchen with a tray. She gave Natasha an encouraging look and began placing plates and cups on the tray.

Natasha stiffened as her father came near and gave her a kiss on the forehead. "Help your mother clean up."

"Yes . . . sir."

He turned to the entryway to get his coat and Natasha followed. "Father."

"Yes?"

"You will let me know the moment you hear anything?" She helped him on with his coat.

"Of course." He put on his fur hat and gloves and moved out into the darkening afternoon.

Natasha shoved the door closed. His words had said yes, but she doubted their sincerity.

CHAPTER TWENTY-TWO

Petrograd

January 10, 1918

"Natasha, you're not chopping."

"No?" Natasha tried to focus on her hand—the cabbage—the knife. "No, I'm not." She took a deep breath and the effort made her hand tremble. She set down the knife. "Last night I had another dream of Prince Vladimir and Empress Anna. They were walking in a forest with Agnes. The sunlight was shining through the birch leaves, and it was peaceful and beautiful . . . so beautiful." Her words and thoughts drifted away.

Her mother took the chopped cabbage to the soup pot. "Was there more to the dream?"

Natasha began chopping again. "I . . . I don't remember."

Her mother returned to her side. "I'm sorry if your sleep is troubled with dreams of things I've told you. Perhaps your father is right. Perhaps I shouldn't share my beliefs or the stories from my childhood."

"No. I want to know those things. Besides, it was a good dream. I don't remember all of it, but for once I felt Agnes was safe."

"Perhaps today we'll hear something."

"I've hoped that for a week, but Father always tells me to be patient." Impatience colored her words. "And the Bolshevik leaders have been so busy fighting to control the Constituent Assembly, that all *my* effort to get information has failed." She finished the chopping and pushed the remaining cabbage to her mother. "It doesn't surprise me. We are all so anxious at the offices that no one has time to think. The people voted more anti-Bolshevik delegates into the Assembly and now we have to . . ." She stopped talking and shook her head. "Drivel. It's all drivel. I don't really care about any of that right now. I only care about Agnes and her family."

"Let's put a few lentils into the soup," Svetlana Karlovna said, going to the pantry.

"Peace, Land, and Bread," Natasha mumbled.

Her mother returned with a handful of lentils and put them into some warm broth to soak.

Natasha shook her head again. "I stood next to a young girl at the bakery while we waited for our bread ration. She told me her system for eating bread. She said she takes a small bite of bread and counts to thirty. She does that between every nibble. She says it makes the bread last longer."

Svetlana said nothing as she added a pinch of salt to the soup. Then she spoke softly. "It has not gone the way the Bolsheviks intended."

"No," Natasha answered. "But any new government takes time to get on its feet."

Her mother's voice strengthened. "Father John of Kronstadt said that if Russia ceased to be Holy Russia, she would become nothing more than a mere horde of tribal savages intent upon destroying each other."

"A priest said that?"

Her mother brought a cloth to clean the cutting board. "Yes, ten years or so ago . . . just before his death."

Natasha took the knife to the sink for cleaning. "The Bolsheviks are trying to keep us together—keep us more firmly united. It's the White Russians who want to rip things to shreds—they are the ones intent on destruction."

"Isn't it the Bolsheviks who want to take God out of our lives?"

"They . . . we just don't see what God has done for the people. Hundreds of years of *Holy* Russia, and hundreds of years of struggle and sorrow. Hundreds of years of rules and rituals that made sure nothing changed. The priests are always urging the people to be humble and accept their fate." Anger and tears filled Natasha's voice, and she growled to regain her control. "Is that what Agnes should do—be humble and accept her fate?"

"God did not take Agnes and her family away, Natasha. Do not attribute evil acts to God."

"But, of course, even though God is all-powerful, He can't intervene in the madness?"

"He gives man freedom to choose."

Natasha angrily swiped at the tears on her cheeks. "Well, that certainly excuses Him, doesn't it?" She began to cry in earnest.

"Natasha?" Her father walked into the kitchen, and Svetlana went immediately to help him with his coat. He brushed her away and stepped toward his daughter. "What is it?"

Natasha glared at him. "I'm upset about my friend. I don't know what's happened to her."

Ivan Alexseyevitch took off his coat and handed it to his wife. "I've had word."

"What?" Natasha said, her voice cracking.

"Yes. Just today. You may want to sit down."

"No. Just tell me where they are."

"They've been sent back to Finland."

"They have?" A bit of color came back into Natasha's cheeks.

"Well, Johan and Alma have been sent with their youngest daughter, but . . ."

Natasha stared at him. "But? What do you mean, but? Where are the others?"

"They've been sent to a work camp in Siberia."

Natasha stood unmoving. The blood in her veins seemed to have stopped its flow. She could hardly hear as her father's words droned on.

"The Committee decided that Johan and Alma were too old to be of much use in the camps, and Linda Alise too young, but the others were all strong and healthy. It will be good. They can work for the state and pay back some of the wealth they took from the people."

"Stop!" The word came out an angry hiss. "Stop!" Natasha gripped the back of the kitchen chair. "They are the most innocent of people. They don't deserve this. What do they have to pay back? What do they owe the state?" Her voice became hysterical. "They won't survive . . . Agnes won't survive!"

"Calm down! Of course she'll survive," her father said in an offhanded tone.

"Which camp? Where were they sent?"

"I don't know."

"You don't know?" Natasha backed away. "I hate the Bolsheviks! I hate God!"

"Natasha Ivanovna! That's enough!"

Natasha turned her vitriol on her father. "You didn't even try to save them! You wanted punishment for them! Well, I'm going to save them, no matter what it takes!" She turned and ran up the stairs to her bedroom. She slammed the door, went to her dresser, and pulled out the blue book. With her hand trembling with fury, she riffled through the pages and found Agnes's note. *"It can save us."*

Natasha laid the book on the bed and paced around her room. She tamped down her anger and fear, and worked to clear the fog of anguish from her mind. Agnes had given her these riddles for a purpose. If she could calm her tumbling thoughts, she could work on the meaning. *Be still.* She closed her eyes and the words floated into her awareness.

> *Whoever makes it, tells it not.*
> *Whoever takes it, knows it not.*
> *And whoever knows it, wants it not.*

"What does someone make that he doesn't want known?" she mumbled. "A mistake? A lie?" She studied the words. Did those answers fit with the second line? "Whoever takes a mistake knows it not. No. That's not it." She kept talking to herself, forcing her mind to concentrate on the words. "Whoever takes a lie knows it not. That works better. And whoever knows it, wants it not. Whoever knows a lie, doesn't want it." She stopped and looked out her window.

Thick snow obscured everything in the darkness, and she only saw the white flakes because of the glow of a single streetlight. If the answer was a lie, then she had to flip it for the actual answer—the truth. But it wasn't reasonable that Agnes would give her such an esoteric clue.

Natasha stared again at the first line on the paper. *Whoever makes it, tells it not.* "It has to be something one actually makes . . . something tangible . . . and once you've made it, you don't tell anyone about it. Something you want to hide, but something you want someone else to take." She growled in frustration and began pacing again. "Think, Natasha, think! You've had harder riddles than this. Please, please, please. Help me figure this out!" she pleaded. She rubbed her temples. "And when the person takes it, they don't know what they've taken. Something fake . . . something untrue. Fake diamonds! No, you don't make diamonds. A bad promissory note . . . false money." She stopped. She held up the paper of riddles. *It can save us.* "Money," she whispered. "Whoever makes it, tells it not. Whoever takes it, knows it not. And whoever knows it, wants it not." *Counterfeit money.* "So very smart, little squirrel." And because of the arrow pointing south she knew the true answer wasn't counterfeit money, but *real* money.

It can save us. Everything fell into place. She looked at the first numbered clue. She knew it was a location—the Rostral Columns. If the Lindlof family had secreted away money, then the other three riddles might be hiding places. Hadn't Agnes said they were hiding money in case their goods were taken from the home? A sense of surety ran through Natasha. The childish riddles that she and Agnes had played all their lives might indeed be the means of saving them.

Her optimism was blunted as she thought of dear Mr. Lindlof trying to come up with a plan to save his family—a way to get them all safely to Finland—and the fear he must have felt to settle on such a desperate solution. And what of sweet Agnes, scribbling riddles in the middle of the night to let her know in case something went wrong. Yes, and something had gone wrong. The Bolsheviks had come in the middle of the night to arrest the entire family, and the money had been lost to them.

In her mind's eye, Natasha saw Erland running from the policeman, Arel with the bloody cloth to his cheek, and Agnes stumbling into her arms. She shook her head. No. She wouldn't dwell on those images or be debilitated by sadness or deterred by the impossibility of the task. Somehow she would find out where her friends were being kept, and if there was money hidden at the three locations, she would use it to barter for their freedom.

When she thought of all the barriers confronting her, the logical thing would be to give up, but that she would never do. Agnes had entrusted her with the family's last hope, and she would not fail her friend.

Natasha put the note back into the blue book and placed it under her pillow. She *would* figure out the other clues, but not tonight. Tonight her mind needed to work on unraveling an essential piece of the puzzle—finding an undetected route to the Rostral Columns.

NOTES

1. **Father John of Kronstadt** (October 19, 1829–December 20, 1908): A Russian Orthodox monk. Father John lived simply, preaching basic doctrines of kindness and service. Nine years prior to the revolution, he prophesied that if Russia ceased to be Holy Russia the country would disintegrate into warring tribal factions.

CHAPTER TWENTY-THREE

The Ural Mountains

January 1918

The train swayed along the endless track, locked in the colorless bite of winter. Agnes was cold. The hard benches inside the train car offered no comfort or relief. It was as if they said, *"You deserve this. Bad people deserve bad treatment, and you are an enemy of the people."* She had never felt like an enemy to anyone. When she was at school at the Smolny she tried to be kind, even when one of the girls had ceaselessly taunted her. Hadn't she borne that with quiet meekness? Hadn't she returned charity for mistreatment? Hadn't she followed the Savior's teachings? Someone started coughing—a raspy cough that went on and on. Agnes closed her eyes. *Lord, where are you?* It wasn't the first time that thought had come to her mind over the past several weeks.

The wheels clattered over a crossing and Agnes imagined a bridge and a river. They were moving down the eastern side of the Ural Mountains and into Siberia. Agnes pulled her ragged coat tighter and retied the shawl around her shoulders. It did no good. Even with her many layers of clothing, the cold seeped through and settled on her skin. Her broken heart generated no heat and could not be called upon to revive her. She didn't want to die, but could see no escape if the cold continued to whisper in her ears and encase her body. Her eyes moved slowly over to find Erland, curled in the corner of the boxcar like a mongrel dog. Several men sat off to the side of him, but ignored him as though he didn't exist.

Agnes wanted to go to him and feed him warm soup, but she had nothing. She feared to move, and standing was out of the question. She crept her hand along the bench until she found Alexandria's ankle. She laid her hand on her sister's felt boot and patted it three times. Alexandria stirred, but didn't wake. Agnes worked to keep her mind inside the dim interior of the boxcar. Anything outside of that was deep, dark water in which she'd drown. Her numb lips formed letters and she whispered their names. "Johannes, Oskar, Arel, Erland, Alexandria." If she kept saying their names she would keep them alive. *We are all going together. That's a good thing. At least to the same town or village. . . . That's what we've been told. All of us here on this train. Well, not all of us.* "Johannes, Oskar, Arel . . ."

"Agnes."

Was she speaking her own name out loud?

"Agnes," the voice came again.

"What?" she barked hoarsely.

"Shh . . . it's Arel." He took her hand. "Here's a biscuit." He joggled her hand. "Here, can you feel it? Grab it with your fingers."

Her fingers curved inward involuntarily.

"Good girl. Now, eat it."

"Why?"

"It's food. Eat it."

Arel's voice went away, and she slowly brought the biscuit to her mouth. "Do what your brothers tell you to do," her father had said. *No! No! I can't think of Father. That way lies madness. I can't think of his words or I'll see his face . . . and Mother's face.* "Where are you?" she whimpered.

Alexandria stirred and sat up. She too had a biscuit in her hand. "Porter, some tea, please," she said in an imperious, but groggy voice.

Agnes chuckled and her sister started giggling. *How is this possible?* Agnes wondered, looking at their bleak surroundings, and even bleaker circumstances. *Perhaps we're going mad.* Would there be warmth in madness?

Alexandria slid her arm through Agnes's. "What would I do without my big sister to help me?"

Agnes ate the stale biscuit in silence. Her physical presence had to be enough for her sister; she had nothing else to offer.

The train whistle sounded and it seemed a hundred miles away. *It's dancing off into the dark night to find an ear to hear it,* Agnes's tired brain conjured. "Somewhere in a simple wooden house is a peasant family huddled around their giant stove, eating dried apples and blini, and the youngest child will perk up her ears and say, 'Listen, Papa. The great train is calling.'"

"What are you mumbling, Agnes?" Alexandria questioned. "Are you all right?"

"What? Yes. Yes, I'm fine." Agnes went back to eating her biscuit, wondering if the green-eyed soldier from the women's battalion was safely back at home, sleeping by the warm stove, and taking care of the family cow. *Dear Father, where are we? Can you see us? Please . . . take care of us . . . of Papa and Mama . . . and Linda Alise . . . I . . .*

She was in the Summer Garden and Elder Lyman was speaking of God's love for the Russian people. A soft breeze blew against her face and she heard Mother Russia singing. The boxcar swayed back and forth, back and forth, back and forth, and her body slumped to the side. She felt hands lift her legs and place them on the bench. She saw Natasha Ivanovna's face and her long hair braided with flowers, then . . . nothing.

CHAPTER TWENTY-FOUR

Sergey Antonovitch sat close to Natasha Ivanovna in the council meeting. Several times he reached over and touched the back of her hand—his glances encouraging her participation in the discussion. She made a few simple comments, but her mind was thinking of the task she had set for herself that night and not of preparations for the agitprop train. It was the perfect opportunity. The room at the university where the meeting was being held was only a few blocks from the Rostral Columns. It was bitter cold and the late afternoon sky was dark with clouds swollen with snow. Few people would be out.

Professor Prozorov was talking about motion picture cameras and assigned Dmitri Borisovitch to find film stock over the next few months. There was a process to clear the images from used stock and they would certainly do that, but the professor wanted new film also if they could get their hands on some.

Natasha caught only bits of the conversation concerning Lenin's vision for the use of the camera for propaganda. She was planning her excuse for leaving the meeting and the route she would take to the columns. Each time she saw herself stepping out onto the Mendeleevskaya Boulevard, her heart beat hard against her chest. How much time would it take to get to the columns? What if she'd read the riddles wrong and there was nothing to find? She chided herself silently. *Enough, Natasha Ivanovna. Now is the time to be brave for Agnes and her family.*

She leaned close to Sergey and whispered in his ear, "How much longer?"

"What?"

"The meeting—how much longer will it last?"

"An hour or so."

She nodded. "I need to go out."

"Of course," he answered, keeping his eyes on the professor.

"And I may walk over to see if my father is in his office."

Sergey turned to look at her. "Why would you do that?"

"Is there a problem, Comrade Gavrilova?" Professor Prozorov asked, removing his glasses imperiously. The scowl on his face registered displeasure at being interrupted.

The man was an arresting figure with his dark hair and full beard, and since meeting him, Natasha had been intimidated. "No, Professor, sorry. There's no problem," she answered as she stood. "I just need to go out."

Sergey started to rise. "I'll go with you."

"No, don't be silly. They'll be talking about the speeches and you'll be needed for that." She pulled her coat from the back of her chair. "I'll return shortly."

Sergey's eyes narrowed.

"Really," Natasha assured. "I'll be fine." She smiled at him. "Pay attention." She looked up at Professor Prozorov. "Sorry to interrupt." She moved to the door and stepped out into the hallway quickly before anyone else could detain her. She shut the door respectfully and took a breath. As she raced down the dim hallway, she put on her hat, mittens, and scarf, retracing in her mind the path she would take: from the building onto Mendeleevskaya Boulevard, then east on Birzhevoy Street, past the Naval Museum, and out onto the square where the huge columns stood flanking each end of the small park. She would have to check both columns as each had a male and female statue allegorically representing Russia's main rivers. If luck was with her, she would find the correct male statue immediately.

Natasha stopped with her hand on the door handle. She took a deep breath and moved out into the late afternoon gloom. The frigid air stung her cheeks and she hunched into her coat, wrapping her scarf higher on her face. The snow made a squeaking sound under her boots and the loudness made her anxious. Even though she could see no one else on the boulevard, she loathed drawing attention to herself.

She hurried, being careful to maintain her balance on the slick street. An errant wind clawed at her scarf and the bottom of her coat. She kept panic from her mind by repeating the details of her route—east on Birzhevoy Street, past the Naval Museum, and onto the square. In her thoughts the distance seemed compact, but as she moved along, the blocks seemed to stretch into miles. Her breathing was raspy and she heard herself whimpering. *Stop it, Natasha Ivanovna. The Naval Museum is not far ahead. Just keep going.* Through the darkness she raced, determined not to fail her friend.

How many times had she analyzed the meaning of Agnes's final words to her? How many times had her friend's angel face troubled her dreams? The riddles on that paper were significant and were carrying her to a possible means of escape for her friend. *It can save us.* Natasha set her jaw. She had to have figured it correctly. Her heart would accept no other outcome.

Another stiff wind blew down the corridor of buildings, nearly stopping her progression. Natasha lowered her head and pushed on. She came out into the square and glanced up quickly to find the nearest column. The monolith stood close to the Neva River, whose waters were frozen by winter's frigid blast. She remembered a day when Mr. and Mrs. Lindlof had included her on a family outing to the frozen river. The boys had pulled the girls about on sledges while the parents ice-skated. They'd gone home to hot soup and kissel.

A large truck drove across the palace bridge, and Natasha glanced up to find the driver frowning at her. *He thinks I'm crazy for being out in weather like this.* She crossed the street and headed for the column. Her teeth began to chatter and she folded her arms across her chest. At the base of the brightly painted monolith sat the huge marble statue representing the Volga River. She had laughed at Agnes once when she'd admitted feeling anguish for the poor stone giants confronting winter in only thin drapes of fabric.

Natasha set her jaw against sorrow. She made sure she was alone before clambering up onto the column's stone foundation. She had never been this close to the monument, and the symbolic prows of ships that protruded from the column loomed large overhead. Natasha had to work quickly before anyone came by. She moved around the statue, searching for hiding places in the folds of stone fabric—behind the ankle, behind the bronze oar the bearded figure held. Nothing. She looked quickly into the two ship prows which were low enough for someone to reach, but again—nothing.

Natasha jumped from the stone base and ran toward the other statue. Her feet came out from under her and she vainly grabbed at the air for support. Pain shot through her hip and arm as her body slammed into the ground. She gritted her teeth, fighting to control the pain and keep tears away. *Get up! Get up, Natasha Ivanovna! You must not lose this chance.* She pushed herself onto her knees with her uninjured hand, pausing to steady herself before standing. Her head throbbed and her hip burned with pain, but she assessed that nothing was broken. She forced herself to move.

Slowly she hobbled forward, whimpering in frustration at her snail's pace. Without question, Sergey Antonovitch would be suspicious of the time she was gone. What could she tell him? She ignored the pain and walked faster.

As she came around the side of the statue, she was confronted by a group of young men smoking and sharing a bottle of vodka. They seemed as startled by her sudden appearance as she was with theirs. She'd been so intent on her mission, and not falling again, that she hadn't even heard their subdued voices until she was upon them. Hope and opportunity drained away, and Natasha felt tears pressing against the back of her eyes.

One of the young men broke from the group of five and approached her. "Gave us quite a scare, Miss. We thought you might be the Winter Witch come to freeze our blood." His friends chuckled, and the slovenly young man gave them a jocular grin. "But you're not that, are you?"

The man was close enough that Natasha could smell the unwashed stench of him. She stepped back and didn't answer.

"What are you doing out here in this freezing dark all by yourself?"

"Waiting for my father," Natasha said firmly.

The young man stopped and glanced around. "Out here?"

"Yes. He's a professor at the university. His office is just there." She pointed toward the institute of literature.

A large truck pulled to the side of the road and honked.

"Hey, Pavel!" one of the friends called. "The truck from the factory is here."

Another of the men drained the last of the vodka and tossed the bottle onto the street as he moved toward the truck. "Come on, Pavel! Work over women."

"Too bad," the young man said, leering at Natasha. The horn honked again, and he threw down his cigarette butt and slouched away.

Natasha shuddered as she watched the truck turn onto the Birzhevoy Bridge and head off into the Petrogradskaya District. She was alone again. She looked over at the statue representing the Dnieper River. She pushed back her doubt and moved with determination to the column.

As she began climbing the stone base, her arm and hip throbbed with pain, but she ignored them. She hunted again around the base of the statue: ankles, folds of stone fabric, bronze oar. As she pushed her hand behind the oar, she thought she felt something soft and yielding, but she couldn't be sure. She withdrew her hand and stripped off her mitten. The subzero air bit into her flesh, but she didn't care. She shoved her hand back into the space. Her fingers felt only cold, hard surfaces, and then they touched fabric.

She grasped the object and drew it out. She stared at the tied cylinder of cloth in her hand and could not stop the tears of relief. *It can save us.* She was curious what was inside, but now was not the time to investigate. She put on her mitten and shoved the package into her coat pocket. She felt the shock and adrenaline leave her, and her stiff body complained of each movement as she climbed slowly down to the street. Wiping the tears from her face, she gave the silent marble giant a smile of gratitude and moved off.

As she hobbled back to the university, her mind churned with thoughts of finding the other two packets, of finding out where Agnes and her siblings were imprisoned, and how she could get the money to them. She also wondered what she was going to tell Sergey Antonovich.

When she reached the building she noted that several of the once-lighted windows were dark. Had the meeting ended already? How long had she been gone? Was Sergey looking for her?

She opened the front door of the building and stepped inside. She yelped with fright and surprise as she was confronted with Sergey, Dmitri, and Professor Prozorov standing near the entrance. The men stopped talking abruptly when she came in and she noted their stiff appraisal. The look on Sergey's face was a mix of anger and suspicion.

"Where have you been?"

Natasha blinked. "I . . . Have you been looking for me?"

"We were just about to. Where were you?"

"I went to see if my father was in his office, but I fell."

"Fell?" Some of the anger dropped from Sergey's face.

"Yes. I fell hard. I think I might have blacked out for a time."

Sergey reached down and took hold of the bottom of her coat which was indeed soaked with water. The suspicion on his face was replaced with concern. "Oh, my dear, I'm so sorry. I knew I should have come with you."

"No, it's all right. I didn't break anything."

"Where are you injured?"

"My hip and left arm seemed to have taken the worst of it."

"Here, let's take a look," Professor Prozorov interjected.

Natasha clung to her coat. "Oh, no, it's all right. My mother will look at it when I get home."

The professor reached for the collar of her coat and tugged. "I know a little about medicine, comrade. Let me evaluate the truth of the matter."

Natasha reluctantly allowed him to remove her coat, then took it from him, and held it close. She offered her left arm to him. He undid the button on her cuff and slowly pushed back the blousy sleeve. Even in the dim light of the hallway, the garish purple bruise along her elbow and upper arm indicated a vicious fall. Professor Prozorov probed the bones of her elbow and Natasha cried out in pain.

"Enough!" Sergey Antonovitch shouted, glaring at the professor. "She's had a bad fall, it's obvious."

"Yes, it is obvious." He nodded at Natasha as Sergey gently buttoned her sleeve. "I'm sorry, my dear. We need to get you home. May I offer my automobile?"

"Yes," Sergey snapped, "that would be appreciated."

Natasha did not understand this curt interchange, but she didn't care. She was beginning to feel nauseous from the pain and anxiety, and if she could ride in an automobile instead of walking to catch the streetcar, it would be heaven.

"Yes, thank you," she mumbled. "A ride in your automobile would be . . ."

"You don't have to say anything," Sergey whispered in her ear as he helped her on with her coat. "Dmitri, you go with the professor to get the auto. Natasha and I will wait here and watch for you to drive up."

Dmitri's eyes jumped from Sergey's face, to her face, and back again.

Odd, Natasha thought. *He looks guilty about something.*

The two men left to get the automobile, and Sergey slipped his arm around her waist. She leaned against him and he kissed her forehead. "I'm so sorry you were hurt."

She felt his concern was genuine. She looked up at him and he kissed her on the mouth.

She'd thought the fall would be disastrous and expose her secret outing, but she now knew it was the accident that brought her not only an alibi but sympathy. She put her left hand in her pocket and wrapped her fingers around the precious bundle. Surely now there was hope.

"Your arm must hurt."

"What?"

"For you to protect it like that."

"Oh, yes. . . . It feels better when I give it a little support."

Sergey kissed her forehead and her cheeks. "I'm sorry, Natasha," he whispered as he kissed her. "So sorry for the doubt."

Her eyes flew open. "Doubt? What doubt?"

Sergey looked as though he'd been caught saying more than he'd intended.

"What do you mean, Sergey Antonovich?"

"Never mind. It's Professor Prozorov. He sees treachery behind every corner."

"Treachery?" She stepped back. "Does the professor suspect me of something?"

"No . . . no . . . well, yes. I mean, not really, but he is suspicious of everyone. His cousin was killed by White Russians, so now he thinks everyone is plotting."

"And what does he think of me? Does he think that I ran off to inform the White Russians of our meeting?"

Sergey's silence indicated that that was exactly what Professor Prozorov had thought.

"That's absurd."

"Yes, that's what I told him. And, of course, now he knows he was completely wrong."

Natasha looked at Sergey with a grim expression. "How can we trust a man like that? He will be over our lives for months, Sergey Antonovich."

"Don't overreact, Natasha. He is a brilliant man."

"Just because he's a professor, Sergey, doesn't mean he can't be dangerous."

"He's just being cautious."

"Cautious?" She winced as the bruises on her hip and side twisted. She leaned down to catch her breath.

"Ah, let's get you home," Sergey said, his voice a mix of concern and frustration. "Your health is the most important thing right now."

Professor Prozorov's auto pulled up in front of the building and Sergey whispered in her ear, "Let's not tell him we talked about this." She frowned at him, but nodded. "Besides, we might find his diligence and paranoia useful."

She stopped. "Useful?"

"Against the many radicals who want the Bolsheviks to fail." He opened the car door.

She nodded again and climbed in, but in reality she was too tired to care. Other things had taken on greater meaning, and the shouted slogans of "Peace, Land, and Bread" and "All Power to the Soviets" had begun to sound like the shrill voices of children in a schoolyard.

CHAPTER TWENTY-FIVE

SIBERIA

February 1, 1918

Ekaterinburg. Agnes and Alexandria stood pressed together with the other female prisoners on the platform of the train station. They had become so used to the smell of unwashed bodies that they were embarrassed by the disdainful looks and comments of the guards who surrounded them. Ekaterinburg. Agnes glanced again at the faded sign on the side of the train station hut which feebly announced the town's name. Ekaterinburg. It was an unknown place—a place of desolation and lost souls. *No one will know where we've gone.*

A woman, shivering with fever, was pulled from the group. A guard barked for her name and checked his list. She was taken away. A young woman started to faint and an older babushka caught her. The woman motioned for the group to press in. Everyone moved closer together to prop up the girl as the woman slapped her face several times. A guard looked over, but did not approach. Names were called, lists checked, and more of the sick taken away. Agnes heard jangling bells and the clop of horse's hooves. She reached for Alexandria's hand. The wagons were coming to take them away, and they must stay together.

She strained to see the knot of male prisoners at the other end of the platform. She thought she could make out Johannes's face, but all of her other brothers' faces were missing. And where was Erland? Had he been taken away with the sick?

The guards yelled at them to move to the wagons, herding them around the side of the station hut and out to the frozen and snow-covered road. Four powerful workhorses stood harnessed to four wagons. As Agnes watched the huge beasts stamp and snort and shake their heads, she calculated that only a small percentage of the emaciated prisoners would be riding in the wagons. The two wagons were nearly full with the sick male and female prisoners.

She leaned close to Alexandria. "I think we're going to have to walk. Are you able?"

Her sister pressed her pale, cracked lips together and nodded. "Do you think it will be far?"

Agnes pulled her hat over her ears. "No idea."

The men were closer now as the guards loaded them into the wagons, and Agnes searched anxiously for her brothers. Alexandria was the first to discover them. She grabbed Agnes's arm and whispered urgently. "Look! There's Oskar getting into that wagon with Erland. Oh, Erland isn't well."

It was true. Agnes watched as Erland crawled into the wagon and was pushed onto the wooden floorboards by Oskar. Erland hadn't seen a doctor since the night of their arrest, and she knew there was internal damage that wasn't healing.

Guards were reaching past her and Alexandria, dragging women to the wagons. The babushka was put on, and she pulled the fainting girl with her.

"Agnes!"

She heard her name called and looked quickly back to the knot of men. Johannes and Arel stood staring at her, intent on catching her eye. It had been risky for Johannes to call out her name, but she was grateful for the connection. She gave the two a weary smile. Someone pushed against her back and she nearly fell.

"Let me onto the wagon!" a woman pleaded as she shoved past. "I have a bad foot."

"There's no room," the guard said. "You will have to walk." He raised his voice. "The rest of you will have to walk."

Agnes found Johannes's face again, and he nodded his encouragement. Agnes and Alexandria nodded back.

The drivers called commands to the horses, and the wagons moved forward, creaking and groaning under the weight of their human cargo. Agnes turned her face forward, took Alexandria's hand, and walked.

In the darkness of the afternoon, she could see the outlines of buildings and church domes that testified of the town of Ekaterinburg.

Why this town? Why send us here—so far away from everything?

They walked beyond the town and into a forest of pine trees. The scent was strong and clean, and Agnes wanted to wander off and fall asleep under the protective boughs of one of the beautiful giants.

"Agnes! Don't close your eyes!" Alexandria snapped.

Agnes obeyed her sister's voice, and as the world came into focus again, she found herself bumping against the woman on the other side of her. The woman seemed oblivious of her presence, but Agnes mumbled an apology and moved back to her sister. Her toes were numb, and she stamped her feet, attempting to encourage circulation. Alexandria clutched her little brown suitcase against her chest—her face a mask of determination. Agnes knew that the suitcase held a meager store: a lightweight coat, a sweater, the new gloves she'd worn to the theater, and a picture of the Savior that Elder Lyman had given to her when she was five. *Thirteen years ago.*

People were beginning to fall, and several times she or Alexandria stumbled over a crumpled body. All the women helped each other to stand and move forward, bonded by necessity and a common foe.

"Do they want us to die out here?" Alexandria mumbled. "Why would they bring us all the way out here to work in a work camp if they just wanted us to die?"

A guard rode up beside them on a dappled gray horse that seemed to blend into the opaque surroundings. "Shut up there!" the guard yelled. "No talking!"

"How far?" Agnes asked.

"Not far. Keep walking and don't talk."

A half a mile later they broke the cover of the forest and came out into a clearing unprotected by the trees. The wind blew slivers of snow into their eyes, and with daylight long extinguished, it was difficult to see much farther ahead than the lead wagon. Agnes lowered her head and trudged on.

It seemed like only a few minutes later when Alexandria shook her arm. "Agnes, look there. That must be the camp."

They were going into another forest, but this time the tall pine poles stood tightly side by side and formed a square.

"Someone has cut off their arms and green hair," Agnes complained.

"Agnes, are you awake?"

Agnes nodded.

"Well, stop mumbling nonsense. Someone will think you've gone mad."

"Haven't I?"

"No. Now stop it."

Agnes heard the fear in her sister's voice, and shook her head to clear her thoughts.

The gate of the wooden kremlin stood open, and as the lead horse passed under the portico, Agnes shuddered. *Dear Lord, please be with us in this lonely place.*

As they entered the enclosure they were confronted by a wall of a large building, thirty feet in front of them. The lead wagon angled to the left around the side of the building, and the women followed. Agnes held back.

"Agnes?"

"I want to see where the men go." Just before she was forced to move around the building, Agnes saw the men's lead wagon angle right. She caught up to Alexandria. "They're not going off to a separate compound. They'll be here with us."

"That's a blessing," Alexandria responded.

They came to a stop in front of the two-story building. The look and smell of the wood indicated it was new; perhaps it had been completed in the last months of autumn before the cold weather set in—completed even before the Bolsheviks seized power. Perhaps the Provisional Government had built it, and now the Bolsheviks were laughing in their faces as they used the fortress for their own grim purposes.

Agnes brought her mind back to making a map of the compound. Steps led to a front porch which ran the entire length of the building that she assumed was the prison headquarters and the place where the guards slept.

She was turning to look behind her when the lead guard dismounted and met the commandant of the prison on the porch. The guard handed the stern, broad-shouldered man the packet containing the lives of fifty-eight people—sixteen women and forty-two men. It was only then that Agnes realized she could no longer see the men. A fence eight feet high ran the entire length of the compound from the steps of the headquarters to the back prison wall. She could hear the horses whinny, a shuffling of feet, and the muttering of a few bass voices, but the wall effectively sliced the prison into two sections—sections where a foot apart might as well be a hundred miles.

"How will we know if they're all right?"

Alexandria squeezed her hand. "We'll find a way."

The commandant nodded to the head guard, who in turn ordered his men to conduct the prisoners to their quarters. Agnes almost started crying with relief when she thought about being inside away from the wind, of being able to lie down, of finding water to bathe. Though perhaps water was too much to hope for.

As they passed the long barracks building, Agnes could hear the muted rumble of voices. How many prisoners already occupied the camp?

All sixteen of the new female arrivals were led to a door at the far end of the building. Inside was stark. Lit by a few lanterns, Agnes could make out the unadorned pine plank walls, a few high windows, no chairs, and one small heating stove. Thin mattresses and blankets were stacked in one corner, and in the opposite corner was a partition with a hallway beyond which Agnes deduced was the way to the latrine.

They were ordered to get a mattress and blanket and line them up in two rows in the center of the room. The women complied, but a tussle broke out when two women went for the one remaining mattress and blanket. The guard ordered the louder of the two women to be taken out.

"Where are they taking her?" Alexandria asked as she rolled out the mattress next to her sister's.

"I don't know . . . probably to one of the other rooms."

"And where are the sick ones?"

"I think we passed an infirmary at the other end of the building."
Agnes watched as some of the concern drained from Alexandria's face.

"Oh . . . well . . . that would be good. Maybe Erland will have a bed."

"No more talking," the guard said. "Tomorrow you will be up at five,
assigned to your work details and your bosses. You and you," he pointed to
two women, "shut down the lights."

Agnes and Alexandria put their blankets together and laid down close
to each other for warmth. The last lantern was extinguished, plunging the
room into melancholy darkness.

The guard hesitated at the door. "There are guards on each tower, comrades, but they really aren't necessary. We are two hours from town and you
would freeze in half that time." He went out into the dark night, shutting
fear and loneliness into the room.

Agnes wondered if Alexandria was praying. Her heart wanted to pray,
but resentment and pain kept the words from her lips. Her only reassurance
was her own determination to keep them all alive. *Johannes, Oskar, Arel,
Erland, Alexandria.* Before exhaustion took her into a fitful sleep, Agnes
thought of Natasha Ivanovna—how she and Arel and Natasha Ivanovna
danced at the burning of Maslenitsa on New Year's Eve. The warm fire
leaped high into the sky and Natasha Ivanovna was laughing, and in her
raised hand was a cloth bundle.

NOTES

1. Soviet work camps fell into basically two categories: **penal work camps**
housing criminals who had actually broken a law, and **"special work camps"** which
incarcerated persons under suspicion of actions against the state, mostly clergy, aristocrats, wealthy merchants, and intellectuals. Those sent to "special work camps"
were mostly sent without trial or recourse. Under Stalin these work camps became
the gruesome **Gulags** where millions of Russians perished.

CHAPTER TWENTY-SIX

*"What is the foundation of the rights of man? The Lord Almighty has orga-
nized man for the express purpose of becoming an independent being like unto
Himself, and has given him his individual agency. Man is made in the likeness
of his Creator, the great archetype of the human species, who bestowed upon him
the principles of eternity, planting immortality within him, and leaving him at
liberty to act in the way that seemeth good unto him—to choose or refuse for himself, to be a Latter-day Saint or a Wesleyan Methodist, to belong to the Church of
England, the oldest daughter of the Mother Church, the old Mother herself, to her
sister the Greek Church, or to be an infidel and belong to no church."*

Natasha looked up from her reading as her bedroom door opened. She
slipped the blue book under her bedcovers, but not before her mother noticed.

"Are you feeling better?"

"Some."

"May I sit with you?"

"Well, I . . ."

"Natasha, I know about your book." Svetlana Karlovna approached the
bed. "And I know it means a great deal to you."

"How do you know that?"

"You've hidden it from your father so he wouldn't take it away from
you."

Emotion filled Natasha's face as she brought the book out from under the covers. "Mr. Lindlof gave it to me."

"Ah." Her mother sat down on the end of the bed. "But why else do you treasure it?"

Natasha ran her fingers over the impressed gold letters that spelled out *Articles of Faith*. "I didn't at first. I was going to throw it away . . . but . . . I couldn't."

"And now?"

Natasha's eyes filled with tears. "Now it is precious to me and I don't understand why. It goes against everything Father has taught me, against atheism, and against many of the things I write for the Bolsheviks."

Her mother moved further onto the bed, pressing her back against the wall, and bringing her knees to her chest. She looked like a young girl and Natasha smiled.

"It surprises me that you would care for such a naïve book, Natasha, even though the English must intrigue you."

"But mother, it's not naïve. The writer, Professor James Talmage, is brilliant. I'm sure that's why Mr. Lindlof gave it to me. He knew I would be captured by the science and philosophy."

"It sounds like a very odd book."

"No, it isn't. I'm just not explaining it well." She gathered her thoughts. "Professor Talmage is a scholar and an apostle."

"What do you mean . . . apostle? Such as the apostles of Christ?"

"Yes. Arel Lindlof once told me that in their church they believe in modern-day prophets and apostles. In fact . . ." She hesitated before saying the name, "Agnes told me about a time when a Mormon apostle came to Russia. She met him—an Elder Lyman."

"An American apostle?"

"Yes. She and her family were with him in the Summer Garden when he said a prayer for Russia."

"Oh, Natasha, you must speak more slowly."

Natasha tampered her enthusiasm. "Sorry, Mother. It just feels like I've opened a door into a whole new room—ten rooms—rooms I never knew existed."

"And these rooms are filled with scholars and prophets and apostles who come to say prayers for Russia?"

Natasha smiled. "Yes."

"Why would a small American church be interested in Russia?"

"Agnes said that Joseph Smith—"

"Joseph Smith?" The blunt American name was difficult to say, and Svetlana attempted it again. "Joseph Smith? And who is he?"

"Was. He's dead now, but he was the first Mormon prophet." Natasha could tell by the look on her mother's face that she was trying to absorb concepts that she herself had been intently pondering for weeks now. "Is it too much?"

"No, I want to hear about it, only, not everything at once."

Natasha nodded, deciding to leave out Joseph's First Vision, visits of angels, and gold plates. She smiled to think of how much spiritual information the Lindlofs had managed to sneak into her head over the years. "Joseph Smith was a young man from Vermont, America, who was inspired by God to start a new church."

"When was this?"

"I think Agnes said the Church started in the early 1830s . . . I can't remember exactly. Then in 1843, the Prophet was prompted to send missionaries to Russia."

"I never heard about missionaries coming here."

"They didn't."

"Why not?"

"Joseph Smith was killed before they could come."

"What do you mean, killed?"

"He was shot dead by an angry mob while he was in jail. He and his brother were both killed."

Her mother looked stricken and she made the sign of the cross several times as if to ward off evil. "Were they bad men—this Joseph and his brother?"

"I don't think so. Agnes always spoke about Joseph Smith with great tenderness." Natasha ran her hand over the book, working to control her emotions. "Besides, we know very well that innocent people are sometimes mistreated and put into prison."

Svetlana nodded. "Yes, we do know that." They were silent for a time. "But an apostle finally did come?"

"Yes, Elder Lyman in 1903, when Agnes was eight years old."

Her mother got a curious look on her face. "I think I might remember that day. The Lindlofs came out of their home all dressed in good clothes . . . and a huge carriage came to fetch them. I asked where they were going, and Alma said to the Summer Garden for an outing. Alma was pregnant with Linda Alise, and I remember thinking it odd that she was going out in her condition." Svetlana's face brightened. "Yes! It was that day. They came back in the afternoon for dinner, and several men were with them. I was so curious I pretended to sweep the threshold so I could see what was going on. I remember a large, good-looking man in American dress." She sat reminiscing. "That must have been him," she said quietly. "That must have been Elder Lyman, the apostle."

"And where was I?" Natasha asked, fascinated by her mother's story.

Svetlana shook her head. "I don't remember. With your father somewhere, I suppose." She crossed herself again. "What if it were true? What if I saw an apostle of God?"

Natasha was confused by the longing she heard in her mother's voice. "But your faith is in the Orthodox Church."

Her mother looked at her straight on. "And how do you see the Church, Natasha?"

Natasha found it an odd question. "It doesn't really matter what I think."

"Today, it does. I want to hear."

Natasha sighed. "Everything is structured, static. The devout are good people, but it seems that you do things only because of tradition—all the bowing, lighting of candles, and kissing icons—it seems . . ."

"Lifeless?"

Natasha stared at her mother's innocent face, then nodded. "Yes, lifeless."

Tears formed in her mother's eyes. "I have always felt that there was something more. In my heart there has been a question, an emptiness." She brushed the tears from her cheeks. "I want to open a door into new rooms, Natasha. I was foolish not to ask questions of Alma Lindlof . . . or perhaps

I was afraid of what your father would do." She held out her hand for the book, and Natasha gave it to her. "What is it called?"

"Articles of Faith."

"Written by Professor Talmage?"

"Yes. But everything is based on the thirteen articles of faith set down by Joseph Smith."

"The *Prophet* Joseph Smith."

"Yes."

Svetlana handed the book back to her daughter. "Will you read them to me—these articles of faith?"

"Really?"

"Yes. I would like to hear what the Lindlofs believed."

Natasha opened the book to page one and began reading. She read slowly as it took her time to translate from the English into Russian. "Article One: We believe in God, the Eternal Father, and in His Son, Jesus Christ, and in the Holy Ghost. Article Two: We believe that men will be punished for their own sins, and not for Adam's transgression. Article Three: We believe that through the Atonement of Christ, all mankind may be saved, by obedience to the laws and ordinances of the Gospel." Natasha glanced up to see her mother's hand move toward her chest, and she was sure that her mother was going to cross herself again as was her custom, but her hand merely rested on her chest as if to measure the beating of her heart.

"So simple," Svetlana whispered. "So pure and so simple."

Natasha laid the book on her lap, surprised by the thought that had jumped into her mind. She hesitated, not wanting to change what she and her mother were sharing, but the words would not be silenced. "Mother, I need to tell you something."

"Yes, Natasha, what is it?"

"Father must not know."

Svetlana did not answer.

"You must promise me this."

Her mother finally nodded, and Natasha smiled and took her hand.

"The night the Lindlofs were taken away, Agnes gave me something."

"What?"

"Riddles." She brought out the folded paper from the back of the book.

"But they're not just riddles. They're clues to money the Lindlofs hid before they were arrested."

Her mother frowned at her. "How do you know this?"

Natasha got quickly out of bed and ran to her dresser. "The night I was at the university—the night I fell—I wasn't going to father's office, I was following the clue to the Rostral Columns." She returned to the bed and handed her mother the bundle. "And I found this. Open it." She watched excitedly as her mother undid the ties and unrolled the cloth. Ruble notes plus silver and gold rings, and a few gold coins winked up at them.

"Oh my," her mother said.

Natasha slid back under the covers. "Yes. Against her father's wishes, Agnes told me they were trying to escape to Finland, and they were afraid the remains of their goods might be confiscated by the Bolsheviks."

"And the hidden money?"

"No. She didn't tell me about that. Only after I'd solved the first two riddles did I figure out what they were trying to do. Of course they never thought they'd be arrested." She handed her mother the paper. "When Agnes gave me the riddles she said, 'It can save us.'" Tears rolled down Natasha's cheeks, but her words were defiant. "And that's what I'm going to do—find the money that can save them."

Svetlana handed her daughter a handkerchief. "But you don't know where they're being held, and Johan and Alma are in Finland by now."

"I know, but I can't worry about that." She blew her nose. "I can only do what my friend has asked me to do. . . . Then I'll wait until I can give the money to them."

Svetlana Karlovna sat looking at the riddles. "How can I help you?"

Natasha's heart filled with love for her mother. This was not letting things brush past—this was not being timid and following orders. She'd seen her mother assert herself a few times, but in this she was putting herself in danger. "Thank you, Mama."

Svetlana nodded. "What is it you need?"

"Help in solving the other two riddles."

"But you and Agnes were the ones to do riddles. I have no skill at it."

"I think you can look at them with new eyes."

"Old eyes and an old head."

"You are not old." Natasha gave her mother a saucy look. "And I think you are much wiser than you let on. Now stop stalling and look at riddle number two. It's a location, and I think I have a few things figured out, but I'm not sure."

"It's very short."

"It is."

Svetlana read. "'The African kings fly to the north river's shore.'" She read it again, and then shook her head. "I have no idea what that means."

Natasha smiled. "That's why it's a riddle. The meaning is hidden. For example, there are two objects because 'kings' is plural, and 'the north river's shore,' I think, could mean the north bank of a river."

"So, two African kings on the north bank of a river?"

"Yes, but 'African kings' are probably not actual kings. And why Africa?"

"Maybe they're African jungle kings."

Natasha sat straighter. "Yes! Lions! Where are there two lion statues on the north bank of a river?"

Svetlana shook her head. "But lions don't fly, and Agnes wrote that these creatures *fly* to the bank of the river."

Creatures. The word stuck in Natasha's brain. *Lions* that fly. Part lion, part bird. "Griffins."

Svetlana's face registered surprise and delight. "Griffins! Yes. It must be. The two griffins on the north end of the bridge over the Griboyedov canal."

Natasha gasped. "The Bank Bridge!"

Svetlana looked in wonder at the simple riddle. "Your friend is very smart."

Natasha gave her mother an exuberant hug. "Yes, she is!"

"And you think they've hidden money there?"

"I'm sure of it." Natasha took the paper. "And now for the final hiding place." She read.

> *One season.*
> *One place.*
> *Two women of grace*
> *Stand present and past—*

Laurels extending, abundance expanding.
Two creatures divided
One vanquished, one free.

She looked up from the paper into her mother's stupefied face. "That's all of it."

"All of it? It's quite enough," her mother said. "I don't even know where to begin."

"It will take a little time, but we'll work it out. You are much better at this than you give yourself credit."

They heard the front door open and close. "Svetlana Karlovna?"

Natasha hid the paper, and her mother scrambled from the bed.

"Oh dear! What time is it?"

Natasha glanced at the clock on her dresser. "Just before four."

"Svetlana?" came a more pointed call.

Her mother rushed to the door. "He's early and I haven't even started the tea." She opened the door and called down the stairs. "Yes. I'm here Ivan Alexseyevitch. I was just checking on Natasha."

Natasha followed her mother to the top of the stairs. "Mama, thank you for today. I'm glad I no longer have to face this alone."

Her mother turned and gathered her into her arms. "We will pray for a good outcome." She kissed both of Natasha's cheeks, and then hurried down the stairs.

Pray for a good outcome. Was there an actual, omniscient Being that listened to the prayers of her mother, the prayers of the tsar, the prayers of her friend? Surely it was impossible, but . . . perhaps not. Natasha's mind still had doubts, but her heart clung to the hope that the prayers of her dear friend did find access to an unknown realm.

Natasha turned back into her room and saw the blue book on the bed. She picked it up and thumbed through the pages. Was there an answer here? How could faith stand against the logic and power of government? How could faith feed men, or take away their poverty? She opened the book and read.

CHAPTER TWENTY-SEVEN

Petrograd
February 2, 1918

Sergey Antonovich's apartment was cold. He sat at his table in his coat and mittens reading *Pravda* and drinking weak tea. He'd only had enough wood to heat the one pot of water and then it was gone. He cursed the tsar, the greedy bourgeois merchants, and the Provisional Government for bringing such hardship to the people. He gulped down the last of the tepid tea and looked at the clock—one in the afternoon, and though a pale light came through the window, there was no heat to it. *Hang on for two more months,* Sergey told himself. *Two more months and warmer weather will come and you'll be on the train.*

He heard footsteps in the hallway and a knock at his door. Who could that be? He was not expecting anyone.

He opened the door to find Dmitri Borisovitch and Nicholai Lvovitch, their arms full of wooden slats and their faces beaming.

Sergey laughed. "Ah, comrades! What's all this?"

"It's wood, Sergey Antonovich!" Dmitri Borisovitch said, stepping into the room.

"We knew your stove had been starving of late, so we came to feed it."

Sergey laughed again. "What did you do, tear down someone's house?"

"Fence," Nicholai said pragmatically, dumping the slats by the stove.

"You did not," Sergey asserted.

"Oh, yes, we did," Dmitri countered. "As comrades, we have no need for fences that separate us, so we are taking them down."

"Here are a few dry pieces to get things started," Nicholai stated, handing Sergey some smaller slats he'd just broken apart with his beefy hands.

"Thanks, Nicholai." Sergey put the wood in the stove and started it. "Thanks to both of you."

"Ah, there's more!" Dmitri said dramatically. He reached into his pocket and brought out a packet wrapped in butcher paper. "Sausage!"

Sergey was stunned. "How did you manage that?"

"We took wood to the butcher."

"You are lucky not to have been caught by one of the members of the Housing Committee."

Dmitri scoffed. "Those lunks? They're too busy being important and monitoring how much electricity is being used. They don't see what goes on under their noses."

Sergey shook his head. "All I'm saying is that it's hard to run on slick streets."

"Yes, comrade, I understand you," Dmitri answered. "But it's harder to live when you're frozen."

Laughing at his friend's bravado, Sergey brought out a pan to cook the sausage.

◆　◆　◆

After the meal the three friends sat around the table. The room was almost warm and the hot food had done much to back anxiousness into the corner. The men had spent several hours talking about and arguing over many topics. Sergey had been especially angry over the arbitrary acts of sabotage perpetrated by anti-Bolshevik forces—acts that destroyed factory machinery and shipments of goods, or rerouted food away from the starving people. Dmitri brought up the priceless cache of wine from the Winter Palace that the Kronstadt sailors had been ordered to destroy. He banged his fist on the table and went on and on about the waste, until Sergey scolded his ranting. "Enough, Dmitri Borisovitch. It is the duty of the Commissar for the Fight against Drunkenness—"

Dmitri scoffed. "What a title." He continued in a mocking voice, "I am the Commissar for the Fight against Drunkenness and I say you must not drink ever again! Wedding party? No! Naming day? No! Christening? Ah! You miserable dog! I'll cut out your liver."

Sergey and Nicolai howled with laughter, imploring Dmitri to stop. He told them he would as soon as they agreed that the better idea would have been to give each family in Petrograd a bottle of wine for their New Year's celebration. Then they could have said thank you to the tsar and toasted him for his generosity. The three friends toasted the idea with a shot of vodka.

The conversation turned to the agitprop train and Professor Prozorov.

"How goes the search for film for your camera, Dmitri?"

Dmitri exhaled dramatically. "Ah! Now there's a topic to make me angry. Two weeks of scrounging and I've come up with three canisters. Three canisters! And the stupid American filmmakers gobble up hundreds of canisters just to make mindless films to entertain." He stood and put more wood into the stove. "And of course the war makes everything impossible."

"Another promise out the window," Nicholai Lvovitch grumbled. "Peace, Land, Bread. I haven't seen any of it."

"It takes time for a new government to get established," Sergey instructed. "You must be patient, Nicholai."

"Patient? That's easy for you to say. You are a crafty speaker, and Dmitri is a filmmaker. No worries for you. Chairman Lenin will use you two to work for the government. But me? I tell you, if this war isn't over soon, I'll be on my way to the front line, and with my luck, I'll be shot the first day."

Sergey slapped his shoulder. "A treaty with the Germans will be coming. Trotsky says by March."

Nicholai grunted. "I hope so."

Sergey slapped him again. "Yes! Good! We must all hope. The war will end in March, and then in April the three of us will be off on the train."

Dmitri gave his friend a cunning grin. "The four of us."

"What?"

"The *four* of us will be going on the train. Surely you haven't forgotten Princess Natasha Ivanovna Gavrilova?"

Sergey grinned back at him and poured them each another shot of vodka. "No, of course not. It would be impossible to forget Natasha Ivanovna, with her beauty and intelligence."

"And influential father."

Sergey downed his shot in one gulp. "That too."

"And has Professor Prozorov given up the idea that she is a spy for the White Russians?"

Sergey smacked his glass down on the table. "Absurd man. Has he never read the things she's written for the party? Trotsky has used her words in speeches and sent out her pamphlets to the countryside! She embodies the very ideals of the Soviet!"

Dmitri laughed. "Yes! Yes! Calm down, comrade. We know how you feel about her. Prozorov is an idiot, but a very powerful idiot. Let's just hope she never gives him reason to doubt her."

Nicholai nodded as he finished off his vodka. "Or he'll send her off to a work camp, just like you did her friends."

Sergey grabbed the front of Nicholai's shirt and yanked the big man around. "What did you say?"

"Wait! Wait! Comrade!" Nicholai sputtered. "I'm sorry!"

Sergey Antonovich's face was livid with rage. "You vowed never to speak of that!" He dragged Nicholai to his feet.

"I . . . I know. I'm sorry, it just came out!" Nicholai cowered, anticipating a blow. "Remember, Sergey Antonovich, that I agreed with you. I thought you were right to send in the report on that greedy family."

"Shut up, Nicholai Lvovitch!" Dmitri said, moving to come between them. "You're not making it better."

"But, I—"

"Just shut up!" Dmitri tried to push the men apart. "Sergey Antonovich, he meant no harm. He forgot, that's all. He just forgot."

"And what if he *forgets* when Natasha Ivanovna is around?"

"I won't! I won't!" Nicholai vowed.

Sergey snarled at him. "Do you think she'll understand that I did it for her own good?"

Nicholai pried Sergey's hands from his shirt and stumbled back. "I'm sorry, comrade. I won't talk of it ever again."

"You'd better not, or I swear I'll—"

"Enough, Sergey Antonovich!" Dmitri snapped. "He meant no harm. He's your friend."

"Right now, he isn't." Sergey glared at Nicholai. "Get out of my house."

Nicholai Lvovitch did not move. He stood staring as though he did not understand the meaning of the words.

"I mean it. Get out."

Nicholai glanced over to Dmitri, who nodded and tried to give him a look of reassurance.

Nicholai picked up his coat and lumbered to the door. "Stay warm," he said as he moved out, and shut the door behind him.

Sergey paced for a few moments, and then slumped into a chair. "Stupid oaf."

Dmitri sat too. "You know him. We've been friends since we were children."

"Yes, and we used to forgive his foolish blunders, but now his stupidity could cost me."

Dmitri nodded. "I'll keep an eye on him."

Sergey clasped his hands in frustration. "I just thought the Housing Committee would come and confiscate all their goods and force them to live with other families. I thought to humble them—the bourgeois merchant and his daughter filling Natasha's head with all sorts of nonsense."

"Of course," Dmitri encouraged. "You feared she was being misled."

Sergey stood and began pacing. "And then the police came and took them away. You should have seen her face, Dmitri. When Natasha told me that her friend had been sent to a work camp . . . I . . . I looked at her face, and it was like part of her had died." Sergey gripped the back of the chair. "I never meant for that to happen. I never meant for the Lindlofs to be sent away."

"Of course not," Dmitri cajoled. "You had no way of knowing." He handed Sergey another drink. "I think there must have been other wrongdoings you knew nothing about. They could have been giving money to the White Russians, or distributing anti-Bolshevik propaganda. Or perhaps it was that strange religion of theirs. Perhaps some of their neighbors turned them in for that."

Sergey nodded. "Perhaps."

"Yes, that's it. You can't know for sure it was your report, can you?" Sergey shook his head. "No."

"Then let's forget about it. What do you say we put more wood in the stove and play a game of cards?" He stoked the fire, and then fished around in the desk drawer, and brought out a deck of cards.

"I can't lose her, Dmitri Borisovitch. I won't."

Dmitri sat down and began shuffling. "No, of course not." He set the deck in front of Sergey. "High card deals." They both picked cards. Dmitri drew a seven and Sergey drew a king. "Ah, see there," Dmitri flattered, "you are lucky in everything. Natasha Ivanovna will be with you forever."

NOTES

1. The circumstance of Sergey reporting the Lindlof family to the secret police is consistent with the tenor of the revolution and changing feelings concerning allegiance. Loyalty to the State became more important than loyalty to family or friends. Lenin wrote several works declaring the need for children to be separated from the archaic ideas of their parents, especially when it came to government and God.

CHAPTER TWENTY-EIGHT

PETROGRAD

February 3, 1918

"What did you tell Father?"

"That we were going out to look for traveling shoes for you."

"Ah, that was good," Natasha said, helping her mother over a slick area on the walkway. "Shoes are hard to come by, so if we don't return with a pair, it will be all right."

It was a cold day, but the sky was blue and the sun was shining. Natasha smiled. So few clear days. Luck must be on their side. Even the leafless trees along the Griboyedov canal did not seem so forlorn today. She was glad she'd told her mother about the riddles and the hidden money. The prospect of retrieving the bundles did not seem as frightening now.

"Careful," she said as another ice patch presented itself.

Her mother took her arm. "You must be careful too, Natasha. You have not fully recovered from the last fall." She altered her pace. "Perhaps we should slow down."

Natasha was eager to get to the Bank Bridge, but the memory of her fall at the Rostral Columns made her hesitate. "You're probably right. It's just that my feet want to keep up with my heart."

"I know. My heart is racing too."

They walked in silence, passing only a few people along the way. It was midmorning so most working people were at their jobs and the shoppers were home with their meager purchases. They could see in the distance a few lines of people waiting for galoshes or candles or milk. Natasha shook her head. Sometimes people stood in lines without knowing what was for sale. If it turned out to be galoshes in the wrong size, people bought them anyway. They could always trade them later for something they truly needed. Her mother had bartered for a suitcase that way. She'd stood in line to purchase a hammer then traded it with a neighbor for the suitcase.

"For your trip in April," her mother had said as she presented it, and Natasha remembered the mix of pride and melancholy in her voice.

The canal made a gentle bend, and Natasha's trepidation grew as she knew they would soon be able to see the Bank Bridge and the griffins that stood guard there. Would their plan work? Perhaps there would be too many people passing by. Perhaps someone would look out one of the windows of the nearby buildings.

"There they are," her mother said in a whisper, bringing Natasha's thoughts back to the task at hand.

Four impressive statues sat at each corner of the bridge: artistic black griffins with their gold wings lifted skyward and the cables for the suspension bridge extending from their mouths. Natasha's heart sank as she saw several people walking past on the far side of the bridge and a young couple idling on the bridge itself; their concentration was obviously on each other with touches, smiles, and whispered conversation, yet Natasha knew that they would be sure to notice if she began searching about the statues for the hidden bundle.

"I suppose we will have to wait until they leave," her mother said.

"That may be a while," Natasha answered as she and her mother walked back and forth on the south side of the canal. "Even though it's cold, it doesn't look like they have plans to leave any time soon."

Svetlana turned her back on the canal, closed her eyes, and bowed her head.

Natasha was perplexed. Was she trying to pray the couple off the bridge?

After a time, Svetlana began walking again and Natasha followed. "I think we should let them in on the secret," her mother said with a smile.

"What? We can't do that!"

"Yes, I think that's exactly what we *must* do. You go and search, and if there are any questions, I'll answer them." Natasha hesitated, but her mother patted her arm. "Trust me."

Natasha didn't stop at the griffins on the south side of the canal, knowing that the clue led to the statues on the north.

The couple ignored Natasha and her mother as they passed by, and even when Natasha began searching around the legs of the mythical beasts, the couple barely glanced at her.

"There's nothing here," Natasha whispered to her mother.

"Check the mouths," her mother answered in a perfectly conversational tone.

As Natasha climbed up on the statue to check its mouth, the young man took his arm from the girl's waist and frowned. "Hey! What are you doing there?" he asked, coming near the statue.

Svetlana turned a smiling face to him. "It's a game. She's looking for a clue."

"A clue?" the girl asked, forgetting the boy for a moment and staring up at Natasha.

"Yes. She and her friend play this game. They make up riddles that lead them to different places around the city. When they find the clue at one location, it leads them somewhere else."

"How delightful!" the girl said, stamping her feet to warm them.

"It's a girl's game," the young man scoffed.

"That's what her friend's brothers always said," Svetlana chuckled, "until they got lost on such a quest." She smiled at them. "Things are not always what they seem."

"I found it!" Natasha said jubilantly, as she brought the bundle from the griffin's mouth. "I found it, Mother!"

"How clever," the girl said, moving to Natasha as she jumped down from the statue. "Is that it? Is that the next clue?"

Natasha looked at the girl's eager face. "Actually, this is the final location of this hunt . . . so . . . this is my prize."

"A prize? How delightful. What is it?"

Natasha put the bundle into her pocket. "Oh, we've hidden many things over the years: candy, coins, childhood trinkets." She walked to her mother. "I can't show you because it's part of the game, but I can tell you a couple of the riddles that led me here, if you'd like."

"Oh, yes! That would be fun."

Natasha smiled at the round-faced girl as her boyfriend shook his head. Natasha stalled for time. "Hmm. Which two should I pick?" The girl watched expectantly. "All right, here's one. 'The palace you eat.'"

The young man stepped forward. "That's the whole riddle?"

"That's the whole riddle," Natasha answered.

"'The palace you eat,'" the girl recited. "What's the second one?"

"'The African kings fly to the north river's shore.'" Natasha smiled over at the young man, who was frowning in concentration. "Not as easy as you thought?"

The girl giggled. "I'll probably figure them out first."

"That's very possible," Natasha agreed.

The girl beamed at her.

"It's time for us to be getting home, daughter," Svetlana said. "We've a meal to prepare."

"Food," the young man said abruptly. "Now that's something I can understand."

"And I know just what to serve you," the girlfriend giggled.

"What?"

"The palace you eat!"

The women laughed as the young man growled. "Come on," he mumbled. "I *am* hungry now."

"Thank you for sharing your game," the girl called back.

"You're welcome," Natasha answered. "Good luck with the riddles."

The girl waved, and then the pair was gone down the lane.

Natasha pulled the bundle from her pocket and looked at it in wonder. "We did it, Mama! We did it!"

"We did."

"How did you know that we were supposed to let the couple in on the riddles?"

Svetlana only smiled and took her daughter's hand. "Come now. Let's get home and hide that treasure."

◆　◆　◆

Natasha and her mother stopped talking abruptly as they neared their neighborhood. The euphoria Natasha had carried from the Bank Bridge melted like June snow. In front of the Lindlofs' home were two wagons, a truck, a half a dozen people, and a flurry of activity. Crates, mattresses, satchels, and suitcases were being unloaded and carried into the Lindlof house. A young boy was trying unsuccessfully to drag a trunk over the threshold. A square-faced man with bushy eyebrows cuffed the boy on the side of the head and picked up the trunk. A woman stood by the truck, barking instructions. She held a child on her hip while another clung crying to her skirt. A government official walked about, pointing at things and checking items off a list. Natasha was close enough to see the badge on the upper sleeve of his black coat.

"Oh no, Mother. What are they doing?" Natasha picked up her pace, determined to stop this slovenly group of riffraff from inhabiting the home of her friend. She stood in front of the doorway, blocking entrance to a tall, thin man of about thirty, who was attempting to maneuver a large crate to the door. It was difficult to tell his actual age as he seemed to be missing all of his front teeth. Natasha winced as he yelled a profanity at her, but she stood her ground.

"What's this about?" the man snarled, chewing each word like a piece of tough meat. "Get out of my way."

"No! You take your things out of this house!"

"And who are you to say anything? Move aside!"

Natasha glared at him.

Svetlana Karlovna arrived at her daughter's side as the official from the Housing Committee intervened. "Comrade, what's wrong here?" he asked the thin man.

"This trollop won't let me into my house."

"How dare you!" Natasha hissed. "*Your* house? I know the owner of this house and it certainly isn't you!"

"Natasha, calm down," her mother warned softly, but her words were lost in the ensuing chaos of noise.

The square-faced man now joined the fray, shoving Natasha to the side and demanding answers. The woman screeched her defiance while the baby on her hip wailed in fright.

"They can't move in here. This house is owned by a different family— not these people," Natasha yelled.

The official checked his papers. "No, it is being leased to four families . . . well, three families and one single gentleman."

Natasha started to protest, but the official gave her such an angry look that she closed her mouth.

"The former inhabitants were enemies of the state," the official said. "Their house has been confiscated to house these families. It is a much better arrangement."

A small man in an oversized cap crept from the house and ushered his wife and little ones inside.

"See, I told you," the thin man said, a condescending grin twisting his mouth. He shoved Natasha away from his crate and picked it up. "If you are friends with enemies of the state," he grunted, "we'll be watching you."

The square-faced man leaned down to stare into Natasha's eyes. He smelled of tobacco and cheap wine. "My wife and I lived in a cellar with rats before this place was offered to us." He straightened. "The Bolsheviks know how to take care of people." He grinned at the official. "Long live the worldwide proletariat!"

From each according to their ability, to each according to their need, Natasha thought. But what if a person is a lazy brute who drinks away his ability? Natasha gave the government official a scathing look. "And how do the Bolsheviks change men's hearts?"

"What's that?"

"How does the state make them better men, more caring men? And how does the state know it's not giving things away to the scabs of humanity?"

The official's face reddened with anger.

"Natasha, don't," her mother warned.

"Are you speaking malicious words against the state, comrade?" the official snapped.

"I'm just asking questions, comrade. Are we no longer allowed to ask questions?" Natasha held the official's gaze.

"Not if those questions sound like the words of an anarchist."

The drunk man emerged from the Lindlofs' home, a look of smug victory smeared across his ugly face.

Natasha felt hot emotion knot in her chest. She had forced pain and fear into hidden recesses of her heart, but now those places were tearing open, spilling their contents of rage and sorrow. "I am not an anarchist, comrade! I am a simple soldier of the state, but I have questions!" Her mother took her arm, but Natasha jerked it away. She advanced on the government official. "I have questions that need answering, comrade. Who will answer them? Who will answer why they took my friend and her family, comrade? Who will answer that?"

"They were enemies of the state!" the official yelled.

"Not true!" Natasha yelled back. "I tell you, not true! They always helped others! They were good people!" She felt hands on her arms again and went to pull away, but this time the grip was strong and did not release her. She screamed and twisted in an effort to escape. "Let me go!"

"Natasha," said a deep voice in her ear. "Natasha, calm down."

"Let me go, Sergey Antonovich! Let me go!"

"Your father is watching," came Sergey's furtive reply.

The hot emotion turned to ice and her body slumped forward. Sergey Antonovich kept her from falling and pulled her body back against his. He folded her in his arms and walked her away from the angry official.

"I should write up a report on her!" the official yelled after them, his tone punitive and resentful.

Sergey was about to turn back, but Natasha's mother stopped him. "Take her in. Take her in. I'll talk to him."

Natasha righted herself and pushed away from Sergey's embrace. "I can walk, Sergey Antonovich."

As she approached the house, she looked up and found her father standing in the doorway, his dark eyes fixed on her face. The last of her bravado drained away. Sergey placed his hand on her back and she stood straighter, yet as they passed by her father into the house, his icy demeanor made her catch her breath. She reached into her pocket and folded her fingers around the packet, chiding herself for her outburst. She could not afford to let anything jeopardize fulfilling her promise to her friend. She walked into the parlor and slumped down on the sofa.

"May I take your coat, Natasha?" Sergey asked.

"No. No . . . I'm cold. I want to keep it on."

Sergey sat down beside her, took hold of her hands, and rubbed them between his. "You shouldn't have gone out on such a cold morning."

Natasha nodded. "I know, but I needed traveling shoes."

Her father came into the room and Natasha could tell it was his intent to reprimand her even though someone other than family was present. "Sergey Antonovich comes by to call on you, and what do we find? We find a fishmonger caterwauling in the street."

Sergey Antonovich stared at his boots. Natasha looked at her father straight on, and he stared her down.

"What did I say about your behavior? What did I tell you? Answer me!"

"To lower my head."

"Yes, and I certainly did not see that today."

"She was upset to find people moving into her friend's home," Svetlana Karlovna said as she moved quietly into the room. "I think it's understandable."

"I didn't ask your opinion," Ivan Alexseyevitch replied.

Natasha felt the calm and mercy her mother had brought into the room evaporate as her father continued. "She puts us in jeopardy with her behavior. Is that to be understood? To make any sort of anti-Bolshevik statement is very dangerous during this volatile time. Why would you do such a thing, Natasha? Why would you put your position at the Smolny and my position as head of a soviet in jeopardy?"

She parroted her mother's words. "I was upset to find people moving into Agnes's house."

"Well, accept the truth of it. You're a grown woman now, not a child, and the Lindlof family will never live there again."

Natasha's mother stepped forward. "Ivan Alexseyevitch, please."

"No, Svetlana! It's time for her to not only write the words of the Bolsheviks, but to *live* the words of the Bolsheviks."

Natasha set her jaw against emotion and pressed her fingers against the packet of treasure in her pocket. She lowered her head and spoke softly. "Father is right. The cause of the proletariat is far more important than any petty emotion I may have for my lost friend." She glanced over at Sergey. The color had drained from his face and his eyes held a haunted look. She looked quickly back to her father. "I'm sorry for my childish heart. I will set it aside and get on with the work at hand."

Her father studied her for a few moments. "Yes. Good." He turned to his wife. "Svetlana, don't you have a meal to prepare?" She nodded tersely. "I have work to do in the study. Call me when the meal is ready." He turned back when he reached the parlor door. "Join us for dinner, Sergey Antonovich. I want to hear how plans are coming for the Red Train."

"Yes, sir."

Her father and mother left the room, and though Natasha kept her face emotionless, the tears spilled from her eyes and ran down her cheeks.

Sergey kissed her mouth and tried to brush the tears away. "Oh, my darling girl, how can I help?"

"Bring back my friend and her family."

Sergey looked shocked. "I . . . I wish I could, but . . ."

"But you can't. I know." Sergey reached to brush away more tears, and Natasha stood. "Don't look so pained, Sergey Antonovich. It wasn't your fault." She wiped the rest of the tears away with the sleeve of her coat. "I must help Mother with the meal." She moved to the door. "Will you be all right here by yourself?"

He gave her a feeble nod, and she exited.

◆　◆　◆

Next door at the Lindlof home, the square-faced man was hanging a red banner out a second-story window. On the heavy muslin fabric was painted a propaganda picture—two shafts of wheat surrounding a crossed hammer and sickle.

The official from the Housing Committee smiled as he read out the words displayed prominently underneath the emblems, "All Power to the Soviets." He waved up at the drunken man, and then went back to checking his official papers. "Yes. A much better arrangement. A much better arrangement for everyone."

CHAPTER TWENTY-NINE

PETROGRAD

February 10, 1918

Natasha yanked another paper from the typewriter and threw it in the heap of discarded missives at her feet. She picked up the heavy machine and set it on the floor next to her desk. Four hours of work and not one good idea. She stretched her back and decided to go upstairs to the room where they served tea and sometimes bread. She looked over at the girls hunched over their sewing machines. Only three now worked where there used to be twenty. Well, fabric was hard to come by.

Natasha moved out into the madness of the hallway. There was always such chaos and urgency at the Smolny. How did anything get accomplished? She passed the big room where discussions and talks resonated. She could hear Trotsky's voice and several others in a heated debate about the Brest–Litovsk negotiations with Germany. Plans for ending the war weren't going well. She was writing flyers assuring the working masses that peace was coming soon—declaring that the war would end and the brave Russian soldiers would be marching home. Natasha shook her head. The soldiers would come home, but at what a bitter price. Trotsky, as the Foreign Affairs Commissar, was trying desperately to insure that peace would come without reparations or reprisals, but she knew the German command would exact their pound of flesh.

Natasha made her way through the crowds of people in the hallway, greeting several individuals as they rushed by, and being asked by a few how her work was going. She looked around at all the haggard but earnest faces and felt a solidarity envelope her. *We're doing the best we can—trying to make men less selfish. Why does it seem like such an impossible task?*

She put her kopeks down for tea and a piece of dark bread, and made her way to a small table at the far end of the room. It was cold, but it was always cold. She took a bite of bread and chewed it slowly, sipping her tea to make the wad soft enough to swallow. She glanced around and drew the riddle paper from her pocket. She knew the final riddle by heart at this point, but she liked to see the words in front of her. She and her mother had been picking apart the riddle for days and it was nearly solved. On Sunday they would go to the location and find the last bundle. With two successes already, there was no doubt in Natasha's mind that they would find the last of the Lindlofs' money. She took another sip of tea and smoothed the paper on the table.

> *One season.*
> *One place.*
> *Two women of grace*
> *Stand present and past—*
> *Laurels extending, abundance expanding.*
> *Two creatures divided*
> *One vanquished, one free.*

She tapped her finger on the paper. *One season, one place.*

She and her mother had thought at first it might be the Winter Palace, but Natasha knew Agnes would never send her to a location so large and inaccessible. They had finally settled on the Summer Garden; it was the Summer Garden no matter what the season, and Natasha knew the place held a special meaning for the Lindlof family. *Two women of grace stand present and past.* They were sure this stanza referred to a statue, but there were many marble statues in the park and they didn't know if the two women of grace were two female statues standing near one another, or two women represented on one statue. She and her mother would go to the gardens on Sunday and search. *Laurels extending, abundance expanding.*

A warm hand gripped her shoulder and she jumped, knocking over her cup of tea. She snatched up the paper and shook off the wetness from the one corner. "Of all the stupid things!" She spun around to confront the person who had startled her. "Sergey Antonovich! What are you doing here?"

His contrite look made her bite back some of her anger.

"I'm sorry, Natasha. I didn't mean to frighten you. I was here listening to Chairman Lenin's speech and I thought I'd come to find you."

"Oh . . . oh, I see," she said, distractedly blotting the last of the wetness from the paper with her coat sleeve.

"If you're busy, I can just—"

"I need a towel to mop this up."

"I'll get one." He turned quickly to the long table where workers were ladling soup and cutting loaves of bread.

Natasha made sure his back was to her, and then folded the paper and put it into her pocket.

Sergey returned with a kitchen worker.

"Oh, for goodness sake," Natasha said. "All I needed was a towel."

"I know, but she insisted."

The girl bobbed her head and smiled. "I'm glad to do it for you, comrade." She set to work on the spill. "I am happy to serve one of the writers for the Bolshevik cause."

Natasha frowned. "How do you know I'm a writer?"

The girl's head bobbed again. "One of the other workers pointed you out. She had one of your pamphlets and she showed it to me. It was about a chicken with no head. It was very good."

Natasha was shocked into silence.

"Yes, she does great work for the cause," Sergey interceded.

The worker glanced over at him, covering an embarrassed smile with her hand. "Yes, comrade, and you are a great speaker. My friend and I attended a rally where you spoke against Kerensky."

Sergey looked pleased. "Well, you are quite the little Bolshevik, aren't you?"

The girl giggled. "I am, comrade." She knelt at his feet to wipe some wetness from the floor. "My father died in the war and my mother died last winter from consumption." Sergey offered his hand to help her stand, and she took it shyly. "Thank you, comrade." Girlish adoration showed on her face as Sergey smiled at her. She looked down self-consciously to the dirty towel in her hand. "Anyway, my sister and I work here now. She is a typist." She said this last with great pride, and Natasha felt a twinge of sadness as she contemplated the girl's circumstance.

"I'm sorry about your parents," she offered.

The girl looked surprised. "Oh, we do all right, comrade. Just last week my sister and I were able to get butter!"

Someone from the long table called her name and she turned. "Well, I have to get back to work." She bobbed her head several times. "Thank you for talking to me."

"We are proud of you, comrade," Sergey said with his most charming smile.

The girl giggled. She gave a slight bow to Natasha and left.

Sergey's self-important smile dropped when he looked back at Natasha. "Is something wrong?"

"What do you mean?"

He put his hand on her arm. "Your face looks like a storm."

She moderated her features, but not her emotion. *"My sister and I were able to get butter?"* she recited. "Is that not a bitter statement against the dreams of the Bolsheviks?"

Sergey frowned. "Natasha, you know it takes time."

She moved past him. "Yes, I know, I hear the sentiment over and over." He caught up to her and she kept walking. "I write that propaganda all the time, Sergey Antonovich. Citizens! Be patient as your land is redistributed and lies fallow for lack of industry; be patient as your son is slaughtered in the bloody trenches of war; be patient as your child's teeth fall out for lack of milk."

Sergey grabbed her arm. "Natasha!"

She pulled away from him. "There has to be a better way, Sergey Antonovich."

"People's teeth fell out under the tsar and the Provisional Government, Natasha. The Bolsheviks have only been in power a few months. We must have time."

They were quarrelling in the hallway, but the flow of workers took little notice. People were always discussing or arguing or yelling about something in the halls of the Smolny. It seemed the fabric of the Soviet doctrine was woven of loudness and contention.

"The Bolsheviks need time?" Natasha spat back at him. "How much time? Lenin doesn't even know how we will get to this grand Soviet utopia—it's an experiment. And will the experiment take a few months, a few years—fifty years? How long will it take for the government to force men's hearts to see the needs of others before the needs of self?"

"The leaders are trying to show the way, Natasha Ivanovna. Look at how little money they take, how simply they live and dress, how hard they work."

"And how long will that last?" She moved around a Red Guard. "Besides, they are a handful, Sergey Antonovich. Our country takes up one-sixth of the world and has one hundred and fifty million people. I think the dreams of the Bolsheviks will only come true if we force men with threats and guns."

"You can't mean that."

Natasha stopped walking. "I do."

"So you feel our journey on the agitprop train in the spring will be for nothing?"

Natasha considered the many ramifications of her answer.

"Natasha?"

She looked at him straight on. As she thought about Agnes in the work camp, of coercion, and the twisting of men's hearts and minds, she wanted to answer "Yes" to Sergey's question, but she had to play the game. "No, Sergey Antonovich," she answered softly. "I have hope that we will teach the great ideals of Socialism, and that the simple villagers will understand and embrace the doctrine."

Sergey studied her face. "Of course, that is what we *all* hope. It is their government after all . . . the government of the peasant farmer and the worker."

Natasha gave him a wry smile. "Are you preaching to me, Sergey Antonovich?"

"No, it's . . . it's just that I don't understand your ambivalence of late."

She began walking again. "I have much on my mind."

"Is that all it is?"

She moved into her office and Sergey followed. She didn't like the insinuation in his voice. "What do you mean?"

"You're not having second thoughts about going on the train?"

"No."

Sergey turned to the seamstresses. "Why don't you take your break now?" he snapped at them.

The three girls stood immediately and went out.

He turned back to her and Natasha tried to discern the look on his face. "There's no need to be upset, Sergey Antonovich."

He put his hands on her waist. "I'm not upset. I'm worried about you." He leaned over and kissed her neck. She pulled back and his grip tightened. "See. You are different of late."

There was a knot in her stomach, but she kept her voice calm. "It's Agnes."

Sergey released his grip and stepped back. "Agnes? What about her?"

"I don't know where she is, and I'm worried about her."

Sergey took a deep breath and nodded. "Of course, I'm sorry. I should have been more aware of your anguish."

Natasha moved to the window and shoved it open onto the cold day.

"I'm sure she's fine," Sergey said.

"You can't know that."

"Well, they're not in a penal camp, only a special camp."

Natasha rounded on him. "How do you know that?"

"I . . . I don't for sure, but it would make sense. They weren't convicted of a crime—just of being enemies of the state."

"Oh." Natasha turned back to the window, the cold air biting into her cheeks. "Oh, of course . . . just enemies of the state," she said bitterly. Sergey moved toward her but she stopped him with her voice. "I must get back to work, Sergey Antonovich."

"Of course." He took his hat from his pocket. "May I call on you, Sunday?"

Natasha made the reply as offhanded as possible. "Perhaps in the evening. Mother and I will be out most of the day."

"Still trying to find traveling shoes?"

"Yes, that's it. I must be ready for the spring." She managed a smile and Sergey smiled back.

"Until Sunday then."

After he'd gone, Natasha closed the window, and then stood for a long time looking through the frosted panes at the muddy street below. Images of white cows, work camps, marble statues, and Agnes's perfect face swam in front of her vision. A voice kept repeating in her head, *My sister and I were able to get butter.*

Natasha placed her hand on the cold glass. The trusting acceptance in the girl's words beat into her head, blocking out the elevated promises of the party. What could she write now that would have any meaning or truth?

NOTES

1. The people of Russia, especially those who lived in the cities, had lived with deprivation for years prior to and following the Bolshevik Revolution. In March 1917, bread rationing was enforced and people were expected to live on a quarter of a loaf of bread a day. There were massive marches and protests demanding food. During the Russian civil war—which lasted from 1918 to approximately 1921—crime was rampant, diseases spread, industry fell apart, and starvation reached catastrophic levels. Just prior to the end of the civil war it was estimated that nearly 7.5 million Russians had died from starvation.

CHAPTER THIRTY

SIBERIA

February 12, 1918

They had learned to keep their heads down: when standing in line for the count, when standing in line for the thin broth, when working in the laundry, and especially when being lectured or commanded by one of the guards. The weeks had brought realization, and the slaps across the face had brought submission.

The women worked mostly in the camp: cooking, cleaning, scrubbing, and sewing. The men processed lumber. Every morning, before the sun rose, the shuffle of boots could be heard leaving the camp for the forest and the lumber mill. The second day in camp, Agnes had surreptitiously asked one of the old-timers what jobs the men did. "Logs mostly," the scrawny woman had answered, keeping her eyes fixed on the one small boiled potato on her plate. "Cut, saw, ship. Sometimes us women get to go out to the mill and hack off tree limbs. That's good work."

Yes. Agnes had learned that some jobs at the camp were better than others. Today she and Alexandria had been assigned to empty the twenty-gallon latrine pots and then scrub their dormitory floorboards alone. The boss of their work gang of fifteen was the babushka who had helped the young woman that first night in Ekaterinburg.

Her name was Vera Speranskaya, but everyone called her Little Mother. She was very strict, but they all knew it was to keep them alive. Little

Mother made sure their bread ration wasn't short, the work duties were rotated fairly, and the guards kept away from the girls who wanted to be left alone. It seemed the soldiers preferred the most recent crop of women— before their teeth went bad and their bodies lost their soft curves. Agnes knew Little Mother had saved her and Alexandria several times during that first week in camp.

There were others in the gang who accepted the soldiers' advances because it meant favors, leniency, and sometimes extra soap. Little Mother was a pious woman, and after a few weeks of gentle lecturing, and an insistence that all gifts given by the soldiers be shared equally among the gang, the women of Gang 38 received the reputation of being cold fish.

Agnes dipped her stiff-bristled brush into the bucket, then sloshed the tepid water out onto the floor. Alexandria worked beside her, and as they neared the center of the room, the door to the dormitory opened. A blast of cold air crept across the floor, chilling the soapy water on Agnes's hands. She heard the thump of several pairs of boots crossing the room toward them, and she quickly glanced sideways at Alexandria, trying to give her a look of fortitude.

Where is Little Mother? Agnes thought in a panic. *Please, Lord, send the Little Mother to help us.*

They kept their heads down, their eyes on the floor. A pair of boots came into their field of vision, and Agnes could sense Alexandria trembling beside her.

"Comrades!" The deep voice barked. "Stand up!"

They did as they were told, never lifting their heads or looking up at the voice that commanded them.

"Agnes? Alexandria?"

Agnes shook her head to clear the confusion from her brain. She thought she'd heard Johannes speak her name.

"Look up, comrades," came the guard's voice again.

The women obeyed and Alexandria squealed with delight. She rushed past the smiling guard and into the arms of Johannes, Oskar, and Arel. Agnes stood frozen in place, unable to comprehend what she was seeing.

"Go on," the guard said, his tone soft and encouraging. "It's not a dream."

Agnes stumbled into Johannes's arms, dropping the brush, and cling-
ing to his frost-covered coat. "How? How is this possible?"

No one answered her. They held tightly to each other, trying not to
waste one precious moment.

"You smell like pine pitch," Alexandria said finally, and they all
chuckled and wiped away tears.

"How are you?" Johannes asked anxiously.

Agnes knew he was evaluating their thinner faces and worn looks,
and hating the restraints that kept him from helping them. "Don't worry,
Johannes," she said with surety. "We're fairly well off, and the woman who
is our boss watches out for us." She looked into the faces of Oskar and Arel,
noticing for the first time Erland's absence. "Where's Erland?" she asked
abruptly.

Johannes took her hands. "He's not doing well. He's in the infirmary.
That's why we've come to get you. This guard is going to take us to see
him."

Agnes felt fear wash through her. "Why is he helping us?" she asked.
She looked with suspicion at the guard who was standing and listening at
the door.

Arel smiled. "I take it you've been saying your prayers?"

"Yes. Though I think Alexandria is better at it. But what does that have
to do with anything?"

"It has everything to do with everything. You see, we've been praying
too—praying for help, praying for a miracle." He made a grand gesture
toward the soldier. "Well, there is our miracle."

The guard grinned at them. He was a large man, some years older than
Johannes, with a bushy beard and mustache. He walked forward to meet
them as Arel continued. "He has just been sent here to be the assistant
commandant."

Agnes flinched. That didn't sound like a miracle.

"Agnes, Alexandria, may I introduce Andre Andreyevitch Orleansky."
Arel put his hand on the guard's shoulder and Agnes and Alexandria
gasped, waiting for the angry reprisal. It did not come. Arel gave them a
reassuring look. "Comrade Orleansky is my friend. He was the soldier with
Bruno and me in the war."

"The . . . the one who helped you escape?" Alexandria spluttered.

Arel nodded. "The very man. Isn't that a miracle?"

"It is," Agnes said, her voice a mix of reverence and wonder. She stepped forward, forcing herself to go against weeks of indoctrination and submission. She looked into the soldier's face. "Thank you. Thank you for helping my brothers."

Andre Andreyevitch nodded. "I am sorry that Bruno died. He was a good young man. But your brother's prayer was only that he'd get home to see his family again, wasn't it? And that happened."

"Yes, we were blessed to have him home with us," Agnes said.

"And I was blessed to hear that prayer and spend those weeks with Arel and Bruno," Andre Andreyevitch replied. "I learned much."

"How did you come to be here?" Alexandria questioned.

Andre Andreyevitch grinned. "I tend to play whatever part gets me through difficulties, Comrade Lindlof. When the Bolsheviks seized power, and then pardoned all war deserters who would pledge allegiance to the Soviets, I took them up on the offer. My uncle had become important in one of the military committees and he said he would help me." Andre Andreyevitch shook his head and grinned again. "My uncle actually recommended me to a post near Moscow, but for some strange reason I was sent here."

"Yes—for some strange reason," Arel said.

There were steps on the porch outside the door, and everyone stiffened. Andre Andreyevitch raised his rifle and pointed it at Arel. The door opened and Little Mother stepped inside. She recovered from her shock almost immediately. "What's happening here?" she questioned, just the right combination of sternness and acquiescence in her voice.

Andre Andreyevitch became official and brutish. "The commandant sent me to gather these two female prisoners," he snapped.

"And the men?"

"They have all been ordered to the infirmary."

"Why?"

Andre Andreyevitch glared at her. "I don't know. I am just following orders. Now give them over."

The Little Mother glowered back at him, but finally turned slightly to the girls. "Get your coats."

They moved to obey.

"Don't expect them back until after supper," Andre Andreyevitch said without excuse.

The Little Mother stared at him. "These two are hard workers. They'd better be returned to me exactly as I give them to you," she said fearlessly.

"You don't have much to say about it," Andre Andreyevitch said officiously, "but don't fret. No harm will come to them."

Agnes and Alexandria returned to the group, dressed for the fierce cold of outside. Their heads were bowed and the proper humility colored their demeanors.

"Come on then," their guard snapped. "Out into it." He pushed them from behind as Johannes opened the door.

The stinging cold bit Agnes's face and she hunched into her coat. The sadness that normally came with the cold did not come. She knew it was the warmth of seeing her brothers again and having a miracle evident in all their lives that kept the melancholy ache from her heart.

♦ ♦ ♦

Their bodies had not been fully warm since arriving at the camp, and Agnes sat with her siblings by Erland's sickbed feeling guilty for the opportunity of escaping, even for a short time, the persistence of winter. She had seen depredation leech compassion from the soul of many of the prisoners and she vowed to not let that happen to her.

She looked over at Erland. He sat up in bed trying to smile and converse with his brothers and sisters, but every word was an effort, and his emotion usually came in tears. His skin was a sallow hue and the glint of his eyes was absent. Agnes bit her bottom lip and took his hand. The abuse he'd suffered the night of their arrest was finally taking its toll. Did the Cheka policeman know or care what a precious life he'd damaged on that horrific night? *Dear Erland who was always active and teasing—the brother who ate the most and was the most annoying.* She fought back tears and forced herself to concentrate on the conversation.

"Our gang is probably the best," Oskar was saying. "We can cut and haul five trees an hour."

"And you get to work together?" Erland asked, his eyes moving from one brother's face to the next.

"We do," Oskar answered, the tone of his voice growing somber.

"I'm so glad," Erland said. He turned slowly to Agnes. "And you and Alexandria are together?" She nodded. "That's good. I've prayed for that."

"Oh, Erland!" Alexandria sobbed. "We've missed you." She laid her head on the mattress and he patted it.

"You're here now. That's all that matters."

"And we'll be able to come more often with my friend helping us," Arel said.

"And when you're better, you'll work with us in the gang," Johannes declared.

Erland gave a weak smile. "Let me start by chopping down saplings, will you?"

The brothers smiled at him.

Andre Andreyevitch came into the room with the medical orderly. "It's time to go."

Alexandria wiped her face on Erland's sheet and stood up. They all put on their coats and hats, but stood around the bed, unable to move away.

"Go on now," Erland said. "Don't get into trouble on my account."

"We pray for you every day," Arel said, his voice husky with emotion.

"I know," Erland said, leaning back onto his pillow. Agnes plumped it for him and he smiled. "You are an angel."

The orderly came to the side of the bed with a notepad and a look of annoyance. "If you stay one more moment," he hissed, "I will report you, no matter what the assistant commandant says."

They knew it was bluff, but as they did not want to mar their chances for future visits, they turned away reluctantly. Alexandria kissed Erland's forehead, and Johannes finally let go of his hand. Agnes turned back at the doorway and waved, but Erland had already laid his head on his pillow and closed his eyes.

CHAPTER THIRTY-ONE

PETROGRAD
February 15, 1918

Snow had fallen during the night and a soft white stillness covered the city of Petrograd. Natasha and her mother rode through the wonderland in a small black cab, which got stuck in snowdrifts at every other intersection. The women had finally had enough of the cabman's bad temper and foul language and asked to be let off at the military complex. As they walked across Mars Field, adjacent to the barracks complex, they were relieved to be away from the mad driver and to be able to talk about the riddle and the final hiding place. They would reach the Summer Garden in a few minutes and they were anxious to find the statue—or statues—quickly.

"I think it will be two women on one statue," Natasha said confidently.

"That's what we should look for first then," her mother concurred.

"But we'll keep our eyes open for any statue that has a woman with laurel leaves or a laurel wreath," Natasha added.

"Yes."

Her mother's breathing was a bit labored, so Natasha slowed her pace. The deep snow was mid-calf, and though it was beautiful, it hampered their movement.

"Perhaps we should come another day," Natasha suggested.

"Shall we let a little snow stop us?" her mother answered.

Natasha smiled. "No, of course not. I just thought it might be difficult."

"For me?" her mother quipped. "Remember, I'm a country girl, Natasha. When my sister and I were young in Sel'tso Saterno, we'd trudge through snow up to our waists to go out and milk the cows."

Natasha grinned. "Oh yes, and it was very early in the morning and the temperature was a hundred degrees below freezing."

"Mind your manners."

Natasha only laughed and pulled her scarf more snugly around her neck. "We still haven't figured out the meaning of—'Two creatures divided, one vanquished, one free.'"

"It will probably make sense when we find the right statue," her mother said.

"*If* we find the right statue."

"Don't doubt yourself. Your friend has faith in you."

They came to the edge of the military parade grounds, having encountered no one, and continued on to the south gate of the Summer Garden. They moved into the wintery park and were immediately encased in a reverent solitude. They could hear the sound of trucks and automobiles at a distance, but here the women seemed detached from the noise and cares of the city. Though leafless, the black trunks of the oak and elm trees created an enchanting forest. It was easy for Natasha to imagine the stone images coming to life when no one was looking.

"I wonder where the Mormon apostle stood when he gave his blessing," her mother said quietly.

Natasha was surprised by her mother's inquiry, and a little disheartened that that important story of her friend's life hadn't come to her own mind. "I don't know," she answered. "Agnes never told me the place. Do you think the statue may be there?"

Her mother rubbed her face with her gloved hands. "Well, it would have been a good place to start."

Natasha nodded and fell into her own thoughts. She remembered Agnes trying to tell her about the day with the apostle—about how he loved the Russian people, and about the beautiful blessing. She also remembered that she'd been irritated with Agnes's excited chatter, even to the point of telling her friend not to talk about it, that she didn't care about silly superstitions like God.

The look of devastation on Agnes's angelic face had been—Natasha pulled her thoughts to the present. "Let's get started," she said, her voice carrying a note of frustration that had nothing to do with the day.

The walkways were covered with snow, but the hedges and statues clearly marked a passage through the park. Natasha could see ten statues just from where they stood, and she looked over at her mother in dismay.

"We'll keep looking until we find it," her mother reassured, surmising her daughter's worries.

They left a trail of footprints in the pristine snow as they searched the extensive garden. There were many statues of women: women with books, women with musical instruments, women standing near animals. There was even a woman holding a laurel wreath, but she was a singular figure leaning on an obelisk, and did not fit any of the other clues.

Natasha and her mother were nearing the north side of the garden that faced the Neva River. They'd been searching for an hour, and Natasha was cold and discouraged. They had seen more than forty statues but none had satisfied the demands of the riddle.

"Perhaps this is the wrong place," Natasha said dejectedly. Perhaps we need to start over."

"No," her mother answered. "I think this is exactly the place the Lindlofs would choose. This garden has a special, almost sacred, meaning for them, yes?"

Natasha nodded.

"Well then, let's keep looking for a little longer."

Natasha nodded again, glad for her mother's optimism. "There are a few statues around Tsar Peter's old Summer Palace. We can check those, then move over to the west side."

Her mother turned in that direction and Natasha followed. They hadn't gone twenty steps when Natasha pointed. "Mother, look there . . . at that large statue!" She quickened her pace. "I think there are two figures on that statue!" She struggled against the snow, frustrated with her slow progress, but as she neared the statue, her heart seemed to verify that this was the monument of Agnes's riddle. Natasha stood quietly staring at the exquisite marble masterwork as her mother came to her side. "This is it. Don't you see? This is the one."

"I think it is," her mother agreed. "This is a statue representing Russia's victory over Sweden. The one figure is Winged Victory and the other woman symbolizes Russia."

"'Two women of grace stand present and past,'" Natasha quoted. "And see how Winged Victory extends a laurel wreath over Russia's head?"

"Yes," her mother said softly. "And how the statue of Russia holds a cornucopia in her left hand? That is the symbol of abundance."

Natasha stared at the statue, mesmerized by its beauty and the way it fit the riddle exactly. "'Laurels extending, abundance expanding. Two creatures divided, one vanquished, one free.'"

The foot of Winged Victory rested on the head of a lion, and Natasha moved forward, putting her hand on the lion's mane.

"The symbol of vanquished Sweden," her mother said, coming to stand beside her. "And the eagle represents peace and freedom."

"My friend is brilliant, isn't she?" Natasha said, a tremor of emotion in her voice. She reached up and touched the eagle's wing.

The peaceful moment was shattered as they heard the wrenching of a door and the jangle of keys. Both women turned quickly to see an aged groundskeeper coming from the old palace.

"Hurry! Look for the bundle," her mother commanded. "He hasn't seen us yet."

Natasha set to work, her hands fumbling over the stone. She shoved her hand into the maw of the cannon, behind the leg of Russia and the eagle's wing. *Nothing!*

"Hurry, Natasha, he sees us."

Natasha reached into the opening behind the lion's head and felt the familiar give of the packet's covering. "It's here! I have it!"

"He's coming over," her mother warned.

"What are you doing there?" the old man called.

Natasha started and dropped the packet into the snow. She bent down to pick it up, hoping the old man hadn't seen her. Moments later, her hope was broken.

"What's that you've got there?" the groundskeeper demanded.

He was thirty feet away and Natasha knew she had to think of something fast. She turned her back on him, and took her time standing. Just as he reached them, Natasha took a deep breath and turned. The man's face was rough and lined, but his gray eyes were keen and full of suspicion.

"I asked you what you have there."

Natasha held out a soggy handkerchief. "This? It's my—"

"I know what that is," the man snapped. "What's in your other hand?"

Natasha held it out. "Nothing, comrade."

The man growled. "Don't say comrade to me. I'll have none of the Bolshevik tripe spouted at me."

Natasha's mother nodded. "Yes, we agree, but one can't be too careful these days."

Natasha could see the old man's irritation fade, but duty was obviously foremost on his mind. He narrowed his eyes at Natasha. "What did you drop?"

"My handkerchief was the only thing—"

"Didn't look like no handkerchief to me," the groundskeeper said, coming to stomp around the base of the monument. "And what were you doing to the statue?"

"Just brushing away the snow with this," Natasha said, holding out the handkerchief again. "We wanted to see the details of the fine work."

The man snorted. "Sounds like a tall story to me. Two women out on a snowy day to look at statues? Bunch of nonsense." He glowered at them. "I think you'd better be on your way. Go on now."

Natasha's mother nodded and gave him several small bows. "Yes, sir, whatever you say." She took Natasha by the arm. "Come, daughter, time to get home and prepare our evening meal."

They moved as quickly as the snowdrifts would allow out toward the main gate. Natasha looked back once to see the groundskeeper examining the statue. *Did he think we were saboteurs, planting bombs in the park?* She shook her head. Well, the anti-Bolshevik factions weren't above destroying machinery and food, so why not statues? And what of the gangs of ruffians who attached themselves to the Bolshevik cause? They assaulted people in the streets and set fire to property in the name of the proletariat movement, when in actuality they cared nothing for the political ideology, but wanted only the free bread offered by the Soviet police. *From each according to their ability, to each according to their needs.* It was madness.

"What did you do with the packet?" Her mother's words brought her mind back to the garden.

"I put it in my bodice," Natasha answered smugly. "My scarf covered it."

"That was quick thinking," her mother said with an admiring smile.

The women walked together out the north gate of the Summer Garden, and Natasha felt a sudden wash of relief. "All three, Mother! I've found all three of the Lindlofs' packets."

"Yes, my darling. You've done well."

"*We've* done well. Thank you for your help." She took the packet from her bodice. "Now I just have to find how to get the treasure to them."

"I believe a way will open," her mother said as they walked along the prospect fronting the frozen Neva River. "I would have liked to have gone over to the Church of the Resurrection and said a prayer of thanks, but the Bolsheviks have turned it into a storehouse."

Natasha took her mother's hand. The image of the church saddened her. She remembered her mother taking her inside the church several times when she was a child. The beautiful pictures that covered the walls and ceiling were all done in glistening mosaic, and sparkled like jewels. She hadn't understood what the pictures meant, but even as a child she knew the people who made the pictures must have felt deeply about what they were creating.

She touched the bundle in her pocket and drew her coat tighter. The icy wind and drop in adrenaline made her shiver. "They have to be so cold in the work camp. Cold and hungry. What do they have to eat, and what if they're sick?" She felt the press of tears behind her eyes. "I can't stand the thought of someone hurting Agnes. I can't stand the thought of any of them being mistreated."

They came upon three Red Guards standing near the Marble Palace. Natasha stopped talking and steadied her emotions. The guards glanced at them before returning to their conversation. One was saying something about the electricity being turned off, and another was complaining about the holes in his boots.

Natasha shivered again.

"I say we find a cab," her mother said. "I still have a little money."

Natasha nodded.

As they searched for a cab, she heard again the sounds of the city: automobiles, streetcars, the movement and voices of people, but something was missing. It took her a while to place it, but then it came to her—the sound of church bells. All her life the church bells had rung. Now they were silent. Maybe it was childish, but she missed their comforting assurance.

NOTES

1. The Resurrection Church to which Natasha's mother refers is the Church of Our Savior on the Spilled Blood, the site of Tsar Alexander II's assassination. It is within walking distance from the Summer Gardens.

CHAPTER THIRTY-TWO

SIBERIA

March 1, 1918

Arel surreptitiously watched Erland as he hacked limbs and branches off the felled trees. He'd been working with the gang for a week now, and though his spirit seemed strong, his body struggled. Arel knew that Andre Andreyevitch had done Erland a favor by ordering him from the infirmary at the first sign of improvement; all the prisoners knew that the infirmary wasn't a good place for anyone's health.

Gaunt and permanently bent, Erland actually worked with the women of Gang 38, and Arel was glad Agnes and Alexandria could keep a close watch. He knew that his sisters were doubling their efforts to cover Erland's unproductive attempts. The men had hauled in twenty logs that morning and the pace of the work was brutal. Arel knew they couldn't slack as the workers had been promised an extra ten minutes at their meal break if they brought in twenty-five logs in the morning. The Lindlofs needed those ten extra minutes; Andre Andreyevitch had secretly sent word that he would meet with them during the break.

Oskar came up beside Arel as they hauled the twenty-fourth log to the mill. "I wonder what news he has for us?"

Arel shrugged as a guard rode by on his skittish gray horse. The animal stamped and snorted before moving off.

When the soldier was out of earshot, Oskar continued. "Do you think it might have anything to do with getting us out of here?"

"I don't know," Arel answered. He made himself look busy with keeping the log on the sledge.

Johannes was guiding the huge workhorse down the packed trail. He glanced back at his brothers and gave a warning look.

"Johannes thinks we should be quiet."

Oskar grinned. "Oh, he does, does he? Does he think the guards are going to harm me? They wouldn't dare." Johannes shot them another glance and Oskar waved. "The commandant would have their heads. They know I'm the best worker on the gang—even with my bum leg."

Arel knew it was true. During their months in the camp, all of their bodies had hardened to the work, but no one's more so than Oskar's. He seemed to thrive on the cold, work, and meager meals, and the guards often made bets as to how quickly he could bring down a tree. Arel also knew that he and his brothers' constitutions were tougher than the other men who smoked or chewed tobacco or drank the vodka doled out from time to time. Oskar had once traded his ration of vodka to a rat-faced little prisoner for a tin of smoked fish and three ounces of sugar.

Prisoners were allowed letters twice a month and packages once a month, but of course the Lindlofs never saw their names listed on the post board because no one knew where they were, and a letter had to first be sent to the camp and checked by the censors before a prisoner could write back. One prisoner received a package from his wife every month like clockwork.

Arel saw movement out the corner of his eye and turned to look into the deep green of the forest. He saw a beautiful silver fox disappear behind a tree. Arel took a deep breath of pine and steadied his emotions. *Somehow we'll get through this. Somehow. Please, God, let Mother and Father know we're all right.*

They reached the mill with log twenty-four, and shortly thereafter two other groups in their gang brought in logs. The boss congratulated his men on their great effort and sent them off to the cook station. Arel admired the boss, but kept well out of his way. Comrade Golubev was seventy years old and fiercer than any man Arel had ever seen. Even Cossacks or Red Guards who were taller and heavier could not match the determination in his eyes or the strength of his overlarge hands. Golubev wore the black, padded jacket and pants with his number over the right knee like the rest of the prisoners, but that was where any other similarity ended. He wore the birch-bark shoes and leg straps of an ancient country peasant, and carried himself with the pride of hundreds of years of Russian serfs. Even the meanest guards left him alone.

Gang 38 had been given their break also, and Erland staggered over to join his brothers. Johannes gave him a supportive nod and Erland smiled weakly.

"I didn't even drop the hatchet today," he said slowly. "Alexandria and Agnes said I did well." His breathing was labored.

"Of course you did well," Oskar said.

"It's not . . . not like working with the men though," Erland wheezed.

"And fortunate for you," Oskar answered. "Us men are a bunch of louts. Ah, but the women . . ."

They came to the food tent and got into line with the other men waiting for rice, fish broth, and a lump of bread. Erland was so worn out that he stumbled on the threshold and fell into the man in front of him. The man grunted and turned to cuff him, but Oskar interceded.

"Sorry. Sorry, comrade. Just an accident."

"Keep that skeleton away from me," the man barked, crossing himself absentmindedly. "He looks like the bringer of death."

"And you look like a pig. Oh, no, excuse me, you *are* a pig," Oskar barked back.

The dirty man turned to fight, then evaluated Oskar's fitness, and walked away, muttering. The brothers smiled as he found another place in line.

"Thanks, Oskar," Erland said, picking up his soup bowl.

"It's my job as your big brother."

The kitchen orderlies slopped soup and rice into their bowls and handed them each a lump of bread, after which they went to find a place where they could sit together. As they moved about, they searched the other side of the room where the women sat until they found Agnes and Alexandria. The brothers and sisters shared furtive glances, then went about their business.

The brothers pressed themselves into a small space at the back table and set to eating at once. The tent was cold and if they wanted their bodies to have any warmth from the soup they had to eat it quickly. They ate half the bread and tied the other half into their grubby handkerchiefs. They would eat this precious morsel in the late afternoon when their stomachs were growling with hunger.

Arel saw Erland put all his bread away, and his heart twisted with sadness. He knew Erland found it difficult to swallow, and that the bread his body needed so badly would be given to Agnes and Alexandria.

"What were we talking about before that pig man interrupted us?" Oskar asked, sopping up the last grains of rice and broth with a small mouthful of the heavy black bread.

"Women," Erland said, bobbing his head and grinning. "Yes, women."

"That was it!" Oskar chuckled. "Such a good topic."

"Remember how we all loved Natasha Ivanovna?" Erland said softly.

They all nodded, trying not to let the image of Natasha's dark hair and eyes sink too deeply into their bereft hearts.

"Yes, and I think Arel still loves her," Oskar said. "Ah! Look at his face! It's true." The brothers grinned at Arel's discomfort. "Poor boy," Oskar continued, "in love with a beautiful Bolshevik."

"That's enough," Johannes said. "From what Agnes has told us about the note, Natasha Ivanovna may be our only hope of ever getting out of here."

They all sobered at the pronouncement.

"I wonder if she's figured out the riddles?" Arel wondered.

"She and Agnes were very good at figuring out those games," Oskar conceded.

"Yes. It was smart of our sister to leave those clues," Johannes said. "I thought the money we'd hidden was lost to us forever."

Oskar shook his head. "And you don't think Natasha Ivanovna will turn it in to the authorities?"

"No," Arel said immediately. "She loves Agnes. She'll do anything to help her."

"We just have to keep praying that Natasha Ivanovna is as true as she is beautiful," Erland said. His chuckle turned into a cough and he grimaced in pain. He laid his head on the table to control the spasms.

Johannes rubbed his back as the other brothers watched helplessly. Finally Erland quieted. He made a pillow of his bony arms and closed his eyes. Johannes kept his hand protectively on his brother's back.

"What should we do?" Arel whispered.

"Let him rest," Johannes answered.

At that moment Andre Andreyevitch came into the tent. A few prisoners glanced over at him, then back to their bowls, many stopped talking, and even the kitchen orderlies found jobs to occupy them elsewhere.

The assistant commandant looked imperiously around the room. When his eyes found Golubev and the Little Mother, he motioned for them to join him. The gang bosses ambled forward, showing just the right amount of humility. As bowls clattered and the conversations resumed, the assistant commandant spoke to the bosses. The look on his face was angry and all the prisoners hoped their names were not on his lips.

The bosses turned and Arel knew that the Little Mother would be calling out Agnes and Alexandria, and that Golubev would be summoning them.

"Erland, sit up," he said gently, reaching across the table and taking Erland's hand. "Johannes, put his mittens on him. His hands are like ice."

Johannes was able to rouse Erland and get his mittens on just as Golubev came to their table.

"You four . . . the assistant wants to see you in the mill office." He leaned over the table and growled at them. "You'd better not be in any trouble, because I can't afford to lose you off the gang."

They didn't answer, but stood to go out. Johannes supported Erland by grabbing a wad of fabric at the back of his jacket and holding his arm. His body was so emaciated it was like handling a marionette.

As they walked out into the frigid afternoon, Agnes and Alexandria fell in line behind them. None of them spoke and they all kept their heads down. They walked into the warm mill office and the scent of pine was overwhelming. Andre Andreyevitch stood with his back to the stove and a smile on his face. When he saw Erland, the smile dropped.

"Sit him down. Sit him down in the clerk's chair."

Johannes maneuvered Erland into the chair, taking care not to bump his brother's thin arms against the wood.

"I've sent the clerk and the mill foreman on an errand into town." He moved to check Erland's condition. "They weren't too happy, but what of that?"

Erland straightened as the assistant commandant approached. "I'm fine, sir . . . just a little tired."

"I can send you back to the infirmary."

"No, sir, thank you. I'd rather stay with my brothers."

"Are you sure?"

Erland nodded.

Andre Andreyevitch shook his head, then turned and picked up an old sack. He set it onto the clerk's desk. Something solid clunked inside it when he set it down. He opened the top of the bag, reached in, and pulled out a charming birch-bark box. It had been lovingly crafted by a country artisan with carvings all around the sides and a perfect replica of a squirrel carved on the top.

Agnes gasped. How did he know? How did he know that Natasha's pet name for her was "little squirrel"? She could not stop the tears, and she felt Arel's arm around her waist.

"Are you all right, Comrade Lindlof?" Andre Andreyevitch asked.

Agnes steadied herself and removed her coat. "Yes, sir, I'm just not used to the warmth."

"Of course," he said, "how silly of me. Please—all of you—take off your coats."

Everyone complied except Erland.

When he had their attention again, Andre Andreyevitch continued. "I have finally come up with a plan for you to retrieve your money, if"— he looked meaningfully at Agnes—"by some mad chance, your friend has found it." He put his hand on the box. "You will send this box to your friend, and she will send the money back to you in it."

They all stared at him as though he were mad. Johannes finally spoke.

"But Natasha Ivanovna must write to us first."

Andre smiled. "Alexandria will write a letter to the camp as though she were Natasha Ivanovna. It will have the needed addresses, and I will fake the post. The censors never really check the outside that carefully, they are more interested in the letter's content." They all nodded. "Then Agnes will write to her friend and put two letters in the box."

"Two letters?" Agnes questioned.

Andre Andreyevitch nodded, removing the lid from the box. "One here." He pointed inside the empty box. "And one here." He flipped the box over and pressed the carved pinecone on the bottom of the box. No one heard the latch move, but, as they watched, Andre Andreyevitch pushed the bottom panel to the side, revealing a two-inch gap between the false bottom and the actual bottom.

The brothers smiled at each other, but Agnes shook her head. "Others have told me that the guards go through all boxes and packages thoroughly, and prisoners are never allowed to keep any box, or jar, or container."

"Yes, that's true." Andre grinned. "But, you see, all empty boxes and containers are brought to the assistant commandant."

"That's convenient," Oskar said.

Agnes persisted. "But what if they find the secret compartment while they're going through the contents?"

Andre Andreyevitch gave a little shake of his head. "You give our guards too much credit for intelligence, Comrade Lindlof. Here again, we will have a safeguard. You will instruct your friend to put into the box the typical things most prisoners receive: sugar, salt, baked goods, paper, pencils, letters, and photos—that sort of thing. Then, on the very top, she will lay a couple of two-ruble notes."

"Is that a bribe?" Alexandria broke in.

Andre Andreyevitch smiled. "No, just the opposite. The guards aren't allowed to touch money—too much temptation for thievery. Any box containing money is immediately brought to me without being searched."

Agnes looked at the eight-inch square box and nodded. She picked up the lid and ran her hand over the squirrel carving. "I think this might work."

Alexandria clapped and Erland looked hopefully at his siblings.

Andre Andreyevitch handed Agnes the other part of the box. "Your brothers tell me that you and your friend, Natasha Ivanovna, are good at figuring riddles."

Agnes smiled. "Yes, Assistant Commandant, we're very good." She pressed the pinecone on the bottom of the box to see how it worked, then replaced the lid and handed the box back to him. "Won't the guards who do the post wonder how we came by such an item?"

Andre Andreyevitch shook his head. "It may be your letters inside the box, Comrade Lindlof, but it will be my handwriting on the wrapping. I will bypass the checkers and send it out from my office."

"Then why the two letters?"

"One can never be too careful, right? What if the box is checked along the way, or at the post station in Petrograd? The censors will read the letter inside the box and find nothing remarkable about it, but your friend will be able to discern the hidden meaning."

Agnes nodded. "I'm sorry. I shouldn't be questioning your planning. We're very grateful for your help."

"I'm glad for your questions. It makes me consider everything. Please, if you think of any other questions, let me know, all right?" Agnes nodded again, and Andre Andreyevitch looked around at the other members of the family. "It's time to put you back to work. If anyone asks why I called you, say that someone made a negative report about your behavior and I had to check it."

Arel stepped forward and extended his hand. Andre Andreyevitch took it. "Thank you, Andre Andreyevitch. You are a blessing to us."

"Just keep praying that this works." He looked at Alexandria. "Get started writing the letter from Natasha Ivanovna, and you"—he looked at Agnes—"start creating the riddle and letter for your friend."

As they left the mill office, Agnes knew that they all felt a whispered hope—a hope that had eluded them for months. God had guided things to this point. They just had to keep faith that He would not forsake them.

Erland stepped out into the snowy work area whistling a well-known Bolshevik rally song.

"What are you whistling that for?" Oskar asked, swatting at him with his hat.

"Put on your hat," Erland scolded. "You'll catch your death."

Oskar shoved the hat on his head. "Well, stop whistling that song."

"But, brother, I want everyone to think I'm a happy little Bolshevik so that no one is surprised when they let me stroll out of this camp."

The siblings laughed and Agnes was amazed and heartened to hear Erland teasing again. There *was* hope! Somehow all the complicated plans would work, and come spring they would find themselves reunited with their parents and Linda Alise.

They heard the work whistle blow, and Johannes growled at them to lower their heads and put on somber looks. Agnes did as she was told, knowing the serious mask hid a heart that, for the first time in a long time, felt happiness.

CHAPTER THIRTY-THREE

"Lenin had to bring peace, Sergey Antonovich. The Bolsheviks promised peace and Trotsky couldn't stall the German command any longer." Dmitri Borisovitch stood by the window while Sergey paced near Natasha's desk. The seamstresses had left the Smolny for the streetcar an hour before and Natasha envied them. For the past twenty minutes she had been sitting and listening to Sergey and Dmitri argue about the Brest-Litovsk war treaty.

Sergey slammed his fist down on her desk. "After all the months of wrangling, Trotsky knew it was useless. Did you know the Russian delegation signed the final draft without even reading it?"

Dmitri nodded. "But it's peace, Sergey Antonovich."

Sergey rounded on him. "Peace? At what cost? Lithuania, Livonia, Estonia—gone. Twenty-five percent of our fertile farming area. Sixty million people. Seventy-five percent of our iron ore and coal deposits! It is a high price for peace!" He kicked a chair across the room.

A dark figure appeared in the doorway. "I agree with you, Comrade Vershinin. The treaty is a hangman's noose around our neck, but what could we do?"

"Commissar Trotsky!" Sergey gasped. "I'm . . . I'm sorry. I've just been so angry since hearing the report."

Leon Trotsky walked into the room, and Natasha stood. She noted the strain on the man's face and felt a rush of pity for the futility of his efforts. *A government cannot force men to change their hearts.* She shook her head to clear the thought.

"Are you all right, Comrade Gavrilova?" Trotsky asked as he came to her side.

"Yes, Commissar. I . . . we've all been upset by the report."

"I understand. But we will not give up hope, will we?"

"No, Commissar."

"We thought our glorious Socialist revolution would inspire the workers of other countries, especially the workers of Germany. We thought the proletariat would rise up against their imperialist government and the war would end." He rearranged a few things on Natasha's desk. "That did not happen."

"But the Soviet ideal will continue here," Dmitri Borisovitch stated emphatically.

Trotsky looked into his eager face and smiled. "Well, for a while anyway." He absently picked up a blue book from Natasha's desk. "The Bolsheviks never planned for Russia to stand alone. The dream is for a worldwide dictatorship of the proletariat." He set the book down and Natasha unobtrusively slid a flyer over the top of it. Trotsky's mind seemed to wander. "Workers of the world unite. The worldwide dictatorship of the proletariat . . . a lofty goal." He shook his head. "Well . . . anyway, Germany will now turn its anger and guns away from us and we shall have time to work on our own problems." He looked at Natasha Ivanovna and smiled. "And we will hope that Germany loses the war and keeps nothing of what she took."

"It is what she deserves," Natasha answered coldly.

Trotsky gave her a wry smile. "We will have you write something about it, Comrade Gavrilova."

"I would be glad to."

"But first you will write to the Russian people—a stirring proclamation of the Bolshevik fulfillment of peace."

"Yes, Commissar."

"And Comrade Vershinin, you will give speeches." He turned to Dmitri. "And you . . ."

Dmitri shrugged. "Yes, I know . . . I will keep looking for film."

Commissar Trotsky gave him a puzzled look while Natasha and Sergey laughed. Sergey thumped Dmitri on the back. "Dmitri Borisovitch is our filmmaker on the agitprop train."

"Ah, of course," Trotsky answered. "You're the one who brought pictures from the Winter Palace on the day of the revolution."

Dmitri brightened. "Yes. That was me."

"Well, with the three of you, we should have the entire country enlightened in no time."

"We'll do our best, Commissar," Sergey said, and Natasha noted the commitment in his voice.

A courier came to the door, stopping abruptly when he saw Trotsky. "Commissar Trotsky, Chairman Lenin wishes to speak with you."

"Yes, I'll be right there." He turned back to the three. "It's late. You should be off to your homes. Go. Go on, now. Get some sleep. We need you bright and healthy."

"Yes, Commissar," Natasha said. She was grateful for his command because it meant she wouldn't have to stay and listen to any more of Sergey's diatribe about the war treaty. As Trotsky was leaving the room, she slipped the blue book into the pocket of her coat. She said good-bye to Dmitri and Sergey, and headed for the streetcar. She too was upset by the unfolding events in the country, but those worries occupied only a little corner of her head. She put her hand on the book in her pocket and took a deep breath of cold night air. The weeks were flying by and soon it would be April. Normally the thought of the approaching spring made her smile, but all it did now was bring a wash of anxiety.

She heard the sound of the approaching streetcar and ran to catch it.

◆　◆　◆

It was late when Natasha arrived home. The house was still and cold. She grabbed one of her mother's currant rolls and crept up the stairs to her bedroom. She had removed her coat and slipped the blue book into its hiding place when a soft tap came to her door. Natasha jumped. "Yes?" she said softly.

"May I speak with you?" came her mother's voice.

Natasha opened the door. "Yes, of course."

Her mother entered the room. She carried a package. "This came for you today in the post."

Natasha's heart started beating so fast she had to place her hands on her chest to calm it. "I've never received a package."

Her mother held it out to her. "I'm sure it's from Agnes Lindlof. It doesn't have her name, but it is from Ekaterinburg and that town is in Siberia."

Natasha took the package. "Oh, Mother. It means she's alive."

They were speaking in hushed voices, but Svetlana moved her daughter away from the door. "Your father is asleep, but still, we must be very quiet." She tucked a strand of Natasha's hair behind her ear. "No loud weeping."

Natasha grinned through tears. She sat on her bed and patted the coverlet for her mother to join her. She ran her hand along the brown felt wrapping tied with cord. She removed the large address card from under the cording, and frowned. "This isn't Agnes's handwriting." She looked again at the box. "Would you bring me my scissors, please . . . out of my sewing basket." Her mother went to retrieve them and Natasha worked to keep up her spirits.

"It has to be from her," her mother said, returning with the scissors.

Natasha nodded and cut the string that attached the address card to the package. She studied it again before handing it to her mother. She cut the knot of the main cord and slipped the binding off the felt. Her hands were trembling as she removed the covering. When she saw the birch-bark box with the carving of the squirrel, the tears came freely.

"It *is* from her." She took the lid carefully from the box and saw the letter sitting inside with her name beautifully penned on the cover. "Oh, my dear, dear friend." She wiped her eyes on her sleeve, took out the letter, and opened it. She steadied her voice and read.

Dearest Natasha,
    I and the others are well.

Natasha looked up quickly. "The others? They must all be together then!"

Her mother put her hands over her heart. "That is a miracle, isn't it?"

Natasha continued reading.

We are working for the people and it is good.

"I'm sure the Bolshevik censors liked that," Svetlana commented. "Your friend is very smart."

Natasha ran her fingers over the squirrel carving. "Yes, she is."

You have always been a Treasure to me, dear friend. I remember whenever I was sad or Down, you would always say, "Poor Makar. The Pinecones always fall on the head of poor Makar."

Natasha paused, staring at the letter. "I never said that." She read on.

Or, you would tell me a riddle to cheer me up, like this one: I'm weightless, but you can see me. Put me in a bucket and I'll make it lighter.

Please write to me, and if you would, please return the box filled with good things.

Your friend,
Agnes

"That's all?" Svetlana asked, disappointment coloring her voice. "She has the chance to write a letter and that's all she writes?"

Natasha smiled. "This isn't a letter. It's a clue."

"A clue about what?"

Natasha picked up the box. "About the treasure and how to get it back to them."

Her mother stared at her. "How did you figure that out already?"

"Agnes and I have been doing this since we were girls." She handed her mother the letter. "See how she capitalized 'Treasure' in 'You have always been a Treasure to me'?" She ran her hand over the box. "She knew we wouldn't be able to just put the bundles inside, because the guards would find them straightaway."

"'Down' is capitalized also," her mother said.

Natasha turned the box over, mumbling to herself. "'The Pinecones always fall on poor Makar.'"

"And what of the riddle?" Svetlana asked. "'I'm weightless, but you can see me. Put me in a bucket and I'll make it lighter.'"

"That's an easy one," Natasha said, looking up. "The answer is a hole."

Her mother read it again silently. "Of course! A hole. But what does that have to do with the box or the treasure?"

Natasha stood and paced. "A hole . . . a place where animals hide . . . an empty space." She stopped and turned the box over again, running her fingers over the image of the pinecone. "Poor Makar. The Pinecones always fall on his head.'" Natasha applied a slight pressure on the pinecone on the bottom of the box and felt a small movement along the edge. She took a breath, then slid the panel to the side, exposing the hiding place. Another letter was nestled inside.

Her mother sat with her mouth opened. "How did you do that?"

Natasha took out the letter, handed her mother the box, and sat back onto the bed. "Years of practice."

"Svetlana!" Natasha's father's voice came down the hallway.

Svetlana Karlovna stood. "Oh, dear!" She gave the box back to Natasha. "We'll talk tomorrow when he's gone to the university." She kissed her daughter on the top of her head. "You are a genius!"

"Svetlana!"

She moved quickly to the door and opened it. "I'm coming, Ivan Alexseyevitch!" She turned back to Natasha. "When you first told me about these riddles and helping the Lindlofs, I thought it was foolishness."

Natasha nodded. "And now?"

"I think there's a very good chance of helping them." She went out the door, and Natasha heard her footsteps padding down the hallway.

Natasha lit fire to two pieces of wood in the stove, put on her night-gown and socks, and slipped into bed. As she nibbled on the roll, she read the letter from her friend. The *real* letter.

My dear Natasha,

If you are reading this you have figured out the clues in the first letter. I have no doubt you have accomplished this.

I have been praying that you have found your way to the money we had hidden to aid us in getting to Finland. If not, there are three hiding places: the Rostral Column, the Griffin on the north of the Bank Bridge, and the statue of Peace and Abundance in the Summer Garden by the old Summer Palace. There you will find money, gold coins, and some silver rings hidden in bundles.

Once you have found the bundles, open one and take out half the money for use in sending back the box, for purchasing the things for inside the box, and for your own use. We insist on this.

You are to place a couple of two-ruble notes on top of the goods you send. This will ensure that the box is checked and handled by the assistant commandant of the camp. I am not mad in suggesting this. God has sent Andre Andreyevitch Orleansky to be the assistant commandant. He was the man who escaped from the war with Bruno and Arel, and he is willing to help us. I know you don't believe in such things, dear one, but to us it is a miracle.

Except for Mother, Father, and Linda Alise, we are all here at camp 206, three or four miles outside Ekaterinburg. I cannot write of my loneliness for Mother and Father, or for you. If I do, I will begin to cry and ruin my paper. Paper is nearly impossible to come by—even though there are trees all around us.

We eat mostly gruel or soup made with cabbage and potatoes, and sometimes a bit of fish. But we always have bread and it is enough. I long for fruit. Some in the camp have bad teeth and scurvy from lack of fruit. Perhaps you could send us some dried apple slices? We will have to give some to the guards, but that's just the way of things. Alexandria had an extra sweater and coat when she arrived at camp, but she gave them away. One woman only had an old blanket to wrap herself in, so we are better off than most, but Alexandria could use some warm socks and I could use a pair of gloves.

Our brothers are with us, which is another miracle, and we see them once in awhile. They are holding up. Remember how they used to pester us? I am sad because the room on the paper is running out and there is so much I want to tell you.

Send the box to me at the camp number and the name of the town. Also write, "Culture and Education Section." They handle the post.

My heart longs to see you and the Griboyedov canal, and the great Neva River. My heart tells me my parents are safe and that is comforting. If you hear from them, please let them know where we are. We have such gratitude for what you are doing for us.

I love you, dear friend.

Agnes.

Natasha read her friend's words over and over again until the stove grew cold and the candle spluttered out. As she curled beneath her covers, she folded the letter and put it carefully under her pillow, making sure of its placement many times as she drifted off to sleep. In her dreams, she saw a ragged woman wearing a blanket for a coat, a squirrel jumping from the lid of a birch-bark box, and a quiet pine forest where Prince Vladimir walked. She walked in the forest too and calmness enfolded her.

Hold on, dear Agnes. Your treasure is coming.

NOTES

1. **The Treaty of Brest-Litovsk** brought about an end to the war between Russia and Germany. The terms of the treaty were harsh for Russia, but Lenin accepted them so that the Bolsheviks could concentrate on their country's tenuous condition in the aftermath of the revolution.

CHAPTER THIRTY-FOUR

SIBERIA

April 3, 1918

"Alexandria, look! You can see through the windows," Agnes whispered.

"That's what windows are for," Alexandria answered groggily. She curled herself into a tighter ball on the thin mattress and clutched her blanket closer. "It's dark. You can't see anything."

"Dawn is coming. Besides, I can always see the thick frost on the windows even in the middle of the night."

"Shut up, will you?" someone growled. "They'll be waking us soon enough."

Just then the banging on the pipes began, and all the women groaned. "What did I tell you?" The woman sat up. Her short dark hair was smashed down on one side, and her eyes were puffy from sleeping hard. She glared at Agnes. "Next time you wake me up early, I'm throwing you out into the snow."

No one paid any attention. They put on coats and boots, and focused on the pattern of the day. Some went to the drying room for the dry socks, some went to get the bread ration, and some shambled off to the latrine. Alexandria walked over and put her hand on the high window. "No frost," she said. She looked over at Agnes. "You're right. No frost."

They smiled at each other, and Agnes knew that her sister was feeling kindred feelings. Winter's harsh grip was letting go. In a month there would be warm sun, and meadows filled with flowers, and perhaps fresh fruit. Her thoughts drifted back to the first time she ate peaches. They had been sent to her father from a count who was very impressed with a gold necklace made for his countess. Agnes remembered the exquisite workmanship of the necklace, and though the payment was substantial and the peaches were delicious, she figured neither gave sufficient homage to her father's abilities. The count should have lavished him with honor and a room full of rubles.

Agnes looked down at her shabby coat tied with a rope. She had been so young.

Time and experience had a way of teaching what was truly valuable.

"I'm going to wash my face," Alexandria said, and Agnes turned to follow.

◆　　◆　　◆

Little Mother hurried the gang through the morning routine, anxious that they not be late for the morning's turnout. After two weeks of not being chosen for the mill rotation, they were headed there today, and with the temperatures above freezing, the gang was restless to step out through the gate and into the illusion of freedom.

Most of the men's gangs worked at the mill every day so Agnes had high hopes that she and Alexandria would see their brothers.

The whistle blew and the women pushed their way to the outside. It was still extremely cold in the pale morning light and the prisoners' breath exhaled in white puffs. The tool wagon was at the head of the line, followed by three guardsmen on horseback; then the men came bumping into place, settling ranks with five men in each line. The women followed suit at the back of the procession.

The officer of the watch was yelling something at those counting the prisoners and Agnes used the opportunity to speak with her sister. "Did you see them?"

Alexandria shook her head. "There was too much confusion."

Agnes put her gloved hands in her armpits and stamped her feet. "They just have to be at the mill today."

A guard walked up and hit her in the upper arm with the butt of his rifle. Agnes yelped. "No talking, and hands behind you."

Agnes obeyed and the guard moved away.

The captain of the watch was speaking the daily sermon and a hush fell over the prisoners. "You will keep strict column order on the line of march. You will not straggle or bunch up. You will not change places from one rank of five to another. You will not talk or look around to either side, and you will keep your arms behind you. A step to the right or left will be considered an attempt at escape, and the escort will open fire without warning. First rank, forward march!"

The tool wagon led out and the guards and prisoners followed. As Agnes passed under the fortress portico, her heart lifted. *Somehow we'll get through this.* She didn't turn her head, but glanced out the corner of her eye at Alexandria. Their neighbors in Petrograd had seen Alexandria as the weak and pampered Lindlof girl—always attending parties and the theater; always with the prettiest frocks. Oh, if they could see her now—never complaining or whining about her circumstance, never expecting more, and working harder than many of the country women in the gang. A swelling of emotion nearly made Agnes reach out for her sister, but she caught herself and continued the rest of the way concentrating on the frozen, rutted track and her prayers.

Within a short time of reaching the mill and being assigned to their work details, they found their brothers. The men were put to work sawing logs into planks and the women to bagging sawdust, and although the sawdust made Agnes's nose and face itch, it was a perfect means for getting close enough to the saws to whisper questions as the men finished one saw cut and reset the saw for the next swipe. Agnes and Alexandria made sure to position themselves near Johannes and Arel's saw. When there was a lull, they moved in with their shovel and burlap bag to scoop up the sawdust.

"Where are Oskar and Erland?" Agnes asked at the first pause.

Neither group stopped moving or working.

"They're chopping today," Johannes answered.

Agnes's face lit up. "Erland's chopping? Is he feeling that much better?"

Johannes did not look at her. "No. He's not better, but he needs Oskar to look out for him." This admission came at a cost, and Agnes stared at Johannes's stricken face. The screech of the saw blade against the log stopped conversation and made the women step back.

"What do you mean?" Agnes asked when the next pause came.

"Oskar's strong. He does his work and Erland's work as well . . . so the guards leave them alone."

"I see." Agnes lifted a scoop of sawdust to the bag, but only half made it inside.

"He's not doing well then," Alexandria said.

Johannes shook his head as the saw bit into the log.

Alexandria was doing the shoveling now. "Why doesn't Andre Andreyevitch put him back in the infirmary?"

"He's tried. Erland won't go."

Anger washed Alexandria's face. "What do you mean he won't go? You force him to go."

Johannes's face became even more anguished. "I can't, Alexandria. He won't leave our sides."

The saw cut again, but the sisters didn't move back. They stood resolutely, trying to absorb in a moment what their brothers had known for weeks. They were going to lose Erland.

"Give him a blessing," Alexandria insisted as she followed her brothers to the stack of timber.

"We have," Arel said gently as he and Johannes hefted a log.

"Wasn't he promised he'd get better?"

"No," Johannes said. "The blessing talked about how much God loved him and the peace of the gospel."

The log was fit into the chute and Arel turned on the power.

Alexandria started weeping. Agnes dropped the bag and wrapped her sister in her arms. Agnes knew they all felt the knife pain of sorrow, but for Alexandria it was worse. She and Erland were closest in age and shared a special bond. It was Alexandria who understood his swing in temperament, and while the other siblings were often annoyed with Erland, she was always calm and forgiving of his antics.

A commotion arose outside. The large mill doors were open and Agnes watched as several guards ran past. When the gang boss, Golubev, went past the door, Arel turned off the saw, and he and Johannes ran for the entrance.

Agnes followed, dragging Alexandria with her.

"What's happened?" Alexandria whispered, fear evident in her voice.

Agnes knew. Something told her that the nightmare they'd just learned about was coming true. Her mind was numb and her legs wooden as she made her way over what seemed like miles to the door of the mill. When they stepped outside, Alexandria broke free of her grip.

There was news being passed about by the workers outside, and Agnes caught words like "hurt," "killed," "collapsed."

"What's happened?" Alexandria cried out again. "Are they talking about Erland?"

"I don't know," Agnes said, unwilling to let the feelings of her heart pass her lips.

The guards were trying to restore order, but they were caught up in the drama and their efforts were halfhearted. They did manage to keep the curious prisoners in a contained area, but when Arel and Johannes saw Oskar emerge from the forest carrying Erland in his arms, their grief propelled them forward.

"Stop!" a guard yelled, but the brothers did not obey. "Stop, or I'll shoot!" The guard raised his rifle.

"No!" Agnes yelled, running to the guard's side. "No! No, don't shoot!"

The guard fired, but the bullet missed.

"Comrades! Stop!" Agnes screamed in panic.

Her brothers stopped at the sound of her voice, and Arel fell onto his knees. The guard moved forward to apprehend them.

"They were just concerned for their comrades," Agnes called after him.

Alexandria came to her side. "This isn't happening."

Agnes took her hand.

Oskar was close enough now that Agnes could see his face filled with loss. He had set his jaw against the flood of emotion, but his body trembled with grief. He walked past his brothers as the guard yanked Arel roughly to his feet. They shared a look of sorrow. Agnes and Alexandria stood silently, wiping tears away and swallowing cries of anguish.

"Bring him to the mill office!" a voice behind them barked, and they turned to see Andre Andreyevitch motioning Oskar to the office. "You two, help." He shoved Agnes and Alexandria forward. "And you"—he pointed at the guard—"bring those prisoners in here."

There was confusion and scuffling as they maneuvered themselves into the office. Oskar sat down near the stove with his back to the wall, cradling Erland in his arms. Johannes and Arel were shoved through the door, the guard following after.

"Leave them!" Andre Andreyevitch commanded. "Send someone for the wagon, and then stand guard outside."

The guard nodded and went out. As soon as the door was shut, the siblings gathered around Oskar and Erland.

"He's not dead. He's not dead," Oskar kept repeating.

Agnes knelt beside them and took Erland's skeletal hand. "No, he's not dead."

The others knelt around as Andre Andreyevitch stood in front of the door. Alexandria removed Erland's prison cap and gently brushed back his sparse hair.

"He said he was just going to sit down for a minute," Oskar blurted out. "Just sit down for a minute."

"Oskar, it's all right," Johannes said.

"There was a stump under this big pine, and . . . and I didn't worry about it."

"Oskar . . ."

"I thought good . . . good, he'll get some rest. You know how tired he's been lately." Tears streamed down Oskar's face. "And the guards didn't care because I do the work of three anyway. They always get their quota. I looked over at him once and he was just sitting there and . . . and then five minutes later the gang boss yells and I look over and he's . . . he's lying on the ground. Just slumped over like a broken doll."

Johannes gripped Oskar's shoulder. "Oskar, stop. There was nothing you could have done."

Oskar looked up at his brother and Agnes could see his eyes begging for exoneration. "We told him he had to eat," Oskar said. "We told him."

Alexandria collapsed into weeping.

"Dear Father," Arel prayed, "please, bring us your peace. Please bring peace to Oskar and to Alexandria." Tears filled his voice, but the words pierced through to every heart. "Bless Erland . . . dear Erland. And, if it is Thy will, take him home to Thee. We love him and know that he will find rest with Thee . . . that his sorrows will be at an end."

As Arel was speaking these words, Agnes opened her eyes and looked at Erland. His body went slack in Oskar's arms and his face relaxed. Oskar moaned and wrapped his big arms around his brother's shrunken frame. Agnes felt a tangible peace surround them, as warm and encompassing as the heat from the stove.

A knock came to the door.

"You two, step back!" Andre Andreyevitch snapped at Johannes and Arel. "Women, dry your tears."

Agnes knew the assistant commandant was doing what was necessary to maintain the ruse and keep them all safe, but she could see what it was costing him. He knew their hearts were wounded with the death of their brother and though he may have wanted to give them time to grieve, he could not.

Andre Andreyevitch opened the door and the first guard of the compound stepped inside. "Commandant, the wagon for the sick prisoner is at the front."

Andre Andreyevitch stood straighter. "The prisoner has died." He pointed at the brothers. "The three of you carry the man to the wagon."

Oskar would not relinquish Erland's body, so Arel and Johannes helped him to stand, then followed him numbly outside.

"And get a blanket to wrap around him," Andre Andreyevitch told the guard.

"But why? He's dead."

"Just do as you're told."

"And the prisoners?"

Andre Andreyevitch swallowed. "They will each receive two days in the cell."

"Only two days? Such disobedience requires five days at least."

"Are you questioning my command?"

"No, sir."

"Then follow my orders."

The guard scowled, but left the office without another word.

He pointed at Agnes and Alexandria. "And you two get back to work."

The two stumbled forward in a daze. They came out into the yard to find several prisoners milling about as if unsure what to do. Andre Andreyevitch set things to right quickly.

"All of you, back to work! Gang bosses, get your people working!"

The order was followed immediately.

The sisters stood staring at the wagon as it pulled away until the Little Mother barked at them to get back to work.

Andre Andreyevitch came up behind the two as they made their way to the mill yard. He spoke in a low whisper. "My heart is aching for you, but there's nothing I can do. You understand, don't you?"

Agnes and Alexandria nodded.

"I actually came to the mill today to give you a message." He waited as they passed by a guard. Just before they reached the large doors of the mill, he spoke. "Agnes, you will find your name on the listing for the post. A certain box has arrived."

Agnes gasped and turned to look at him, but the assistant commandant was already walking away, barking harsh orders at any derelict prisoner.

◆ ◆ ◆

Agnes stood in the assistant commandant's office. It was late and "lights out" would be issued at any moment. She did not know exactly what time it was as none of the prisoners had clocks or watches. Time was kept by the ruling power.

Andre Andreyevitch slid open the bottom of the birch-bark box and three cloth bundles and a letter fell out onto the desk.

Agnes was stunned. The plan had worked! Her emotions were too mangled to feel the complete joy of the moment, but she did know that this money could save the rest of them.

Andre Andreyevitch pushed the bundles across the table to her. She picked up the letter and pressed it to her heart, then slid one bundle into each of her boots. The smallest of the bundles she pushed back to the assistant commandant. He shook his head.

"We insist," Agnes answered. "If you were caught helping us, you would be shot. Take it, please. My friend Natasha has used some of the money to buy the goods and pay for the post, but I'm sure there is enough left to help you out of most difficulties."

"Miss Lindlof . . ."

"Please. I know you would help us for nothing, but we won't allow it."

Andre Andreyevitch smiled. "Behind that angel face is a firm determination."

"Yes. Now, put it away quickly before a wood sprite comes in and steals it."

The assistant commandant took the bundle and hid it under some papers in the side drawer of his desk. He then took off the lid of the box and began to rummage through it.

The office door opened and the commandant of the camp came into the room. Agnes's heart crashed against her ribs as she stared in horror at the bottom of the box still in its open position.

"Good evening, Commandant," Andre Andreyevitch said with formal correctness, smoothly sliding the bottom of the box back into its proper place. "May I help you?"

The weasel-eyed leader came close to Agnes, stripping the head scarf from her head and running his hand across the back of her neck. "Such a shame we make them cut their hair. Bet yours was luscious wasn't it, hey? What do you say to that?"

"Yes, Commandant."

He chuckled. "Yes, of course . . . luscious. What is your name?"

"Prisoner 146377, Commandant."

He swore. "Not that. Your name."

"Agnes Irene, sir."

"Agnes Irene? What kind of name is that?"

Andre Andreyevitch broke in. "Is there something you needed, sir?"

The commandant turned to glare at him. "Yes, there is something! I just don't come in here unless I have a reason." He pointed at Agnes. "What is she doing in here so late at night? Were you planning something naughty with the little Matryoshka doll, Lieutenant?"

Agnes saw color come into Andre Andreyevitch's face and anger snap into his eyes. "No, sir," he said sternly. "Prisoner 146377 had a parcel which contained some questionable items."

The commandant displayed comic disappointment. "That's all?"

"Yes, sir."

The signal was sounded for "lights out" and the commandant gave Andre Andreyevitch a malicious grin. "Oh, now see . . . you may have to keep her all night anyway." He walked over to peruse the contents of the box. He took out Natasha's letter, the ruble notes, the socks and gloves, a can of tobacco, a bag of dried apple slices, chocolate bars, three tins of salmon, a small icon of Jesus, and a jar of caviar.

"Hey, hey, what's this?" he said, tossing the jar of caviar into the air. "A prisoner can't have caviar! What do we think . . . we're in the middle of a bourgeois dining room?" He put the jar in his pocket. "That would never do. The members of your gang would tear you apart for that. And this?" He picked up the tin of tobacco. "Disgusting. Women don't smoke. Surely you don't smoke . . . a beauty like you?" He glanced at Agnes and shook his head. "No, of course not." He put the tobacco in his pocket along with one of the chocolate bars and a tin of salmon. He picked up the icon of Jesus. "Throw that in the trash. No need for that." He handed it to Andre Andreyevitch. He looked at Agnes and smiled. "And those ruble notes will go into your account."

"I have an account?"

"Of course, comrade. We keep all your money safe for you for when you leave here. If you leave here." He took her head scarf out of his pocket and dangled it in front of her face. He glanced back at the assistant commandant. "Don't wear this one out, Lieutenant. She looks like a white lily from the hothouse."

Agnes grabbed the scarf from his hand, and he laughed at the embarrassment in her face.

"Oh, how I miss the frothy women of the tsarist regime. The Bolsheviks have turned all the women into such equals that they've begun to look like men." He rubbed his hand across her cheek. "Not this one though . . . not this one. Little Matryoshka doll."

Agnes pulled her head back, but the commandant grabbed her hair, leaning in and nuzzling her neck.

Andre Andreyevitch stood abruptly. "The reason you came in, Commandant?"

The commandant chuckled and stepped back without releasing Agnes's hair. He ran his fingers over her lips as he spoke. "I'm cutting the bread ration. You will inform the kitchen." He turned to Andre Andreyevitch, who nodded. "You'd better tell this morsel to inform her package sender about what is and isn't allowed." He took the jar of caviar from his pocket, kissed it, and walked from the room.

Agnes stood looking at the floor.

"I'm sorry," Andre Andreyevitch said softly. His voice was mellow and tender, and Agnes nodded.

"May I go now?"

"Yes." He handed her all the remaining goods—even the icon of Jesus—and she wrapped the treasures in her scarf. She kept the icon in her hand.

"Do you have a hiding place for the bundles of treasure?"

"Yes," Agnes answered. "We've been planning."

"Good." He brought out the second tin of salmon from behind his back and walked near to give it to her. "You can't actually have this tin, so I would suggest you give it to the guard outside the door. He's a good person to have on your side. Tell him I said to escort you back to your dormitory."

"Yes, sir." She turned to go, and then hesitated. "Thank you for your help today." She watched remorse cross his face.

"I wish I didn't have to put Arel and Johannes in the cell, but . . ."

"No, we understand. We do. Your authority would be questioned if you didn't punish them. They will be all right, Andre Andreyevitch."

The assistant commandant shook his head. "Where does your strength come from, Agnes Lindlof? Does it come from your faith?"

Agnes looked at the image of Jesus in her hand. "Yes."

"How? In all this madness, with all this sorrow—how can you still believe?"

She looked up. "I hear His voice."

Andre Andreyevitch's eyes narrowed.

"Not like a mad person, Commandant, but as a stillness . . . a voice in my head that whispers peace and compassion."

"Compassion?"

"Yes. Christ suffered greatly, so He understands my heartaches and my pain."

"And they aren't just your own thoughts?"

Pain washed her face and tears fell. "No. My thoughts are of loss and anger and revenge." She wiped her tears. "The Bolsheviks hope to silence God."

Andre Andreyevitch nodded.

Agnes's eyes held sorrow. "The Bolsheviks are fools." She turned and walked from the room.

NOTES

1. The marching orders given by the captain were taken from the book *One Day in the Life of Ivan Denisovich* by Aleksandr Solzhenitsyn. Solzhenitsyn spent eight years in a Soviet labor camp from 1945 to 1953.

CHAPTER THIRTY-FIVE

PETROGRAD
April 13, 1918

Dmitri Borisovitch had collected twenty canisters of film, and Natasha Ivanovna watched him as he strutted around the loading platform at the train station looking as though Lenin had personally patted him on the back. He spoke to her at length about his amazing procurement, then hurried off to snap at the baggage handlers and instruct them on how to place the film in the boxcar.

"He's going to pass out from exertion," Natasha said offhandedly.

"He does seem overanxious," her mother answered.

They had been standing together on the platform watching the bustle and saying little. Natasha was grateful. So many thoughts and feelings were bumping around inside her that she found speech difficult. Even when Sergey Antonovich had come to her, talking with excitement about the journey, she had been reserved. He'd finally tired of her short answers and gone off to find Professor Prozorov.

"I don't want to go, Mother."

"I know."

"I want to be here to receive Agnes's letters."

"Of course, but I promise that if letters come, I will keep them safe for you."

"Thank you." Natasha looked over at Dmitri Borisovitch as he bossed around one of the baggage handlers. She sighed. "Do you think the box reached them in good order?"

Her mother took her hand. "Natasha, you mustn't worry about things over which you have no control."

Natasha nodded.

"You did everything that was asked of you."

"I did."

"Then leave it in the hands of God."

Natasha found it interesting that she no longer felt that coil of resentment snake up her spine when her mother spoke of God, or when she saw a ragged babushka crossing herself when she passed a church. She still did not know if God existed, but over the months, her vehement declarations about Him had faded in certainty.

Natasha watched as her trunk was loaded. "I guess there's no turning back."

"Turning back?" her father barked as he came to stand beside them. "Why would you be thinking about that? I'd give my best suit to be going on this journey."

Natasha forced enthusiasm into her voice. "Of course, I'm honored to be going. I've just never been away from you two for so long a time."

"Nonsense," her father scoffed. "You're a grown woman. Besides, you'll have Sergey Antonovich to look after you." He handed her a newspaper. "Here, I bought you *Pravda* to read on the train."

"Thank you."

The train whistle blew and a few moments later Professor Prozorov came up to them, shaking hands with Natasha's father and giving her an unctuous smile. "Fifteen minutes to boarding. Do you have everything?"

"Yes."

He looked away from her to her father. "We have a printing press on the train, Professor Gavrilov. Did your daughter tell you that?"

"No, she didn't."

"Well, I'm surprised. It will mean that her written words will be going out to thousands of ignorant peasants."

Natasha was standing close enough to her mother to feel her body tense in anger.

"And we have moving picture cameras and film, and an entire boxcar for the visual artist who will be doing the posters. No greater way to use their talent than to serve the state."

"It is thrilling, indeed," Natasha's father said with a more subdued enthusiasm. "The ideals of the Soviets spreading across this vast country —thrilling."

Professor Prozorov sobered. "Yes, Professor, exactly right . . . well put."

"And you will be sure to keep watch over my daughter?"

Professor Prozorov looked puzzled. "Why, yes. Yes, of course." He glanced over at the train. "Now, if you'll excuse me, I have to check on the final details."

Professor Gavrilov's next words halted his departure. "I'll come with you, if you don't mind. I'd like to see that printing press."

"Why, yes, Professor Gavrilov, I'd be glad to show you." Professor Prozorov turned back to Natasha. "Be sure you're punctual. You know Russian trains—always right on time."

"Yes, Professor," Natasha said flatly.

The two men moved off, and Svetlana Karlovna blew out a breath of air. "Ignorant peasants? How dare he say something like that?"

"I've told you, he's not a nice person," Natasha stated. "I'm sorry for what he said. People from the city always think they're better than the country folk."

"And intellectuals think they have the answer to everything."

Natasha smiled. "I promise not to be haughty during my time with Uncle Petya and Auntie Anna."

"My sister is brilliant, and even though my brother-in-law is *just* a farmer, he is one of the wisest men I know," Svetlana declared.

Natasha took her mother's hands. "Yes, it's true. I love them dearly and my cousin Irena Petrovna . . . I can't wait to see them."

Her mother nodded. "How fortunate that Novgorod was the first stop of the propaganda train. But it is sad that you have only three days to spend with them."

Natasha found it funny that her mother never called it the agitprop train or the Red Train, but always the propaganda train. She smiled at the dear woman and found her eyes filled with longing. "Mama, are you all right?"

"Oh, I just miss home—the magical little wooden house in Sel'tso Saterno." She shook her head. "It's silly to dream, but I wish I were going with you."

"I wish that too," Natasha said. "I've never traveled to see Auntie Anna and Uncle Petya on my own."

"Yes, you were eighteen the last time we were all there together."

"So long ago. Will I even know my cousin?"

Svetlana Karlovna smiled. "I think you will find her little changed. Irena Petrovna is still the same simple girl you played with years ago."

"Will she ever leave her home?"

"No, I'm sure she won't. Her childlike innocence would not understand much of the wider world."

The train whistle blew a loud blast and the women jumped.

"Oh my goodness!" Natasha said. "Does this mean I have to get on board?"

"I think so," her mother answered, a note of reluctance in her voice. "Now, Uncle Petya will be at the train station in Novgorod to pick you up."

"Yes, I know."

"It's only four miles out to Sel'tso Saterno, so you can spend the evenings and mornings with your family, then work for the Bolsheviks during the day."

Natasha laughed and hugged her mother. "Yes, dear one, I know. We've had it all worked out for weeks."

Her mother wiped her tears away. "Yes, I'm just being silly."

Natasha turned toward the train, then hesitated. "Thank you, Mama, for all you've done to help me—for getting the money to Agnes, and . . ."

Sergey Antonovich and her father showed up at that moment, and the rest of her sentiment went unsaid. The look in her mother's eyes told her she understood.

Sergey took Natasha's arm. "Natasha Ivanovna, we need to get onto the train!"

"Yes, of course." She hugged her mother and father.

"We're very proud of you," her father said in a raised voice.

The whistle blew again and the train began to move. Professor Prozorov stood in one of the doorways motioning for them to hurry. "Come on! Come on, Sergey Antonovich! What are you thinking?"

Sergey pulled Natasha away from her parents. "Good-bye Professor . . . Svetlana Karlovna. I promise to watch out for her."

"You are the pride of Russia!" Professor Gavrilov shouted after them.

Sergey waved his cap as they ran. "All power to the Soviets!"

They scrambled onto the train just as it began to pick up speed. Natasha turned in the doorway for one last look. Her mother put her hand on her heart then held it up in a final wave.

Sergey Antonovich gave Natasha an exuberant hug. "I feel as though our life begins this day, Natasha Ivanovna!"

She nodded, but she wasn't thinking about her life; instead she was thinking of a life imprisoned in a work camp on the other side of the Ural Mountains—a precious life that she wondered if she'd ever see again.

♦ ♦ ♦

The sun was setting in crimson streaks when the train pulled into the station at Novgorod. Dark clouds, still heavy with winter, rolled over the countryside, and the wind shook the budding branches of the trees. Natasha was unconcerned with the threatening weather; she felt as though she was coming home.

The strong smell of moist dirt and pine trees unlocked her mind to memories of summers spent in Sel'tso Saterno: working in the garden, wandering the forest trails, and pretending to be a magical empress in her aunt and uncle's enchanting wooden house. It had been the house of her grandparents, and when they died, it had passed down to Aunt Anna. Natasha knew the house would have gone to her mother had she not married a city professor and gone to live in St. Petersburg.

Natasha understood the sadness in her mother's eyes over abandoning such a place, for she well remembered the first time she saw the cottage winking at her through the leaves of the trees. To her four-year-old eyes it seemed like a giant baker had decorated a splendid cake and then misplaced it in the middle of the forest. Wood, carved in lacy swirls and eyelets, hung on every roofline and surrounded every window. The carved panels around the doors were done in flowers, leaves, and birds in flight, and all of the intricate scrollwork was painted in vivid tones of turquoise, rose, and yellow. Over the years, the colors had faded from their former splendor, but Natasha felt it only added to the cottage's charm.

Shimmering into her thoughts came Agnes, pressing a strawberry to her mouth and reaching out her hand. Natasha reached for her, but she disappeared within a stand of birch trees.

Movement startled Natasha awake and brought her gaze to the window of the train. Sergey stood to gather his notebook bag from the luggage rack. He smiled at her. "I thought you had plans to stay in Novgorod for a few days."

"Oh!" She stood abruptly. "I was dreaming."

"I could tell."

"Where are Dmitri Borisovitch and Nicholai Lvovitch?"

Sergey chuckled. "Gone, minutes ago."

She glanced back out the window. "But they're not letting anyone off yet."

"Shortly," Sergey answered, bringing her satchel from the rack. He pulled her close and kissed her. "Are you so anxious to abandon me for your country relatives?"

"Yes. No. I mean . . . I'm not abandoning you. I haven't seen my family for six years. I'm excited to see them."

"Of course, I understand."

The train whistle blew, cutting off Natasha's need for a response, but as Sergey took her arm, she wondered if he did indeed understand.

They stepped off the train into a crowd of curious townsfolk, and Natasha wondered what they thought of the agitprop train with its metal face studded with red flags, and the overly eager students pouring out of the train to shove pamphlets at them and call them "Comrade." Novgorod was close enough to Petrograd for the events of the revolution and the Bolshevik ideology to have reached them, but Natasha knew that distance was only a small part of the barrier over which the Bolsheviks were climbing.

"What does your uncle look like?" Sergey asked, scanning the crowd.

"Jolly."

"Jolly?"

"He's always smiling." She chuckled and Sergey gave her a disgruntled look. "He's a short, stocky man."

"That's half the men here," Sergey said without judgment.

"He has, or did have anyway, a close-cropped, brown beard and mustache."

A man, woman, and girl rushed at them from the side. "Natasha Ivanovna?"

Natasha turned at the sound of her name and her face brightened. "Auntie! Uncle! Irena!" She ran into their arms. "I never thought you'd all come to get me."

"We couldn't stay behind," Aunt Anna said, laughing.

"I had to come," Irena said, patting Natasha's face. "Look at you. So beautiful."

Natasha took her cousin's hands and kissed her cheeks.

"You're tall," Irena said. "You're as tall as Papa, and much taller than me and Mama."

"And you're as pretty as an angel," Natasha replied.

Irena's eyes widened. "Well, some angels are pretty." She patted Natasha's face again. "Did your friend come with you? She was a very pretty angel."

"No, not this time. Do you remember her? That was a long time ago."

"I do remember her. She was like sunshine."

Pain wrapped a band around Natasha's chest. "Come," she said to change the subject. "I want you to meet someone." She turned and Sergey stepped forward. "This is my friend, Sergey Antonovich Vershinin."

Irena stared and Aunt Anna curtsied. Uncle Petya took his hand. "We're very happy to meet you. Anna's sister, Svetlana Karlovna, has written much about you."

"Oh, yes?" Sergey answered. "None of my secrets, I hope."

Uncle Petya laughed. "Just how fond you are of our little Natasha Ivanovna."

"Well, that is no secret."

Natasha could tell her cousin was mesmerized by Sergey's voice and face, unlike her aunt, who was now giving the handsome young man a good country once-over.

"Sergey Antonovich!" Dmitri called from a distance.

Sergey looked over, and Dmitri motioned that he should come join their group. He was handing out pamphlets as Nicholai Lvovitch helped set up a small platform in the center of where a crowd had gathered.

Sergey turned to Natasha's family. "Excuse me. I guess it's time for me to make a speech. Are you staying?"

"Oh, no, not tonight," Uncle Petya said. "We want to get home before full dark and the storm, and our old farm horse walks like she's going backward. But one of the nights I pick up Natasha from her work here, I'll stay to listen."

Sergey shook his hand. "Fair enough." He kissed Natasha on the forehead. "I'll see you tomorrow." He lifted his cap to Aunt Anna and bowed to Irena.

They were silent for a moment after he'd gone, then Irena sighed and said, "Is he really a Bolshevik?"

Natasha put her hands over her mouth to cover her laughter. "Oh, my dear cousin, I have missed you." She looked lovingly at her aunt and uncle. "Let's be on our way. I can't wait to be inside the magical cottage."

Irena smiled broadly. "And you will be sleeping in my room with me."

"Of course," Natasha said, placing an arm around her cousin's waist.

"Your bags?" Uncle Petya asked.

Natasha held up her satchel. "I have everything I need in here."

"Young people," Aunt Anna said as they walked from the platform, "traveling about the country with little more than the clothes on their backs."

"Well, at least she's not wearing red," Irena said.

"What?" Natasha spluttered.

Her parents tried to shush her, but Irena went on innocently. "We thought you might come all dressed in red with a picture of Lenin in your pocket."

Natasha laughed again, and after a time, her family joined her.

◆　◆　◆

Natasha lay in the dark of Irena's bedroom listening to her cousin's soft snores and the patter of rain on the roof. Her cousin had prayed at her icon station, climbed into bed, and talked and talked before falling asleep in the middle of a sentence.

Natasha was tired, but her mind kept tying and untying events and questions. On the train she had read from Talmage's book, and now her mind brought up images of the lost ten tribes, feelings about the man Jesus, and questions about the existence of God. Thrown in for good measure, Prince Vladimir tromped about, leading a fairy-tale white cow through the forest.

"That's enough now," she'd finally whispered, giving her senses over to the soothing sound of rain and the smell of pine logs burning in the stove. She drifted out of consciousness to the pleasant vision of Agnes painting the scrollwork around the windows of the little cottage.

CHAPTER THIRTY-SIX

Siberia

April 15, 1918

"What do you mean, you're building a fence in Ekaterinburg?" Agnes asked as she dumped the kitchen garbage into the pit.

Arel put his hand on her arm. "Stop. Listen to me. Andre Andreyevitch could get me only a few minutes to talk to you, so please listen." Agnes nodded. "For the past three days, we've taken boards from the mill to build a tall fence around a house in Ekaterinburg—the Ipatiev house."

"Who lives in the house?"

"No one. The owner was told to get out."

"What? How do you know that?"

"The guards talk, Agnes. Do you think we don't hear? Besides, Andre Andreyevitch said he's heard the Bolsheviks are going to imprison someone very important there. That's why the fence is so tall."

"But you don't know who?"

Arel's eyes took on a haunted expression. "No, but can't you guess?"

Agnes stared at him, the pain in her stomach increasing. "The tsar?"

"I think the tsar and his whole family."

Agnes felt a wave of nausea pass through her. "They don't deserve such treatment—especially not the children. And with the tsarevitch so ill . . ." Anger and tears filled her voice. "Why can't the Bolsheviks just leave them alone?"

Arel looked around anxiously. "Agnes, keep your voice down."

She pressed her lips together and nodded. "I'm sorry, Arel. I just can't stop thinking of the pictures . . . the pictures of Olga and Tatyana in their nurse's uniforms, helping the wounded soldiers, of Anastasia with her mischievous smile, or pale little Alexei in his sailor's uniform."

"Perhaps I shouldn't have told you."

"What have they done to deserve such treatment?"

"What have *we* done?" Arel said solemnly.

Agnes stopped ranting and tears jumped into her eyes. "Yes. What have *we* done?" she whispered. She held him close. "I'm sorry, Arel." She stepped back. "I haven't even asked how you and Johannes are doing after your time in the cell."

Arel took a quick breath. "We survived. It wasn't as bad as I'd heard, and Andre Andreyevitch snuck food to us."

"He puts himself in jeopardy for us far too often. What if others become suspicious?"

"Don't call on trouble, Agnes," Arel said gently. He hated to see her once round face gaunt and pale, her hands dirty, her eyes filled with fear and anguish. "Perhaps I shouldn't have told you about the tsar. We have enough sadness already."

"No, I'm glad you did. I'll tell Alexandria and together we can pray it isn't true."

He held her at arm's length and looked into her red-rimmed eyes. "How are you—you and Alexandria?"

"We've not been sick, and we work hard," she said flatly.

"Good little Socialist."

Her look turned hard. "Never. I will never support a government that forces people's will and silences God."

Arel looked at her in wonder. "No, of course not."

"In my heart and soul I know that every day the Bolsheviks move us further and further from Elder Lyman's vision."

Arel nodded. "I'm afraid that's true."

"But that is the Russia I want, Arel. I want the beautiful Russia of Elder Lyman's prayer—the Russia of destiny." She wiped the wetness off her cheeks with her coat sleeve. "And I'm afraid I won't live to see it."

"Please, don't say that. We will get out of here. Natasha Ivanovna has sent the money, so there's a much better chance." Agnes didn't respond. "Oh, please, Agnes, don't give up hope." He took her gently by the arms. "The money is well-hidden, right?"

"Yes."

"So, you see, there's a way to get us out."

"We have the money, Arel, but there's no one to bribe. We might be able to get one of us out somehow, but five of us? Impossible."

"What we need is a miracle."

She looked into his face. "Yes."

"And doesn't the Lindlof family believe in trusting God?"

Trust God. She was back in their home on the Griboyedov canal and looking into the dear face of her father. She nodded. "Yes, we believe in trusting God."

The assistant commandant came around the side of the building. "Comrade Lindlof, I need to return you to the dormitory."

"Yes, sir." Arel looked back to Agnes. "Perhaps your gang will be on the mill crew sometime soon, and we can talk again."

"Yes, I hope so."

He kissed her cheek then walked quickly to Andre Andreyevitch. He offered a furtive wave before the two disappeared around the side of the barrack.

Agnes looked down into the garbage pit, wondering if the silver writing set her father had crafted for the tsar was now in some rubbish heap, and if the grand duchesses had ever found the notes she and Bruno had secreted inside. She shook the odd image from her mind, picked up the garbage bucket, and returned to the kitchen.

CHAPTER THIRTY-SEVEN

SEL'TSO SATERNO

April 17, 1918

Irena Petrovna ran her hand over the smooth surface of the icon stand. She hesitated, crossing herself, and bowing as was her custom before moving to the silver plaque with the enameled inset of St. Basil. The eyes of the image looked beyond her, and over the years, Irena had come to believe that the tender saint was looking into heaven. *What did he see there?* she wondered.

Reverently she pressed her forehead to the plaque, whispering a prayer of gratitude and petition; gratitude for the chance to labor in this sacred edifice, and petition that the doctor would be able to heal Father Dobrosky of the lung sickness which was choking the old monk to death. He had been the shepherd of their country church through her life and her mother's life, and as she looked at the ornately carved icon screen located at the back of the nave, she thought of all the times she had watched the humble monk appear through the screen's central royal doors. Even as a little girl she loved to stand with her mother and the other common worshipers and peer into the holy sanctuary once the doors were open.

Irena cherished her small wooden church with its unadorned bronze cross above the one-domed cupola. Most of the other churches in the area were made of brick and limestone, and painted a dazzling white. Most had five cupolas and were filled with venerated symbols of worship. Irena closed her eyes and pictured the bright gold dome of the Holy Sophia Cathedral in Novgorod. Christ was represented by the central dome surrounded by the four smaller domes for Saints Matthew, Mark, Luke, and John.

She had been very young the first time she walked with her mother the three miles from their village of Sel'tso Saterno into Novgorod to see the prominent cathedral. The size and splendor of the edifice struck her with fear and amazement. She thought perhaps it was the only place where God would hear her prayers.

Irena opened her eyes and looked around at her chapel's simple embellishments. She knew better now; she knew that true worship found its place no matter the size or grandness of the church. Besides, the monks who sang in her country church had the voices of angels which lifted her spirit from the muddy world and nearer to the fire of heaven.

Irena brought her cloth to the surface of the plaque, rubbing left to right, top to bottom. Sound and sense retreated as she performed her task. She shivered with reverence, or was it cold? She looked to the high windows filling with the orange glow of morning. With the sun, the chill inside the small church would retreat slightly, and by the time young Father Keronin returned for the service, the worshipers would find the temperature comfortable.

Irena wondered why the Father had locked the beautiful carved doors this morning when he left. He had never done that before. She hadn't asked because it was not her place, and she trusted that he had his reasons. Her mind floated back to her work and her heart was happy. She felt no remorse at not being a university student like her cousin, Natasha, or a married lady like the other girls in the village. Her mother had always told her that God would find a place for her simple mind, and indeed He had.

Irena smiled as she worked. It was lovely seeing her cousin again after so many years, and even though Natasha spent her days in Novgorod working for the Bolsheviks, in the early morning and at night they were able to spend time together cooking, sewing, chopping wood, and chattering away like schoolgirls. Irena loved their walks in the evening gloaming when Natasha would talk about her life in Petrograd and her friend Agnes.

She remembered Agnes from the summer she had come with Natasha to visit. Agnes had blue eyes and a golden heart, and Irena could tell her cousin grieved for her friend, but still she would not send her prayers to God for help. At night when they'd lie in bed telling each other fairy tales and talking about faith, her cousin seemed unsure about God. It was hard for Irena to understand. She yawned and moved to clean the next icon. She had come early to the church, allowing Natasha to get a little extra sleep. Her cousin had been very tired the night before when she'd returned home from her day in Novgorod. Irena thought that the work Natasha was doing for the Bolsheviks did not make her happy. But what did she know? She was just a simple country girl who cared more about God than government.

Irena reached toward the wooden icon of St. Peter and heard a voice, muffled and indistinct, but without question, it was a voice. She held her body perfectly still, her hand frozen in its advance toward the holy relic. The voice came again. Her eyes flickered to the face of the apostle. She crossed herself and bowed.

"I hear you. I hear you," she whispered, her voice imbued with worship. "But I don't know your words."

Now several voices.

Irena stepped back, looking fearfully at the shadowed frescos that covered the walls: angels with wings and staffs, princes with swords, saints with books of judgment. Her heart pounded as faces stared and hands reached out. The passionate eyes of Boris and Gleb looked down at her. *Nothing to fear,* she told herself as she pressed her hand to her chest. *They are the noble sons of Prince Vladimir. They are martyrs and saints.* Yet she could focus only on the metal of their sharp swords.

"What are you trying to say to me?" she asked them. She had always believed the voices of saints and angels would be beautiful and soft, but these voices were loud and angry. She dropped her cloth and put her hands over her ears to shut out the din. "Have I done something wrong? Has pride crept into my offering? Are you here to punish me?"

There was pounding on the front doors. Irena turned quickly and fell over the uneven surface of the stone floor. She crawled forward yelling. "What? What is it you want? Go away!"

"Open this door!" a voice rasped.

Irena stood and ran to the door, pressing her hand against its aged surface. "No! No, I can't. It's not time to open the doors!"

"Stupid girl!" the voice barked. "Open the doors or we'll break them down!"

Irena willed strength into her slender arms. "Go away, you bad men!"

"Just open the doors!"

"I don't have the keys!" Irena yelled.

A knife blade shot through the narrow slit between the doors, piercing Irena's hand. She screamed and fell back. Father Keronin came running through the royal doors of the icon screen.

Why is he coming through there? Irena wondered in her fright and confusion. *It isn't time for the service, and his keys are still jangling on his belt.*

"What's happening here?" he called as a crash came against the doors. The priest looked over at Irena Petrovna, who was kneeling on the stone floor and cradling her hand. Large drops of blood dripped onto her white apron. The priest crossed himself and grabbed an ancient pike off the wall. The doors shook again as another crash sounded. One of the old hinges snapped and the door sagged inward. A yell went up from the men on the threshold and instantly another thrust was leveled against the wood. The doors gave way, hinges squealing, the splintered planks grating against the floor. Two young men kicked the remnants away and rushed into the room.

The priest blinked as light poured into the dimness of the sanctuary. He was afraid, but filled with wrath. He raised the pike. "How dare you break into the church!"

Four other men joined their companions.

The priest's eyes were adjusting to the light, and he glared at them. He was small in comparison to their brutish peasant stature, but his was the strength of indignation. "How dare you pollute this holy place. You are not from our village." He squinted at them. "I saw you in Novgorod. You came on the train with the Bolshevik artists."

A man with dark hair and full beard shoved his way to the front of the group. "Now stand back, Father. We don't wish you any harm."

Father Keronin stood his ground. "You've already done harm," he spat, glancing over at the bleeding girl.

The leader followed his look. He grunted when he saw the red stain on her apron. "Dmitri Borisovitch, take care of her."

"Yes, Professor." He detached himself from the group and moved toward the girl.

As he approached, Irena screamed and pushed herself to her feet, smearing blood on the stone floor. "Don't! Don't hurt me! You . . . I saw you. You broke down the door! You bring evil to this place."

"This place has been evil for a long time," the leader barked. "Now, stay still, comrade, and let Dmitri help you."

Irena ran.

Dmitri swore and ran after her.

"Leave her alone!" the priest yelled. "She's simple. She doesn't understand." He wavered, torn between helping the innocent girl or protecting the sanctuary.

Professor Prozorov took the opportunity to grab the priest's wrist and wrench the weapon away from him. The priest yelled out in fury and pain as he felt several bones crack under the pressure of the man's large hand.

"Nicholai Lvovitch, tie him up if he's going to be so much trouble."

The priest began to weep as another trespasser with thick straw-colored hair began tying his hands with rough rope. The priest gritted his teeth against the pain. "Why? Why are you doing this?"

The leader ignored him, turning his attention instead to the others in the gang. "Everything goes into the wagon—plaques and panels off the walls if they'll come down, icon stands, candle stands, priest's robes, and especially jeweled miters . . . if they have any in this backwoods church. Don't worry about the icon screen. Others will come to tear it down and paint over all the frescos on the walls."

The priest stared at the man as if a demon had suddenly sprung out of the stone floor. Dmitri returned with the girl, holding her roughly around the rib cage. She was nearly unconscious from shock and fear.

"Put her down!" Professor Prozorov growled. "Go help get things cleared out."

Dmitri obeyed, allowing the girl to fall to the floor. The professor knelt by the prone figure. He took off his glasses, put them into his pocket, and gently picked up the bleeding hand.

Irena gave a terrified cry and tried to slide her body away from him.

"Leave her alone!" the priest yelled. "She's an innocent."

"And she'll be dead if I don't get this bleeding stopped." He stripped off the girl's head covering and wrapped it tightly around her hand. When he had it tied off, he pulled her over against the wall, sitting her next to the priest, then stood to supervise as two of his men went by carrying a wooden panel painted with the image of St. Clement.

"You're stealing the holy artifacts?" Father Keronin asked, his voice taut with anguish and disbelief.

The leader turned to glare at him. "Why would I want to steal trash?"

Nicholai Lvovitch went past carrying an icon of Elijah and the mosaic of St. Basil.

"Stop!" Irena called. "Where are you taking them?" Her blue eyes stood out in her bloodless face.

Nicholai stopped to smirk at her. "To the cart, little comrade. I don't know where they'll end up after that—on the train and then to Petrograd, maybe. Our Bolshevik leaders will decide what to do with them." He moved on. "Maybe burn them."

"Burn them?" Father Keronin struggled against his bonds. "No! No! Those icons are hundreds of years old."

Professor Prozorov grunted. "Maybe they've outlived their usefulness."

The priest stared at him blankly. "Why? Why would you do that? Why would anyone do that?"

"To get out from under the yoke of superstition, to set the people's feet on a better path," Prozorov answered. "All religion does is exploit and befuddle the working class. That domination is over."

The priest, his face wet with tears, stared at the dark-haired man with realization. "You're not a peasant. You try to look like a peasant, but you're not."

The big man smiled. "There are no peasants or tsars or bourgeois merchants anymore." He paused before adding, "As there are no more professors. Now, we are all comrades."

Candlesticks, icons, jewel-encrusted plaques, and silver crosses were all carried unceremoniously from the sanctuary. The two believers could hear with wrenching clarity as each article was thrown into the wagon. Dmitri walked by with an exquisite silk embroidery of St. Sergii draped around his shoulders.

Irena pressed her wrapped hand to her eyes and cried. "Please, St. Sergii, come and stop them. Please, please, please." Her lips turned blue and she fainted.

"Irena Petrovna!" the priest called out, sliding over to her.

At that moment Natasha Ivanovna came running into the nave. "What's happening here?" she yelled, seeing only the chaos of men carrying out the holy artifacts.

"Ah, Natasha Ivanovna," Professor Prozorov said. "So glad you decided to join us."

"What are you doing? We never discussed destroying a church."

Professor Prozorov's face showed malevolence, but his voice was controlled. "We? Why would you think you'd be included in any of the Central Committee's grander plans?"

"Where is Sergey Antonovich?"

"He's in Novgorod, organizing things for our departure."

Nicholai Lvovitch came in carrying a jewel-encrusted miter. "Comrades! Look at this headdress! This must be the biggest prize of all!" He saw Natasha and his eyes went immediately to his boots. He hurried past her without speaking another word.

Irena called to her in a voice that was little more than a whisper. "Natasha, please . . . please make them stop."

Natasha spun around. "Irena?" She saw her cousin feebly attempting to push herself into a sitting position, and then she saw Irena's bloody hand. Natasha cried out and ran to her. "What happened?"

"These evil men stabbed her," the priest said through gritted teeth.

"What?" Natasha knelt by her side. "Who? Who did this?"

"She got in the way. It was an accident," Professor Prozorov said.

Natasha glared at him. "Is this what you call working for the people?" She held her cousin close. "Is this serving the people?"

One of the looters came quickly into the nave. "The alarm has been sounded in the town."

Professor Prozorov reached into the pocket of his coat and brought out papers. "I have the orders from our leaders, but just in case, take out your pistols."

"Yes, Professor." The man went to tell the others.

The professor looked down at the semiconscious girl. "Hopefully the doctor will be among the gathering crowd." He shook his head, disgusted by the weeping priest. "What is your place, priest? What are you good for? Nothing, but weeping and drinking and robbing the working man of his meager wares and wages. And for what? To chant words over him when he is born and words again when he is dead."

Father Keronin had managed to free his damaged hand and was gently patting Irena's face. He gave the professor a reproachful look. "You are a stupid man if you think destroying the church will destroy our faith."

Professor Prozorov pulled the other pike off the wall. "In a few days, a committee will come with workmen and soldiers and saw off the cross from the top of the dome. They will paint these walls and put in desks and chairs. This building will become a government office space, which means it will finally be serving a purpose."

Natasha was sickened by the professor's callous arrogance. She put an arm gently around her cousin's waist and carefully looped her uninjured arm around her neck. Irena whimpered. "Come on, dear one," Natasha encouraged as she lifted her. "I'll take you to your mother."

"Put her down," Professor Prozorov ordered.

Natasha stared at him. "I'm taking her to her parents."

"No, you're not." He advanced on her. "Put her down."

Natasha was trembling with rage as she placed Irena back onto the cold floor.

"Natasha?"

"Shhh, Irena . . . your mother and father will be here soon."

Professor Prozorov grabbed Natasha's arm and yelled to the others still in the room. "That's it! We're done here. Everybody out!"

Irena reached up and took Natasha's hand. "Don't . . . don't go with them. Stay with me. Stay here with Papa and Mama and me."

Natasha attempted to pull away from the professor. "I'm going to stay with her until her parents come."

"No, actually you're coming with the rest of us." He wrenched her away from her cousin's grasp and dragged her toward the entrance.

"Let me go!"

"Nicholai Lvovitch, take her to the wagon."

Natasha struggled to free herself. "You can't do this to me!"

Professor Prozorov gave her the unctuous smile that Natasha had grown to hate. "You? Who are you? You are not an individual, Comrade Gavrilova, but a servant of the state." He turned and walked from the room, stepping over the splintered doors, ready to face the angry townspeople.

As Nicholai Lvovitch pulled her from the church, Natasha saw that bewilderment and guns were keeping the simple farmers at bay. Her aunt and uncle were in the crowd, their eyes fixed on the gaping hole ripped into the holy sanctuary. Her aunt was weeping. When they saw Natasha, they brightened, and Natasha knew they expected Irena to follow. When she did not emerge, they ran to their niece.

"Where is she?" her uncle demanded.

Natasha was glad Professor Prozorov was busy with the main group of villagers and did not notice their interchange. She saw several guns pointed at her uncle's back. She kept her voice as still and steady as possible. "Irena is in the church. The priest is caring for her. Please stay calm."

Her aunt frowned at the threatening men. "I don't understand what's going on."

"I don't either, Auntie."

"Get to the wagon!" the professor snarled at Nicholai Lvovitch.

Nicholai started walking, but Natasha resisted. She turned to her family. "Wait until we've gone, then help Irena. She's been hurt."

Her uncle stood in front of Nicholai Lvovitch. "Irena's hurt? What do you mean, Natasha?"

Her aunt started to move to the church, but Natasha grabbed her hand. "No! Wait! She'll be all right. You just have to wait until we've gone."

"Are they taking you against your will?" her uncle asked. He gave Nicholai a threatening look.

Tears rolled down Natasha's face. "It's all right, Uncle. Don't worry. I'll be all right."

Her aunt walked alongside her. "Will you be coming back to the cottage?"

"No."

"But, your clothing . . ."

Natasha smiled at her aunt's sweet concern. "Keep them for Irena. Tell her it's a gift for her naming day."

Nicholai Lvovitch shoved her onto the buckboard of the wagon and climbed up. Dmitri sat on Natasha's other side, casting her a malevolent look. The rest of the men piled into the wagons. Professor Prozorov mounted his horse and brandished his official papers. He took up the reins and commanded the gang forward.

Natasha looked back to see her aunt and uncle disappearing into the church. The remaining townsmen looked fierce and many women cried as the gang moved off down the track. The wheels of the wagon bounced along the rutted road, and from the pile of sacred relics, the eyes of St. Basil looked up into the cloudless morning sky.

NOTES

1. Thousands of churches nationwide were destroyed or their contents confiscated during the years of Soviet rule. Many were turned into government offices, schools, or cultural centers. A conservative estimate indicates that in Moscow alone some 300 churches were destroyed or repurposed.

CHAPTER THIRTY-EIGHT

Melting snow ran in rivulets down the streets toward the Iset River, turning the packed earth into an oozing sludge that sucked at the workers' boots and stained the bottom of the women's skirts. Alexandria and Agnes knelt on the wooden floor, scrubbing off the mud of a dozen workmen.

Seven women from Gang 38 had been ordered to the large house in Ekaterinburg to scrub floors, wash walls, and paint the first-floor windows with white paint. The male prisoners had been finishing the tall fence that enclosed the house and bringing in crates and a few furniture pieces.

"If someone comes in again with muddy boots, I'm going to yell at them," Agnes said. She tossed her scrub brush into the bucket of murky water and pushed her hair away from her face with a wet hand.

Alexandria sighed and sat back on the floor. "I think they've finished bringing in crates."

"I hope so," Agnes mumbled, taking a piece of soft cloth and rubbing up the last traces of water from the beautiful wood. "We've cleaned this front entry six times!"

"I suppose it could be worse," Alexandria said. "We could be painting white over the windows or washing down the walls."

Agnes let out an exasperated grunt. "I'd rather be doing either of those things."

Alexandria stood and moved her bucket to the side. "Or, you could be back at the camp, gutting fish or emptying the latrine pots."

"You're right," Agnes said. "I didn't mean to complain." She picked up the bottle of floor polish and poured a pool of coffee-colored liquid onto the floor. The two sisters picked up clean rags and set to work rubbing the polish into the wood.

A guard came into the room and Agnes glared at him. "Careful of the floor." The young soldier skirted his way around the edge of the room and out the front door.

Alexandria giggled. "He looked like his mother just reprimanded him."

Agnes smiled. "Rightly so." She continued to polish in ever widening circles, proud of the shine she and Alexandria were restoring to the neglected floor.

The front door opened and Agnes was about to issue a reprimand, when two nuns crossed the threshold. They walked into the entryway carrying baskets and smearing mud from the bottom of their habits as they crossed the foyer. They stopped abruptly when they saw the women on their knees, polishing.

"Oh! Oh, dear!" the older nun chirped in a thin, reedy voice. "We're sorry."

They backed their way to the door and began taking off their shoes.

"Oh, sisters, please don't worry," Alexandria insisted. "We will just have to clean it again anyway."

The younger of the two nuns moved to her. "Are you sure? Because we don't mind going to the back entrance."

Alexandria looked up. "No, please, you're welcome here."

"Are you the house servants?"

"No, we're—"

Agnes interrupted. "We're here for today. We're helping prepare things." She and Alexandria stood.

The older nun joined them. "Yes, we've been sent from the monastery with eggs, milk, and cheese." Her head wobbled and a tear leaked from the corner of her eye. "It's very sad, isn't it?" the old nun mumbled. "If the Russian people knew of his circumstance, their hearts would break. Well, they have thrown him into the lion's den here, that's for sure. One wonders why God would allow it."

Agnes stood in rapt attention. The old nun's words seemed to confirm the rumors she'd heard for weeks. This wasn't to be the prison for a high-ranking baron or Provisional Government leader, but a dungeon for the Russian tsar himself—Tsar Nicholas and his family!

"Come along, Mother," the younger nun cajoled. "We need to get these things delivered." She took the woman's arm and tugged her gently toward a side door. Agnes knew her efforts were meant to stop the old nun's indiscreet babbling.

As the holy women left the room, Agnes turned excitedly to her sister. "Alexandria! Did you hear that?" The look on Alexandria's face halted the next words on Agnes's lips. She moved to her sister and took her hand. "What is it?"

"The tsar and tsarina will walk on these floors, Agnes. Tsarevitch Alexis and the grand duchesses will walk on these floors."

The tone in her voice conveyed not excitement, but dread, and as Agnes looked around the cold, cavernous room with its drab walls and cheerless light, the bleakness of the situation twisted her heart. Three hundred years of the Romanov dynasty reduced to a few rooms in an old house in Siberia.

Alexandria started as they heard the movement of horses and wagons arriving at the front of the house. Shouted orders were being given, but they could not make out the words. Together, they ran to the window. A corner of glass was free of paint and Agnes peered out, catching distorted forms of people and movement.

"What? What do you see?" Alexandria begged.

"I think there's a tall, blonde woman, and a portly soldier, and . . ." Agnes stepped back. "The Grand Duchess Marie."

"What?" Alexandria ran to the window and looked out. "It *is* her. It is! She is surrounded by guards, but I see her face clearly."

"What are you doing?"

Agnes and Alexandria turned quickly to find the Little Mother glaring at them.

"We . . . we couldn't help ourselves, Little Mother," Alexandria stammered. "It's the Grand Duchess Marie."

The Little Mother's face drained of color. She crossed herself then looked down at the floor. "Quickly! Get this floor done! We were supposed to be out of here before they arrived!" She grabbed the buckets of dirty water. "I must go and alert the others."

Agnes's heart was hammering in her chest as she raced to grab her polishing rag. She and Alexandria worked feverishly, attempting to make the floor presentable. They neither talked nor looked at one another, concentrating only on the task. They were together on the far side of the room when the door opened and a knot of people entered. They were speaking in muted tones, but Agnes could hear an older female voice making comments about the "dreary" house. Someone answered her in French, and a rumbling male voice spoke words of reassurance. A harsh voice commanded the group forward and the door slammed.

Agnes tried to melt into the shadows. Her heart pounded and she knew it was only a matter of time until she and Alexandria were discovered. She so wanted to look up to see if Tsar Nicholas II was actually standing in the room, but she held her curiosity in check and kept her eyes at a level where she saw only plain skirts, worn boots, and traveling satchels.

A pair of boots detached themselves from the group and walked toward them. Agnes gasped and took Alexandria's hand. The guards in this place were probably stern and uncompromising, and she braced herself for rough treatment. Instead a gentle voice spoke to them in perfect Russian.

"Ladies, would you please stand?"

Alexandria gripped her hand so tightly that Agnes whimpered. She glanced at her sister and noted the look of panic in her eyes. They stood, pressing close to each other, and hardly daring to look at the person who had addressed them. When they finally did, they found themselves staring into a face they'd seen many times on placards and posters at school, on coins, and in cinema newsreels—a handsome face with a large mustache and well-trimmed beard.

Alexandria curtsied and bowed her head, and Agnes quickly followed her example.

"Your Grace," Alexandria said in a voice that sounded too calm for the circumstance.

"Ah, please stand straight," Nicholas said kindly. "You no longer have to bow to me, or the once-royal family."

"But we wish to," Agnes replied. "You deserve our respect." She looked into the tsar's haggard face and saw the briefest of smiles.

Tsarina Alexandra remained aloof, but Grand Duchess Marie timidly approached. A full smile softened the tsar's face when Marie reached his side. "My daughter, Marie Pavlovna. And will you kindly tell me your names?" he asked.

Agnes had to swallow several times before croaking out, "Agnes Lindlof, and this is my sister Alexandria."

"We are pleased to meet you," Nicholas said. "Will you be staying here with us?"

"Oh . . . Oh, no, Your Grace," Agnes said. "We were only brought here for the day. We are prisoners from the work camp."

"Impossible," Marie whispered. She looked earnestly into the girls' faces. "What could you possibly have done to offend the Bolsheviks?" She took Alexandria's hand. "So young. You look to be my age."

Alexandria nodded, and Agnes saw tears well up in her eyes. "I'm seventeen, Duchess."

"Ah, seventeen." A tear slid down Marie's cheek. "And I am nineteen." She dropped Alexandria's hand, quickly brushing the tear away, and changing her mood. "And here is your sister." She held Agnes's hand for a moment. "My sisters and brother will be here soon."

"Why are they not with you?" Agnes asked. The duchess lowered her head, and Agnes could tell she was struggling for the words. "I'm sorry; it's not my business."

Marie looked at her father for permission and he nodded. "They had to stay back in Toblosk because our little Alexis is unwell."

"My heart aches for all your suffering," Alexandria said. "We pray for your family every day."

Nicholas looked at her steadfastly. "How kind. It is good to hope that some still think of us with fondness."

"What's the meaning of this?"

The booming voice filled the entryway and the two guards came to attention, while the prisoners adopted submissive demeanors. The big soldier stormed over to Tsar Nicholas and Marie. "Step back." He motioned for one of the guards to come forward. When the soldier was within arm's reach, the big man hit him across the face. "They are to speak to no one! Do you understand?"

"Yes, Commissar," the guard said, wiping blood from his lip.

The big man turned on the tsar. "I am Alexander Avadeyev and I have been assigned by the Central Soviet Committee to be commissar over this house for the remainder of your stay." He looked over at the tsarina and a malevolent smirk planted itself on his face. "Ah, Grigory Rasputin's toy." He took several steps toward her. "I'm sorry to have to report that something has gone wrong with the plumbing, Your Highness, so you won't have running water for a week or two." He motioned around the room. "Not quite the Winter Palace, but I'm afraid it will have to do. We lovingly call it the House of Special Purpose."

A shiver of fear ran down Agnes's spine and she slid onto her knees.

The commissar was immediately aware of her. "You. You two finish your work and get out."

"Yes, Commissar," Alexandria said, kneeling down and picking up her polishing cloth.

"The rest of you follow me," the commissar directed, laughing loudly as he moved toward the side door. "I will show you the other lavish rooms."

As the entourage followed, Grand Duchess Marie quickly bent down to address Agnes and Alexandria. "I will pray for you. Be brave."

Before they could respond, she was gone. They heard the echo of footsteps fading away down the hall and the commissar's hateful voice barking orders . . . then . . . quiet.

The silence in the room was oppressive, and Agnes spoke just to rid the room of the painful images. "Grand Duchess Marie was beautiful . . . even in plain clothes and an old coat . . . she was beautiful."

Alexandria's voice was husky with emotion. "I can't stand the thought of them being under the thumb of that loathsome man!" An anguished growl rose up from her chest. "I can't stand it!" She picked up the bottle of polish and threw it against the opposite wall. The glass shattered, staining the wall with brown splatters.

At that moment the Little Mother entered the room followed by the other five women of Gang 38. She stared at Alexandria, who still had her hand in the air. "Have you gone mad, girl?"

Alexandria burst into tears. "We saw them, Little Mother. We saw the tsar and tsarina. And . . . and the Grand Duchess Marie. They were here . . . in this room."

The women in the gang stood reverently as though they were in the nave of some great cathedral. The Little Mother crossed herself and moved over, squatting beside Alexandria who now had her face in her hands. The gang leader patted her back and looked over at Agnes.

"Did they look well?" she asked.

Agnes hesitated, and then shook her head. "No. You could tell their imprisonment has been harsh."

The Little Mother pressed her lips together. She stood, waving the women to the door. "The wagon is here to take us back to the camp. Come now."

Agnes helped Alexandria to stand. "But where are our guards?"

"Who knows?" the Little Mother said with a shrug. "The commissar has been making them run errands here and there all day."

"Wasn't he afraid we'd escape?"

"Where would we go? With the high fence, this house is just another fortress prison."

Agnes nodded as she and Alexandria followed the Little Mother toward the door. They stopped in the small cloakroom to retrieve their coats and boots, and Alexandria turned back to look into the entryway.

"Should I clean that?" she asked, staring at the wall.

The Little Mother stood by her side. As she buttoned her coat she appraised the mess. "No. Let the commissar do it."

"But won't we get into trouble?"

"What's he going to do—put us in a work camp?" The Little Mother turned to lead the women of Gang 38 to the wagon.

Agnes took a parting look at the damaged wall. A sick feeling dropped into the pit of her stomach. To her eyes, the stain of brown was not floor polish, but splatters of dried blood.

NOTES

1. In April 1918, Tsar Nicholas II and his family were imprisoned in the Siberian town of Ekaterinburg. They lived in the Ipatiev House under very restrictive conditions for only seventy-eight days.

CHAPTER THIRTY-NINE

Moscow

May 2, 1918

"Six days of fighting," the wagon driver was saying. "Six days, and there was snow and cold and I was driving my sleigh around, and boom! A cannonball exploding here—and rat-a-tat!—a machine gun there, and my poor horse with the devils shooting all around. Moscow didn't go the same way as Petrograd. You were organized—one day and poof!—the Bolsheviks are in power. The Junkers put up a fight here. Six days!" He crossed himself as they passed a church.

"Are you a Christian, then?" Sergey Antonovich asked.

"Menshevik, Christian, Bolshevik . . . I go along with anyone that will feed my horse." He laughed raucously and slapped his leg in glee.

Natasha wondered how the scrawny driver kept his horse on the right side of the street with all his hand gestures and turning around to see his passengers' reactions to his stories. The man's clothing was stained and decrepit, and his face coarse with stubble.

"One day I come around the corner of the Nikitskaya and rat-a-tat! Here's all this machine-gun fire. I pull my horse off to a side street and wait, but I watch these boys—little waifs—waiting by the side of a building. When the firing stops, they run across the street like it was a game. Rat-a-tat . . . rat-a-tat." The wagon driver shook his head. "Most didn't make it."

"How are things now?" Sergey Antonovich asked to get him onto another subject.

"Well, you know what they say, 'He who is fated to hang won't drown.'" The man chuckled at his own cleverness and Natasha politely joined him. Sergey scowled and Natasha knew he was offended by the comic Muscovite's flippant attitude. In fact, she'd noted that Sergey had been tense since their departure from Novgorod. He had not been happy with her explanation of the incident at the church in Sel'tso Saterno, and now he spent most of his time with Dmitri and Nicholai. She didn't care, as her thoughts were more often on home, and Agnes, and the words from the *Articles of Faith*.

After leaving Novgorod, and receiving a tongue-lashing from Professor Prozorov, she had snuck off by herself to read. When she'd opened the book, she was surprised by the words that met her eyes.

Chapter 23
Submission to Secular Authority
> Article 12—We believe in being subject to kings, presidents, rulers, and magistrates, in obeying, honoring, and sustaining the law.

She'd cried herself to sleep that night in worry for her cousin and in confusion over church and state. The priest's invective against the Bolsheviks echoed in her tangled thoughts: *"You are a stupid man if you think destroying the church will destroy our faith."*

"And you've come from Petrograd on that Red Train?" The wagon driver's words brought Natasha back to the present.

"Yes," Sergey answered. "We've actually been to the towns and villages in the countryside."

"So, where have you gone?"

Sergey proudly listed their travel. "We've been south to Yasnaya Polyana, southwest to Mozhaysk and Borodino, and northeast to Kastreeva and Vladimir."

"My, my, my! You have been busy," the driver said, sounding impressed. "And did you never go north?"

Sergey hesitated. "Yes . . . we did, of course. We went to Khatkova and Sergiev Posad."

They had come to a stop, and the driver turned in his seat to give Sergey a questioning look. "Sergiev Posad?" he said with amused interest. "And were you well received in Sergiev Posad?"

Natasha knew the man was goading them, being well aware that any attempt to spread the message of Socialism and atheism in Sergiev Posad would have been met with scorn.

"It was difficult," Sergey said tensely.

"You mean the monks from the St. Serguis Monastery did not come out with open arms to greet the Bolshevik faithful?"

"Be careful there, little man," Sergey warned.

The driver chuckled. "Just a joke, comrades. We must be able to laugh at ourselves. All I'm saying is that it will be difficult to get the monks to change their tune."

Sergey leaned toward the man, his voice cold and threatening. "And what will they do when the Bolsheviks close their gates and put them into prison?"

"Hmm." The driver clucked his tongue several times and his horse's ears flicked. "I suppose they will have to chant beautiful hymns to the rats."

"Don't mock us."

The driver laughed. "No, no, comrade! I understand your work. You are teaching the peasants about a better way of life."

Sergey shifted in his seat. "We are explaining the Soviet ideals."

"Ah, of course . . . the Soviet ideals: 'Peace, Land, and Bread.' 'All Power to the Soviets.' 'Everyone is equal.'" The man clucked again to his horse. "There's a good nag . . . just as good as the car that takes Lenin from here to there."

They crossed the bridge over the Moscow River and for the first time on their journey together the driver was quiet. When they reached the other side, he let out a sigh and crossed himself.

"Are you all right?" Natasha asked.

"It's the place where my friend died during the fighting. They found his body on the riverbank."

"I'm sorry," Natasha replied.

The driver waved his hand in the air in a dismissive gesture. "Be afraid to live, little beauty, but do not be afraid to die." They came to the east side of the Kremlin wall and suddenly the little man's jollity returned. "So, this is your first time in the great city and you want to see the sights. Well, here is one! Just look at that—one of the great walls of the Kremlin . . . hundreds of years old!" His tone became reverent. "Inside those walls beats the heart of Mother Russia."

Natasha felt a rush of emotion. "Can you take us to see the Cathedral of St. Basil the Blessed?"

The driver's head bobbed several times. "Yes, of course. The beautiful cathedral. The cupolas all swirled and brightly painted."

"And the Brotherhood Grave," Sergey interrupted. "That is the main thing we wish to see."

The driver slumped in his seat and flicked the lines over the rump of the horse. "Yes, comrade," he said with a sigh. "I can take you to see the graves. I was there with my friend's widow on the day the coffins were put in. I can tell you the whole story, but are you sure you wouldn't rather see Pushkin's statue, or go to a bar and drink vodka?"

◆　◆　◆

Their driver's name was Plekhanov, and after he had tied his horse to the post ring on the northeast side of the Kremlin, he guided them up the hill toward Red Square and the cathedral. Natasha had seen many churches in her lifetime, but this edifice was fantastical and mesmerizing. Photographs showed the shape, of course, but not the color, and her eyes and emotions could not take in the splendor.

"See, not one bit of damage," Plekhanov was saying. "Some reports went out that the cathedral had been flattened during the fighting." He shook his head. "Such nonsense. What a business. Boom! Crack! Fighting all around. Some damage to the Kremlin wall and one of the churches, but nothing of the sort of nonsense the papers were screaming."

Natasha turned to see what Sergey Antonovich thought of the magical structure, but he had his back to the church. He was staring instead at the base of the north Kremlin wall where, beneath a row of leafing linden trees, ran a fifty-yard long swath of earth.

"Is that the grave?" he asked.

Plekhanov turned. "Huh? The grave? Oh, yes, that's it."

Sergey began walking across the square, the two following.

"I'll tell you, it was cold the night we dug."

Sergey did not stop, but glanced back at the driver. "You helped dig the grave?"

"Yes. Yes, of course, for my friend who had died." He caught up to Sergey. "The ground was frozen, but there were hundreds of us digging. It was dark, but the Committee put torches up there on top the wall."

Sergey stopped at the edge of the dirt and looked down the length of the massive grave site. "How many are here?"

Plekhanov crossed himself. "Five hundred, comrade. Maybe a few more than five hundred."

Sergey's head drooped and he reached out toward Natasha.

She took his hand and stood close to him.

"Tell us," Sergey said in a choked whisper.

Plekhanov seemed momentarily at a loss for words. He took off his cap and rubbed his hand over his short hair. He hit the cap against the side of his leg several times, then brought it to rest over his heart. "You must understand, young ones, these are painful memories for me."

Sergey nodded. "Yes, Comrade Plekhanov, we do understand, but it is important for us to know."

Plekhanov cleared his throat. "Hmm. Yes, of course." He put on his cap and folded his arms across his chest. "I went early to escort Madame Dybenko to the square. That is my friend's widow. It was gloomy—sometimes snow—but hundreds of people were marching to the square. Many had red banners on poles. Snap! Snap! Snap! That's how they went in the stiff breeze." He rubbed a hand across his stubbly face. "We went to where the coffins were waiting. Just rough wood coffins with red stain brushed on. My friend Pasha Dybenko was a factory worker. There were many factory workers who died." Plekhanov stamped his feet as if they were cold. "Some of the coffins had names on the top lid, some of the lids were off with a father and mother weeping over a son." Sergey shook his head. "We found Pasha's coffin because I'd nailed his fur hat on the top. He was always proud of that hat." His voice cracked and Natasha reached over to touch his arm. "Big strong soldiers came and lifted the coffins onto their shoulders. Tears . . . tears were . . . streaming down their faces." Plekhanov took out his handkerchief and blew his nose. "We followed them into the square and there were thousands of people. I think a band was playing . . . yes, yes . . . there was a band playing, and the people were singing, and on the Kremlin wall"—he pointed—"all along there, they'd hung huge red banners that said things like 'Martyrs of the World Social Revolution' and 'Long Live the Brotherhood of Workers.' They had to lift the coffins over the hills of dirt we'd piled up from the digging. Up over the hills and down into the pit. One old babushka tried to jump in after her loved one. Others held her back, but she was kicking and scratching, howling like a wounded animal." Plekhanov crossed himself and fell silent.

"And there were no priests to say prayers?" Natasha asked gently.

Sergey frowned at her. "Of course not. The Russian people no longer need priests to pray them into heaven. We are building a kingdom on this earth far brighter than any heaven can offer."

Natasha stepped back. An emotion washed over her, and she was shaken when she realized it was not anger or sadness, but fear.

Plekhanov studied Sergey Antonovich warily. "It is true that all the churches were dark that day, comrade." He pointed across the square. "Even the blessed Iberian Chapel, which always has candles burning, was locked tight." He looked at Sergey straight on. "But I tell you, comrade, I said prayers for my friend, and they made me feel better . . . and I'm sure prayers were in the hearts of most of the Russian people that day. Their lips might have been singing the *Internationale,* but their hearts were praying for peace and understanding."

Sergey gave him a condescending look. "How sad." He turned away from them. "You two leave me alone now. I'll meet you back at the wagon."

As she moved across the square with Plekhanov, Natasha looked back to see Sergey walking the length of the grave site. She sighed and turned her gaze to the Cathedral of St. Basil the Blessed.

"You are not as Bolshevik as your friend," Plekhanov said, giving her a crooked smile.

"Why do you say that?"

"I see how you look at this church," he answered simply. "There is hope in your eyes for heavenly things."

"I don't believe in . . ." She could not finish the sentence. She looked up at the simple cross on the highest dome and started crying.

Plekhanov patted her back. "Ah, you may not believe, but you hope."

"Yes. Yes, I do hope. I want the people of this beautiful country to have joy and contentment."

"And is this why you ride around on the Red Train, because you think the Bolsheviks can bring joy and contentment?"

Natasha wiped her eyes on her sleeve and evaluated him. "Are you an anarchist?"

"Me?" he chuckled. "Heavens, no! I can't afford to be carted away. Who would feed my horse?"

"But you don't believe governments are any good."

"Oh, no, no, comrade. We must have governments. With governments we have stability . . . well, with good governments, anyway. The better the government, the better the stability."

"You don't believe the Soviet government will bring that stability?"

He gave her a sad smile. "I think our dear Mother Russia will suffer for many years."

Natasha nodded. "There is great wisdom in you for a common man."

Plekhanov tipped his hat to her. "Only one of the proletariat, comrade, and we actually do have some wisdom. In fact, it's the intellectuals who think they're the only ones who can think."

Natasha laughed and dried the last of her tears.

"So . . . what will you do?" Plekhanov asked.

"I have no choice. I must stay with the train."

"It will not be easy now that faith has planted a little seed in your heart."

Melancholy enveloped her. "I know." She looked up again to the brightly painted cathedral and the sadness retreated a step. She thought of Agnes saying her prayers, of the people silently praying at the Brotherhood funeral, of millions of her countrymen lifting their sorrows and dreams to God. How could a government silence those holy words, or keep a benevolent Heavenly Father from hearing?

She looked into the scruffy face of the wagon driver. "Will you pray for me, Comrade Plekhanov?"

He gave her a kind smile and nodded.

NOTES

1. Portions of Plekhanov's description of the events in Moscow were taken from John Reed's book *Ten Days That Shook the World.*

2. The Kremlin wall necropolis in Moscow emerged in November 1917, when pro-Bolshevik victims of the October Revolution were buried in mass graves on Red Square. Lenin's mausoleum, initially built of wood in 1924 and rebuilt in granite from 1929 through 1930, sits in the center of the gravesite. After the last mass burial was made in 1921, funerals on Red Square were reserved as the last honor for notable politicians, military leaders, cosmonauts, and scientists. John Reed is the only American buried there.

3. The route taken by the Red Train that Sergey and Natasha work on is fictional.

CHAPTER FORTY

MEDVENKA
May 17, 1918

Natasha Ivanovna was soothed by the gentle motion of the train. The sound and sensation allowed her to escape the reality of the street meetings and propaganda. She did her work for the proletariat dictatorship, but her writing had become mere repetition. Fourteen days earlier at the Kursky Station, Sergey Antonovich had had to drag her onto the train. She'd watched Moscow slide away into the afternoon gloaming, thinking of Comrade Plekhanov, and his friend Pasha—Pasha who'd given his life for the revolution, and whose favorite fur hat was now buried with him in the Brotherhood Grave.

Over the weeks, the wagon driver's words about government and faith mingled in her thinking along with edicts of communal living and ways to efficiently run a rural soviet, and, despite the fact that she worked hard to keep them at a distance, thoughts of home also edged their way into her mind. She wouldn't let these stay long because they always included images of Agnes and her family, of the celebration of the New Year when she and Agnes and Arel had danced together, and of police trucks driving off into a dark night.

Natasha sat straighter in her seat and stretched her legs. The blue book fell to the floor and she bent down to retrieve it. She was nearing the final chapter—article thirteen. She smiled to think of the day Mr. Lindlof had presented the book to her. Did he know then what the words would come to mean to her? She breathed deeply and looked out the window. She loved to watch the landscape roll by with its forests, streams, and charming villages: Chekhov, Tula, Orel. So many of the fairy tales from her childhood seemed to come to life in the country settings: enchanted cottages and balalaika players, country festivals and dancing bears, houses that walked about on chicken legs, and magical birch trees.

"Natasha Ivanovna?" Sergey's voice came unexpectedly into the train corridor.

She slid quietly off the seat and onto the floor, knowing she would be hidden from sight behind the canvas-covered printing press. She'd found the place of solitude not long after they'd left Moscow, and she now waited anxiously for the times when the press was dormant so she could hide away.

The door to the compartment was shoved open and she held her breath.

"Stupid girl," Sergey's disembodied voice mumbled, and Natasha felt a jab of pain in her stomach.

The door closed and she crawled back up onto the seat. *Stupid girl?* She chided herself for being surprised. As the train moved south, her enthusiasm for the work waned while Sergey's increased, and she knew it affected their relationship. They still talked, but she quickly lost interest in his rhetoric and he grew irritated with her complacency. And recently his kisses had become more ardent, but less caring. He neglected her for arguments and discussions with Dmitri and Nicholai, yet insisted she be by his side each time he gave a speech.

His speeches were passionate, and Natasha could see their impact reflected in the faces of the simple Russian peasants. For them, Sergey Antonovich embodied Russia's dynamic future where the Communist system would create prosperity, equality, and unity. Sergey was warm and persuasive, and many a village babushka came timidly to him at the end of a speech to touch the sleeve of his coat or pat his face.

The compartment door opened again, and she jumped. She looked over to see Nicholai Lvovitch staring at her.

"Natasha Ivanovna? Where have you been? We've been looking for you."

She stood. "Me? Oh . . . oh, I'm sorry, Nicholai Lvovitch. I must have fallen asleep." She put the book into her satchel and climbed up onto the seat. She edged her way around the printing press and Nicholai helped her. "Is something wrong?"

"Professor Prozorov has called a meeting."

She let out an exasperated breath of air. "Professor Prozorov is always calling a meeting."

Nicholai Lvovitch stopped in the corridor and turned to her, a look of genuine concern on his face. "Natasha Ivanovna, you must be very careful what you say."

"What do you mean, Nicholai?"

The big man swallowed and looked around. "Professor Prozorov does not like you."

"I've known that for a long time," she said seriously.

"Yes, but he has asked us all to watch you."

"What?"

"Shh . . . shh . . . keep your voice down."

"Watch me? Does he think I'm a spy or something?" she hissed.

"No, not a spy . . . of course not. But he doesn't trust you. You don't care about the revolution like you used to."

Natasha lowered her head. "I . . . I . . ." She stammered for words to refute the accusation.

Nicholai Lvovitch put his hand gently on her arm. "I understand, comrade. Your heart is at home and with your friend in Siberia."

She looked up into his broad face. "How do you know about my friend?"

He flushed with guilt. "Well, I . . . I found out from Sergey Antonovich. He explained it to me and Dmitri."

"Explained it?"

"He was upset for you . . . and . . . and so he told us." He turned and began walking down the corridor. "Come on now. No time for talking."

She started after him. "Nicholai!"

"No. I mean it. We must get to the meeting. You've caused enough trouble already."

"What do you mean by that?" She called for him to stop, but he lumbered along as though he didn't hear her.

A minute later they reached the dining car where the rest of the workers were already assembled. Nicholai dropped her at the side of Sergey Antonovich and went to stand in the shadows at the back of the room. She looked at him, wondering why such a slight misstatement would cause him such discomfort.

"Where were you?" Sergey asked.

She turned to him with an engaging smile. "You don't need to know all my secrets."

He gave her a questioning look, but before he could reply, Professor Prozorov arrived.

"Good. You're all here," he said, his eyes resting for a moment on Natasha. He looked up. "The conductor has informed me that just before we left Kursk, the stationmaster received a telegram that a contingent of the White Army may be in the area."

The tension in the room jumped and several of the workers called out invectives. Dmitri Borisovitch stood, his voice rising above the others. "So why did we leave Kursk? We would have been safer there!"

This sentiment was repeated and the din increased.

Professor Prozorov shouted them down. "Enough! Quiet! There is reason to believe the anarchists are closer to Voronezh, which is well east of here."

Natasha scanned the room and many of the workers looked riotous.

The professor spoke loudly. "Command decided that it would be better to send us on to Medvenka."

Dmitri clenched his fists. "Command decided? Decided from where . . . Moscow?"

Professor Prozorov stared him down. "That's enough, comrade. We all knew this calling came with risks. We talked about it in our meetings. We set plans. Have you forgotten?"

Dmitri grunted and sat down.

The professor continued. "We have taken the red flags from the engine so as not to draw undue attention, and our escort of Red soldiers are on alert. They are armed with rifles, and we have field guns. We also have pistols and ammunition for all the workers. Those will be distributed after the meeting."

The four female workers found each other's eyes, trying to make a display of courage. The artist Sedova turned her face to the professor. "But there is only forest between here and Medvenka. We will be without any hope of assistance for what, four hours?"

Professor Prozorov gave her that unctuous smile that Natasha hated. "Comrade Sedova, we are well prepared to defend ourselves. Let's not try to look over the mountain." With that he ended the meeting, ignoring questions and assigning Nicholai Lvovitch and several others to distribute the pistols and ammunition.

Natasha knew that any anger Sergey had felt toward her was swept away by the threat of attack, and she was willing to forgive his unkind slight. Perhaps he'd called her "stupid girl" out of frustration—everyone was on edge.

Sergey stood as soon as she did. He wrapped her in his arms and kissed the top of her head. "We'll get through this."

"Yes, of course," she replied.

He pulled her more tightly against him. "It's been difficult. I'm sorry."

She couldn't breathe. She stepped back and put her hands on his chest. "I understand, Sergey, I do. The revolution is the most important thing."

He covered her hands with his. "Yes. Yes, that's it." He was just about to kiss her when Nicholai Lvovitch came up. He held out a pistol to each of them.

"The women are getting together to be trained, Natasha Ivanovna. You must join them." He looked at Sergey. "And you are to join Dmitri and me for a drink of vodka."

◆　◆　◆

Natasha sat in her secret hiding place reading her book. "Article 13— We believe in being honest, true, chaste, benevolent, virtuous, and in doing good to all men . . ." Something flew past the compartment window and she looked up. Her heart thudded against her ribs and she strained to look toward the back of the train to see if the object had been something other than a bird. The tension on the train was palpable, and as soon as the women's training session had ended, she'd sought solitude.

As the hours passed and Medvenka drew closer, she grew hopeful that they would arrive without incident. It was foolish not to have considered the dangers of the trip, and surely her father had been aware that a train full of Bolshevik faithful would be a target for opposing factions. Of course, they were accustomed to the anarchists and saboteurs in Petrograd, sneaking about in the shadows for fear of the large numbers of Red Guards. Natasha shivered. Out here they were isolated and the White Army was strong. She yelped in fear when Sergey Antonovich pushed open the door and leaned against the door frame.

"Sorry, didn't mean to scare you. Nicholai Lvovitch told me I might find you here." He stepped into the room and locked the door. Natasha noted Sergey's voice. His speech was slurred and louder than normal, and she doubted that he'd shared only one drink with his friends.

Sergey walked to the printing press and frowned at her. "How do I get over there?"

"You have to climb across the seat."

"Ah." He made his way clumsily to the small rectangular piece of seat directly across from her. He sat down and composed himself. "You shouldn't go off by yourself, Natasha. Safety in numbers, you know."

Natasha nodded. "You're probably right. I just needed to think things through." A piece of red fabric flew past the window. "Did you see that?"

"Yes, of course. I think the engineer is throwing out the red flags. He doesn't want to be caught with them."

Natasha felt sick. She put her hand on the pistol sitting at her side. "I don't know if I could shoot someone."

"I'll protect you." Sergey leaned forward to take her hand. "What's this?" He picked up the blue book.

Natasha forced herself to remain calm. "It's just a book."

Sergey flipped through the pages. "Not just a book. It's in English." He stopped to read over a page. He looked slowly up at her. "It's a religious book."

"Actually the content is more philosophical."

He glowered at her. "Do you think I'm stupid?"

She could see the vodka fueling his anger. "No, of course not. I admire your brilliance."

He ignored her attempt at flattery. He flipped to another page and read silently, his lips pressed together in a hard line. "Is this what's been twisting your mind? Is this what's been turning you from our cause?"

"I haven't turned from—"

Sergey slammed the book against his hand. "Don't lie!"

She pressed herself back against the seat. "Sergey, be calm. Let's talk about this calmly."

His tone became menacing. "And here I admired your intellect. I admired all the words you wrote . . . and your beauty." He went down on his knees in front of her. "And all the time you were laughing at me behind my back. Laughing at everything I was passionate about." He grabbed the side of her neck and forced her mouth down to his.

She pushed him away. "Stop! Sergey, stop!"

He slid his hand to her throat and held the book up for her to see. "Do you think I'm going to let this come between us?"

She whimpered. "It's just a book . . . please . . . give it to me."

"Where did you get it? Who gave it to you?" Her silence angered him and he shook her. "Answer me!"

"Agnes's father."

His grip loosened and momentary doubt crossed his face. "What?"

"Mr. Lindlof."

Sergey swore and threw the book against the compartment door. "Will I never be rid of that hateful family?"

"What do you mean?"

His grip tightened again and he pulled her down onto her knees. "Who do you think sent in the report on them?"

Natasha saw smug triumph in his eyes. "No. Impossible."

His free hand slid around her back and he pressed her to him. "I knew how you cared for them, and how they were polluting your mind. I had no other choice."

Angry tears jumped into her eyes. She tried to hit him, but he pinned her arms. She struggled and screamed, but he was stronger, and he covered her screams with his mouth.

The compartment door was kicked open and Nicholai Lvovitch came stumbling in.

Natasha gasped for breath. "Help! Help me, Nicholai Lvovitch!"

Nicholai took out his pistol and aimed it at Sergey Antonovich. "Let her go!"

Sergey stood and pulled Natasha up by her hair. "Get out! This has nothing to do with you!"

"Leave it!" Nicholai roared. "The White Army is stopping the train!"

The squeal of brakes on the track affirmed his words. Fear printed itself onto Sergey's face. He made his way to the door, shoving Nicholai Lvovitch aside with a snarl. He ran down the corridor, wrenching the pistol from his pocket.

They could hear gunfire and men shouting. Nicholai Lvovitch nodded at her. "Come on, Natasha. I'll help you."

She grabbed the gun and shoved it into her satchel. She clambered across the seat and jumped down by his side. "What should we do?"

"We'll jump from the train before it stops and run for the woods. There's thick cover in the trees." Nicholai moved quickly down the corridor.

Natasha scooped her book off the floor and followed. "Dear Lord, watch over us," she prayed as she ran.

The train was only moving a few miles an hour, so when Nicholai reached the exit portal, he didn't hesitate. Natasha tamped down her fear and followed, stumbling and rolling into the tall grass and undergrowth. When she regained her bearings, she located Nicholai a few yards ahead of her. She heard the sounds of a major engagement happening on the other side of the train and thought perhaps she and Nicholai might have time to make it to the woods, but when she glanced back, she was horrified to see three mounted soldiers wheeling around the back side of the train, obviously intent on killing anyone attempting to escape. Someone shot at the riders from inside the train and the soldiers became focused on saving their own skins. They were unaware of the two figures disappearing into the dark shelter of the forest.

NOTES

1. **The White Army:** The anti-Bolshevik military forces typically formed from remnants of the former tsarist army. This fighting force was the nemesis of the Communists during Russia's civil war from 1917 to 1921.

CHAPTER FORTY-ONE

KURSK

May 23, 1918

"Get up!"

Natasha felt something hard kicking at her leg.

"Get up!" the voice came again insistent and harsh.

Natasha opened her eyes and saw the farm woman and her thin son staring at her.

"You have to get out of my barn!" the woman hissed. "The White Army is coming!"

Natasha sat up.

"If they find you here . . ." The woman threw Natasha her satchel. "They'll burn my place down!"

Nicholai Lvovitch was shoving his coat into his carry sack. He ran his hand over his newly acquired beard and jerked his head at her to get up. She quickly put on her boots and stood.

"Thank you for helping us," she said to the woman.

"Yes, yes. Now get going."

The thin boy held out a small piece of bread to her, his sunken eyes never leaving the morsel.

Natasha shook her head. "No, you eat it. I still have some of what you gave me last night."

The boy shoved the bread into his mouth and ran from the barn.

Natasha and the woman joined Nicholai at the barn's entrance. The woman pointed. "Take that trail into the woods. In a mile or so you'll come to a wagon track. Another three or four miles and you'll come to Kursk."

Nicholai nodded. "Thank you."

"You can catch the train there. Now, go!" She shoved them out into the early morning dimness.

Natasha followed Nicholai into the forest. She felt woozy from waking so abruptly and from lack of food, but she kept her pace. Over the past days she had learned to trust Nicholai Lvovitch's sense of direction and knowledge of the land, and she knew he was grateful for the money she had sewn in the hem of her skirt.

They had stopped at a small home one night, asking for food and a place to stay. The farmer was surly and unwelcoming until Natasha offered him a gold coin. Since then, the two escapees had relied on each other for survival.

They had heard from a family sympathetic with the Bolshevik struggle that most of the people from the Red Train had been taken captive and were locked up somewhere in Medvenka. She and Nicholai did not talk about the night of their escape, but kept their focus and energy on getting back to Petrograd; though Natasha found that focus could not keep away the bad dreams. The first night in the forest, as she lay curled under her coat, she'd dreamed of Sergey Antonovich's hand around her throat, and last night she'd walked with him by the Griboyedov canal. As they'd talked about the great ideals of Socialism, she'd watched as Red Guards sawed the crosses off the St. Nicholas Cathedral.

"Are you listening to me, Natasha Ivanovna?"

Nicholai's words brought her to the present. "I'm sorry. What did you say?"

He held a branch until she had moved past it. "We will probably be in Kursk by early evening. We should plan what to do."

"Eat supper," Natasha answered.

Nicholai chuckled. "Yes, I'd like that. Six days of walking and very few meals."

"I want meat pies and apples and cake."

"Stop, Natasha Ivanovna! I may start running and you could never keep up."

"Don't challenge me, Nicholai Lvovitch. My friend Agnes and I used to—" She stopped talking abruptly, checked her emotions, and walked on in silence.

After a time, Nicholai cleared his throat. "I . . . I'm sorry about your friend." Natasha nodded, and he continued, emotion washing his tired face. "And I'm sorry about the church and your cousin in Sel'tso Saterno." He began weeping. "I've been wrong about so many things." His sobs grew more intense and he bent over and put his hands on his knees.

Natasha moved to him and patted his back, knowing that years of fear and anguish were escaping with the sudden apology. "It's all right, Nicholai Lvovitch. Many have believed the lies. It all seemed like a grand cause, didn't it?"

He nodded and wiped his face on his sleeve. He took a deep breath of cool morning air and calmed his emotions.

Natasha held his large hands with her slender fingers. She waited until he looked into her eyes. "You saved my life, Nicholai Lvovitch. I can never repay you for that. That act will do much to wipe out other things in the heavenly books."

His eyes widened in surprise. "You believe in heaven?"

"'We believe all things, we hope all things, we have endured many things, and hope to be able to endure all things.'"

"Where is that from?"

She smiled to herself. "I think the Apostle Paul might have said it."

Nicholai Lvovitch was clearly taken aback. "I never took you for someone who read the Bible."

She gave him a wry smile. "No, I would suppose not." She began walking and Nicholai followed.

"Is the blue book you read a small, traveling Bible?"

"No, but it does have many spiritual things in it." She stepped over a log. "When we have time, I'll tell you about it." She walked faster. "But for now, let's get to Kursk and some warm food."

"And then the train home!" Nicholai Lvovitch said brightly, the last vestiges of sadness gone from his voice.

Natasha nodded, but did not reply. *Home.* She wanted to see her mother and eat her cooking. She wanted to sleep in her own bed and take a proper bath, but she did not want to go back to work for the Bolsheviks, she did not want to see the strangers living in the Lindlof home, and she did not want to be without her dearest friend. Agnes's angel face came unbidden into her mind and Natasha pressed her hand against her chest to ease the pain of loss. She looked at the blue sky and beautiful birch trees and walked on toward Kursk. With every step, words from the thirteenth article of faith whispered in her ear and offered comfort: *We have endured many things, and hope to be able to endure all things.*

CHAPTER FORTY-TWO

Moscow

June 2, 1918

"I have bread, Citizen Plekhanov! Bread!" Nicholai Lvovitch plunked down the satchel on the old man's table and took off his cap. "Bread, cheese, and a few figs."

The older man clapped Nicholai on the back. "Wonderful! I'm going to keep you to be my gatherer. What do you think, Natasha Ivanovna? Can I keep him through the winter?"

Natasha folded the newspaper she'd been reading and joined them at the table. "I don't think his aging parents would like it."

Plekhanov grinned. "Ah, yes . . . well, I probably could not keep him fed, anyway." He picked up one of the figs. "These look good. Quite a find!"

"It's nothing," Nicholai mumbled shyly.

"Nothing? Ha! Since most of the fruiterers have closed up shop, these are a treasure."

"Oh, and I brought this for the horse." Nicholai rummaged in his coat pocket and brought out an apple. "It's shriveled, but . . ."

Plekhanov took the apple, put his hand over his heart, and gave a little bow. "My old nag is grateful. I will go and give this to her. You two eat."

Natasha watched the old gentleman as he shuffled to the door. He put on his hat and gave the apple a little flip in the air before exiting.

"I'm glad you said we should come here, Natasha Ivanovna. He's a good man."

"Yes, he is. We need to leave tomorrow though. I've cabled my parents and they're expecting me."

"Of course." He handed her a slice of bread and some cheese. "I'm glad for the rest, but I take up a lot of space in this little hovel."

Natasha nodded. "We both have imposed long enough." She sat at the table to eat her food.

"I can't figure out this Plekhanov," Nicholai said with a chuckle. "Is he a Bolshevik, a counterrevolutionary, a Christian—"

"Or a crook?" Plekhanov said brightly as he walked into the room.

Nicholai's face reddened. "I'm sorry, friend. I wasn't making judgments."

"No, no, Nicholai Lvovitch. I'm glad I have you guessing. That's what I want to do with the Bolsheviks. I want to keep them confused as to who is this Comrade Plekhanov." He took off his cap and slapped his leg with it.

Natasha laughed. "Plekhanov the fox."

He winked. "I think soon we will all be hiding our true identities."

Natasha handed him a fig and nodded. "You are one of the wisest men I know."

Plekhanov threw back his head and laughed. "And this coming from the daughter of a university professor!"

"Study doesn't make you wise. My father has read much of the Bible, yet doesn't believe a word of it. You, on the other hand, have read many of Lenin's and Trotsky's writings and think they're misguided."

Plekhanov sat at the table. "Here is the problem, little fox cub, the world is a wicked place—a wicked and muddy place. Who is to find their way through? The government says 'go this way' and they force a man to be caring and share his crust of bread, but if the government isn't there with a big stick, the man will eat all the bread himself. It's just the way in this muddy world."

"That's what I've always thought," Nicholai Lvovitch stated. "So, if there is a God, why doesn't He tell us how to go?"

Plekhanov grew quiet. "Perhaps He tries, Nicholai, but we're not listening."

For a few minutes they ate in silence, then Natasha spoke. "Nicholai and I will be leaving tomorrow."

The old wagon driver's head bobbed up and down as he tore off a chunk of bread. "Yes, yes. I knew I couldn't keep you forever. I would, though. Oh, yes, I would."

"We must get back to our families."

Plekhanov shoved bread into his mouth. "I understand. But, what will you do there now, Natasha Ivanovna? What will you do in the grand red city of Petrograd? Will you go back to work for the Central Committee?"

Natasha glanced over at Nicholai Lvovitch then back to Plekhanov. She shook her head. "No. I can't do that. I can't write words I don't believe."

"Ah." Plekhanov ate his fig. "And your father? Will he allow that?"

Natasha gave the little man a wry grin. "I guess I will have to play the fox too, my dear friend. I will be a seamstress or a teacher or even a typist for my country, but I will not write the propaganda of the state."

Plekhanov grinned back at her. "Your heart will not allow it."

"No."

The horse whinnied out in back, and Plekhanov patted Natasha's hand. "And now my nag and I will take you both for one last tour of the great city before you leave, yes?"

"Yes, dear friend. We would like that."

CHAPTER FORTY-THREE

SIBERIA

July 17, 1918

Agnes discovered the assistant commandant kneeling by the kitchen garbage pit. He was retching and sobbing, and it frightened her. She was reluctant to approach, but she didn't want to go for help either. Finally compassion overtook her fear and she set down her garbage bucket and ran to him.

"Andre Andreyevitch," she said softly. "What is it? What can I do?"

The big man groaned and continued sobbing.

Agnes looked around and drew near him. "Is it one of my brothers?" He shook his head. "Please, stop. You're scaring me."

Andre Andreyevitch put his hands over his face. "Evil . . . a great evil is on this country. Our soldiers would never do it . . . never," he said, weeping. "Hungarian guards. The commandant sent them to the house . . . he sent them last night."

Agnes stepped back. "What are you talking about, Andre Andreyevitch?"

He moaned and rocked back and forth. "This darkness will never go away."

His words were madness, and her body went cold at the sound of them.

"Shh . . . shh, you're not making sense."

"Yurovsky didn't want the Russian soldiers," he choked, and Agnes thought he would retch again. "They'd never do it . . . they'd never kill innocent children." He let out a sound like a wounded animal. "So much darkness!"

The banging of pots and voices from the kitchen masked his cries, but Agnes knew it was only a matter of time before he was discovered. "Look, Andre Andreyevitch, it's morning. The sun is up."

He stood abruptly, wiping the sick from his mouth with the sleeve of his coat. "It will never be morning again."

Agnes was shocked by his visage. She had never seen a face so bereft of hope.

Andre Andreyevitch staggered out into the view of one of the towers and the guard was immediately alert. "Stand still!" the guard yelled, raising his rifle.

"I'm the assistant commandant, you ignorant dog! Stand down!"

The guard saluted and turned to look in another direction.

The encounter seemed to sober the assistant commandant. He took a ragged breath and pressed the heels of his hands against his swollen eyes. He stumbled back into the shadow of the building and Agnes kept him from falling. His arms dropped limply to his sides. "They've butchered the royal family." He turned his tortured face to look at Agnes, and new tears fell. "All of them . . . the tsar and tsarina . . . and the grand duchesses. Shot them . . . stabbed them with bayonets."

"Stop!" Agnes hissed. "Stop!" Her mind refused to understand his words.

But Andre Andreyevitch could not stop. The gruesome words fell from his mouth like vomit. "The new commissar of the house, Yurovsky—he shot the little tsarevitch in the head."

Agnes grabbed the front of his coat and shook him. "Stop it! Stop it!" she screamed. "You don't know what you're saying!"

"The Hungarian soldiers shot them! They've told us!"

Agnes shook him again, but her arms were going numb. "Don't. Don't," she whimpered.

"Olga tried to make the sign of the cross before she died," he said flatly. "But they killed her. Murdered them all. They threw their bodies down a mine shaft."

Agnes staggered back. "Not true." She saw splatters of brown polish on a wall, but now those splatters were blood—the blood of the tsar and his family. "Not true."

Andre Andreyevitch wept again. "It is true, little sparrow. God help us, it is true."

Agnes went down on her knees. She saw Grand Duchess Marie's beautiful round face and heard her words, *Be brave.* Then darkness and oblivion enveloped her.

NOTES

1. On the morning of July 16, 1918, the tsar's entire family was taken to the basement of the Ipatiev House and slaughtered by bullet and bayonet. The family doctor, Botkin, a lady-in-waiting, Anna Demidova, the cook, Kharitonof, and the footman, Trupp, also shared the Romanovs' fate. Word had been received that the White Russian Army was on its way to Ekaterinburg to free the royal family. The Bolshevik leadership feared that Tsar Nicholas, if released, would become a rallying point to all those who opposed Soviet rule. Thus, the order was given for him and his family to be executed.

CHAPTER FORTY-FOUR

Quiet. No voices. No banging of the pipes. No shouted orders. Agnes opened her eyes and looked to her familiar high window. It was white with light. She sat up. Something was wrong. Even though the summer extended the light from early morning until late at night, Agnes knew the time for roll call was long past.

Other women were also sitting up and reacting to the phenomenon, anxiously questioning the silence. The Little Mother crawled stiffly from her mattress and moved to the door. She paused with her hand on the doorknob. Alexandria pressed herself against Agnes's shoulder as the door opened. They heard the murmur of men's voices. As one, the women scrambled to their feet. They followed the Little Mother out the door and into the yard. No guards stood there with rifles. No guards on horseback. No guards on the towers. Women ventured into the yard from the other dormitories—huddled together like deer in a clearing.

The men's voices indicated movement toward the back of the headquarters building and the main gate. The women moved in that direction. No ordered lines. No lines of five. In a mass they ran toward the east wall of the fortress. When they reached the back of the building they were stopped by the sight of two hundred male prisoners staring out at the road and forest now framed by the wide-open gates.

Alexandria took Agnes's hand. "What does it mean?"

Agnes shook her head.

A young woman, who had come to the camp only a week earlier, walked out to the gaping maw.

"Don't!" someone yelled.

"It's a trap!" others added, their voices strained and strangled.

The girl hesitated then walked out. She kept walking, never slowing, never turning back.

The dam broke and, with a roar, the prisoners surged forward. Agnes and Alexandria clung to each other as the press of bodies moved them inexorably toward freedom.

Agnes tugged Alexandria back from the maelstrom. "We have to find our brothers!"

They turned from the crush and saw Johannes immediately. He, Oskar, and Arel were moving directly to them. Johannes grabbed their arms and pulled them toward the side of the headquarters building.

"We have to keep our heads," he stated hurriedly. "Go and gather your things. Secure the money and make sure you have an extra pair of socks. Strip your blankets and bring them."

"What's happened, Johannes?" Alexandria yelled.

"I don't know," Johannes admitted. "But we don't have time to talk about it now. God has blessed us with this opportunity to escape and we're not going to miss it." He hugged them both fervently, and then smiled. "And don't forget your boots." The sisters looked down at their stocking feet in wonder. Johannes pushed them. "Hurry! Go!" They ran toward their dormitory. "Meet us back here!" he called. He turned to his brothers. "Let's get our things." He started moving toward the men's side, but Arel did not follow. "Arel, come on!"

"I think we should look for Andre Andreyevitch."

Johannes stopped and frowned at him. "He's gone with the rest, Arel."

"Maybe," Arel said calmly. "But I still think we should look."

"Arel—"

"You and Oskar go gather our things and I'll search." He turned to move around the side of the building.

Oskar gave Johannes a crooked smile. "As I always say . . . never question one of Arel's inspirations."

They followed their brother. He was already up the steps of the headquarters building and to the door when they caught up with him. Arel didn't hesitate. He walked through the main office and down the hallway that led to the assistant commandant's office. They heard a knocking sound and pressed themselves against the wall. Arel reached to open the door.

"Arel, be careful!" Johannes hissed.

Arel stood to the side and pushed the door open. The knocking became more distinct. A body lay on the floor—a dark stain on the back of the military jacket and a pool of blood seeping from underneath the stunted frame. The brothers moved into the room.

"It's the commandant," Arel said as he moved near.

The knocking came again from behind the desk and the three men rushed to the source. Andre Andreyevitch lay curled in a ball—his right arm bloody, his left hand holding a pistol which he rapped feebly against the floor.

Arel knelt by him, laying a hand on his shoulder. "Andre Andreyevitch, we're here. We've come to help you."

The body shuddered. "I knew you'd find me."

As Johannes ran to gather their things, Arel and Oskar worked quickly to ready Andre Andreyevitch for leaving. Oskar stripped off the man's military jacket while Arel tore a Bolshevik banner from the wall and wrapped Andre's injured arm with strips of red. Oskar found a civilian suit in a trunk. They threw the jacket over Andre Andreyevitch's shoulders as they lifted him. As he struggled to support his own weight, he looked down at the figure on the floor.

"He tried to take my money."

Arel focused on the corpse and saw one of their bundles in the commandant's hand. The felt was ripped and gold coins and ruble notes lay just out of reach of the rigid fingers. Oskar knelt and scooped up the money.

Andre Andreyevitch took a ragged breath. "I should be dead. I guess he was so drunk he couldn't shoot straight. He hit me on the head with his pistol, but I got one shot off. I . . . I blacked out after that."

"Quiet," Arel instructed. "You've lost a lot of blood."

"Let's get out of here," Oskar said, placing Andre Andreyevitch's arm over his shoulder.

They stumbled past the commandant's body and out into the hallway. Just as they emerged, Agnes and Alexandria entered the front office.

Agnes gasped. "What's happened?"

"We'll explain later," Arel grunted, trying to keep the assistant commandant on his feet. "Let's go."

"Wait!" Agnes cried. "The box! I want the box!"

Andre Andreyevitch nodded weakly. "In the trunk . . . office."

Agnes ran.

"Agnes, we don't have time!" Arel yelled after her.

He and Oskar dragged Andre Andreyevitch outside where Johannes met them at the bottom of the steps. He had two carry sacks, and a string of sausages around his neck. Alexandria stared at his unique necklace.

"What?" Johannes asked innocently. "I thought I'd stop at the kitchen."

Many of the prisoners were coming back into the camp—running to the dormitories to retrieve whatever meager possessions they'd managed to pilfer or horde.

"Keep your head down," Arel instructed the assistant commandant. "One of the prisoners might recognize you."

Andre Andreyevitch did as he was told.

They made their way to the front gate where Agnes joined them.

"Good," Arel said when he saw her. "Let's hurry before the guards come back."

"They won't be back," Andre Andreyevitch said through gritted teeth. "The White Army is in Ekaterinburg. They came during the night to take the town and save the tsar."

"Oh, no," Agnes whimpered. "They're too late."

"Yes, they've found that out, and now they're slaughtering every Red Guard and Bolshevik they can find. We got word they're coming here." He slumped forward and nearly passed out.

Oskar and Arel held him up. "What should we do?" Arel yelled at him.

"Get us out of here." The effort to speak was taking every bit of strength the big man possessed. "To . . . the mill or the forest."

The group lurched forward, away from the road and the prison—away from captivity and chaos. As they pushed further into the protection of the trees, Agnes thought she heard the distant sound of a hundred horses' hooves drumming against the ground. Her brothers moved faster and she pursued with singleness of purpose, trying not to think of the simple grave they left behind in the unadorned prison cemetery.

◆　◆　◆

"Two hundred rubles," the doctor said without pity. "That will take care of the arm. And another hundred to keep you all hidden for a week while he heals. Your clothes and food will be extra."

Arel glared at the physician. The man's hazel eyes, though small, were determined. Arel opened his mouth to protest, but Johannes stepped forward.

"Yes. Yes, we agree. Though it will take most of what we have, we understand the risk you are taking for us." He held his hand out, not to Agnes, but to Oskar. "Give me the bundle, brother."

Oskar followed Johannes's lead. "How can you do this?" he pleaded, taking the ripped bundle from his pocket and placing it in Johannes's hand. "It will leave us with practically nothing."

"The Lord will provide," Johannes said.

The doctor scoffed. "So, you really aren't Bolsheviks then."

"Would we have been in one of their work camps if we were Bolsheviks?" Oskar said derisively.

"Look here now!" the doctor barked. "Watch your tongue!"

Johannes interrupted. "Please forgive my brother, Doctor. He's worn out. He hardly knows what he says most of the time. We are very grateful that you're helping us."

"As you should be," the doctor blustered. "It will be difficult to hide you"—he glowered at Oskar—"and nearly impossible to find clothes for everyone."

"Perhaps this will help." Johannes laid the cloth open, and the doctor's eyes bulged at the sight of ruble notes, gold coins, and silver rings.

"That's a miracle," the man whispered. "In these troubled times? A miracle."

Johannes smiled as he looked around at his siblings. "Indeed . . . a miracle."

CHAPTER FORTY-FIVE

NEAR NOVGOROD

August 11, 1918

Three days had become ten, and ten days had become hopelessness and sorrow. The money used for passage, food, and bribes was nearly gone, and Agnes squeezed the miniscule cloth bundle in her pocket, hoping to stop the pangs of hunger. She mumbled on like a madwoman. "We don't know where we are . . . Johannes says he knows, but we have to be careful . . . both armies may be looking for us. And why are we going to Petrograd? Mother and Father won't be there." She rummaged in her pocket. "Where's that bit of cheese I had? Someone stole it. What is it you can break with one word?"

"Agnes."

She was suddenly alert and batted at the hand on her arm.

The hand did not release her. Johannes's voice came to her ear. "Agnes, you're mumbling again."

"What?"

"Look at me."

Agnes found it impossible to look at her sister and brothers. The images of gaunt, dirty faces and haunted expressions made her empty stomach roil.

"Look at me."

Agnes squinted as she looked into Johannes's pleading eyes.

"Agnes, you must stop. You're drawing attention to yourself."

Agnes's eyes flicked to the other passengers on the train: grimy, despondent, and fierce.

Her brother's whispered voice came again. "We're almost home. Please, dear one, hold on. Two or three days and we'll be home."

"There is no home there," Agnes said simply.

Johannes's face twisted in pain, and Agnes looked away.

"Sorry, Johannes. I won't mumble anymore."

His hand rested on her shoulder for a long while, then he turned and went back to sit with his brothers.

Agnes turned her attention to worrying a loose tooth. She'd lost two while she was at the camp, and this one had started wiggling just east of Kazan. She'd found it five days after leaving the doctor's home. Agnes rubbed her bottom lip. The doctor was a vile, heartless man, threatening to turn them over to the White Russian army if they didn't pay his extortion fees. The jackal had figured they were keeping secrets when her brothers insisted none of them wanted help from Ekaterinburg's liberators.

We would have been saved by the White Russians, but not Andre Andreyevitch. He would have been slaughtered—slaughtered like the tsar and his children. Blood splattered on the wall. No. We had to escape. We had to walk away from death and graves.

Agnes put her head into her hands and closed her eyes. Three days walking into the mountains, one day on the back of a logging truck, two days on a barge going south on the Kama River. The quiet days on the river were good, until Oskar and the barge mechanic fought over a game of cards. Now they were on a train going as far as their money would take them. Which was not far. Not all the way home. Agnes tried to pull out her tooth and pain shot along her jaw.

Alexandria was beside her, taking her hands away from her face. "Here, hold onto this." She pulled the birch-bark box out of a ragged satchel and placed it on Agnes's lap.

Agnes rubbed her hand over the carvings, outlining the squirrel and the pinecones. Tears fell.

"Agnes, stop. You have to be strong for me."

Agnes rubbed at her eyes. "I'm just hungry. I had cheese in my pocket, but someone took it."

Alexandria put her arm around her. "We'll get something at the next station."

"We don't have enough money."

"We'll get something. Don't worry."

"Where are we?"

"About six hours from Novgorod."

"Novgorod? I know that place." Agnes looked at her sister. "There's a cottage . . . Natasha's aunt and uncle."

Alexandria patted her hand. "Yes, you spent a summer there. Sel'tso Saterno."

"Yes. Are we going there? We could be safe there."

"I don't think so, Agnes."

Agnes went on in a high, animated voice that made Alexandria grimace. "Natasha's cousin Irena is the sweetest girl, and their house is something from a fairy tale."

"Agnes . . ." Alexandria stopped when she saw the hope on Agnes's face. "I don't know, Agnes. Johannes will tell us if it's safe."

Agnes stood. "Of course it's safe. I have to talk with him. I have to tell him." As she turned to move down the aisle, there was a strong tug on the box she was holding. Agnes looked down into the lined face of an old woman. The woman's dark eyes were narrowed and defiant. The younger woman sitting next to her leaned forward and glared.

Agnes stepped back. "What are you about? Keep your hands to yourself."

The younger woman jumped to her feet. "You were about to fall on her, you ugly lout!"

"No, I wasn't!"

"Come on," Alexandria said, pushing Agnes gently along. "Let's go find our brothers."

Agnes resisted. She scowled at the slovenly pair, and then acquiesced to Alexandria's insistent shove. "The old one tried to steal this!"

"No one is themselves anymore," Alexandria said distractedly, trying to keep Agnes moving. "Don't make a scene."

"Well, they're making a scene," Agnes said, pointing at her brothers who sat locked in a heated discussion.

The men's conversation stopped abruptly when Alexandria and Agnes approached, and Johannes was immediately alert. "What is it?"

"That old woman back there tried to steal this!" Agnes barked, holding up the birch-bark box.

"Shh," Johannes warned. "Sit down."

Oskar and Andre Andreyevitch stood and let the women take their places.

"Why is it out of the satchel?" Johannes questioned.

Alexandria dropped her gaze. "I . . . I thought it would calm her."

"Oh, enough of that!" Agnes interrupted. "That's not what we came to talk about. We came to talk about staying for a time with Natasha's aunt and uncle."

"What?" Arel asked.

"Yes. The ones who live near Novgorod. I've been there. It's beautiful."

Johannes's voice was low and gentle. "You spent a summer there."

"Yes."

He shook his head. "We can't, Agnes. We'd put them in danger."

Her eyes filled with tears. "But it's beautiful there, Johannes. The magic house and the lovely little church. It's safe. And they have a garden. There'd be lots of food."

"Agnes . . ."

"Please, Johannes, please. I know them. They would take us in. I know they would."

People on the train were turning to look at her.

Johannes took her hand. "All right. All right, Agnes. I'll think about it."

She smiled and brushed the tears off her cheeks. "You'll see. It's beautiful."

Johannes slumped back, weariness and frustration stamped onto his features. Oskar and Andre Andreyevitch gave him looks of understanding and moved off to sit in other seats as the train continued west into the afternoon gloaming.

◆　◆　◆

The slowing of the train brought them awake. Agnes's head lolled forward and she woke with a whimper of pain. She saw Johannes rub his hand across his face and Arel dazedly looking around like a little boy after a nap.

"Where are we?" Alexandria asked.

Johannes steadied himself and looked out the window into the dark night. "I see a few lights. Maybe a town or a village."

A squeal of brakes sounded and the train slowed quickly. Now they could all see lights winking through the trees.

Andre Andreyevitch walked down the aisle to them. "A man told me this is Viny. The train will stop for a few minutes to unload passengers."

"What time is it?" Johannes asked, running his fingers through his hair and replacing his cap.

"Just hours before daybreak. They say there's a vendor with tea and bread."

"I want bread," Agnes said, sitting forward.

"How far to Novgorod?" Johannes questioned.

"Only about an hour. That will be the main stop," Andre Andreyevitch answered.

"And where our tickets run out," Johannes mumbled.

"I want bread," Agnes repeated. "Please, Johannes."

He focused on her face. "We can't Agnes. There won't be time."

"Please, Johannes. Just give me the money, and I'll hurry and get bread for all of us."

The train was pulling to a stop in front of the small station hut and several people stood to disembark.

Agnes's voice took on a frantic tone. "Please, please, Johannes." She pressed her finger on the glass. "See there! There's the vendor. He still has bread to sell. I see it!"

Johannes stared out the window for a moment.

"Please?"

He growled in frustration and reached into the pocket of his coat for a few coins. "Have Oskar go with you."

She snatched the money. "There isn't time!" She shoved her way past several people moving toward the exit. One fellow cursed at her and another raised his fist.

"Agnes!" Johannes stood as Arel and Oskar made their way to him.

"What is it?" Arel asked.

"Agnes defied me and went alone to buy bread."

"I'll get her," Oskar said as he moved away down the aisle.

"Oh, no," Alexandria choked.

"What? What is it?" Johannes asked, his voice trembling with exhaustion and anxiety.

"There's that old woman and her companion. The one who tried to steal the box." Alexandria's face was ghostly white. "Agnes still has the box with her! I didn't take it back."

◆　◆　◆

Agnes ran toward the vendor. "I . . . I have coins," she panted. "I want to buy bread."

She saw the vendor nod as he held up a round, dark loaf. A few people passed by in a swirl of muted sound and color, but all Agnes could see was the bread. All she wanted was the bread. The coins dropped into the vendor's hand and she felt the rough crust on her palm. She closed her eyes and pressed the loaf to her face, breathing in the smell of yeast and rye.

Suddenly someone grabbed her hair and dragged her back. Her eyes flew open and she saw someone shove the vendor to the ground as he tried to protest. The few other people on the platform had melted into the moonless dark. Agnes clung to her possessions and kicked, but her attacker was merciless as she pulled her far back into the shadows. Agnes twisted around and broke free. She started to run, but the old woman was there to join her companion. She slapped Agnes's face and shoved her.

"Give us that box."

The younger woman yanked at it, nearly prying it loose, but Agnes kicked her. The woman backed away and fell over a wooden bench. Agnes advanced on her, kicking again and again, weeping and snarling. "You—can't—have—it!"

The old woman threw her body against Agnes, forcing her against the wall. Agnes felt a piercing jab in her side and she gasped in pain. She staggered around to see several large, rusted nails protruding from the side of the hut. The old woman lunged at her again, but before she could strike, she was thrown aside by Oskar; her scrawny body landed hard on the platform, her head cracking against the station wall. Her companion pushed herself to her feet, cursing as she stumbled away into a thicket of trees.

Oskar ran to Agnes as she slumped onto her knees. Her grip went slack and the bread and the box tumbled across the platform.

"Agnes!"

"It's not bad. Just some nails." She sagged forward and Oskar caught her. His hand felt a sticky wetness as he laid her gently on the platform. In the shadows all he could see was a dark stain on her blouse. "No, no, no! This isn't possible. Heavenly Father, please help us."

The train's engine engaged, and with a hiss of steam and clank of metal, the train's wheels began to move. The whistle blew shrill and cold, and Oskar looked around frantically, undecided about what to do. He put his arms under his sister to lift her, and Agnes moaned.

"I'm sorry, but I have to get you to the train."

The station mistress poked her head around the side of the hut. "I heard a ruckus. What are you doing there?"

"Help! Help me. My sister's hurt." Oskar grunted as he stood up.

The woman bellowed at him. "You just stay there! I've called the police!" She disappeared back into the hut.

The train was picking up speed, and Oskar wept in frustration. He'd never make it.

"Oskar!"

He looked up to see Johannes and the rest of their party running through the shadows toward him.

♦　♦　♦

The afternoon sunlight danced on the lake and Agnes heard the sweet laughter of her dearest friend. She saw Natasha in the meadow running a race with her cousin, Irena. It was odd. The sun was bright, so why didn't the warmth of it reach her skin? Her body shook with cold. *Has someone put my body into the water? I'll drown. Don't they know I'll drown?*

"Johannes, she's shaking again and pushing off the shawl."

"Agnes, we're right here with you."

Here? Where is here?

"It's the fever. She's delirious. Johannes, we have to take her to Natasha's aunt and uncle's."

Low and urgent voices began to argue.

Agnes moaned and forced her mind away from the meadow and the lake. "There."

"Hush, all of you," Alexandria ordered. "She said something."

Johannes spoke to her. "Agnes, wake up. Can you open your eyes?" She did. "Good girl. Good girl."

"We must go there."

"Get her some water."

Feeling came back into her body and with it an awakening of pain. Clenching her jaw, she focused on her surroundings of pale blue sky and beautiful trees. She let her thoughts drift away with the fluttering of the leaves.

"Agnes?"

She turned her head to look at her sister.

"Stay awake."

Agnes worked to keep her eyes open, becoming aware that she was propped against Oskar. Images flooded into her mind of a man selling bread, of an old woman with sagging skin, of someone's hands on the box.

"The box."

Alexandria patted her hand. "We have it . . . and the bread. You put up quite a fight."

"That old woman . . ." Agnes's hand went to her side.

"Shh . . . never mind," Oskar said quietly.

"Did she stab me? Did she want to kill me?"

Oskar's arms tightened slightly and he kissed the top of her head.

"But *you* killed her."

"No, she was just knocked out. I made sure before we left the station."

"I don't remember after that."

"You fainted," Oskar said.

"For how long? My wound isn't bad."

Oskar tried to make the words light. "I think your body needed a rest."

Agnes looked at the ragged group of people surrounding her, and tears pooled in her eyes. "And you've carried me . . . carried me for hours?"

"Enough of that," Arel said as he brought her water in a tin cup.

"Where are we?"

Johannes crouched down beside her. "I think about fifteen miles from Novgorod. We've been following the train tracks."

"Novgorod?" Agnes's hand trembled, spilling some of the water onto her blouse. "Then we're close to the cottage!"

Arel smiled at her. "Yes. Andre Andreyevitch has gone ahead to see if there's a road or wagon track going in that direction."

Agnes turned her eyes to her oldest brother. "Thank you, Johannes."

"No, Agnes. I'm still against it, but I think I'm being overruled."

"Then, thank you for giving in."

Johannes smiled against his will, and Agnes put her hand on the side of his face. "I promise to get well. If you take me to Natasha's family, I promise to get better."

Johannes nodded, but his eyes stayed fixed on the ground. Agnes knew he was trying to shelter her from his sorrow, but he didn't know the farm. He didn't know the peace and health that they would find there.

Pain shot through her as she turned her body. She clenched her jaw, refusing to moan as she sat forward. *Dear Lord, please give me the strength to walk to the little cottage. That place will heal us . . . all of us. If I go, the others will follow.*

"What are you doing?" Oskar asked as she struggled to stand. He was immediately on his feet.

"I'm standing. You've carried me long enough."

Johannes took her hand. "Agnes, you can't."

"Yes, I can." She was shaky, but she was standing. Her side burned when she tried to straighten, but she pushed through the pain. "Where is my portion of bread?"

Alexandria handed her a chunk, along with a relieved smile.

A cooling breeze whispered through the leaves of the trees and Agnes listened. She hadn't heard the voice of Mother Russia for a long time and the sound gave her hope. She took a bite of bread and began walking.

◆　◆　◆

Irena looked up from hoeing potatoes and saw a group of people emerging from the forest. They walked toward her. *These are the people I saw in my dream—the people with sad hearts.*

She threw down the hoe, picked up her skirt, and ran to the house. "Mama! Papa! They're here! The ones I saw! They're coming!"

CHAPTER FORTY-SIX

PETROGRAD

August 14, 1918

Natasha kept her eyes on the street. She could not look at her friend's house. Several panes of glass were broken out of the front windows—innocent victims of one of the many fights over wine or food. Soiled rags, garbage, and a broken chair lay strewn around the threshold, and mewling voices of discontent seeped out of the house like tar.

Natasha held her purchase close to her chest and made a wide arc around the place. She fought off memories of standing in the Lindlofs' kitchen, chopping vegetables and laughing with Agnes, of sitting around the table New Year's Eve when their voices blended in the beautiful folk song, of Arel kissing her.

Natasha ran to her front door. She knocked loudly to drum out her thoughts, and when her mother opened the door, she pushed past and stumbled up the stairs.

"Natasha?"

"I'm all right, Mama. I . . . I just . . ." She turned and sat down heavily on the step. She hunched over and buried her face in her arms. Tears and anger wrapped themselves around her words. "I can't stand it! I can't!"

Her mother sat beside her.

"Where is she? Where is my friend?" Natasha clutched at the package to keep the pain at bay. "Is she dead? Have they killed her?"

Her mother rubbed her back.

"We've heard nothing! Nothing!"

"What did you buy today?"

"What?"

"Your package. What did you buy?"

Natasha sucked in a large breath of air and stopped crying. Her mother handed her a handkerchief, and she wiped her face. The pain stepped back. This was how her mother had helped her over the weeks since her return home: distracting her grief with work, or talking about mundane things, or telling stories.

"So, did you find what you were looking for, or did you buy something to trade?"

Natasha untied the string and opened the brown paper. "It's a gray sweater."

"Ah, good. The nights will soon be cooler."

"I wanted blue."

"But gray will be just as warm."

"Yes."

They sat quietly, side by side.

Finally Natasha spoke, her voice low and calm. "I had another dream last night of the peasant girl and the white cow."

Her mother nodded. "Tell me."

"It was good. I was feeding the cow pears."

Her mother grinned. "That is because my sister has been sending pears to us from the country."

Natasha smiled at her mother. "Yes, maybe so, and I'm missing them because dear, kind Aunt Anna hasn't sent me any for weeks."

"Yes, you greedy thing. And perhaps you were hoping the white cow would beg some for you."

They laughed together, stopping abruptly when they heard the postman's bicycle bell. The women stared at each other in wonder, and Natasha stood. "The post! Maybe he will bring pears today!" They laughed again.

Natasha pulled her mother to her feet, then ran for the front entrance. She opened the door expecting to find the postman searching through his mailbag for the many letters and packages addressed to her, instead she was disappointed to see him ride past, ringing his bell not for her, but for the usurpers next door. She kicked the door frame. How could fate favor that boorish lot with correspondence? She kicked the door frame again and was about to close the door, when she saw a figure walking toward her. Even though it was quite warm, the man wore an overlarge cloth coat and a cap. A shiver of apprehension ran down Natasha's spine and she stepped back into the shadows of her house. Just before she closed the door, the figure spoke.

"Natasha Ivanovna, it's Arel Lindlof."

Her hands trembled as she yanked open the door. She rushed forward onto the sidewalk and threw her arms around him. "How? How is this possible? How did you get away?"

Arel held her tightly, absorbing her energy and reality. He glanced over to his former home and saw a large, brutish man with unkempt hair taking letters from the postman. The man gave him a suspicious look.

"Natasha Ivanovna," Arel said softly, "may we go inside?"

She was immediately alert, following Arel's gaze to her loutish neighbor. "Yes, dear friend. Come in."

They moved into the house, and Natasha closed and locked the door.

Natasha's mother stood at the bottom of the stairs, her eyes wide, and her mouth open. "Oh, dear boy." She moved to Arel and put her hands on his haggard face. "Come to the kitchen."

"Thank you, but I don't want to be a bother."

Svetlana crossed herself and led the way to the kitchen. Arel took off his coat and hat and handed them to Natasha. He ran his fingers self-consciously through his hair.

Natasha tried not to stare at his gaunt face and haunted expression.

"Your father isn't here?" Arel asked without taking his eyes off her.

"No, he's at the Smolny."

Arel nodded.

"Oh, Arel," Natasha said, covering his hands with hers. "Are you all back? Are you all safe?"

He looked into her eyes and a tear slid down his cheek. "Not Erland. Erland died at the camp."

Natasha sat back and gripped the edge of the table. "And Agnes?"

He did not answer, but brushed distractedly at his tears.

Natasha bit her lip. "Arel, tell me! Tell me what's happened to Agnes!"

He pressed his lips together, a desperate cry sounding in his throat. Natasha stared at him, willing the words from his mouth. "She's very ill. The doctor says it's an infection. We thought she was getting better, but her body is so weak that . . ." His words trailed off.

"Where is she? How long have you been in Petrograd?"

Arel covered his face with his hands. "I just arrived on the train. Andre Andreyevitch came with me, but he's gone to his apartment."

Natasha was agitated with his ramblings. "You've come on the train from where?"

"Novgorod. We're staying with your aunt and uncle."

"Why didn't you telegraph?"

"It's not safe. I came to bring you back with me. Agnes is asking for you."

Natasha stood. "I'll get my suitcase. We can catch the afternoon train."

He looked up at her. "I was praying that you'd come with me, Natasha Ivanovna."

Natasha turned to her mother. "I need you to come with us."

Svetlana nodded.

"Stay with him. I'll pack for both of us." She ran from the room.

Svetlana brought Arel a glass of water and a currant roll. He drank the water slowly, fighting back his emotion. Svetlana took his hand. "I know what Natasha would tell you. She would tell you to have faith."

Arel gave her a questioning look, and she returned a gentle smile. "I know it's strange, isn't it . . . a Bolshevik who believes in God?"

◆　◆　◆

Natasha tied a three-cornered scarf around her head, put the blue book into the pocket of her light coat along with the last of the ruble notes from the cloth bundle, and picked up the suitcases. Her mind was fixed on one thing only—getting to her friend's side. She wasn't concerned with how they'd escaped or why Agnes was ill or why they were all at Sel'tso Saterno. All those stories would eventually be told. Right now, she needed only to see Agnes.

The front door opened and Natasha's heart pounded. *Father! Father's come home early.*

She flew down the stairs to intercede. As she maneuvered her way into the front hall, she found her mother already there.

Her father's brow furrowed as he looked at the suitcases. "Are you traveling, daughter?"

She decided to tell the truth. "Yes. Mother and I are going to Sel'tso Saterno."

Ivan Alexseyevitch turned to his wife. "What's this? Has something happened?"

Svetlana nodded.

"Is someone ill?"

Natasha answered quickly as she heard the chair pushed back in the kitchen. "Yes, but not the family. My friend . . ." Her voice shook with anguish. "My friend, Agnes Lindlof is there at Auntie and Uncle's, and she's very ill."

"Agnes Lindlof? How can she be there?"

"We escaped."

Ivan Alexseyevitch started as Arel Lindlof walked in to stand beside Natasha.

"We escaped when the White Army came in to liberate Ekaterinburg."

"You were in Ekaterinburg?"

"Our work camp was near there, and my brothers and I were on the crew ordered to build a high fence around a certain house. The Red Guards called it 'the House of Special Purpose.'"

Natasha's father looked stricken. "Then the rumors whispered at the Smolny are true? The tsar and his family . . ."

"Slaughtered."

Svetlana Karlovna burst into tears.

Arel went on, his voice bitter and accusing. "Shot, bayoneted, burned."

Natasha put her hand on his arm. "Arel, stop."

Ivan Alexseyevitch stepped forward. "No. I want to hear. I want to hear it all."

"The jailers heard the White Army was coming to liberate the tsar, so they killed them—murdered them in cold blood: the tsarina, the grand duchesses, even the young tsarevitch. They were disposed of because the Bolsheviks knew that many Russians would rally around the royal family—many Russians would not be fooled by the Soviet propaganda." Natasha expected her father to stop Arel's invective, but he stood mute, his eyes fixed on Arel's haggard face.

"When the White Army arrived and discovered the carnage, they went mad. All the Bolsheviks ran—including all the guards at our camp. That's how we escaped."

Everyone stood in tense silence as Natasha's father stared at Arel's face. His gaze moved to his wife and daughter, and back to Arel. "I'm sorry for what you've suffered."

Arel nodded. "My brother Erland died at the camp, and now Agnes is very sick. She's asking for Natasha Ivanovna. She's asking for her friend."

"I understand."

Natasha could tell that Arel was evaluating her father's emotion. "So, you won't turn us in?" Arel asked quietly.

Natasha saw grief in her father's eyes as he took Arel's hand. "I didn't anticipate the brutality. Many of my friends—brilliant men from the university—have been arrested or beaten for asking questions. Instead of brotherhood, it seems we're creating a nation of brutes."

"What will you do?"

Ivan Alexseyevitch shook his head. "I don't know."

"Father, we need to get to the train."

"Yes, but first I have something to tell you. Something to confess." His grip tightened on Arel's hand. "I know where your parents are."

"What?"

"Yes. They telegraphed from Helsinki a month after you were arrested."

"Why didn't you tell me?" Natasha moaned.

"I didn't want you thinking about them . . . communicating with them." He looked back to Arel. "By time that you were gone and we had no idea where you'd been taken."

"*I* knew. I knew where they were. I could have gotten word to them."

Her father looked stricken. "I didn't realize, Natasha. I'm sorry." He released Arel's hand. "So many secrets."

"Yes, it seems we're becoming a country of secrets." She snatched up the suitcases. "And now we really must go."

Her father nodded. "I will walk you to the streetcar." He took the suitcases, avoiding his daughter's eyes. "But, what about money?"

Natasha opened the door. "I have enough."

They walked out into the afternoon sunlight, and Arel turned to look at his old house.

"Don't," Natasha said. "Don't look at it, it will break your heart. We must go forward from here."

He moved to walk beside her as she strode forward with singleness of purpose.

CHAPTER FORTY-SEVEN

SEL'TSO SATERNO

August 16, 1918

Agnes's skin was chalky white and clammy. Natasha sat by her bedside, replacing cool cloths on her forehead and speaking in a soft, encouraging voice. Arel slept a few feet away on a straw mat and patched blanket. His deep snores testified of his exhausted state—truly the exhausted state of everyone in the company. It concerned Natasha that all of them would succumb to illness and despair. She lifted the dressing on Agnes's wound and sponged away the greenish pus. The doctor said infection—infection that a healthy person could overcome, but her friend was not healthy. The Bolsheviks had seen to that. The doctor had also warned about pneumonia. Natasha shook her head as she examined the wounds. They were such small punctures, but they oozed pus and the surrounding skin was swollen and red.

Natasha gently placed a clean dressing on the area and fought back angry tears.

She looked out the bedroom doorway into the small sitting area, and watched her aunt and Alexandria as they stripped beans. Alexandria—the pampered beauty. But the pampered beauty had changed much during her months of servitude. Natasha could tell that she was no longer the self-centered child, but now looked at the world with expanded vision, responding to the needs of others before fretting over her own foolish desires. They had all changed.

Natasha wrapped her arms across her chest to keep the pain that was hidden there from escaping. *Agnes will not die. I will not let her die.*

Agnes's body twitched and Natasha started. She took her friend's hand. "There, little squirrel, that's better. You're getting stronger and stronger all the time. Soon you'll be strong enough to walk out in the meadow with me. You love the meadow and the forests and the enchanted cottage with its beautiful carvings. Remember? And remember how in the daytime we'd take walks and pick loganberries, and at night we'd sit by the fire and crochet." She took a deep breath and forced calm into her voice. "When you're better, my auntie and my cousin Irena will sit next to us and tell us wonderful fairy tales about clever little squirrels, flying horses, and magical white cows." A tear slid down her cheek. "Please . . . please, Agnes. I want to tell you all I've learned. I want to tell you what the little blue book means to me. I want to ask you about God."

Johannes stood listening to these last sentences. "Oh, haven't you heard, Natasha Ivanovna?"

Natasha sat straighter and looked at the man now leaning against the door frame. "What's that, Johannes?"

"God and Lenin no longer live in Petrograd."

"Oh?"

"Indeed. Lenin has moved to Moscow, and God has moved to . . . well, someplace more hospitable than Russia."

She did not answer him, but placed a new cloth on Agnes's head. "'We believe all things, we hope all things—'"

"Don't do that, Natasha Ivanovna."

"What?"

"Quote scripture." He shook his head. "I can't make out your thinking."

"What do you mean?"

"A devout Bolshevik, writing for the state, pushing their propaganda, hating God . . . And now quoting scripture?"

Natasha hung her head. "I know you're angry at the Bolsheviks, Johannes."

He cut her short. "Angry? They've killed my family, they're killing this country, and they're killing God."

Arel sat up. "Enough, Johannes. You'll disturb Agnes."

"Are you sure it's Agnes you're worried about, or your Bolshevik love?"

Arel's voice was low and threatening. "Get out."

Natasha's body stiffened. "Arel, it's all right. I understand."

Agnes moaned, and they all went quiet. Natasha stared anxiously at her friend's face; when she looked up, Johannes was gone.

Irena came into the room. "It's my time to watch her."

Natasha reluctantly gave up her seat, picking up the bowl and stretching her back. "I need to get fresh water."

"I'll manage," Irena said, taking the bowl and pushing Natasha toward the door. "It's lovely out. You two should go for a walk. There's plenty of time before supper."

Arel shoved his mat and blanket under the bed and followed Natasha from the room. A cool breeze greeted them as they stepped onto the porch, and Natasha closed her eyes, letting the soft movement of the wind play against her skin and tousle her hair.

"Are you cold?"

"No, I'm fine. It's delightful."

Arel looked out over the meadow with its array of white and blue lupine, starflower, and dandelion. Soon the flowers would fade, the green grasses would dry and wither, and the first snows would come.

"Let's walk to the church," Natasha said, stepping from the porch.

Arel followed, bringing his thoughts to the woman at his side. He loved her, and had since their youth. At first it was a game he and Bruno had played to see who could tease her the most, then it was a competition between him and Oskar to be noticed, and when she professed her allegiance to the dogma of the Bolsheviks, he alone continued to care for her. He thought about her dark eyes. He thought about the kiss on New Year's Eve. "Tell me about the Red Train," he said abruptly.

Natasha stopped. She turned to look at him, her expression hard. "Why would you ask about that?"

"I . . . I don't know. Your cousin was talking about it, and . . ." He shook his head. "I don't know. I'm sorry."

Natasha looked away from him. "I don't like to think about it." She took a deep breath. "I could have died on that train." She paused. "It was one of the things that made my father rethink the Socialist doctrine. Perhaps that is one positive thing to come from my idiotic trip."

"But you and your father were both so enthusiastic."

"Enthusiastic and foolish. Red banners—shouted slogans—promises. What were those things?" She started walking and Arel stepped beside her. "We're trying to change a society by forcing people, forcing how they should think and feel."

"But you write for the Bolsheviks."

"*Wrote*. Yes, and I believed what I wrote." A smile softened her features. "Then your father gave me this little blue book and told me that only God can change men's hearts."

Arel smiled too. "My father is very sly."

"Yes, and very wise."

They walked in companionable silence for several minutes.

"I'm glad you like the book, Natasha Ivanovna."

She nodded. "There's much to ponder."

They neared the church and Natasha noted that the cross was absent from the domed cupola. The vision brought an ache to her chest. She walked faster. "Oh, no."

"What is it?"

"They've cut off the cross!" She pointed. "See there—on the top of the cupola? There's a red star now. They've taken down the cross and put up a red star." She was running and Arel ran with her. "No, no, no! It's a sacrilege! Please don't let them have done it. Please." She reached the ancient doors and tried the handle. "It's unlocked." She hesitated.

Arel was breathless at her side. "What is it you fear?"

"Prozorov said they were going to whitewash over the frescos in all the churches; paint out hundreds of years of beauty and faith."

Arel held her arm. "Let's not go in. That way we don't have to see it."

"I have to go in." She pushed open the door and walked into the church's cool interior. As her eyes adjusted to the dimmer light, she saw the sacred images standing in defiance of man's finite mastery. She breathed. "They're here. They're still here." She moved around the room, running her hand gently over the muted pigments. Angels, saints, and apostles looked serenely into an eternity she could not see. She stopped next to Arel who was admiring two figures. "They are Boris and Gleb. Sons of the Christian Prince Vladimir."

He turned to her. "How do you know?"

She smiled. "My cousin Irena told me. We've come here together many times." Natasha touched the shoe of one of the brothers. "I've dreamed about their father—the great Prince Vladimir." She spoke earnestly to the painting of Boris. "Yes, and how does your father feel about the Bolshevik's destruction of God?"

"I don't think Chairman Lenin and Prince Vladimir would be on good terms," Arel said.

Natasha grinned. "No. I'm sure they wouldn't."

The two continued moving about the small church.

"So, what were your dreams of the Christian Prince?"

"One time he came to talk to me and he was leading the peasant girl's white cow." She paused. "Do you know it? The white cow from the fairy tale?"

"Yes, I know that story. The white cow who gives up its life to help the orphan girl?"

"Yes."

"And Prince Vladimir came to see you and he brought the white cow?"

"Yes." A smile touched her lips.

"That's a very strange dream, Natasha Ivanovna."

"Perhaps, or perhaps a deep and symbolic vision."

"Then that would make you a visionary."

Natasha shook her head, the smile dropping from her mouth. "I don't think so. If I'd been a visionary I would have seen our futures on New Year's Eve, and I would have warned us. I would have made it all go away."

"The kiss too?"

She gave him a steady look. "No, not the kiss."

At that moment they heard someone running down the path and calling out Natasha's name.

"That's Irena," Natasha said, moving quickly to the door.

The two stepped out into the sunlight and Irena rushed to them. "I thought you might be here!"

"Irena, what is it?"

"Come quickly! Your friend is awake and she's saying your name!"

"Awake?" Natasha took Arel's hand and they ran for the cottage.

♦ ♦ ♦

"Little squirrel, I'm here. It's me. It's your Natasha. Please wake up again. Please." Natasha rubbed the back of Agnes's hand and looked over at Arel. She knew the desperation on his face mirrored her own. "You said she opened her eyes?"

Her aunt nodded. "Yes, dear one. Irena called to me and I came in. Her eyes were open and she said your name."

"I heard her too," Alexandria confirmed.

Arel looked to Johannes. "Perhaps another blessing."

"No. No more blessings. No more prayers. No more." He walked from the room.

Arel stared at the departing form, then down at the floor.

Natasha tapped the back of Agnes's hand. "Agnes Lindlof, open your eyes! Open your eyes, I tell you!"

Agnes's eyes came open and the company gasped.

"Impossible," Oskar said, stepping forward.

Arel moved quickly to the door. "Johannes, she's awake."

Agnes's breathing was shallow and raspy, yet she fought to eke out words. "You . . . you're here."

"Yes, I'm here, little squirrel. Right here. Don't talk now. It's too difficult."

"Must."

Agnes tried to swallow and Natasha noted the effort. She looked at Arel. "Hand me that water, and prop her up a bit."

Arel and Oskar rushed to oblige, gently lifting their sister and readjusting the pillows.

Natasha put the glass to Agnes's lips and she took a small sip. "More?"

"No."

Natasha set the glass aside and took her friend's hand again. Agnes was whispering something and Natasha leaned close.

"Strawberries."

"What?"

"I smell strawberries."

Agnes's eyes closed, and Natasha reached over quickly and rubbed her hand across her cheek.

"Agnes? Agnes, talk to me."

"I'm talking to Erland."

Panic dropped into Natasha's chest. "No, Agnes, don't talk to Erland, talk to me. Open your eyes and talk to me." Agnes obliged. "Hello, dear one."

"We're at the cottage."

Natasha nodded. "Yes, that's right. We're at the magical little cottage."

"My family is here."

"Yes."

There was a pause as Agnes fought for breath. "You saved us."

Natasha pressed Agnes's hand to her cheek. "No, little squirrel. No. I only followed your brilliant clues."

The corners of Agnes's mouth lifted slightly. "What is it you can't see that's always before you?"

Tears pressed at the back of Natasha's eyes. "What can I do for you?"

This time Agnes's voice came with some strength. "I want to go outside."

"Outside?" Natasha glanced around at the others. "She can't go outside."

"That's what she wants, cousin," Irena said, standing unobtrusively by her icon station. "You need to give her what she wants."

Natasha stood up and backed away from the bed. "I can't."

Oskar stepped forward and slid his arms behind Agnes's back and under her legs. He lifted her emaciated body easily and moved her quickly from the room. Alexandria gathered the quilt, and Arel put his arm around Natasha's waist and guided her out.

Wrapped in the quilt, Agnes was set in a rocking chair in the sunny front yard. Johannes sat near her on the porch step. Natasha and Arel sat together on the ground by her feet.

Agnes reached over and placed her hand on Natasha's head. "I remember flowers in your hair."

"Yes. That summer . . . that summer together."

"You read the blue book?"

"Yes."

"Good."

Natasha wanted to block out the sound of Agnes's raspy breathing. She wanted to take away the sickness. She wanted to scream at God.

She jumped when Agnes spoke again.

"Johannes, please tell Mama and Papa that . . ."

Johannes collapsed into sobs. "I was supposed to take care of you."

"Hush," Agnes said softly, wheezing on every word. "You . . . have no . . . power over this."

Natasha felt those words cut into her heart. That's what she hated! She hated that she had no power over anything: the cruelty they'd all suffered, the insidious spread of the Soviet doctrine, the fighting between her countrymen, the coming of winter. Her mind became her enemy as it conjured her mistakes and arrogance. How many families would be ripped to shreds by this brotherhood of the proletariat? How much anger, hatred, and fear would infest her country, and how much had she contributed by writing meaningless words of revolt and change? She hadn't thought about what that change would mean. But that change was killing her friend. Natasha put her head on her bent knees and rocked back and forth. She felt her mind slipping toward madness and she tried to stop her tumbling thoughts. She put her hand on Agnes's arm.

"What two things can God give you?" Agnes wheezed.

Natasha flinched at the sound. "A riddle?"

"A truth."

"Two things God can give me?" She stopped rocking and dissolved into tears. "I don't know. I don't know, little squirrel."

Agnes fought for the breath to reply, and Natasha waited.

"Redemption and peace."

◆　◆　◆

Agnes died that afternoon as the setting sun shimmered through the birch leaves, and Alexandria and Irena were singing a Russian folk song.

Natasha stood and walked off by herself.

She didn't want to look at the still body or hear the cries or prayers. She walked steadily along the rutted track, grateful that she was alone. She had to be careful with grief and doubt. The chrysalis of her faith was not fully dried, so she could not risk the intrusion of sorrow. She felt safe with the birdsong and cool wind rustling the grass. She felt comforted by the small blue flowers by the side of the road and the weathered face of the farmer driving his cows home from the pasture. She felt stronger for the crimson sunset on the horizon. Agnes had spoken often about the voice of Mother Russia, and Natasha heard it now all around her.

She could not think of a life without her friend. Perhaps someday her faith would grow large enough to encompass a world beyond the solid ground, but now she wanted only the things she could hear and taste and feel. Now she wanted only the dirt under her feet and the sweet song of the birds.

She wrapped her shawl more tightly around her and walked on into the night.

CHAPTER FORTY-EIGHT

SEL'TSO SATERNO

August 18, 1918

She was walking in the meadow with her friend, their arms around each other's waist, their hair braided with flowers.

"Daughter Three-Eyes tells her mother that the magical white cow has been helping the orphan girl complete her tasks and the woman kills the cow for its treachery. The sad orphan girl takes the bones of the cow and buries them in the pasture. A beautiful tree grows up over the bones, and every day when the girl waters the tree it bears delicious fruit and droops down its branches to her so she can reach it."

"I love that story," Agnes said.

"I love it too."

"Natasha. Natasha, wake up."

Her auntie's voice erased the peaceful dream and Natasha moaned.

"I'm sorry, dear one, but if you want to visit the grave . . ."

The grave. Natasha sat up. "Yes, I'm awake." Her body felt tired, and she struggled to keep her emotions from overwhelming her. The shutters were open, letting in the soft glow of morning. Natasha went to the window and saw clouds gathering on the horizon. There would be rain by mid-morning. It was appropriate as today they would be leaving Sel'tso Saterno.

In a few hours Uncle Petya would drive them to the train station in Novgorod. She and her mother would return home, and Johannes, Oskar,

Arel, and Alexandria would crowd into Andre Andreyevitch's small apartment. They would stay out of sight as much as possible until they were able to secure train tickets for Helsinki. With the Great War still raging in Europe, and the upheaval in Russia, their escape would be nearly impossible, but they had no other option.

Natasha dressed and took care of her toiletries. She then packed her suitcase, straightened the coverlet, and lingered near Irena's icon station. *We believe all things, we hope all things, we have endured many things.* She picked up the small icon of Mary holding the Christ Child and laid it against her chest.

"You can keep that if you like."

Natasha turned as her cousin came to stand beside her. "May I?"

"Yes, of course."

Natasha put it in her skirt pocket and took her cousin in her arms. "I love you. You are the dearest girl."

"We are all dear girls—you, me, Alexandria, and Agnes." Natasha wept, and Irena took the hem of her apron and dried her tears. "She's fine, you know? She's in heaven and it's a beautiful place."

There was a soft tapping at the bedroom doorway, and the women looked over to see Arel standing there.

"I'm sorry. I didn't mean to interrupt."

"No, not at all. We . . . we were just . . ."

"We're all walking to the church and . . ."

"Yes, of course. We're coming." Natasha swiped the last of the wetness from her cheeks and helped Irena off with her apron. As they moved to go out, Irena caught her cousin by the wrist and leaned close to whisper in her ear.

"That man loves you, you know."

Natasha felt an unexpected blush warm her face. "Irena!"

"Well, he does. He's not as handsome as the other one, but he's much nicer."

"Irena Petrovna Novoskaya! You're trying to be a matchmaker!"

"No, no, I'm not," she said, a shocked expression her face. "God is doing that."

◆　◆　◆

Natasha watched the gray clouds gather and felt a whip of wind bother the hem of her skirt. She stood near a lovely birch tree whose leaves trembled with every breath of air. She glanced over at the grave and the knot of people standing around. She did not want to stand close, and no one had insisted she give up her solitude. Frequently she turned to look down the wagon track, expecting to see Agnes there, expecting to see her wave, a smile lighting her face. To Natasha's mind, seeing her friend in the meadow seemed more likely than her being shut away in the ground.

Natasha pulled her mind from the image. Irena said that Agnes was in heaven, but Natasha didn't know where heaven was. Was it in the sky? Somewhere up among the billowing clouds? She turned her view back to the mourners, becoming aware of the mumbled voices. All was quiet for a time, then Alexandria began singing. The pure voice came back to Natasha on the breeze, and though she couldn't make out the words, the melody entered into her heart, opening up the wounds of loss and revisiting her suffering. She was about to leave the place, when other voices joined in the singing. The music seemed to fill with faith, and Natasha felt her grief and anger succumbing to hope.

She moved forward, drawn now to the group and their shared sorrow. She entered the circle quietly, standing next to Arel and slipping her hand into his. She felt his fingers tighten around hers and was amazed at how natural it felt, as though they'd been holding hands since they were children.

As the song ended, Arel looked over at her, his eyes filled with tears. He gave her a gentle smile, and without letting go of her hand, stepped forward to lay a bunch of white lupine on his sister's grave. The other siblings did the same.

"It's time to go," Johannes said after a minute of silence.

Natasha watched as her Uncle Petya put his arms around his wife and daughter and led them off toward home. Her mother followed them, taking out her handkerchief and dabbing at her eyes. Oskar, Johannes, and Alexandria turned slowly and walked away together, but Arel stayed at the graveside.

"I'm glad there is eternity, Natasha Ivanovna, but it seems a long way off."

"Yes, I know."

"Please, don't let go of my hand."

"I won't." She tightened her grip and he gave her a sad smile.

He looked up at the red star on top of the church and shook his head.

"What?" Natasha asked.

"I'll never understand them. I'll never understand why they want to walk in darkness."

"They find their truth in government."

"I see. Well, enough of that. I want to think only about my kind and sweet sister."

Natasha nodded and pressed her lips together to keep back tears.

"And when I think of this place, I will always see a sacred image over her grave." He took a step back and hesitated.

"My cousin Irena will tend the grave and pray over it every day."

Arel's worried expression softened. "An angel watching over an angel."

"Yes."

They turned and headed toward the cottage. They'd gone several minutes in silence before Arel spoke.

"When did you first think I cared for you?"

Natasha smiled. "I suspected the night of our New Year's celebration."

"The kiss?"

"Yes. The kiss."

"And when did you *know?*"

"The night you were arrested. The look on your face told me."

"I was sure I'd never see you again."

"Yet, here we are."

Arel stopped and put his hands on the sides of her face. "I love you, Natasha Ivanovna. It seems as though I have loved you all my life."

She leaned close to him. "The one-time Bolshevik?"

He kissed her, and it was apparent that politics was not a concern. The kisses continued until several drops of rain splashed on their faces.

Natasha stepped back. "Are you sure this is wise?"

"What?"

"A life together? It will be difficult, Arel."

"Yes, but we will be together. We can face things together."

Natasha moaned and started walking.

Arel caught up to her. "What is it?"

"My heart hurts. It's broken and mended at the same time."

"Do you love me?"

"Yes."

"Then we'll figure it out."

A flash of lightning lit the sky and moments later a crack of thunder pounded their ears.

Arel took her hand. "I think the pagan god Perun is sending his lightning bolts to frighten us."

Natasha started running as the rain pelted down. "But of course you know, Arel, that we Christians don't believe in Perun."

◆ ◆ ◆

Irena had paced around the porch all afternoon praying for the storm to stop, and just before the time arrived for them to leave for Novgorod, it did. She helped prepare food for the trip, loaded suitcases, and shared in the good-byes. And just before Arel climbed into the wagon she latched onto his coat sleeve. "I will take good care of your sister. I will visit her every day."

"Thank you, Irena."

"And I will pray for you and my cousin."

Arel's eyes widened and Natasha smiled. "No one can keep secrets from Irena."

"I like him," Irena said bluntly.

"So do I."

Natasha hugged her aunt and kissed Irena's forehead. "I love you."

Irena took her hands. "I'm glad you found God, cousin. The world won't be so dark."

"Come on, Natasha. Up you go." Her uncle helped her into the back of the wagon where she sat between Arel and her mother.

"We are going home," her mother said softly as the wagon lurched forward.

Natasha nodded, but in truth she didn't know the meaning of the word. Once, she knew what home looked like—she knew Nevsky Prospect, the Statue of the Horseman, and the Winter Palace—but under the Soviets the meaning of all those things would change.

She wrapped her fingers around the icon in her pocket and gazed longingly at the enchanted cottage until the wagon turned a corner and it was lost from sight.

CHAPTER FORTY-NINE

Natasha Ivanovna stood with her husband on the bridge spanning the Winter Canal. Periodic sunlight broke through the lowering clouds and flickered on the waters of the Neva River. Silently she and Arel watched people walking along the Embankment Prospect. A barge made its way upstream and Natasha wondered how far it would travel. Would it go as far as Lake Ladoga, or perhaps all the way to Moscow? She shivered when she thought of Sergey Antonovich working in the propaganda office in the newly established Bolshevik offices in Moscow. She tried hard never to think of him, but infrequently a glimpse of their time together jumped unbidden into her mind.

"Are you cold?" Arel asked.

"No. I sometimes think of the past . . . bad memories I want to forget."

A Red Guard passed close by and Arel adjusted his hat, turned away from him, and looked out across the river.

"Father said he should have your new papers any day."

Arel nodded.

"I wish you hadn't been so stubborn about staying. You could be leaving today with your brothers and sister for Helsinki. You could be seeing your parents."

"Yes, I miss them. But trust me, dear one, it is no hardship staying here with you."

"But you would be safer in Finland."

"And much lonelier. You need to stay here, so here is where I stay." He took her in his arms. "Now, enough. We have been over this before. And remember, you're a Lindlof now, and we Lindlofs trust in the Lord." When she didn't respond, he whispered in her ear, "When the time is right, we'll see them again."

She nodded. "I love your family, Arel. I wish we could all live here together. Live in the country we love."

Arel held her tightly and looked out across the river. "Perhaps someday." He brought out his pocket watch and checked the time. "It's time to meet them in the Summer Garden," he whispered, his breath warm against her ear.

They turned reluctantly from their moment of solitude and immediately Natasha felt sadness and anxiety press in.

As they reached the gate into the garden, the beauty of the place overwhelmed her and Natasha found it difficult to control her emotions. The leaves of the elm and maple trees were dazzling in various shades of yellow, amber, and red, and when periodic shafts of sunlight broke through the clouds, the ground shimmered in a golden glow.

They met in the place where Elder Lyman had given the prayer for Russia. Andre Andreyevitch stood off to one side of the small courtyard as the family embraced. Natasha could tell that he was keeping watch for anyone or anything suspicious. Alexandria put down her carry sack and hugged Natasha so enthusiastically that they both nearly fell. Alexandria's body was bulky with layers of clothing, and Natasha knew it was the only way to ensure they wouldn't be stolen or confiscated along the way.

Johannes looked about the area, his expression unreadable. "Was it so many years ago?"

Arel nodded. "You were what—fifteen or sixteen?"

"Fifteen. Remember Elder Lyman said that I was about the same age as Joseph Smith when he received the First Vision."

Natasha smiled. Visions, angels, and golden bibles.

"That's right," Oskar said. "What a glorious prayer."

"Will we ever see that Russia?"

Oskar put his hand on his brother's shoulder. "I don't know, Johannes."

Arel took Natasha's hand. "I remember how Erland cried because he felt the love Elder Lyman had for us."

"Yes, and I gave him my handkerchief to wipe his grubby face."

"And Mother made that enormous meal for everyone."

They all stood silent, and Natasha knew they were reminiscing about that day, and thinking about the days to come.

Andre Andreyevitch came and stood beside Johannes. "We should be going."

Johannes nodded and extended his hand to the man who had brought them through so much. "Thank you, Andre Andreyevitch. Thank you." The two embraced as Oskar thumped him on the back.

Andre Andreyevitch stood back and chuckled. "Now I know why you were the best logger on your team."

Oskar grinned.

Johannes approached Natasha. He took her hand away from Arel and held it gently. She could see that emotion was keeping him from forming the words he wanted to say.

"It's all right, Johannes. I understand."

"No, I need to tell you. It was wrong of me to judge your heart. I'm sorry." He looked into her face. "My sister loved you. She loved you."

She nodded and he gave her a brief hug. "Come to Helsinki . . . when you can. When the European war is over and the fighting in Russia is done . . . come to us."

"Yes, Johannes. We will."

Arel looked earnestly into his brother's eyes. "Tell Father and Mother . . . tell them . . . I . . ."

Johannes nodded. "I'll tell them."

They all exchanged final embraces, and then the travelers gathered their meager belongings and walked from the park. Arel and Natasha watched them go, strengthening and comforting each other without words and without tears. Finally Arel spoke.

"I have a riddle."

Natasha smiled. "Yes?"

Arel nodded. "What can't you see that is always before you?"

Natasha fought to contain her emotions. "The future," she whispered.

"So, I guess we'll just have to leave things in God's hands."

"A safe place."

"Amazing how hearts can change."

"It's your father's doing, you know. He tricked me with that little blue book of philosophy."

Arel chuckled and held her around the waist. "He just wanted to offer you another way of looking at things."

"Indeed."

"And you've given my heart another way of looking at things."

"Who would have thought that one of those obnoxious Lindlof boys—"

"Who teased you without pity."

"Who teased me without pity," Natasha agreed, "would one day be my husband."

"You know what I think?"

"What?"

"I think we should go and visit the statue of Ivan Krylov."

Natasha brightened. "Oh, yes. I love his statue. It reminds me of when we were children."

They quickened their pace until they were both running in the crisp, autumn air. As they approached the statue, they were enchanted by the halo of golden leaves framing the storyteller's form. The bronze figure of Ivan Krylov sat reading one of his books, looking much too serious for a teller of children's stories, but perhaps, Natasha thought, he was reading the part where one of the characters in the story is in trouble, or perhaps he'd come to the end of the book where the attendant child learns a lesson.

"Isn't it wonderful?" Natasha said breathlessly.

"It is."

Next to them stood a young lad with his face pressed to the iron bars of the fence, obviously mesmerized by the charming iron animals that cavorted around the pedestal of the statue. Natasha smiled down at him. "Do you like his stories?"

The boy looked up at her, and Natasha felt her heart dance for the beauty of the child: his blue eyes full of innocence, his round face beaming, and a mass of honey-colored curls peeking from under his little blue cap.

In one of his chubby hands he carried a large bouquet of colorful autumn leaves, some almost as large as his head.

"Lion!" the little boy squealed, pointing at the fierce lion at the corner of the statue.

"Yes, a big lion," Natasha answered. "And where's the fox?" The boy pointed. "And the bear?" His blue eyes searched past the dog and the sheep and the monkey until he found the bear playing a cello.

"He's a funny bear," the boy giggled.

Natasha nodded. "Yes, he is funny, but he must also be very smart."

"Oh, he is smart!" the cherub replied. "He can play music and he can dance." The boy turned in several circles as Arel and Natasha laughed.

"Kolya!" a woman called.

"That's my mother. We're going to pray at my father's grave."

Natasha reached out and tucked a curl under the boy's cap. "I'm sorry your father died, Kolya."

The curly head bobbed several times. "But he's in heaven with God, and it's nice there."

Kolya's mother came up to them. "I'm sorry. I hope he wasn't bothering you."

"No, of course not," Natasha said.

"He's a beautiful boy," Arel added.

"Thank you. He brings me joy every day." She took her son's hand. "Come on, time to go." She gave a little bow to Arel and Natasha. "Good day."

Kolya bowed too. "Good day. God give you peace."

Natasha and Arel smiled at him. Kolya stopped halfway down the path to wave his handful of leaves at them.

"What an angel," Natasha whispered.

Arel held out his hand to her and she took it. "Never let go."

"Never."

"Time to leave."

She felt peaceful as they walked through the park towards home. Somewhere from the fringes of the park came a rich tenor voice singing the *Internationale.*

Then, comrades, come rally
And the last fight let us face,
The Internationale,
Unites the human race.

She looked over at Arel and he gave her a crooked smile. "I don't know the words or I'd sing along." She laughed. "I could sing a hymn."

What can't you see that is always before you? Perhaps it wasn't necessary to see the future, but only to know that there was a Father who waited for His children to reach out their hands to Him.

The song faded from their hearing as they neared the main gate. A cold breeze rustled the golden leaves and Natasha tied her scarf more tightly around her neck.

Arel beamed over at her. "Did you hear that?" he asked.

"What?"

"Listen carefully."

Natasha smiled. "Ah, yes. Mother Russia is whispering."

NOTES

1. Six Lindlof children were sent to the work camps, some of whom remained incarcerated for ten years. Two daughters are known to have died in prison. In 1928, LDS missionaries from the Swedish Mission visited the remaining Lindlof family in Finland and found only Brother and Sister Lindlof and one daughter, Linda Alise. Arel was the only sibling sent to the work camps who survived. He eventually married a Russian woman and lived the rest of his life in Russia. He has descendants living in the United States. The fate of the other three Lindlof children is a mystery.

2. In 1988, Soviet premier Mikhail Gorbachev broke with Soviet ideology and its traditional stand against religious worship and allowed the Russian people to have a religious celebration honoring one thousand years of Christianity.

In April 1990, Elder Russell M. Nelson offered a prayer of rededication in the Summer Gardens in St. Petersburg.

In July 1990, the Helsinki East Mission was responsible for sending missionaries into Russia. In February 1992, this mission became the Russia Moscow Mission. At the same time, the Russia St. Petersburg Mission was formed.

In 1998, an LDS temple was announced and is currently under construction in Kiev, Ukraine. The temple site is only six miles from the place where, in 996 A.D., Prince Vladimir erected the Church of the Tithes.

BIBLIOGRAPHY

Andrew, Christopher, and Vasili Mitrokhin. *The Sword and the Shield: The Mitrokhin Archive and the Secret History of the KGB*. New York: Basic Books, 1999.

Bryant, Louise. *Six Red Months in Russia*. New York: Arno Press, 1970 [c 1918].

Engels, Friedrich, and Karl Marx. *The Communist Manifesto*. London, England: Penguin Press, 2002.

Kann, Pavel, and Rita Bianucci. *Art and History St. Petersburg*. Florence, Italy: Bonechi Press, 2005.

King, Greg. *The Man Who Killed Rasputin*. New York: Carol Publishing Group, 1995.

Lenin, V. I. *The Communist Manifesto and Other Revolutionary Writings. Marx, Marat, Paine, Mao, Gandhi, and Others*. Mineola, New York: Dover Publications, Inc., 2003.

————. *Essential Works of Lenin: What Is to Be Done and Other Writings*. Henry M. Christman, ed. New York: Dover Publications, Inc., 1987.

Mehr, Kahlile B. *Mormon Missionaries Enter Eastern Europe*. Provo, Utah: Brigham Young University Press, 2002.

Moynahan, Brian. *The Russian Century: A History of the Last Hundred Years*. New York: Random House, 1994.

Orleansky, Alexei. *Russian Fairy Tales*. Translated by Paul Williams. St. Petersburg, Russia: P-2 Publishers, 2000.

Pushkin, Alexander. *Fairy Tales*. Moscow, Russia: English Translation by Raduga Publishers, 1986.

Reed, John. *Ten Days That Shook the World*. London, England: Penguin Books, 1977.

Salomoni, Antonella. *Lenin and the Russian Revolution*. Translated by David Stryker. Northampton, Mass.: Interlink Books, 2004.

Sherrow, Victoria. *Life During the Russian Revolution*. San Diego, Calif.: Lucent Books, 1998.

Solzhenitsyn, Alexander. *One Day in the Life of Ivan Denisovich*. Translated by Max Hayward and Ronald Hingley. New York: Bantam Dell, 1990.

Talmage, James E. *The Articles of Faith*. Salt Lake City: The Church of Jesus Christ of Latter-day Saints, 1899.

Trotsky, Leon. *History of the Russian Revolution*. Translated by Max Eastman. New York: Pathfinder Press, 1980.

———. *The Revolution Betrayed: What Is the Soviet Union and Where Is It Going?* Detroit, Mich.: Labor Publications, Inc., 1991.

Znamenov, Vadim, and Sergei Mironenko. *Nicholas II: The Imperial Family*. Translated by Valery Fateyev. St. Petersburg, Russia: Abris Publishers, 2007.

Zoshchenko, Mikhail. *The Galosh and Other Stories*. Woodstock, New York: Overlook Press, 2006.

———. *The Russian Icon*. Translated by Julia Redkina. St. Petersburg, Russia: P-2 Art Publishers, 2006.